Critics Are Charmed By
NATALE STENZEL and *PANDORA'S BOX*!

"Vengeance is served very cold in this fresh and distinctive tale, a story in which magic and the modern world collide. Romance and snarky wit are a fun mix, and Stenzel definitely delivers both!"
—*RT BOOKreviews*

"This lighthearted romantic fantasy will have readers laughing out loud....Few triangles have been so much fun to follow....Subgenre fans will relish *Pandora's Box*...."
—Harriet Klausner

"*Pandora's Box* is guaranteed to make you chuckle; it also has a heartwarming effect. By the middle, you will have no idea how the author can make everything come out right for all involved, yet Ms. Stenzel pulls it off beautifully. Best of all, there are a couple of sequels in the works. One will be called *The Druid Made Me Do It*, coming in August. Get in on the fun; go ahead and open *Pandora's Box*."
—Romance Reviews Today

THE DRUIDS MADE THEM (NOT) DO IT

Janelle could feel the heat of Kane's body so close to hers, the rigidity of every muscle. It was pure fire underneath that T-shirt, those belted jeans.

She swallowed at the reminder of the Druids' power, their warnings. There were consequences to every action. Kane's very fate proved that.

He tugged the sleeves of her blouse down her arms, let the fabric pool on the floor. Then, carefully avoiding the touch of skin, he unbuttoned her pants. Gripping the zipper tab, he tugged it down, loosening the fabric on her hips. The slacks sagged as the zipper lowered, then finally the pants slid down her legs unaided. He truly intended to get her ready for bed without touching her once.

He took a long step backward. Unnecessarily long. He gritted his teeth. His eyes looked like melted amber. His chest seemed to heave once, and then again. His belly muscles went taut with restraint above a suspicious and impressive fullness in his jeans beneath his belt—his desires and hers…restrained by a heavy Celtic knot.

Other *Love Spell* books by Natale Stenzel:

PANDORA'S BOX

The Druid Made Me Do It

NATALE STENZEL

LOVE SPELL NEW YORK CITY

LOVE SPELL®

August 2008

Published by

Dorchester Publishing Co., Inc.
200 Madison Avenue
New York, NY 10016

ISBN 10: 0-505-52777-4
ISBN 13: 978-0-505-52777-6

Printed in the United States of America.

10 9 8 7 6 5 4 3 2 1

Visit us on the web at www.dorchesterpub.com.

To Steve, the hero behind every book I write, and to our very bright (if spontaneously hurling) children.

Special thanks also to editor Chris Keeslar for emergency brainstorming; and to Julianne Levine, whom I meant to thank a book ago for picking up a certain manuscript on a quiet Friday afternoon...

The Druid
Made Me Do It

Chapter One

"You, Janelle Corrington, will be Robin Goodfellow's guardian on Earth."

Janelle Corrington, onetime child genius and now a dedicated physician, stared at a modern-day Druid dressed in a white robe and pricy sneakers. "Oh, crap."

"That sums it up nicely," muttered Robin Goodfellow, drawing Janelle's ire as well as her attention. He met her gaze with a shrug. "I was just agreeing with you."

"Nobody asked you. *Robin Goodfellow*."

"I hate that name."

"I hate *you*." And she'd never known him by that name. No, when she'd had a fling with Hot Stuff here, several educational years ago, Robin Goodfellow had called himself Kane. Still reeling from her parents' deaths and in between semesters at college, she'd met him at the beach, this mysterious, somewhat older man with dark, curly hair, riveting golden eyes and the body of a god. She'd been hopelessly drawn to the dangerous loneliness in his eyes, the complexity of his mind and his dark sense of humor.

Oh, and did she mention the body of a god? Yes, the body of a god. Not to be shallow or anything, but the body might have influenced her judgment regarding

the rest of the package. Or at least that was the excuse
she'd pled given subsequent events.

After several intense days of mind-blowing sex and
some apparently one-sided soul-baring, he'd walked out
on her while she slept, without an explanation or even
a good-bye. Janelle had awakened alone and confused,
and emerged from the encounter feeling cheap and
newly devastated. She hadn't seen Kane again until today, more than eight years after the fact.

And now this. She glanced wildly around the little protected area inside the state park—a *sacred grove*, for Pete's
sake—peopled with a few dozen Druids and a couple of
pucas, whatever the hell those were. Surprise, surprise,
the primo puca had turned out to be none other than
Kane—a teensy bit of trivia that would freak out any
woman who'd once shared his bed. And then to learn
that Kane was both brother and lifelong tormenter to her
friend Riordan? Janelle almost laughed at the absurdity.

So . . . sure, why not throw puca guardianship into
the mix? An already long-ass day wouldn't be complete
without having oneself proclaimed guardian to a puca.

"Now, Janelle, is that any way to treat an old lover?"

She offered Kane a poisonous smile. "Not at all. In
fact, if I had my way, you'd be swinging—"

"*Excuse* me." High Druid Phil—as identified by the HI,
MY NAME IS badge stuck to his white robe—peered over
his purple-framed glasses first at Kane, then Janelle. "Is
there a problem with our decision?"

"Ya *think*?" Janelle refocused her overheated, bruised,
smudged and sarcastic ire on the white-robed man in
front of her. Hey, sixteen hours in scrubs now filthy with
old blood, fresh dirt and grass stains did not make for a
pretty or patient female. "Like I'm going to accept guardianship duties for Captain Revenge the puca freak." She
stabbed a thumb in Kane's direction. "Unless everything
I've gathered so far is the hallucination I'm hoping it is,
Robin Goodcreep here made life absolute hell for my

friend Riordan—his own brother, mind you. And now you want to saddle me with his betraying ass? What did I ever do to deserve that?"

"Well, you were the one who suggested he be assigned to a guardian rather than be left to roam at will. You said it was reckless, that he needed supervision. I just assumed you were volunteering for the position out of concern for your fellow man."

"Oh, no. Not volunteering. I was merely expressing concern—and mostly for my fellow *wo*man. I'm thinking, now that he's done crucifying poor Riordan, he's liable to go on a heartbreak bender with every gullible human female he can find. I'm not condoning it. But I'm also not witnessing it, disciplining it or wasting precious time on it or on him. He's your problem. You deal with him."

Ignoring Janelle's insults, Kane stepped forward. "With all due respect to the council, I think Dr. Corrington has every right to object to a duty she finds distasteful."

"Ooooh, the Great Puca speaks on my behalf." Janelle mockingly batted her eyelashes. "Now there's irony for you."

But High Druid Phil was already shaking his slightly balding head. He gave Janelle a sympathetic look—which Janelle did not trust in the slightest. "I'm afraid there's no point in debating the subject. Dr. Corrington stated her concern and I immediately endowed her with guardianship authority." He turned to Janelle. "It's too late. You're already the puca's guardian."

Janelle stared at him a moment before turning her outrage on Kane. "You. Get me out of this. Change his mind. Reverse the action. Or cage your own betraying butt inside Riordan's cornerstone. You know, where you confined *him* for the last two thousand years." She still couldn't believe he'd orchestrated Riordan's imprisonment after he had unknowingly slept with Kane's fiancée. Oh, or that both men—er, pucas—were nonhuman and magical.

Kane appeared ready to interrupt, so she waved an impatient hand. "Look, I don't care how you manage it, but you are not coming home with me and I am not your guardian. Get it?"

"I think everybody in the tri-city area gets it, given your decibel level." When Janelle opened her mouth to protest further, Kane held up a hand. "I didn't do this and I can't change it. Talk to the Druid." He continued in a low mutter: "That'll teach me to take the high road. Should've played the royal card and let them eat cake."

Glaring at the convincingly resigned look on Kane's face before studying the sympathetic but unbending expression on High Druid Phil's, Janelle pondered homicide. Actually, any normal person might already be questioning her sanity, given that she was expecting reason from a *Druid* and a *puca*. Granted, her concept of reality was slightly left of the accepted norm. After all, she'd listened to Riordan—well, she'd known him as Teague at the time—describe some pretty fantastical dreams. Something about a man living a fragmented existence, his soul divided between some mysterious, magical self (Riordan) and his human self (Teague), two beings, one consciousness, some freaky powers—but this terminology . . . "What *is* a puca, anyway?"

Kane and the Druid exchanged glances, before Phil cleared his throat and spoke. "We thought you knew. You said you were familiar with Riordan and, er, Kane, and even Riordan's former guardian, Mina. . . ."

"Apparently I wasn't as familiar with all of you as I thought I was. Just give me the definition. Very simple request. Since you are, after all, trying to put me in charge of one, I think I have a right to know exactly what I'm dealing with here." Before she rejected it completely and threw a tantrum to terrify a Druid and even a puca.

The Druid raised his eyebrows over the rims of his glasses and peered at Kane. "Do you want to field that one?"

"Might as well." Kane looked annoyed.

Janelle glanced back and forth between them. "What, is it that difficult? Simple definition, dude. Oh, but I forget. Even telling me your real name is a challenge for you."

"Kane *is* my real name." And the puca had the nerve to look offended. "It was given to me at my birth. Legend and old wives' tales named me Robin Goodfellow."

"And that would qualify as an unimportant little footnote in our—"

"Do you want to talk or to listen?" Kane interrupted.

Patronizing jerk. "Fine. Speak."

"I am a puca. Riordan is a puca. Our father is Oberon, King of All Faerie."

King of the faeries? He didn't really mean . . . Couldn't possibly mean, not literally . . .

"Yes, literally, king of the faeries," Kane continued without pause. "But Riordan and I have different, human mothers. As far as we know, we are the only two puca in existence."

"Why?"

He glanced at her, obviously bemused.

She gestured impatiently. "I mean, why would you be the only two?"

"I don't know. I didn't exactly take a census. We are who we are and—"

"And you're incredibly arrogant and short-sighted. So, what's the significance of being a puca?"

He looked harassed, which was mildly satisfying. "A puca is a shape-shifter."

Her satisfaction gave way to the shock she'd so far held at bay. First faeries, and now—"Shape-shifters . . ." She lost her breath in a whoosh. Okay, maybe she'd already been aware of this on an intellectual, completely abstract level. The puca as shape-shifter. A myth. Facing the myth as a reality, however, and attaching it to a guy she'd once slept with was more than a little jarring. "You're seriously, literally, a shape . . ." Lost it again.

"Shifter. Yes." Kane nodded, an evil glint in his eye. "I'll show you later."

"Oh, you have got to be kidding me."

"You keep interrupting," he chided. And that had to be the Devil dancing in his eyes. What, he was amused now? So much for him being a *repentant* puca. Even if he did change his mind at the last minute and save his brother . . .

"Say something even halfway intelligent and I'll stop," she replied.

"All right. Humans aren't aware of the faerie realm. We like it that way. Those of faerie blood have the ability to glamour. This means we can change people's perceptions and memories to keep our existence secret."

"I'll bet that talent comes in real handy with your human playthings, too. You don't have to suffer morning-after discomfort if your lover 'forgets' the wild nasty ever happened. Ah, but then, a baffling nine months later . . . God only knows how many halflings and fourthlings and whaterverlings wander the Earth in complete ignorance. But do go on."

Kane seemed to be holding on to his temper by a thread now, which was mildly pleasing, and certainly distracting from the frightening faerie talk. Then he spoke. "You think that's what we do? So explain why I didn't erase *your* memory, then."

Janelle recoiled, her senses scattering. She thought she read brief regret in his eyes before he glanced away and proceeded as though he'd never paused. As though he'd never made it personal.

"I've seen the birth, rise and death of many civilizations." Kane smiled, not kindly. "And I'll no doubt live to see the fall of this one as well."

The High Druid looked uneasy. "I hope that's not a threat?" Phil's uneasiness terrified Janelle.

"What?" Kane eyed Phil distractedly. "Oh, no. Not a threat. Just a statement of fact. Everything has a beginning and an end." He turned back to Janelle, who had partially recovered but was beyond managing even a pretense of her former casual disdain. "Oh, look. I finally have your attention."

And then some. She licked dry lips. "How old are you? Exactly."

"I couldn't say. Possibly twenty-three hundred years, give or take a century. We didn't keep exact records in the early days."

"The early days. Right."

He raised his eyebrows, anticipating further comment.

"N-no. Go on. I'm all ears." And light-headed. Really light-headed. She knew he'd lived longer than the average human, but never had she dreamed . . . To be born twenty-three hundred years ago . . . that was old. *Scary* old. He'd seen too much. With all those powers and the ability to get away with everything, he must feel nothing. No wonder he'd left her so easily. But . . . why hadn't he erased her memory of him? She didn't have the balls to ask. And, frankly, she couldn't spare the pride such a question would cost her.

"I guess you could say I've spent the last two millennia . . . angry." He turned his gaze to his brother, Riordan, who so far had stood silently by, just as Kane had requested in the middle of this foolish ceremony. Well, not foolish, for Riordan's future was decided during it. And Kane's future was tethered to Janelle's because of it. So, basically, it had been pretty darn effective and life altering, considering it was run by a bunch of guys in white robes and sneakers hanging out in the park. Thank God the robed guys had decided in Riordan's favor. Otherwise Janelle would have never forgiven herself for arriving too late to act as a character witness in this odd little hearing. According to the Druid's brief recap earlier, it had been a close thing. Until Kane arrived and confessed his own guilt. He'd admitted he'd exaggerated Riordan's offenses and had his brother imprisoned for two thousand years, not to serve justice but to carry out his own revenge.

And all over a woman.

Yep, to be two thousand years' worth of angry because of a dispute over a woman, Kane had to be the biggest misogynist in the universe by now. And eight years ago, Janelle had twisted up the sheets with him and given up her heart to his "tender" care. God, what an idiot she'd been. Expect no mercy at *his* hands.

Which was a good point actually.

Wrenching her gaze from Kane's, Janelle turned back to the Druid, feeling just a little desperate now. "Look, Phil. Let's be honest here. If he's telling the truth about everything—and you seem to believe he is—then how could I possibly wield any influence over him in some ineffectual little 'guardian's' role? According to you guys, your buddy Kane here can change his shape, he can make people believe anything he wants, he lives basically forever, and his daddy's a king.

"Meanwhile, here I am, just an exhausted, seriously indebted general practitioner who splits her worry time between patients and her next malpractice insurance payment. What with patients, the clinic and the grunt work any new-hire salaried doctor owes to the clinic that hired her, I don't spend but ten or so hours in my own apartment each day. If that. I'm too busy working. How could I possibly be responsible for a super-powered, conscienceless freak?"

She glanced uneasily over her shoulder. Well, Kane hadn't whacked her head off or turned her into a jackass yet, so she had to believe he either couldn't or wouldn't hurt her. Let the insults continue. She found them comforting. Like a wall of bricks standing between her and anything that made her feel vulnerable.

"That's a legitimate question," Phil mused quietly. "A puca does have a lot of power at his disposal. As we said, however, he's now lost his ability to glamour, and he's subject to human laws and mores. He can shape-shift, but he can't erase or warp humans' memories of it, so shape-shifting recklessly or for ill gain could land him in a world of trouble."

"Sounds like a small consolation to me." *Distance, Janelle. Just slide away from the guy.* What could he do? She wasn't subject to Druid governance, and somehow she got the feeling Kane didn't welcome her guardianship any more than she did.

Not that she would take it personally or anything. Taking it personally that Kane didn't want her around him would imply that she still gave a shit about him and of course she didn't. Why would she? How could she possibly? Look what he'd done to her. Hell, look what he'd done to Riordan: tortured him for two thousand years. Kane was cold, cruel and heartless.

He just wasn't her kind of guy at all. Not that she'd had much time for guys recently. But still, she thought it was reasonable to expect a guy to have enough happy-go-lucky in his soul to preclude some psychotic avenger act like the one Kane had going.

On that disturbing note, she turned back to survey Riordan and Mina. "You guys are okay, right? Together and here to stay?"

The pair turned to each other with that same sweetly dopey look Janelle had caught on Riordan's face the first time she saw him staring at Mina. "We're together and fine." Riordan smiled at Mina before turning back to Janelle. "I'm whole now . . . but 100 percent human. And very happy."

"What a relief." Janelle smiled, honestly thrilled for both of them. "So that means . . . nothing can harm you or separate you now? Not the Druids, not Kane, not some other faerie jerk?"

Riordan laughed. "Nope. We're clear."

"Excellent! In that case . . ." Janelle waved a cheerful little salute toward Riordan and Mina before turning a false smile on Kane and Phil and his happy little Druidic following. "It's been great, guys. Good to meet you, great chatting with you, have fun in the grove, tell great stories over the campfire, all that good stuff. Be seeing you." *Or not. Hopefully not.*

With another cheery wave and tons of bravado, she turned on a heel and headed off toward the path that would lead to her car, her home and real life.

"Could you live with yourself?" Phil called out to her, his tone calm and disarmingly confident.

Janelle slowed but didn't halt.

"Kane's free now. Disoriented and lost, but not yet evil," Phil continued. "He proved that by coming back to clear his brother—belatedly, sure, but he did come back. He's not all bad. And you have the opportunity to influence him for the good of all."

Her steps were sluggish now, her conscience heavy.

"Two thousand years of vengeance. Now denied. And so he's at loose ends with no one to guide him back to the right path. It could be a turning point for him. For the better . . . or the worse. Without sufficient guidance from the only woman who possesses that power, I'd bet on the latter. I think you would, too. Can you live with that?"

"Damn it." Janelle whirled to face them again. "Of *course* I don't want that. But why does it have to be me? Why not somebody else? Somebody with more personal sway, more knowledge, maybe some freaky magic of his own to wield? I couldn't possibly be your best choice."

Phil shrugged. "I was going to give the leash to Riordan here. I thought it was fitting. You told me not to do that—in effect, accepting the leash on his behalf. And now you're reneging."

"Oh, no you don't. I never agreed to a thing. You're just twisting words and making assumptions you have no right to—"

"I'll do it," Riordan said abruptly, even as Mina dug

her fingernails into his arm and bit back some choice words. Riordan appeared resolute, though. "He's my brother. I'll do it."

Janelle stared at Riordan, then turned to Kane, who looked more sober than she'd ever seen him. He honestly didn't want to burden the brother he'd already tortured for so long. Well, damn it, neither did Janelle. But what about her life? Why her? Fiercely torn, she whirled back to the Druid. "That's not fair either. You can't just—"

Phil overrode them all. "No exchanges. The choice of guardian, once made, is final. Janelle Corrington, the duty is already yours, whether you accept it or not. He is tied to you alone. What you do with that tie . . . well, that's between you and your conscience."

Janelle felt her heart racing, invisible walls rising high and closing in around her. Claustrophobia. This was too much.

"I have an idea." Riordan's voice broke through her panic. Janelle focused on him, as did Phil, his buddies and Kane.

"This is a huge burden that you've forced on Janelle. She's right about that. And she is innocent in all this. Agreed?" Riordan eyed everyone, who all nodded slightly. "All right, then. I propose that she be compensated."

Janelle groaned. "Oh, come on. It's not about money. I don't need freaking money. I need to get rid of the freak. I just want him gone."

"Well, we can't exactly deal in money anyway." Phil sounded apologetic. "Cash is too materialistic for something like this."

"Yes, cash is bad. Very bad. And I suppose your tricked-out tennies and your purple designer specs were free? Maybe you conjured them while chanting naked under the full moon? You know, right before you punished me for speaking my mind by saddling me with puca guardianship. Hypocrites."

Phil looked less than amused. "The eyeglass frames were on sale, and the shoes . . . are comfortable." He shifted restlessly. "I have high arches."

"I wasn't talking about money," Riordan murmured. "How about giving Janelle something truly valuable? Something she'd consider worth the trouble of guarding a puca she hates." He glanced at his brother. "No offense, bro."

Kane shook his head impatiently. "Just tell us what's on your mind. What would compensate Janelle for something this big? Immortality?"

Phil raised a finger. "Um . . . can't do that one either. Try another."

Riordan met and held Janelle's gaze. "How about an ability? For example, the gift of healing . . . with just a thought."

Her heart thudding into her stomach, Janelle fisted her hands in the material of her stained scrubs. Healing with a thought? Such a wonderful thing! But completely impossible. Had to be. "You're bluffing. Teasing. Something."

Riordan glanced at Kane and then at Phil, neither of whom openly objected to the suggestion. Then he turned back to Janelle. "I'm completely sincere. Have you never wished there was more you could do for a patient? Maybe all hope was gone, you couldn't figure out what was wrong or fix it even if you did know . . . I know you've broken your heart over sick patients, Janelle. I've been there when you cried."

Uncomfortable with this exposure, Janelle glanced uneasily at Kane, who suddenly seemed fierce as he stared at his brother. He glanced only briefly at Janelle before focusing on Riordan again.

Janelle turned, shakily, back to Riordan. "You'd better explain."

Riordan glanced expectantly at Phil, who cleared his throat. "As Riordan said, it can be done if you wish it.

The Druids have healing gifts and, with a little passive aid from someone of faerie blood, we could offer the gift to you as well. It comes at a price, of course. Only you will know exactly what that price is. No gift is free. But most are worth the price if used for the right purpose."

"She would put it to the right purpose." That was Kane this time. "But I'll insist on certain conditions as well."

"Now wait just a minute!" Janelle's temper launched. How dare he think that he had any right—

"I insist that the gift be unconditional and permanent, not temporary. She should be allowed to *keep* the power, free and clear, regardless of future events and outcomes."

Janelle, who had opened her mouth to finish her protest, slowly closed it. He was defending her interests. Why? Some ulterior motive? Simple ass-kissing in anticipation of future power struggles?

Unfortunately Phil was shaking his head. He seemed to do that a lot. "You know that kind of guarantee is beyond my abilities. I mean, she can keep the power, but only if you two are successful. If, under her guardianship, you make amends to all your victims."

Janelle stared. "But how do you measure the success of something like that?" She shook her head slowly, still not believing in the possibility. Healing with a thought: literally, this was the Holy Grail of medicine. To have that gift . . . how could she possibly turn it down?

"Essentially, the puca's actions, the purity of his intent, and the honest beliefs of his victims will all be taken into account. Judgment will be rendered based on those factors. Also," Phil continued, a bit more hesitantly, "there are rules associated with guardianship."

"Bureaucracy. Even among Druids." Janelle shook her head. She should really just strive for a lighthearted mood. It would make all of this so much easier to swallow.

"It's actually not all that complicated." Phil paused, obviously striving for particular phrasing. Then he met Janelle's eyes, shied away, and connected with Kane's. "Well, during this phase, while Janelle is acting as your guardian, you two . . ." Phil pointed two index fingers, sort of weaving them in warped figure eights. "Can't, um . . ." The figure eights overlapped and intertwined. And Phil met Kane's eyes significantly.

Janelle was frowning, but her ire rose high in sudden, outraged comprehension. "What? You think I'd even consider doing that with him again? Oh, no. Just consider your condition met and even exceeded. It's not even an issue. It's like promising I won't take a swan dive off the roof of the clinic. No worries on that score, buddy."

The weaving fingers slowed, pointed toward the sky in thought-filled silence, then dropped to Phil's sides. "That's good then. Because that kind of association would produce a conflict of interest, thus forcing us to revoke guardianship—"

Janelle grew intrigued again, if mildly hysterical. Just how desperate was she to get out of this guardianship gig? Was it worth sleeping with Kane again just to escape?

"And that would sort of make it impossible for Kane to succeed on this quest to make amends. Honestly, without you to guide him, I don't see the puca changing his ways enough to even come close to making up to his victims for his offenses against them." Phil raised his eyebrows. "So the Druids would meet, vote your guardianship null and void as well as ineffective, and bye-bye goes the healing gift."

She blinked, refusing to acknowledge the previous half thought, which, if carried to fruition, could only mean a future of whimpering insanity for her.

Still, another thought occurred to her, not that she wished to reintroduce that unwelcome option. She didn't. It wasn't even in the cards, as far as she was concerned.

But she had to wonder. After all, it was just possible that the so-called healing powers didn't even exist. What if they were lying? She would have an out clause, assuming she was willing to risk heart and soul in Kane's bed again. They could in reality be bluffing, just to bribe her to agree to the unthinkable. Or even just lying to their misguided little selves and attempting to rope her into their madness.

Kane glanced at her. "The healing power is real, I assure you. If he's offering to give it to you, then he means it."

Janelle concentrated on him a moment, alarmed that he read her so easily, then turned back to Phil. "Supposing I decide to take you seriously. Are there any other conditions?"

"Yes. You must not combine your abilities with his. Doing so would create an unnatural concentration of power that cannot be allowed. There would be consequences."

"What do you mean by 'combining abilities'?"

"Whenever you, Janelle, use your power to initiate a healing, you would create a vacuum of sorts that would draw upon Kane's magic to complete the process. Kane cannot initiate the healing process, and he should remain passive while you naturally draw upon his power. If he were to attempt to push his magic, essentially forcing it through the energy connection we forge between the two of you, it would result in a mixing—a combining—instead of merely a supplementation. The result would be a volatile new energy that is dangerous and therefore banned by the Druid community." Phil raised his eyebrows and gestured broadly for emphasis. "For your purposes, the key point here is that *Kane must remain passive during the healing process.*"

"What do you mean, 'energy connection' between Kane and me?" Janelle eyed him suspiciously, needing more information though she little understood what was already provided. "Would we be forever tied to each other, even after this guardianship gig? Because that is not in the cards. Not at all."

The Druid was already shaking his head. "Proximity is completely irrelevant as far as your healing ability is concerned. Kane could be clear across town, on the other side of the world, even orbiting Jupiter, and you could still draw on his power. Once you complete your duties as guardian, he will be forever indebted to you—as he should be—but you will be free of him. Clear?"

"I see . . . sort of?" Janelle was feeling a little overwhelmed.

Phil glanced at Kane. "The puca understands my meaning." Then he glanced, with more kindness, at Janelle. "As will you, once you grow used to your abilities."

Janelle nodded quietly. Her *abilities*. She couldn't even fathom growing used to a magical gift of healing. And why on earth would she need to combine something like healing with a puca's power? Fine print. No problem. No reality, granted, or at least not much, but sure, she supposed she could promise not to combine her Druid-imbued magic with puca magic. No doubt her alarm clock would be going off any minute and it would dawn November 1—

"So are we in agreement, then?" High Druid Phil glanced from Riordan and Mina to Kane, and lastly to Janelle. "Guardianship in exchange for healing powers, subject to the stated conditions?"

Nope. Not a dream. The healing gift. So she could really . . . !

Janelle felt the hook slip halfway down her throat, catch on something vital and—*yes!*—hold fast as they reeled her in. Death no doubt would ensue. Eh, well. It wasn't like she had any choice in the matter anyway. "We are in agreement. I will be Kane's guardian if you give me the power to heal with a thought."

CHAPTER TWO ✤

"Excellent!" The High Druid looked dangerously satisfied.

Which felt *just* like Janelle had consigned her soul to the Devil. Maybe she had.

Phil hummed a low note; the Druids, as one, swayed and rocked, the note lazily rising around their circle. The effect, in Janelle's jaded and slightly hysterical opinion, sounded remarkably like an instrumental version of a Jimmy Buffett ballad. Imagine a group of KKK-resembling yuppies humming island music at sunset in the middle of a state park. Janelle fiercely bit her lip. Laughing? Possibly not a good thing right now.

Kane seemed to be eyeing her strangely as well. As though he identified with her hilarity, even welcomed it. She narrowed her eyes speculatively, even as Phil cut off the rolling chant with a businesslike slash of his hand.

The High Druid turned unabashedly to face his lay audience. "Now understand that the healing powers are something you must learn on your own, since I can't be allowed to influence you along this path." Phil shrugged carelessly as he reeled off the conditionals in a voice that was equally careless. Janelle's tension and fear rose accordingly. "I don't know why I'm not allowed to help you. Greater minds, powers, et cetera, thought up these rules long before my time. *Bu-ut . . ."*

The tone of his bright afterthought pierced Janelle's emotional chaos. "Yes?" The word sounded pathetically hopeful, even to her own ears.

Phil smiled encouragingly. "The puca can help you learn your other new talents. I have ordered that mentoring be added to his list of assigned tasks."

Kane groaned quietly.

She goggled at Phil. *"Other* new talents? Um, look, Phil. I appreciate the offer, but I'm more than happy with just the healing bit. That's priceless, as Riordan said, and intimidating all by itself. Any other 'powers' would just get spooky."

"Be that as it may, you did make an excellent point about the balance of power between you and the puca. He could run magical circles around you and you could do nothing to counteract matters. Unless we help you. So . . . every power that he's lost, you will now gain."

Janelle stilled. "What does that mean?"

"You'll have the power to glamour, for one. To influence and erase human thoughts."

"Oh, ick." She backed up a step. "Ever heard of boundaries? *No.* I refuse to go messing in people's heads. Nohow, no way."

"I understand your hesitation. But consider, just for a moment. Suppose your puca here shifted into a fire-breathing dragon in front of the mailman. What would you do?"

She lifted her chin and regarded him stubbornly. "I'd just put on my doctor face and tell the mailman he was looking a little flushed; he should go lie down. There's a bad, hallucinatory bug going around. Very contagious."

"And you call yourself a doctor?"

Janelle shot him a harassed look, but the question smacked her square in the conscience.

"Suppose your puca shifted shape at your office or at

the clinic where you volunteer, and one of your associates busted you talking to his altered form?"

"Altered form . . . ?"

"Dog, horse, predatory bird . . . all are favorites of the puca. But he is capable of many others."

Janelle wavered, physically and mentally. The dragon bit she couldn't even take seriously, but this . . . And Phil was so matter-of-fact. "So he really is . . . a shape-shifter."

"That's what he said."

"And I can prevent chaos, panic and an overflowing mental institution with this power you want to give me."

"Glamour. That's what it's called by those with faerie blood and powers. You can glamour humans; just enthrall them a bit as you adjust their memories of the event. It's a minimal intrusion. We insist, however, that you use the glamour *only* to conceal the effects of puca powers from human detection. Like any other puca power, the glamour also cannot be used in a way that's contrary to the particular human's karma or you will face consequences."

She really didn't want to explore those consequences. At all. She held up a hand. "Okay. Forgive me for being obtuse, insensitive or whatever. But I'm a doctor. A scientist. Let's just say a study of karma wasn't part of the standard curriculum offered in medical school. How about a layman's definition?" She glanced from Kane to Phil.

"All right." Phil paused, obviously performing a mental translation from woo-woo to something more decipherable. "Have you ever heard the saying 'what goes around comes around'?" At her nod, he continued. "That's roughly what we're talking about here. It's like a moral accounting ledger, with good deeds as credits, or an accounting of what is owed to you; and bad deeds are debits, or debts you owe."

"And the idea is to stay in the black? To stay out of the heads of people who are also in the black?" Janelle queried.

"Sort of." Phil folded his hands thoughtfully and continued. "Humans see karma as a nebulous concept that roughly means good will be rewarded and evil will be punished somehow, some way, even if it's not an immediate consequence. Karma, in fact, can be a great deal more forgiving toward errant humans than it is toward magic wielders. A human with a huge karmic debt is protected from magic wielders if he's in the process of performing a good deed. If he thinks he's doing the right thing, a magic wielder can't stop him, regardless of context. He's untouchable, his karmic debt to the magic wielder conditionally suspended.

"But in the world of magic, karma plays a fairly concrete role and can be quite ruthless in its judgment and effects. Karma regulates those who wield magic. A magic wielder with significant karma debt is vulnerable to retaliation at any time from anyone he's harmed—either directly or indirectly—through his actions. Thus, it's in his best interests not to accrue debt in the first place. This is just the universe's way of protecting the weaker species and keeping the powerful from becoming tyrannical. With great power, after all, comes great responsibility—and, necessarily, great accountability."

Janelle shook her head. "Um, that's all good to know, but for the sake of simplicity, let's try for the bottom line here." Somehow, balancing the universe felt just a little beyond her capabilities. "How will I know if something I'm planning to do would go contrary to a person's karma?"

"It's usually fairly obvious, if you're aware of all aspects of the situation." The Druid hedged just a little. "If you're informed and you're honestly trying to help, you should be okay. I would think." He trailed off, raising a hand halfheartedly.

Kane turned and murmured quietly, if bluntly, to her, "It will feel like a sickly heave. In the pit of your belly.

That's the big sign that you're about to screw up." He paused, then continued serenely, "Not that it's always a simple matter to heed the warning."

Janelle studied Kane, trying to read the depths of the golden gaze that had fascinated her so completely eight years ago. It still did. But the things he'd done to her (and to others?), to Riordan . . . To risk himself knowingly, body and soul, for the sole purpose of hurting someone else and getting revenge—that was a lot of anger. Janelle looked away. She had her own anger. Her own pride. But what separated her from Kane was that she wasn't willing to pursue vengeance for *two thousand freaking years*.

Kane turned to Phil. "You have something else for her?"

"Several something elses, which I'm sure she'll find out on her own without my help." He smiled, apparently delighted by all the wonders in store. "But primary among those will be a specific power of detection necessary for her guardianship."

"I'm going to need more detail than that."

Phil nodded at Janelle. "You will be able to detect puca powers at work. If a puca did it, you'll know about it. This way, you'll know if Kane has violated the terms of his punishment. And you can report and react accordingly."

"That makes me a puca lie detector, right? A puca nemesis." Something clicked, emotionally and mentally. And maybe on an even more primitive level. Kane was accountable, not just to the Druids, but to *her*. He couldn't hurt her now. *That's* what she needed to feel safe from Kane.

She slowly turned back to him. "Well, Robin Goodfellow. It looks like I have you exactly where I wanted you eight years ago." She allowed herself the joy of an evil little smile. "Is this the part where you grovel and writhe in agony at my feet?"

"It was a mistake. I shouldn't have done it." Kane attempted sincere remorse. He knew he could do it. He was remorseful about Riordan, right? He'd even *saved* his brother. Just channel that and he'd be good to go.

But Janelle didn't respond to his sincerity, just stared straight ahead.

"I was acting on pure instinct." Kane continued to channel. "It just took over when I wasn't looking. Have you never surrendered to impulse?"

She still didn't speak.

Kane studied her, seriously displeased. Hey, he wasn't a complete jerk. He'd come forward about Riordan and here he was now, taking his punishment like a man. That didn't mean he had to be a saint, did it? Maybe it did. Damn. He knew his brother was grateful over it—but not *entirely* grateful. How could he be after two thousand years? And Janelle didn't seem much more forgiving.

A different tactic, then. Something saintly. "Honestly, I just wanted to make you smile. That's all. You looked so serious and burdened that I thought . . ." Kane sighed. "Obviously, I miscalculated. It won't happen again."

And, honestly, she really had looked burdened. That was the hell of it. That evil smile of hers hadn't lasted long, not even the duration of their walk from grove to parking lot. She wasn't a woman bent on vengeance. She simply wasn't made like him.

"Do I look like an idiot?" she asked.

He started. "What do you mean?"

She shot him an annoyed glance. "You didn't do that . . . that *thing* you do, for *me*. You did it because that little Druid pissed you off."

He cleared his throat. "Druid? What, you mean Phil?" Okay, as a protestation of innocence, it fell a bit short of genuine.

Janelle rolled her eyes. "No, not Phil. I'm talking about the runty, troll-looking guy walking behind us. Short guy, sour expression, exuding contempt in your general direction. Remember him?"

Busted. Kane tried, with effort, to hold back a grin. But

it *had* been awfully satisfying to wipe that sour contempt right off the runty Druid's face.

"I saw the look he gave you—and no, he shouldn't have done that—but grow up, for Pete's sake. Try for dignity. You don't swat a fly with a crowbar, you know?" She blinked, mockingly wide-eyed. "They call that overkill."

"I am a puca and a prince. And he looked at me like I was a piece of crap stuck to the bottom of his shoe."

She shrugged. "I look at you the same way. I don't see you trying to terrify me."

"Well, no. But you're prettier than he is."

"Oh, please." The contempt in her voice made him cringe.

"Okay, I admit that was cheap. And you're absolutely right. It was simply bad judgment on my part. I lost my temper."

"That seems to be a habit for you: the overblown temper tantrum. That's why I got tapped for guardian duty instead of one of those idiot Druids. They're all scared of this legendary temper of yours." She paused. "Given your payback to Riordan, I guess they have cause. So, what happens to me if I piss you off?"

"Nothing." He scowled. "I won't hurt you."

"Uh-huh. And you're just a thirty-year-old human beach bum named Kane who wouldn't dream of walking out on his sleeping lover. Tell me another one."

"I give you my word as a puca and as a prince. It's good."

She eyed him a little doubtfully, but let it go. "Next time—and let's not kid ourselves that there won't be one—*next* time you feel the overwhelming urge to pull a stunt like that, would you at least look around you first?" She pressed her lips together. "The old guy next to him about had a heart attack when you went big black stallion on us."

More importantly, however, given the look on Janelle's face, now pale beneath her freckles, he'd shocked *her*.

She was, after all, in charge of making sure he didn't misuse his powers.

"God, one minute you're you, then I turn around and you're a freaking horse. Same glowy eyes and all, just . . ." She shook her head as though she might erase the disturbing mental image.

He waved a hand. "They were just Druids. They already know what I am."

" 'They were just Druids.' You say that like you *poofed* in front of a pair of caterpillars instead of thinking, speaking, freaking-out human beings. You're screwing up already and we're not even out of the parking lot! At this rate, we don't stand a chance in hell of getting you out of my life."

"And, naturally, removing me from your life is your primary goal now."

"You bet it is," she shot back. "Isn't that your goal, too? Freedom? All your magicky glamouring stuff back? Isn't that what you want? And if so, shouldn't we be cooperating here?"

Kane stared straight ahead. "You're right, of course." And he'd forgotten, just for a moment, how necessary it was for him to get far away from her before it was too late. If it wasn't already. Fate was a bitch, and she was riding his ass like there was no tomorrow. Why Janelle, of all people? Anyone else would have been better.

"All right, then. So we need a plan."

He glanced at her. "A plan?"

"Yes, a plan. For a guy who spent millennia following through on his own plan of vengeance, I'd think plans would be old hat for you. We need something just as focused . . . but flipped, of course. No more vengeance for you, Hatred Boy. We're making nice now. Got any bright ideas?"

He frowned. "Not really. I never expected to be in this position."

"Of saying you're sorry?"

He shrugged. "I've never done it until today."

"Thousands of years and this was your first apology? That is seriously arrogant." She eyed the road intently. "But you did say it today. To your brother, I imagine?"

"Yes."

She shot him a mocking glance. "I'll bet that was like pulling teeth for you."

"It was." More like slicing his testicles off with a rusted knife, but no need to verbalize that. He'd already conceded her point. "It's hard to stop thinking in terms of vengeance, too. It's been a long time for me. I'm not sure that I'm capable of changing course."

Janelle drove in silence for a moment. "In that case, I can't believe the Druids haven't given you up for lost. You should be a heartless husk of a being by now. All that time spent hating. How could there possibly be any good left in you?"

"I'm not sure there ever was." He spoke evenly, attempting to hide his own bewilderment. He'd begun this course with good intentions. Figured a slap on the wrist would be what he'd get, and that would be plenty of punishment. For a royal puca. But no, Phil the Druid had some strength of purpose. And now . . . amends? Making up to everyone he'd wronged? How the hell would he do that? In all honesty, Kane felt like somebody had just dumped him in the ocean and left him to swim toward land he couldn't even see. Disorienting, daunting . . . even impossible.

"Let's put it this way. If there isn't any good left in you, then you'd better create some, and fast. I'm not taking you on for life. A few short weeks will be the extent of my commitment. After that, you're on your own."

"Even if I haven't redeemed myself?"

She didn't respond, but also didn't meet his gaze. A bluff?

"What about the healing powers?" He eyed her shrewdly. "Would you so easily give them up?"

"If holding on to these healing powers means explaining to everyone on a daily basis that they hallucinated the talking horse—no, *jackass*—in my waiting room, then yeah. Maybe I'll have to. My traditional medical skills are pretty damn good, I'll have you know. I'm a good doctor, even without the weirdo Druid help. Don't forget that."

Somehow, he had the feeling she was reminding herself more than him. "So, how do you plan on getting rid of me?"

She shrugged. "Where there's a will, there's a way. Marry a stranger, fuck a puca, exorcise my demon . . . My options are many."

He regarded her silently, attempting not to picture . . . They both knew she wouldn't do it. She'd made that mistake with him years ago. She wouldn't let down her guard enough to repeat it.

"Get that look off your face. That option was not really an option. I was being flippant—as in, demonstrating my complete apathy for you and your fate. I would, however, marry a complete stranger to be rid of you."

Would she? If she did that—He inhaled deeply. She was not his. She *wasn't*. And damn it, he'd left her behind eight years ago. What she did with her life now was no concern of his, *should* be no concern of his, damn well *couldn't* be any concern of his. What he needed was to get done and get gone in a hurry. Like before that eight-year-old prophecy became deadly reality.

"All right, we're here." Reluctantly, or so it seemed to Kane, Janelle threw the car into park and shut off the engine.

Kane looked out the car window at the multibuilding complex surrounding them and the rest of the crowded parking lot. "This is home?"

"One tiny little part of it is, yes."

"It's not what I pictured," he mused. He wasn't sure what he'd pictured. Something unusual and eclectic maybe, not so institutional. But maybe the interior wasn't bland and expressionless.

"Oh, come on. You never bothered to picture my home. There wasn't time, and I detected a certain lack of interest. Or do you always walk out on a woman while she sleeps?"

"Well, actually—"

But Janelle was already climbing out of the car. "Let's make tracks. I've had a long day and I'm craving quality time with my pillow."

Kane climbed out of the car, slamming the door shut. Already walking away, Janelle clicked her keychain remote, triggering the headlights to flash and the doors to lock. Kane followed silently.

Sure, he knew about cars. He'd learned to drive just for the novelty. Had Riordan yet? Probably his human half, Teague, had learned. But Riordan, the magical half? Doubtful. Unlike Kane, Riordan had spent the entire industrial revolution—plus several centuries before and after it—caged in stone. A cornerstone, to be precise, but a special one, originally a small chunk of a much larger Sarsen stone that stood nobly amidst many others in the Avebury stone circle in Wiltshire County, England. Older and larger than the more famous Stonehenge formation, the stone circle at Avebury had baffled and intrigued mankind for most of history. Unfortunately—or perhaps fortunately—mankind didn't have a clue. That circle contained power, drew power, enhanced power, transformed power. . . .

"Are you coming?"

Kane glanced up to see Janelle tapping her foot impatiently. She stood at the top of a set of stairs that Kane had yet to climb. Conceding, he swiftly followed her up the steps and slipped through her open apartment door behind her. A tiny hesitation on his part, and she no doubt would have slammed the door in his face and left him outside to fend for himself.

Inside, he gazed around, curious at first and then baffled. He turned back to Janelle. "You live here? Somebody actually lives in this empty place?" And it *was* empty. Sure, there was a folding table and a chair in what passed for a kitchen/dining area. She even had a small television and a gray couch in the living area. Otherwise, the rooms were mostly barren. Boxes were stacked in one corner, and he saw through an open door—leading to a bedroom?—more boxes.

She tossed him an annoyed glance. "I told you I'm never here. Decorating's a waste of time if you're never around to enjoy it."

"So you just . . . work. No social life, no family time, no friends invited over—"

"Yeah, what of it? I'm busy. I work crazy hours and will for a while yet. I'm a doctor. It's in the job description, especially for the new kid on the block. I have to prove myself. Hence, the extra effort."

"And this is your life."

She glared defensively. "Well, at least I spend it helping people. *You've* spent the past two millennia destroying your brother's life."

She had a point. He glanced away. "I had other interests, too."

"Sure you did." She gave him a peeved look, but then curiosity seemed to win out. "Like what? Seducing brainless humans? Impersonating monkeys?"

Meeting her eyes with every ounce of deadpan in his soul, he initiated the shift. It started deep within himself, his consciousness, his core, moving first inward, then outward. Bones melted and remolded at flash speed, limbs shortening, others lengthening, twisting, spine hunching, skin sprouting hair, fingers lengthening . . .

"Oh, my God." Janelle backed away, pointing a shaking finger at him. "Get it out of my apartment. Out. Yuck. They throw *feces*, you know. No crapping on my floor! Ugh, just *out*!"

"Janelle."

"Aaaaaahhhh! Talks. Monkey talks." She stared, utterly horrified.

Kane gave her a quizzical look. "It's still me. I just shifted shape."

Janelle took a breath, then another, obviously still trembling as she eyed him, her gaze canted downward now at his shorter form. "Just . . . bone and flesh, skin and hair. You're still—"

"Well . . . mostly. I assume instincts and abilities, too. Want me to demonstrate?" He cast a laughing glance toward her dangling light fixture.

"No!" She leapt between him and the fixture, arms spread high and wide as though to block him. "Look . . . could you just shift back? This is too weird. I can only take so much in a day."

Amused, Kane didn't respond at first. "You saw me shift earlier, and it didn't affect you this much."

"In the grove? Hell, nothing was usual in the grove. Pucas and Druids—totally surreal. But this is my apartment. It's reality. My life may be bland to you, but it's sanctuary to me. And *normal*. I'd like to keep it that way. Besides, I didn't see the actual shift then. Actually watching you do it now, just physically change like that while I watch . . ." She shuddered.

Strangely disappointed, Kane reversed the shift, letting the flow consume and contort and solidify into the man she'd met eight years ago. "Better?" He noticed that Janelle had averted her eyes while he shifted.

"Only a tiny bit." She still looked uneasy. "We need to set some ground rules."

"I shouldn't be surprised." He gave her a patient look. "What kind of rules?"

"Like you gotta warn me before you pull that stuff. I studied the human body for years and years. And now I spend every day putting it back together again. Making it well. Making it conform as closely to the healthy ideal as possible. You morphing between man and beast is beyond jarring for me."

He cocked his head in true curiosity. "More jarring for you than, say, for Mina?"

"Yes. And since we're on the subject"—she eyed him suspiciously—"*stay the hell away from Mina.*"

"What's that supposed to mean?"

"I saw you eyeing her. Right in front of your brother, even. The brother with whom you should be trying to make amends. Not evening the score."

"Evening the—" He stared, honestly surprised now. "You think I'm after Mina? My brother's girlfriend? Romantically?"

"I doubt there's anything 'romantic' about it. But would you seduce her if you could? Yeah, I think so."

"Okay, I get it now. You think I would do this out of revenge against my brother."

"Gee, ya think? You locked the guy inside of a rock for two thousand years—"

"Technically, only his magical half was confined, while the human half was reborn."

"Because he did your cheating fiancée behind your back," she continued. "Yes, I think seducing the woman he loves would give you one self-righteous orgasm."

"I could see where you would think that—damn good idea, in fact, if I were in the market for more—but I swear I wouldn't do it. Not now."

"Uh-huh. You know what I don't get?"

He eyed her questioningly.

"Why is it that men, when their girlfriends cheat on them, always choose to go after the other guy? Not that I think they should beat the crap out of the girl, but isn't she more in the wrong than the other guy?"

"Riordan is my brother."

Janelle thought that over a moment while Kane watched the play of emotion on her face. Her intelligence was almost visible, so obvious in the complexity of her expressions and the speed and subtlety of their changing. He didn't intend to let her affect him. Not again. But there was no denying that she still fascinated him, all big blue eyes, freckled nose and silky-straight reddish-brown hair. With a killer intellect, compassion for the wounded and wit enough to cut a man off at the knees. She was every bit the woman she'd promised to become years ago. And it hurt him just to look at her.

Janelle nodded slowly. "You know, that's probably the most profound thing I've heard you say yet. You sound almost human. It's obvious you didn't really love this fiancée of yours. Otherwise her betrayal would have hurt you more than your brother's did. But you *love* your brother."

Kane froze as everything inside of him rebelled at the suggestion. Love Riordan? No. He was simply family. Kane felt reluctantly and irrevocably tied to him. That was all. The woman was just romanticizing.

"You *do* love him. Honestly." Her eyes softened in wonder, though she probably was completely unaware of it. "Or there's no way you could have dredged up two thousand years' worth of hatred for him. Project Vengeance would have bored you silly a long time ago if you didn't care about Riordan."

"So I tortured him for two millennia because I love him? Sure, that makes sense."

She was shaking her head, a quizzical expression on her face. "I begin to see the light. This is what the Druids meant when they said you weren't completely lost. You loved him enough to hate him—then loved him enough to forgive him and free him by admitting your own guilt. I think we can work with that."

Kane was floored. "Women. I just don't get you at all."

"I know. Apparently you didn't get that Druid's daughter you were supposed to marry."

Kane felt that like a slap across the face.

Janelle looked a little thrown, too. "Um, that didn't come out quite right."

"No, you're right. If I 'got' Maegth—*understood* her, as I think you meant to say—I would have realized she was the kind of woman who could sleep with her fiancé's brother. But I never had a clue."

"And you dismissed her from your heart and your thoughts. Fairly easily, too, I would imagine. Yes?"

He nodded slowly. Then shrugged. "Not that it matters any longer. Maegth is long dead and Riordan is now free."

"And he's forgiven you as you have forgiven him."

"Which, I'm thinking, is not the same as having made amends to him."

Janelle nodded. "So the question remains."

Kane closed his eyes and verbalized it: "How do I make amends for torturing my brother for two thousand years?"

The next morning found Janelle seated at her plain little kitchen table, Kane hovering impatiently over her. Given her sleep-deprived state—entirely Puca Breath's fault, since awareness of his presence in her house kept her from dropping her guard for even a moment—Janelle took evil pleasure in extending his impatience indefinitely.

"This is a waste of time."

Janelle, freshly showered and dressed in ragged jeans, T-shirt and flip-flops, blandly yet only briefly glanced at him. "It is not. Lists are never a waste of time." Her voice lilted with both real and phony righteousness. Making lists was a comforting process that occasionally produced decent results, so she was an inveterate lister. She would continue to list. Especially if it drove a certain action-driven puca nuts. Pondering the last item, Janelle scribbled a note just below it.

Kane was still grumbling. "Action is good. Lists are just doodles while you stand in place."

"And we already see where action has gotten you—saddled with me. Try thinking first, He-man."

"Another insult." He sounded almost bored with it all.

"Oh, sorry. I'm supposed to slobber all over you with adoration and gratitude for the way you treated me in the past and for the fix I'm in now."

"Oh, you mean for the horrible healing powers you'll have to endure because of me?"

Ignoring his tone, she glanced up in inspiration. "Hey! Do you think the healing powers qualify as amends to me? Like, maybe we can take my name off your list?"

Kane was already shaking his head. "The healing powers were compensation for the guardian stuff, not for . . . *before*."

She eyed him cynically. " 'Before.' Ooooh, sort of like *Before Kane* and *After Kane*, as though you served as a major turning point in my life. Dream on, buddy. You were just the mistake I made while grieving over my parents' death. You could have been anyone."

"So you felt nothing for me."

"Nada. Other than simple annoyance. You nicked my pride."

He nodded slowly, believing not a word. Talk about mortifying. Too bad for her that he was right. Yep, that was Kane. One life-altering demarcation on two feet. Her parents' death had been the low point of her life, and he'd launched her into the stratosphere immediately after . . . only to plunge her even lower than before. As though that brief healing time had only rejuvenated her pain.

"If I meant so little to you, why do you need to keep reminding yourself and me how rotten I am?"

She forced a ditzy smile and an equally ditzy tone, purely intended to annoy. "Because it makes me hap-py."

"So, this is just going to be your new hobby to take your mind off of playing guardian to me?"

"Sounds like a plan. Plus, I will be made happy by the fact that I get free labor out of you. Did I forget to mention that part?" She bared her teeth in a grim smile.

"What do you mean?" He eyed her warily.

"Well, in case it escaped your notice, I have a job. I work at a clinic. In order to keep the job, I have to actually show up and do the work. Employers are funny that way." Then she brightened, as though preparing to enjoy herself. "Meanwhile, you get to be our new volunteer, responsible for filing and minor office-type busy work. We don't have many volunteers, but out of the goodness of my heart, I made an exception for my 'cousin' who's trying to decide whether to pursue a medical career. You get to play the role of the cousin, in case you didn't get that part. Oh, and you get to run errands. You'll use my car. Don't hurt it."

"I don't need a car. I have magic and—"

"Oh, no." Janelle interrupted him. "In my world, you *will* drive a car."

Kane nodded in reluctant agreement.

Satisfied, Janelle glanced down at her notepad. "So. The list. People you need to make amends to. I have Riordan at the top, followed by Mina, then me. Anyone else?"

He frowned. "Well, there was another involved, but I'm not sure whether he was conspirator or victim or—"

"Another?"

"He went by the name of Tremayne. A simple entity of some kind. A nature spirit, perhaps."

"Um . . . okay." She waited. "I'm going to need more than that."

"Hmm?" Kane glanced up, obviously distracted by his own thoughts.

"Tremayne? Your newest addition to our list?"

"Right. I'll have to look into it. He's something of a mystery to me, then and now. Touched by magic, though, I'm sure of that. And somehow compelled to help us restrain Riordan."

She sighed. "So this Tremayne, um, spirit guy, might have been *forced* to help you, very possibly for each one of those two thousand years?"

Kane nodded reluctantly. "It is possible."

"You really do go all out with your vengeance, don't you? So what happened to him?"

Kane frowned, shaking his head. "The Druid Akker summoned him. I don't know much more than that. Not even how Tremayne might have suffered in the process. Maybe something really terrible was involved."

Janelle sighed. Suppressing her own sense of futility, she added the name to their list and glanced up. "Okay. So, Tremayne, Mr. Spirit-slash-Nature Guy. Anyone else?"

"Harmed as a result of my actions?" Kane asked. He groaned. "Probably. I wonder if the Druids are including every offense I've ever committed, or just wrongs related to my act of vengeance."

She chewed her lip. "They did kind of leave that up to our discretion. Or should I say, they're letting us take wild guesses just to see if we can trip over the right answer. The sadists."

"They like to do that. Always have done. I underestimated them at first, I think." He sounded intrigued, even impressed.

"The Druids?"

Kane nodded slowly.

"Well, I hate to support you and all, but I could see where it would be easy to dismiss them. Trendy sneakers, purple glasses and friendly name tags don't exactly lend dignity or even credibility to their little gathering."

"It could be that they do it on purpose. Kill the mystical element, at least on the surface, to discourage the dilettantes and disarm their enemies."

"Seriously?"

He shrugged. "It's certainly possible. Even clever."

"So you really think they *are* Druids, that they have the real, legendary Druid powers?"

"I have no doubt whatsoever. Hell, I even have proof. Want to see?" He patted the front of his pants, his gaze meaningful.

"Whoa, buddy." Janelle leaned back. "I don't know what you're suggesting, but—"

Wicked humor glinted in his eyes. "The buckle, Janelle. Look at the belt buckle."

She dropped her gaze to a bulky Celtic knot wrought from a heavy pewter-type metal. "Okay, I'm looking. Does it do tricks?"

"It's not mine. It wasn't there when I showed up at the grove, but it was there before I left. Did you notice me changing clothes at any point when we were there? The thing just appeared. I think it signifies a bond. To the Druids."

"Yech." Goose bumps rose on her arms and she rubbed at them in subtle denial. "Hey, I get it! Symbolism, right? Like a Druidic chastity belt?" She swallowed a giggle.

"That's not funny."

"Well, no, probably not for you."

He narrowed his eyes at her in mock warning. "Besides the sudden appearance of unwanted accessories, I also felt my powers lessen as soon as the pronouncement was made. It . . . wasn't comfortable." He grimaced at the memory.

Her amusement faded. "It hurt?"

"It was more like a sudden weakness. With nausea."

"Like you're pregnant?"

He gave her a wry look. "Except that instead of an odd fullness, I feel . . . hollow. So it seems you were right. I *am* an empty husk of a being."

Feeling a guilty flush steal over her face, she turned away so he wouldn't see. "So. Back to the list."

"The list." He sounded disappointed.

"Yes. I begin to think you're right. We have the biggies down, so I suggest we approach this thing directly."

"Meaning?"

"I vote for face time." She smiled brightly. "Let's go visit the first guy on our list. You know, the one who should want you dead. Your brother."

Chapter Three ⚜

"It's like this. I know you guys probably don't know each other very well anymore. Despite your loving him and all—"

Kane grunted and eyed Janelle doubtfully. This love stuff was more than a little ridiculous in his opinion, but probably indicative of her inherently good nature. To believe that there was good in him still, despite overwhelming evidence to the contrary. He didn't deserve it. Hell, if she knew what he'd prophesied eight years ago, she'd probably cast off any thought of guardianship or atonement and run screaming.

"But your brother's a nice guy," Janelle continued without pause, "even though he's suffered. Granted, I really only knew his Teague half, the human half, but I have to believe his Riordan half has an equally good heart."

Yes, Riordan was great. Wonderful. The true white sheep of the family, when Kane was just the black sheep with a good bleach job. "And your point is?"

"I don't think the ideas of vengeance or reparation have really occurred to him." She gave him a frank look. "You live by this stuff. Riordan doesn't. He just wanted his freedom. And to not go insane before he gained it."

Kane frowned. He hadn't considered, not fully. . . .

Janelle was eyeing him with uncomfortable shrewdness. "To be honest, I don't know how he kept his sanity, either half of him—the part that knew he'd been rent in two and caged for two millennia, or the human half, reincarnated over and over again with incomplete memories and freaky suspicions that made him doubt his own mind. You screwed him good, Kane. And all over a woman you've nearly forgotten." Janelle's voice had cooled considerably since the earlier love talk.

"I believe the Druids—and Mina—have already made that point."

"Yeah? Well here's mine. I don't think we have a chance in hell of pulling this off. You can't make up for what you've done to him. There's just no way." She glanced up at the front door they'd slowly approached. Parking the car and walking the last few blocks—sort of a mini–pep rally, or so she'd argued to Kane earlier— would give them a chance to talk about this and prepare without resembling scary stalker types to any onlookers. Again, Janelle's phrasing. And the woman did have a way with words. The pep-rally feeling seemed to have evaporated, however.

"But I've promised to try. And I will," he said, glancing at her. "Do you deny that I owe it to him to at least try to make amends, even knowing it probably won't work? Forget the 'love' foolishness you were spouting earlier. Common decency. Honor. Remorse. They all demand that I try."

"And you have those?" It was a sincere question, springing from honest—and therefore devastating— curiosity.

"Oh, probably not," he snapped. "But we can always hope, right?" He halted at the door and knocked.

Kane and Janelle listened as footsteps approached. Paused. Then a voice—Mina's?—rose angrily, soon accompanied by another female voice, also argumentative.

Words like *vengeful, bastard* and *castrate* penetrated the door, before a male voice interrupted. The others fell to mere murmurs. Moments later, the door swung open.

Riordan and Kane stared at each other for a moment before Riordan leaned against the doorjamb and broke the silence. "So, what did you do this time?"

Taken aback, Kane just shook his head. "Um. The monkey thing? Nothing? You tell me."

Riordan frowned, but stepped back and silently gestured the visitors inside. Mina whispered furiously in his ear all the while, angry eyes following Kane's every move.

Aware of Mina's hostility and her very good reasons for it, Kane backpedaled. "Maybe I shouldn't come in. I could . . . telephone or something."

"Oh, no you don't." This time it was Janelle. "Face time. Period. Sit your butt down." She seemed to have resumed her cause in spite of overwhelming doubts. They would find a way to make amends, her tone said, even if it killed Kane. She was willing to make *that* sacrifice.

Kane dropped onto the couch. *Great. This should be loads of fun. Not to mention completely unproductive.* He watched as Janelle turned to face Riordan, Mina and an older woman who looked like Mina, but was dressed much like a gypsy of old. All four seemed guarded, to varying degrees. Kane grimaced.

Janelle smiled uncomfortably at their host. "Look, Teague. Riordan. God, I don't even know what to call you."

"Riordan, please. I plan to get it added legally as a middle name. Since my family's already overrun with males named Jonathon Teague, it shouldn't be a problem convincing everyone I did it for legal or whimsical reasons—to 'express my individuality,' maybe." Riordan gave her a crooked grin. "So it's Jonathon Riordan Teague. What do you think?"

Janelle cocked her head and smiled. "I like it."

"So, what brings you by?" Riordan cast Kane a wary look.

Janelle's smile faded.

Kane spoke up quietly. "I'm sorry if we're disturbing you. We're not here to cause trouble, just—"

"That's not what the guy on the phone said." Mina issued the challenge.

Janelle turned with a frown. "Guy on the phone? Who are you talking about?"

Mina regarded her quietly. "The *who* isn't important."

"Well, actually it is." Janelle seemed impatient but not hostile. "Kane's telling the truth. We're really not here to cause trouble. Just the opposite, in fact. We're here to make amends so Kane can get the hell out of my apartment and go about his merry puca way. Causing trouble won't accomplish our purposes."

"I guess that makes sense," Mina mused. Then she cast a cynical glance at Kane. "And I can't see you doing without your powers for longer than necessary. You're way too arrogant to let that happen."

"Well, they do come in handy now and again." Kane felt just a little harassed. "Me being so arrogant and all."

Mina stubbornly held his gaze for a tense few moments.

Kane relented. "Janelle's right. I'm not here to cause trouble. I swear it. I'm done with that. Just . . . trying to figure things out now. I want to make amends."

Mina eyed him suspiciously for a moment before relenting slightly. "Fine. Let's talk."

"Excellent." The older woman smiled and plopped down next to Kane before Janelle or Mina could sit there.

"Hi. I'm Lizzy, Mina's nemesis. And you're . . . Robin?"

He studied her, entertained by the wide smile and almost manic curiosity. "Kane, actually—"

"Mom," Mina interrupted.

"Hush, darling. We're just getting acquainted." Lizzy turned back to Kane. "So you're the back-stabbing bastard Mina's been cursing all afternoon." Her smile never wavered.

"Er, yes?"

"Oh, those were her words, not mine. I happen to believe that so many things in life are fated to happen."

"Fate?!" Mina sounded outraged. "Two freaking millennia, Mom! Inside a rock! That's not fate, it's—"

"And if he *hadn't* done all of that," Lizzy overrode her daughter, "you never would have met your Riordan. And you might have even married that jerk you used to live with."

Mina stared at her mother a moment.

Obviously deeming the subject closed and her daughter sufficiently chastened, Lizzy turned to Riordan. "And I would imagine that my future son-in-law would consider the price he paid for his Mina to be not too steep. Correct?"

Riordan glanced at Kane before turning to Mina with a smile. "*No* price was too steep."

Satisfied, Lizzy turned back to Kane. "So, you see. Whatever the reasons for it, your brother is now happy, as is my daughter, and therefore so am I. So what can we do for you?"

Kane eyed her with amazement. "There is no one else on Earth like you, is there?"

Mina rolled her eyes. "You don't know the half of it."

"Oh, unkind." Lizzy fluttered her lashes. Then she turned back to Kane. "I'll imagine you want to discuss atonement. And freedom for you and Janelle. Correct?"

Janelle, now seated on the other side of Lizzy, leaned in toward the conversation. "Very correct. We could guess and guess on our own, but it seemed a lot more efficient to just come right out and ask Riordan." She turned to the former puca. "What would make up for what Kane did to you? Is there anything at all he can do or say to balance things between you again?"

Riordan, obviously dumbfounded, just shook his head slowly. "Honestly, Mina's mom's right. This all turned out exactly as I might have wished."

"Ha. Except for the immortality part," Mina added. "That's kind of a big one."

"Well, yeah, but there are those who might say *you're* the one who took that from me." Riordan grinned at her provokingly.

Mina was suitably provoked. "Me? *I* took that from you?"

He shrugged. "I didn't say *I* was one who would say it. I'm not that dumb. Besides, if it weren't for you, I'd still be inside that stupid rock you inherited from your cousin across the pond."

Mina propped her hands on her hips. "And if it weren't for your idiot brother putting you in there in the first place, you wouldn't have spent two thousand years twiddling your invisible thumbs. Right?"

Riordan sighed impatiently. "Look, we can go round and round on this, but it's not going to change anything." He turned to Kane. "I like who I am and where I am. I like my life as it is. I wouldn't change it. Knowing how it all ends, I wouldn't take back those millennia inside the rock, as unpleasant as they were. I'm a better man now. Mina would have kicked my ass out of her life if I acted now how I used to act." He shrugged. "There's nothing I want or need. And if I haven't said so yet, I say it now. I do forgive you. Sincerely."

Mina grumbled. Riordan poked her.

At a loss, Kane stared at them both. Oh, sure, he understood Mina's reaction. Riordan's floored him, though. "You could ask anything of me right now and I'd give it to you. But you don't want anything. What do I do?"

"Gee, I dunno," Mina responded, wide-eyed and insincere. "Maybe you could do something really wild and figure it out for yourself? Like we should spoon-feed the answers to you." Kane knew Mina was a middle-school teacher, and now he'd bet she was the type who preferred assigning essays and research projects to handing out multiple-choice quizzes.

Janelle groaned and, shoulders bowing just a little, rubbed her face with open palms. The sound drew Mina's attention, and the woman's sarcasm and impatience seemed to melt away. Janelle looked as though she'd had the weight of the world dumped on her shoulders—or at least the burden of playing guardian to one less-than-deserving puca.

"Damn." Mina slid a quick, meaningful glance at Kane. "This is your fault, too, you know."

He nodded. What else could he do? He completely agreed with her. Janelle was in an impossible position and it was entirely his fault. And neither Mina nor Lizzy knew the extent of the problem. The danger to Janelle.

Ignoring Kane, Mina approached Janelle and dropped to her knees in front of her. "I want you to know that you can count on me. I'm on your side. I'll do anything you want to help you out of this mess. Anything. Not for him, but for you." She shrugged and tried a smile. "You know, as payback for making those house calls, treating busted heads and showing up at that stupid grove meeting to stand up for Riordan and me."

Janelle dropped her hands into her lap. "Thanks. I appreciate it." She paused. "As for Kane . . . I hate to defend the guy. Honestly, you don't know *how* much I hate it—"

"I can take a wild guess."

"But I think he really wants to make things right. Really. If that makes it any easier."

Mina shot him a glance. "Maybe."

Riordan was smirking a little as he glanced at his older brother. "Man oh man. You're about as beloved as pond scum right now."

"I get that feeling." Kane stood up. "I also get the feeling we're not accomplishing anything here except bothering you. Janelle?"

Nodding, Janelle gave Mina's hand a quick squeeze and rose to follow Kane to the door.

"Wait."

Janelle and Kane turned back.

Riordan caught up with them, glancing briefly at Mina first, as though gauging her emotions. "There is something. Not something that I want, but a source you might be able to use."

"We'll take anything," Janelle stated bluntly.

"Mina's father. Her real dad—"

"He's not my real dad," Mina broke in fiercely. "He's pond scum to rival Kane's pond scum. He's—"

"He's also a hereditary Druid, although I'm fairly sure he's broken all ties with the grove. His name is Duncan Forbes and he's a descendent of Akker, Maegth's father . . . just as Mina is. I'm not sure if that's key to your solution or not, but it certainly figured into mine. It's all tied together, so maybe it will help you."

Mina looked like she'd swallowed a bunch of nails, but she said not another word.

It was so ironic, Kane decided: the man who'd nearly become his father-in-law had produced the line that eventually gave birth to his brother's wife-to-be. The world was small. Small and not very happy, if Mina's closed expression was anything to go by. Kane looked at her. "More damage. Also my fault."

Mina didn't respond.

Riordan shrugged, slipped an arm around Mina and quietly answered for her. "I'm not sure about fault or no fault. Duncan didn't have to be a neglecting asshole of a father. As an adult, he's responsible for his own mistakes. And he's made some bad ones. It's just possible that he'll see the light now that I've been pardoned and the truth has come out. I'm not his enemy anymore. So, neither is Mina."

"You never should have been the enemy."

Riordan shrugged. "Moot point now. Let me know if I can do anything to help."

"You wish to help me make amends to you. There's irony." Kane offered him a crooked smile and a salute, then followed Janelle out the door and back to her car.

"This one's going to be difficult."

Janelle glanced up in surprise at Cindy, her nurse, a dedicated and normally cheerful professional who could charm anyone into near-comatose contentment. "Difficult? For you?" She widened her eyes for comic effect. "Nooooo. Say it isn't so."

Cindy made a face. "Yes. It is possible. I occasionally do clash with the odd human being or two."

"So what's up, then?" *Oh, wait. Not that. Please let it not be Kane.* Thanks to her guardian duties—was it really only the night before last, as in less than forty-eight hours ago, that this had all started?—she'd had to bring him to work with her today as her new volunteer. This, of course, had made for all kinds of fun explanations that didn't quite float in the workplace. Her co-workers had all eyed Kane with naked curiosity when she'd showed up with him in tow. So far none had outright questioned her "cousin" who was considering a career in the medical field, but that was probably just a matter of time. She just hoped the situation didn't damage her position at the clinic. She loved working here. It was exactly the kind of establishment she'd sought after graduation: four general practitioners in private partnership. As a currently salaried physician working for these four, she had high hopes of eventually buying in to become the fifth partner.

Of course, that goal was assuming—and it was a big assumption—she could win over Dr. Larry Hoffman. An ultra-conservative doctor with contempt for all alternative medicine and a barely concealed streak of chauvinism, Hoffman had been against hiring Janelle. He'd questioned her competence and her lack of experience, and some early work she'd done in college with nontraditional treatments of various diseases—treatments she herself had later found to be ineffectual. Luckily, Hoffman's partners had outvoted him. Janelle hoped that simple time and hard work would change his mind and he would accept her. He'd certainly had plenty of opportunity to observe. The man had been haunting her footsteps since the day she began work, and not always in a purely professional manner.

Her "cousin" Kane morphing into a horse in the middle of the clinic would undoubtedly draw Hoffman's negative attention. Surely Kane wouldn't have done anything outrageous. He'd promised—

"It's the patient in Exam Room Three," Cindy murmured. "He won't disrobe and he won't speak, but he's obviously ill, and his mother's at the end of her rope. And I'm at the end of mine, frankly."

Thank God. Well, not thank God that the kid was ill, or that Cindy was at the end of her rope, but at least Janelle didn't have otherworldly fun to handle. "Did you take his vitals?"

"Of course. His temp is elevated. Blood pressure's—" Cindy's cell phone rang and she frowned at it before glancing apologetically at Janelle. "Our friend in the lab at the hospital, returning my page. Here's Room Three's chart. It's all there." She handed off the folder to Janelle, who absently accepted it as she gazed over Cindy's shoulder.

Kane. What the hell was he doing back here? She'd told him to stay in the file room today unless it was an emergency. She opened her mouth to question him.

Kane just shook his head and pointed to Exam Room Four with a head jerk. He didn't even bother to glance at Cindy as the nurse slanted him a quizzical look in passing. Did the guy even know how to blend in? Camouflage, he'd said, was a puca's specialty. Ha! Without his glamour skills, no way would he disappear in the human world.

Janelle glared at him, raised her eyebrows, and mouthed the word *blend*.

He closed his eyes and nodded, then opened them to direct an intense look at her before pointing once again to Room Four.

Now he was dictating to her? Janelle narrowed her eyes at him. Puca business in no way trumped doctor business. In fact, it was very much the opposite. She shook her head, mouthed "patient first," and reversed course toward room three. Her patient was her top priority.

She heard a heavy exhalation behind her, along with a door opening and closing. Apparently, Kane would wait. How about that? A puca learns patience.

Quickly but carefully, she scanned her patient's chart, noting vitals and symptoms. Then she read Cindy's comments about his reluctance to contribute verbally, his obvious physical discomfort and his refusal to disrobe.

Curious now, she opened the door and strode inside. A young man of about sixteen leaned against the exam table. His mother, obviously flustered, sat in a chair across from him, legs and arms folded and expressing her disapproval.

Janelle offered both of them a wide smile as she closed the door behind her. "Don't you just hate going to the doctor? It's so embarrassing, having to take off your clothes and talk about personal stuff. I hate it myself and I *am* one."

The woman sighed explosively. "I know that. I keep telling him that. I won't judge. You won't judge. He still won't cooperate. I'm surprised I even got him here. But it was either that or call the ambulance—and I understand *that* would have humiliated him completely. So here we are."

Janelle nodded then turned to the young man. "Hi, Shawn. I'm Dr. Corrington."

He just nodded.

"I have seen everything. Literally everything. I'd reel off some examples, but your mom here would probably die of embarrassment and sue me for educating you prematurely."

He smiled reluctantly but briefly.

"What this means for you is that I'm completely unshockable. Almost numb, in fact. You can tell me anything."

"Including 'I don't want to be here'?"

Janelle shrugged. "Sure, but then you'd just be stating the obvious. You look uncomfortable to me. Why don't you have a seat on the table?"

He didn't respond and didn't move, just glanced away.

He was going to be a tough nut to crack. And he looked even paler than when she first walked into the room.

"Shawn!" This from his mother, who seemed to be fighting tears. When he didn't respond, she turned to Janelle. "He was cranky last night after school, seemed really tired, and then this morning . . . he was so much worse. I don't know what happened, why or where he hurts. Nothing. I don't know if he got hurt or sick at school or—"

"Mom!"

"Well, if you're not talking, I need to."

He sighed and shrugged. Seemed actually to be physically reeling now.

Concerned, Janelle stepped forward, catching his elbow to steady him as he listed sideways. As she made contact with his skin, waves of fever and pain washed over her. She nearly snatched her hand back. She'd never felt . . .

Wait. Could it be?

She inhaled deeply, slid her hand down his arm, as though checking the pulse point in his wrist. As she did so, she felt her consciousness waver a bit, her awareness merging into an alien one. Male. Young. Embarrassed as hell. Pain and heat and nausea and something infectious . . .

"A rat bite."

"What?" A mother's horror. "Oh, God. Rabies?"

"No." Janelle, a little woozy from the experience herself, hurried to clarify her abrupt—not to mention unexplainable—diagnosis. "But the wound is infected." She met the boy's eyes. "It's not going to kill him or cause permanent damage, but he does need immediate treatment."

"How did you—?" The boy was muttering, even as he interrupted his words and his thoughts with a wince. He was very pale and seemed mentally blurred.

Janelle strengthened her hold on him. "Lucky guess—which you confirmed." She shrugged with studied casualness. "Your symptoms reminded me of a former patient of mine."

"But how . . . ? Dear God, Shawn, what hellhole have you been haunting? What don't I know? Is it drugs? Prostitution?"

"Where's the bite, Shawn?" Janelle asked him quietly.

His color deepened.

Janelle laid her free hand on his forehead, another contact point, appearing to check for fever. That same merging distorted her vision but enhanced her other senses. Painful embarrassment, dread, impending surrender . . . she followed the waves of heat and poison to their point of origin. Backing out of the merge momentarily, Janelle let her focus drift low, halted, then met the boy's gaze. He looked to be in excruciating pain—both emotional and physical agony.

"Uh-oh." Janelle sang it quietly, just loud enough for the boy to hear. He wasn't going to die from this. At least, not due to physical causes. Emotional ones, however, were another issue entirely. She met his panicked gaze.

No doubt reading the unmistakable intent in her eyes, the boy finally spoke up. "Could we have my mom leave, at least?"

"Shawn," his mother protested.

"Sometimes it's easier to deal with strangers," Janelle murmured over her shoulder. "You don't have to look them in the eye later. I feel the same way. That's why I never go to doctors I consider to be co-workers or personal friends." Janelle gave the woman a bracing smile. "My nurse Cindy's right outside. Could you send her in to assist me?"

Janelle turned back to Shawn as his mother reluctantly stepped outside and closed the door. "It's time to come clean, Shawn. Tell me all about your rat bite."

"You know where it is."

"I sure do. So entertain me. Explain how you ended up with a rat down the front of your pants." She gave him a stern look. "Listen to your doctor. Very closely. I understand sexual experimentation. It's normal—to an extent. But cut it out with the deviant stuff. This kind of thing is very, very bad for the privates. You could end up regretting it for a long time."

"Deviant?" The boy looked confused.

Janelle eyed him cautiously. Hell, she wasn't going to cite the possibilities and give him ideas he might not already have. But he looked panicked, was feverish and in pain. She'd flush him out with silence.

He stared, confused and increasingly tense for a few long moments. Then he licked his lips with what had to be a very dry tongue in a dehydrated mouth. "Look, Doc. My girlfriend and I were just hanging out at her house. In . . . well, in the den. And things got kind of . . . And then it turned out her sister's pet rat had escaped and . . ."

Janelle got a sharp mental picture—in reality, it was the boy's sensory memory—of two mostly naked teens rolling in a pile of pillows, working up to the point of no return. Then, just before the deed . . . a bite, a screech and a scream.

Youch. She silently winced. Nice timing. Sharp teeth and one very worked-up and sensitive target. Not a stellar chain of events, but at least they didn't qualify him as Deviant of the Year. God knew she'd seen uglier things during her days as an intern in the ER. "I see." She cleared her throat delicately. "Smooth move, Romeo."

He just groaned, his humiliation complete.

"Hey, no worries. I'm not saying a word to your mom. That can be *your* job." She bit back her grin. God, what she wouldn't give to be a fly on the wall in his mom's living room tonight. "Somehow, I think the interrogation at home will be worse than the one here. But as soon as my nurse joins us, you'll drop your drawers without an argument."

She let the amusement tug a sunny smile across her face. "Or I'll have to get your mommy to do it for you."

Twenty minutes later, Janelle walked down the hallway, attempting with effort not to skip like a smug little kid. It worked! It had really worked! No, she hadn't healed with a thought—she hadn't even tried that yet—but she'd damn well diagnosed the rat bite as well as the extent of the infection. And she'd followed up with the appropriate but traditional medical treatment. The boy would be good as new—if his delicate psyche could withstand this evening's conversation with his mother.

She hadn't expected the merge thing, granted, and the hearing of her patient's thoughts and feelings during it . . . well, that was less than comfortable. But useful! The embarrassment alone was a dead giveaway. Nothing disturbed a boy more than a potentially deformed penis. Another twenty minutes and a few thoughts of impotence probably would have broken the kid without magical intervention, but she'd spared him that.

Still flying high, she opened the door to Exam Room Four, already squeaking out her triumph before the door closed: "I did it, Kane! I fixed his penis and he wasn't even going to tell me until—"

"Janelle."

She turned to Kane, grinning in her euphoria. She'd done it! No, *they'd* done it. She'd drawn on his magic to accomplish this wonder. This miracle. She stared at Kane, really seeing him as a man for the first time since he crawled out of her bed eight years ago. And not just any man. He affected her like nobody else had before or since. God, he was so gorgeous—was it any wonder she couldn't resist him then or now?—and she could see her own elation, her wonder reflected in his eyes. Almost as though he'd sensed and already shared the experience with her. In a way, he had, and she'd felt him—his magic—there with her, steady, powerful, breathtaking. And now titillating. Energizing. Utterly arousing. And, oh, seducing and . . . Helplessly drawn, she grabbed his shoulders and tugged him low until she lost her breath against his mouth.

The touch of their lips seemed to jar every nerve ending in her body. And then it was as though her nerve endings had grown additional nerve endings, her hormones reproducing like horny little rabbits to race around her bloodstream and perform crazed bunny flips in her belly. Janelle could hardly breathe through her libidinal meltdown. Given Kane's uneven breathing, the way he clutched her body against his, and . . .

She could feel Kane's emotions! He was stunned, aroused, pleased . . . alarmed. It was just like when she'd merged with her teenage patient. The healing gift. She'd felt the boy's physical discomfort, his emotional dismay, could even feel his instinctive withdrawal from her touch on his wrist and forehead. But this time it involved more than the physical and mental sharing of information. The arousal, for example. And thank God. Getting turned on by all her patients would be a bad, bad thing.

Getting turned on so completely by Kane . . . that was nearly as bad. And the connection was so complete with him. She felt threatened to her needy, overheated core as he deepened the kiss and she willingly followed his lead.

Her world became a heated jumble of sensation, her experiences mingling with his. The rebounded physical sensation of her lips touching his, the outline of her body, curves plumped against hard flesh. Her sensations and thoughts, hunger and craving, magnified by his similar, if more aggressive, feelings and urges, all set to spiral out of control. He could drop her on the floor and have her naked and willing in a matter of seconds. And he knew it as well as she did. Just as he knew how much it mortified her that she couldn't refuse herself or him. Regardless of the consequences.

The Druid's words floated back to her: *Only you will know exactly what that price is.*

This? This was the price of her healing gift? Dear God. Pulling back in one shaky lurch, she stared into Kane's eyes, seeing awareness there—awareness of *her* emotions, *her* physical reactions, *her* thoughts. Stunned by the completeness of their exchange, she retreated a step, shifting her focus away from his eyes.

And only then did she realize they weren't alone. She blinked as though awakening to—

Oh, boy. This was bad. She closed her eyes, breathing heavily and feeling a little sick as reality dropped on her head. Here she was, a respected physician getting it on in the exam room with a puca posing as her first cousin and in front of . . . whom? Reluctantly, she peered over Kane's shoulder at the strange man. A colleague? Potential patient? Any one of a number of people who'd cheerfully revoke her medical license and self-respect.

Whoever he was, he had looks to kill and . . . the same eerily golden eyes as Kane.

Janelle leaned weakly against the closed door, her gaze seeking out Kane's. "Oh, God. Not another brother. I really can't take this. So, what rock did this one crawl out of? Or maybe you—"

Kane cleared his throat before she could comment further. "Dr. Janelle Corrington, this is my father. Oberon. King of All Faerie."

And His Highness appeared royally pissed off.

CHAPTER FOUR ✧

"So. This is how you make amends to your brother for two thousand years' worth of betrayal?" King Oberon spoke softly, his words slicing deep.

Still reeling from the feel of Janelle against him—almost *inside* him—Kane regarded his father. "Actually, I—"

"Now just hold on a minute there, Mr. King of All Faerie." Janelle tipped her chin high, in a pose Kane had grown all too familiar with in the past two days. "How did you get in here?" Kane noticed she still leaned against the door, her thoughts in a jumble. Had she guessed that he could read them yet?

"Just who do you think you are to dictate where I can and cannot go?" Oberon, used to being feared and obeyed, didn't bother raising his voice.

Janelle straightened and took a stern step forward. "I'm one of the doctors who run this joint. That's who. Explain yourself and your reasons for being here before I call security and have you thrown out."

That would get ugly. Kane hurriedly spoke up. "Janelle, he's here because I called him."

Janelle turned an expressionless gaze on Kane. "You invited this *fairy king* to a doctor's office? During business hours? We have patients and nurses and other doctors running all over the place. Are you gonna gallop your horsey butt up and down the hallway next? We're trying to run a clean and semisane practice here."

"So you're saying I should have called him at your home."

"If you had to, then, yeah. That would have been just a little more discreet."

"Are you two finished now?" Oberon interrupted. Without waiting for a response, he turned to his son. "I assume you called to give me an accounting of yourself."

"No, sir, I didn't. I assumed you'd already heard about—"

"Your High Druid nearly disgraced himself giving me the details, but at least he was man enough to do the explaining. And why did I know nothing of this vendetta of yours? I thought you agreed that Riordan's exile was sufficient punishment." Oberon tossed his hands high. "Apparently not."

Kane attempted patience. "I didn't tell you about the rest because I didn't want to put you in the middle of our—"

"And if you weren't calling me to give me the details, why the hell did you bother calling me at all?"

Kane's temper flared. "Let me finish a sentence and maybe I'll tell you."

"There." Oberon raised royal eyebrows. "You finished one. Speak."

"I am not a dog." Kane narrowed his eyes. "And, effective three days ago, I also am not your heir. You disowned Riordan two thousand years ago. He should be your heir." His temper draining in the face of what he had to do now, Kane screwed up his courage and every iota of honor he might actually have. He had no choice. "I wish to be disowned."

Obviously stunned, Oberon regarded his son speechlessly.

"You know it's the right thing to do."

"You can't be serious. The boy's lived inside a rock for two thousand years. He can't rule the realm when I'm gone."

Like Oberon would ever give up the ghost anyway. Kane strove for patience. "He's a grown man, made wiser by excruciating experience. He also has compassion. God knows he's treated me more fairly than I could possibly deserve. He would rule well." And Kane meant every word of this. He hated every damn one, too, but they were all true.

"But, see, there's another good point. He's a man. As in, *human*. He now has a lifespan only slightly longer than that of an insect. What kind of ruler would a human make?"

"A compassionate one?" Kane replied calmly.

"Maybe. But I don't even know if the elders would approve of this. We've never encountered this situation before. A human to be King of All Faerie?" Oberon's tone and expression pronounced the idea absurd.

"So convince the elders. We've both wronged Riordan— you by consistently favoring me." Kane paused. "And I . . . well, we both know what I did. I jailed him unjustly for two thousand years. He could do the same to me—would be perfectly justified in doing so—but he hasn't asked for it. *That* is a good example of why he deserves the throne. He's rational and compassionate."

"And he will be dead inside of fifty years," Oberon ended quietly.

"Hello?" Janelle looked appalled. "Fifty years isn't exactly nothing. And as for 'insect' . . . Geez, why don't you just exterminate us all now if our little human lives are so insignificant?"

Oberon frowned thoughtfully. "We have considered it in the past, but the issue was set aside for some reason I forget now. Perhaps we should take it up—"

"Oh, for Pete's sake." Janelle glared.

Oberon waved dismissively. "As for young Riordan—"

Kane sighed impatiently. "Dad. He's less than a half century younger than I am."

"Do not interrupt. As for your brother . . ." Oberon shook his head. "I guess I will have to consider." He regarded Kane broodingly. "I suppose I must at least attempt to disown you."

Kane nodded.

"Why?" The word burst from Janelle as if she couldn't stand it any longer. "Why does he have to be disowned? Why do either of your sons have to be disowned?"

"Titania." Father and son spoke in unison.

Janelle widened her eyes, as though to encourage more, preferably meaningful, explanation.

Kane was amused in spite of himself. Here he was, severing ties with his family, his past, his people. He was even giving up all claim to the throne for which he'd been groomed . . . and still she could entertain him.

"Do you all need a little help with this?" she asked with exaggerated simplicity. "I'll start: Titania is . . ." She raised her eyebrows in invitation.

"My wife." Oberon spoke shortly.

"And not my mother," Kane added, his tone matter-of-fact.

"Oops?" She glanced from father to son.

"And also not Riordan's mother." Kane managed with difficulty to keep his expression bland. His father was bound to be irate as it was.

Meanwhile, Janelle eyed Oberon with open disapproval.

The king scowled. "It was at least two thousand years ago." He seemed to consider that sufficient explanation.

"What, you were young and frisky? The nubile faerie king sowing his magical oats?"

"Easy, Janelle." Kane spoke quietly.

She ignored the warning. "So were you married to Titania when the boys were each born?"

"No. I was merely engaged to Titania when Kane was born . . . but married to her when Riordan was. And yes," Oberon forestalled the question, "Titania was enraged. Even today, she's not enamored of either of the boys."

"What he means is she will only tolerate one of us at a time. She likes having us at each other's throats. The favored son has the honor of living at court with Oberon and Titania."

"And that was you?" Janelle asked Kane.

"That was me."

"Living with that pair versus living in a rock. Tough call." Janelle shook her head. "So are you guys done here? I have a patient waiting."

"If you have a patient waiting, why were you seducing my son in your examining room?"

"Just had to get that little dig in there, didn't you?" She scowled, her cheeks pink. "I'll keep everyone out of this room for exactly fifteen minutes more. Then I'll need you both to leave."

She opened the door, slipped out and let the door slam shut. Kane eyed it for a thoughtful moment.

"Tell me that's not your guardian."

Kane turned back to his father. "You know she is."

"You've lain with her."

"Years ago." Kane paused. "Well, a few years ago." Eight years, almost to the day. He'd counted all of them in spite of himself. In spite of his vow not to care.

It couldn't be her. He'd refused to believe it then and he refused to believe it now. And yet . . . she was the only woman in two millennia who'd made him feel anything at all beyond lust. Every other woman had left him cold. And he knew that for a fact because he'd tried. One woman after another. He shook his head. He'd had a hell of a good time, but after a while . . . it had all seemed meaningless. Until Janelle.

Maegth the Druid maiden who wasn't so maidenly had known how to curse every bit as well as her father.

With painful and devastating precision. Riordan didn't know it, but Kane had been damned every bit as much as Riordan. Possibly more so. Riordan, after all, had Mina now. Riordan had also had Maegth. And Janelle was a loyal friend to Riordan, even as she distrusted Kane with every particle of her being. Not that she lacked cause. Yet Kane wanted her. Again. And again.

Oberon regarded Kane with utter disgust. "At this rate, maybe I really should reinstate Riordan. You've failed before you've even begun. Lusting after the forbidden already."

"Who are you to talk? Bad enough that you seduced my mother, an innocent, completely unaware, but then to go after that poor soul who mothered Riordan—"

"I loved your mother." Oberon spoke fiercely. Kane's mother had been a human princess.

"And Riordan's?"

Oberon looked uncomfortable for a moment before he shrugged it off. "It's not for you to judge. Look at you. Look what you've done. To Riordan, to yourself. To me." He shook his head before eyeing Kane with disappointment. "You leave me no choice. I concede to your wishes. Consider yourself . . . disowned." He looked ill at ease now. "Excuse me while I go try to crown a human to be a faerie prince."

Grumbling, Oberon opened the examining room door, his image evaporating with his first step into the hallway. The king knew how to make an exit.

"Now just slow down. Take a deep breath and tell me again." Her head ringing, Janelle held the phone to her ear as she stared accusingly at Kane. It was evening, and they were back at her apartment. It had been a long day, with the second half of this particular day a whole lot less eventful and yet more annoying than the first half. She pinched the bridge of her nose, mostly just to distract herself from pounding temples.

Mina was still ranting in her ear. "And now he's a freaking faerie prince. I'm marrying a faerie prince—who is really a human. Is that even legal? Can Oberon do this to us? Did Kane put him up to it? Because I can damn well do without the honor. Do you have any idea what kind of havoc running a damn faerie kingdom can wreak on a human happily-ever-after? I'm a teacher. Riordan's an entrepreneur. Does any of the above sound in the least like we want the headache of woo-woo politics, especially when the subjects won't even want to be ruled by us? I mean, Riordan's not even likely to live long enough to get the throne, so all we're getting is the hassle of him being an unwanted heir. The kingdom was supposed to be Kane's. He can damn well keep it."

Janelle lifted the phone from her ear, regarded Kane evilly, and handed it over to him. "Your future sister-in-law has a few issues to discuss with you."

Kane eyed the phone as he might a poisonous snake. Or maybe an ugly troll? What did a puca consider frightening, dangerous, and/or repulsive, anyway? Good question. Janelle lowered the phone just a little. "Do trolls exist?"

He looked startled. "Excuse me?"

"Trolls, pixies, brownies, gnomes—all the miniature magicky types. Are they real?"

"Those? No." He lowered eyelids over glinting gold irises. "But dragons and unicorns are." He grabbed the phone even as Janelle's jaw dropped open.

"You're kidding, right? Seriously?"

But he was already speaking into the phone. "Hello, Mina. This is Kane. Janelle said there was something I could do for you?"

The ranting grew louder. Kane flinched, held the phone away, then resolutely tucked it back against his ear. He nodded, obviously listening closely. After a moment he sighed. "Yes, that was me. Riordan is the heir and that's the way it should be. I'm not fit." He paused, flinched again. "I know he's not a faerie. Neither am I. But we're the only sons Oberon has. The rest are female."

"Excuse me?" Janelle stepped closer now. "Why can't a female be heir?"

He regarded her and the phone with mock awe. "Did you two rehearse that?" He shook his head, obviously enduring continued rants. "I didn't make up the rules. Try convincing Oberon. He's the one who insists on a male heir, based on long-standing precedent, although not everyone agrees with him. Hell, Titania thinks *she* should rule. Actually, I think she does rule to some extent. But you can bet she'd do her best to snatch the official crown when and if Oberon ever kicks—" He broke off his own words, eyebrows arching high. "All right."

He handed the phone back to Janelle, who heard that the line was disconnected. "What happened?" She was almost afraid to ask.

"Titania's there." Kane sounded unconcerned.

"*What?* Stepmommy Dearest? With Mina and Riordan? But she hates Riordan, you said. And now Riordan has no powers, and Mina's as human as . . ." With a groan, Janelle slipped aching feet back into her shoes and grabbed her purse, while Kane watched curiously. "Well, what are you standing there for? Aren't you the guy hoping to make amends? Saving Riordan's ass from Stepmommy Bitchiest might be a good place to start. Let's go." She scrambled for her keys, muttering and wincing over her feet. "I swear I never thought I'd one day be called upon to referee faerie family feuds."

"This is how you make amends to your brother? Hello? Does he look like he feels all fuzzy-warm and forgiving now?" Mina glanced from Janelle to an annoyed-looking Riordan, and back to Kane. "We don't want this. Take it back."

"Yes, Kane. Take it back." Titania spoke quietly, her breathy voice a low taunt. "You know you want to."

Janelle resisted staring at the woman. No, not just *woman*. *Faerie*. No, make that faerie queen. Or *scary* queen. The woman had the impossible body of a center-fold, the breathy voice of Marilyn Monroe, huge, almost cartoon-like blue eyes, and this thread of evil uniting the shiny pieces into one truly disturbing whole. Oberon slept with *that*? Yech. Maybe it was a fetish. A twisted, terrifying fetish.

"You know I can't take it back. It was Oberon's decree that you replace me as his heir."

"But at *your* instigation." Riordan spoke with certainty.

Kane nodded. "So, you're not pleased."

"In my shoes, who would be?" Riordan was blunt.

Titania laughed low, the shadowed silver of her voice rippling along Janelle's spine. Eerie woman. Too beautiful for real life and reeking of danger.

Definitely a fetish.

Janelle cleared her throat and risked a glance at Titania. "Could *you* change it? You are the faerie queen. I assume that means you have the power of a queen? Maybe even veto power over the king?"

Her Royal Highness shrugged, gravity-resistant breasts lifting high beneath a wealth of golden hair. "I suppose I could try. But it would be such an effort. Now, if you'd like to offer me a little *incentive* . . ."

"What kind of incen—" Janelle began.

"*No.*" Riordan and Kane spoke in hard unison.

Janelle and Mina eyed them in surprise. Titania, not surprised at all, merely waved a dismissive hand. "As you wish. Well, I'll leave now that I've greeted our new crown prince." She smiled flirtatiously at Riordan, which visibly raised Mina's hackles. "It's just so amusing to have a human for an heir to all of Faerie."

"Yeah. Hilarious." Mina spoke with low warning.

Riordan put a restraining hand on his fiancée's arm, even as Titania laughingly vanished in a display of min-iature fireworks.

Janelle stared, then shook herself free of the shock. "Could that woman *be* any scarier?"

"No kidding." Mina looked pale beneath her irritation.

Riordan and Kane eyed the women with interest before Kane spoke. "Most humans consider Titania almost too beautiful to look upon."

"Oh, she's hard to look upon all right." Janelle shivered. "Do *not* turn your back on the faerie queen."

"It's probably the breasts," Mina muttered scornfully. "Human males would stare at those and miss the great wellspring of evil altogether."

Janelle nodded in silent agreement. "So, she was here just to stir things up? About the heir business?"

"Yeah. And speaking of the heir business . . ." Mina turned to Kane while Riordan looked merely resigned. "What were you *thinking*? Are you trying to sabotage our future?"

Janelle intervened quietly. "It was a dumb move. I'll give you that much. But I think he really was trying to do the right thing."

"Given his usual affiliation in the war between good and evil, I suppose he is most unfamiliar with the good part. He was bound to screw up something as simple as 'doing the right thing.'" Mina dropped onto a chair with a huff.

"Riordan was disowned when he was cursed. Kane was just trying to undo that along with the other bad stuff."

"Disowned is one thing, Kane. But I was never intended to be heir. That was always you." Riordan spoke quietly.

Kane frowned but didn't deny the truth of those words.

Janelle watched him attentively. This was hurting Kane. Immensely. Giving up his family, his heritage, the throne . . . She supposed it was possible he was willing to trade the throne for his freedom. That might qualify as amends. Except, Riordan didn't seem to want it. And Kane knew this. Was it guilt that drove him? Justice? Or the drive to fulfill his quest and be done with it?

"So why did you do this?" Riordan persisted, to Janelle's great relief.

"I think it should be obvious why. Let me quote the wise words of my guardian: Two. Thousand. Freaking. Years." Kane shrugged, his voice and words mocking, even as his gaze briefly and seriously met Janelle's. "Somebody who can sustain anger for that long should not be in a position of power over others. Period."

"Maybe not," Riordan mused. "But I think it's also reasonable for a people to want their ruler to be of the same species. They don't want a human to rule them."

"You're not just a human, though. You're King Oberon's son. The more-deserving son."

"And I probably won't outlive my father. I have a human lifespan now, remember? I'll live another fifty years or so, tops. That's a drop in the bucket to someone of faerie blood. They might as well have no heir at all."

"What is it with you faerie types that you shrug off a human lifespan as negligible?" Janelle glanced back and forth between the two men. "As if it's barely worth living at all."

"And if that's how you thought," Mina quietly regarded Riordan, "why did you agree to live as a human? With me? That was basically a death sentence for you." She shook her head slowly. "You could have had magic and eternity."

"Mina, we've already been through this. An eternity without you would qualify as a death sentence for me. A *life* sentence"—Riordan grinned, clearly enjoying his double meaning—"would constitute a human lifetime and beyond, but with you by my side. I want to spend always with you. Together through all."

Mina, who'd slugged his shoulder at the mention of

life sentence, went soft and wide-eyed as he finished his statement. "You really mean that?"

"You know I do." Riordan edged closer, his voice dropping.

"And that would be our cue to leave." Janelle sidled toward the front door, with a thoughtful-looking Kane following. They slipped out, fairly certain that neither Mina nor Riordan noticed, if they remembered they'd had visitors at all.

As Janelle silently descended the porch steps, Kane kept pace at her side. "He really meant that."

"What?" Her thoughts elsewhere, Janelle frowned at him.

"Riordan would rather limit himself to fifty years with Mina followed by death than live an eternity without her."

Janelle glanced quickly away. The utter bemusement in Kane's voice should not bother her. It shouldn't, damn it. "Lifetime, unconditional commitment. I could see where you'd be unfamiliar with those concepts. One night is generally sufficient in your eyes."

"I never said that."

"You didn't have to. You could never see yourself, under any circumstances, giving up immortality for a woman." She said it as a statement but meant it as a question.

"Isn't it a primal instinct for all of us to stay alive?" he hedged.

"Yes. That's why people pay me, remember?" She raised her eyebrows pointedly. "But we're intelligent beings, capable of consciously acting contrary to those primal instincts, given a sufficient motivation. A mother dying to protect her young. A soldier undertaking a suicidal mission for the sake of his country . . ."

Kane looked at her. "Yes, I do believe there is a time and occasion for sacrifice. But I do not take my immortality lightly. It's who I am. It's my life. I have a definite birth, as do all my people, but then we can live indefinitely without aging, immune to disease and able to recover from most injuries. It's what we know—part of our world, part of our identity. And immortality is important enough to our people that I have serious doubts whether a mortal Riordan will be accepted as ruler, no matter how hard Oberon argues in his favor. Worthy or not, I do know Oberon relies on me as his backup. He needs someone of his blood to take the throne after he is gone."

"So your push to have Riordan named heir to the throne is all just a publicity stunt for you. A sham, a pretense of payback." She cast him a cynical, seriously disappointed look. "It's so easy to offer what you know can't be accepted."

"No. I don't expect you to believe me, but that's not my intent at all. Riordan deserves at least that the attempt be made, if not also the throne in fact. Independent of my fate, independent of the actual identity of our future ruler. He deserves that we accord him this respect."

"And all at no cost to you." She quickened her steps and turned to head down the sidewalk in the direction of her car. Before she got two steps farther, however, Kane grabbed her by the sleeve and pulled her to a stop.

Heart pounding, she turned to face him. At least he'd grabbed her sleeve. No skin-to-skin contact, so he couldn't send her into a lather of hormones or read her thoughts.

His next words proved that wrong. "Yes, I can."

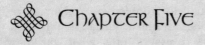 ## ChapTer Five

Janelle glanced up in surprise. Kane didn't mean, *couldn't* mean—

"Yes, I do mean. For such an intelligent woman, you've been in denial about this for a while." Kane looked impatient now. "If I'm going to do this—make amends to everyone I've hurt—then logic tells me I can't start by hiding something like this from you. Or letting you hide it from yourself."

So he knew when she—

"Yes, I knew."

"Oh, God. Stop that. Right now." *Mary had a little lamb. Its fleece was*—

"White as snow." His eyes twinkled. When she goggled at him with horror, his amusement faded. "I'm sorry if this upsets you, but it's just how it is. And now that you know, you can guard yourself against me."

"But I thought it was just because of the healing thing."

"The healing thing? You mean the mind connection." His eyes darkened with the memory and his voice grew husky. "Oh, sure, everything was intensified—and I do mean everything—right after you drew on my magic to diagnose that boy. But even under normal circumstances,

I can read your thoughts when you're projecting them." He shrugged, his expression now matter-of-fact. "And you project them a lot. You're an honest person, so it wouldn't occur to you to shield your thoughts from me."

"No, actually, it wouldn't occur to me to shield them because in my world, people can't read each other's thoughts!" She inhaled sharply, feeling violated. Utterly. She wrapped her arms around her waist.

"I'm sorry."

She glanced at him and then away. "So you've always known everything—"

"Before you spoke? Yes. Like I said, you project."

She frowned, pinching the bridge of her nose. The throb in her temples had escalated to sheer pounding.

"Touch your temples."

"What?" She let her hand fall to her side and eyed him blankly, her thoughts scattering. Probably *projecting* as they scattered, too, damn it.

His lips twitched slightly. "Touch your fingers to your temples. It may take the pain away."

She started. The healing bit. Could she heal herself? Carefully, she raised her hand as though it belonged to someone else. As though she were picking up an inanimate tool. A scalpel. A syringe. She applied it to her temple. The disorientation was milder, but the pounding felt like it was in stereo now.

"No, this makes it worse." She started to drop her hand.

Kane caught her shirt cuff and gently replaced her hand. "Focus. Don't just react. Find the origin of the pain, the discordance, and realign."

"How could you possibly know—"

"I've spent time around Druids. I know how they think. It may not work the way I'm telling you to do it, but I have a feeling it will. What can it hurt to try?"

Janelle inhaled deeply, tried to think above the cacophony in her head. As she exhaled, the pulsing seemed to sharpen, and she tried to follow it to its source. She made progress . . . but the pulsing intensified, scattering her focus, and she lost it. "I can't."

Kane just held her hand in place, his eyes meeting hers. "Focus. You can find your way."

Janelle tried another deep breath. And then another. Followed the pulsing again, held on until . . . *There*. Somehow, she could sense the discord, knew she could tune her mind to it. Instinct took over and she mentally soothed enlarged blood vessels and irritated nerves, neutralizing the chemical imbalances.

As she did so, she noticed the pounding in her head easing to a mild throb, to a subtle pulse, and then fading completely away. She dropped her hand and stared at Kane. She was mildly fatigued by her efforts but nearly euphoric over the results. Amazing. A miracle. She could do this now?

He met her eyes, a surprisingly sweet smile tugging at his mouth. He seemed genuinely pleased for her.

"I *am* pleased for you. Why wouldn't I be? So little compensation for what you're enduring because of me. I'm glad if it pleases *you*."

Her pleasure dimmed. "Do you know what would please me even more? No, don't say it. Of course you already know. But do me the honor of letting me speak my own damn thoughts. Okay?"

He nodded assent, but it was just a formality. As they both knew.

"You know what would really please me? What would please me is if you would teach me how to shield my thoughts from you."

He was obviously unsurprised. "I can try."

"Why just *try*? I'm all for *do*."

"Well, it's a skill, like so many other things in life. Some master it better than others. I have . . . well, to be honest, I don't know whether you'd even be capable of fully shielding your thoughts from me and from others like me."

Janelle stared at him, her heart thudding. "That's not acceptable."

"I can understand that."

"Don't be so damned understanding. I don't need it and I don't trust it. You can read my thoughts. Do you know how humiliating, how degrading that is? How violated I feel?"

"Look, I don't intentionally—"

"Oh, don't give me that. You're telling me you can't just ignore my thoughts and emotions? Just mentally block them? I don't buy it."

"You're right. Normally I can block them. I do it all the time. But with you it's harder."

"Why?"

He met her eyes, his own lit with a desire she shared. Utter awareness. "You know why. You read my thoughts, too."

In the examining room. The kiss. Yeah, the one she'd so far managed to at least partially suppress. The intimacy had been complete to the point of overstimulation of body, soul, heart and mind. It was staggering.

"Frankly, I don't see any way possible for me to successfully ignore you. Or your thoughts. And no way in hell I could suppress any detail of memory surrounding that kiss."

She smiled tightly. "Oh, but I'll bet you can guess— yes, even without reading my thoughts—why *I* might want to suppress it. It's—ooh, surprise again!—*because* you can read my thoughts. All the time. This is just not fair. What if you wore an MP3 player? You could listen to music or books on tape. Wouldn't that drown me out?"

He smiled, obviously entertained by what he considered utter foolishness. "You'd make me walk around with music blaring in my ears twenty-four hours a day?"

"Well, not while I sleep." She frowned. "No, I take that

back. You definitely have to use it while I sleep." Oh, good Lord. What had she dreamed last night?

"Nothing, really. You were awake most of the night."

The throbbing at her temples began anew. She eyed him, feeling all sorts of violent, decidedly *un*-Hippocratic urges. "Look. Even if you can read my thoughts. Would you mind not making it quite so obvious to me? Like, by not responding to all of them? I'm a physician. They teach me not to kill. And yet I want to, so very badly right now."

He opened his mouth—

"And if you say you understand this, I will follow through on the urge. Don't tell me pucas can't be killed. I don't see anyone surviving a beheading. And I know how to wield a blade." She'd briefly trained in surgery, after all, even if she had chosen family practice.

He looked thoughtful a moment. "I guess killing me would take care of the problem for you. A dead ward leaves the guardian essentially unburdened."

"Oh, sure, that would work. Murder as a viable solution for a doctor who swore to protect life. I have an MP3 player. Until I master this shield thing, I'd appreciate it if you made use of it. Not constantly. Not permanently. Just frequently."

"That's not going to happen." When she glared at him, he just held her gaze. "I can't be absent in mind and still complete my task. And I can't afford to hang around long enough for you to master mind shields."

She raised her chin, suppressing any thought of hurt feelings. There was no reason to be hurt. She didn't care. Would not. "So now you're the one cutting out on me?"

"You were right. I need to get out of your life so you can return to your healing and your good deeds. Unhindered."

"My healing and my good deeds. Like I'm the closest thing to a fairy godmother around here." She waved off his objection. "Let's just go, okay?" She nodded at the house behind him. "They've been staring out the window at us since we got out here."

He eyed her curiously. "That matters?"

"There you go again. Testing my Hippocratic oath." Dismissing him, she whirled and stalked down the sidewalk in the direction of her car.

"Look, I thought you'd at least appreciate my honesty."

"Nope. Too pissed about the reality, thanks." She stalked a little faster, only getting angrier when he easily matched her pace.

He said, "So let me get this straight. After helping curse my brother and thereby earning the wholehearted approval of Akker and the ancient Druids, I throw that away by coming clean to everyone. I talk my father into welcoming my brother back into the family and his will, only this manages to piss off both my brother and his fiancée. Then I make the mistake of telling a woman the truth for her own good and I still get nothing but grief and contempt. What am I doing here?"

Janelle snorted. "I'm weeping for you. Deep inside. Really. Now get in the car." She double-clicked her key remote and swung her own door open while Kane rounded the car to the passenger side.

"Life was much simpler before I discovered the inconvenience of a conscience," he murmured to himself as he slid into his seat.

"What was that?" she muttered distractedly. She clasped her seat belt and slipped the key in the ignition.

"Nothing important." He clasped his own seat belt.

She cast him a sharp look. "Something about a conscience? What would you know about a conscience? Besides a momentary aberration in the middle of a state park we both know and love."

"You're right, of course."

She stilled and turned quietly to face him. "So, what about that aberration? Why?"

"Why what?"

"Don't be deliberately obtuse. Why did you come to Riordan's rescue? God knows I showed up too late to do anything for him, assuming I even could. Why did you confess? You didn't gain a thing by doing it."

"And that confuses you."

"Big time."

He gave her a mocking look. "What about that 'love' you're so convinced I harbor for my brother?"

"If you harbored it days ago, you must have harbored it centuries ago. And yet you did nothing to help him until now. Why is that? Something must have happened recently to inspire this sudden act of mercy."

Kane shrugged unconcernedly. "In all honesty, I could not help him before now. His path was set. He could not be freed until this time, with this guardian and in this manner. It was foreseen."

"Not in detail, though, right?"

Kane turned away.

"Oh, great. More secrets. Like this is fair. If I were you, I'd just take a little walk in your head and gather up the answers for myself. I can't do that. Suppose you give a little, just to make this arrangement a little less uncomfortable for me. Can you do that?"

"So you want me to confess to you? Is that it?" He eyed her with amusement. "Is this punishment for what I did to you way back when?"

She stiffened. "Let's leave way back when where it belongs and deal with the here and now. Tell me where your head is. Right now. Tell me what prompted you to speak for your brother."

He stared out the windshield a moment. "If you'd arrived at that Druid Council meeting a few minutes sooner than you did, you might have heard a little something about that. It seems"—he glanced at her and then away—"that I grew a conscience at some point. An infantile one, no doubt, but a real one."

"Just out of nowhere. For no reason. One day, no conscience; next day, you're weeping for the brother you condemned. Just a random change of heart." She stared at him. "I'm not buying it. Something happened."

He sighed. "Not something. Someone."

"Someone? Who? Mina? Look, buddy, I hope you're not thinking what I think you're thinking. And by the way, if I *were* you, I'd already know what you were thinking, but I don't, which really sucks. As your guardian, I really think I should have access to your thoughts, just as you have access to mine. The way things are, I'm at a complete disadvantage."

"So we compensate, like you suggested. Just what do you think I'm thinking?"

"Mina. She's Riordan's." Janelle glared at him. "Sure, she's wonderful and all, but she loves your brother and your brother loves her. They basically walked through the fires of hell to be together. You can't fight that and win."

"Right. You think I want Mina." He nodded blandly.

"It makes sense, don't you think? Riordan slept with your woman way back when. If you slept with his woman now, it would both even the score and stroke that temperamental ego of yours back into proper form."

"I like Mina. She seems great. I think my brother chose well."

Janelle's stomach knotted and she fisted her hands against the urge for violence. "See? So paws off, buddy." She'd never been a violent woman before. What was her problem now?

"Mina's not the one I was talking about."

"Then who? Some other girl you met?"

"You could say that." He turned to face her. "It was you."

Janelle studied Kane for a baffled moment, even as he studied her just as closely. Her reaction seemed very important to him. "Me? Now that makes no sense.

I hadn't seen you in years before we met again at Druids' Grove."

"True. *You* hadn't seen *me* in eight years. Not since I left you that morning." He lifted a shoulder casually. "But it could be that I checked in on you every once in a while after that."

"Checked in on—You've been spying on me?"

"Not with intent to harm or anything like that. Just . . . looking out for you, sort of. From a distance. I was a bastard to you. I knew that. I honestly never meant to be—at least, not that much of one, but . . ."

"But what?"

Her words seemed to interrupt his thoughts, almost as though he'd been speaking mostly to himself, with his focus distant in time and place. He realized now that she was in the car with him. "But maybe my focus . . . was elsewhere. You were collateral damage that I regretted. I mostly just wanted to make sure you were okay. I hurt you at a vulnerable time, what with your parents' recent deaths. I was willing to glamour if necessary to help you past all of that." He appraised her. "But I didn't have to. You did it all on your own and came out ahead. I've always admired that."

"Great. Wonderful. And I'll try really hard not to be freaked out by my own monkey-man-horse stalker-slash-guardian angel. But that still doesn't explain a change of heart days ago."

He studied her, eventually arriving at the obvious conclusion that she wasn't about to let the subject drop just to make life easier for him. "Fine." He shrugged. "It was Paul."

Now that, she hadn't expected. "Paul?"

"Yes. It was late at night on a holiday weekend, not quite a year ago, and you were on call. You hadn't seen him in years." He eyed her significantly.

She colored and looked away. "Nope, not since he dumped me for somebody else. Someone willing to forfeit enough work hours to make time for a relationship. I remember. Go on."

"You were covering for another doctor, one who was part of another practice and who was away on vacation at the time."

"A pediatrician." She spoke quietly. "Duties shuffle pretty widely over holidays. Since I don't have family, I usually offer to cover wherever I'm needed." It kept her busy on those days when she didn't want to think about what she was missing. "So you were watching me then?"

"It was the holidays. I knew you were alone." He shrugged off the subject, his gaze growing distant with recollection. "I remember you looking at Paul, at his crying wife, at the pale baby in her arms. And at the time you were thinking . . ." He hesitated.

She wasn't as kind. "I was thinking that it could have been my baby, had things been different." Her voice was toneless.

She hadn't loved Paul. Oh, sure, she'd liked him. She'd just never given the relationship a chance to develop into anything deeper than that. She'd been too busy with work, and frankly, too afraid to let anyone that close.

No, it was just the idea that hurt when she saw him again. The foregone possibilities. And those had hurt more than she'd ever expected. She was lonely; she'd once dated him and levered him into pushing her away, and now he had a family. She was still lonely. But that was her own fault, not Paul's nor his wife's nor, for Pete's sake, that helpless little baby's. Still, her first reaction had been less than generous.

"But you didn't dwell on that part," Kane continued in a wondering voice. "You went to the hospital with them because Paul and his wife needed a familiar face, somebody to intercede for them, and you had connections at the hospital to get that baby the best care. If you hadn't acted so quickly, the baby might not have made it."

"I was doing my job."

"You were being selfless. To help a man who hurt you and the wife you believed in your heart—at least for a moment—had taken your place and lived the life you could have lived. You set all of that aside to help another woman's baby. They thanked you. You smiled and shrugged it off." He paused and continued more quietly. "Then you went home to be alone again."

"I was just doing my job," she ground out between her teeth. "That's all."

"No. Well, sure it's the truth, but it's not all. Your actions were generous and full of heart. That's just who you are, Janelle. It . . . it humbled me." He smiled, mocking himself now. "In that one act, given all the acts leading up to it, including my callous behavior years ago, you became my conscience."

Janelle was appalled. This was her reward for doing her job in spite of sour grapes? "Oh, no. No, you don't. I don't need that kind of burden. You go attach your new-found conscience to somebody who can live up to it. It's not me."

"It is you. But it's not intended to be your burden. My conscience is my own burden, as it should be. But I might look to you occasionally for a little guidance." His eyes twinkled, as though he knew his words terrified her.

She shook her head slowly, then, fumbling, turned the key in the ignition. Erratic moments later, they were coasting along in traffic, Janelle staring a little dazedly out the windshield. "You know, I didn't sign on to be your conscience."

Kane laughed, seeming almost freer for some reason, now that he'd explained his actions. "Yes, you did. You're my guardian, remember? That makes you the ideal person to be my conscience. Besides, a conscience requires empathy, doesn't it?"

She chanced a glance at him. "Empathy helps."

"Empathy requires feeling. I have very little of that—"

"That's reassuring."

"Except with you." He frowned and seemed to shake his head a little, as though to negate his own words.

"Let's not go overboard, shall we? If you start declaring your undying love for me," she mocked, her heart pounding, "I'm shoving you through the windshield."

"Actually, this isn't a romantic pronouncement, just a statement of fact. A fact I would change if I could. And the unfeeling part isn't so much a fact as a curse."

"A curse. You are cursed with a lack of feeling."

"Literally? No, not lack of feeling . . . although some might argue that." He smiled without humor. "In reality, I'm cursed with the inability to love romantically."

Love romantically? He didn't mean . . . no, she wasn't going there. Back to the point. "You were literally cursed? By whom? The Druid again?"

"His daughter."

Janelle gave him a wide-eyed look. "Oh. More vengeance? You guys must have made a fun couple. So what was the curse, anyway?"

He looked rueful now. "I believe her words were something about me acting in an unfeeling manner toward her and thus reaping what I sowed. She cursed me to be unfeeling in fact as well as action. No woman would ever move me again. Except one."

"And this is where I come in?"

"It's . . . possible that you are the exception." And he seemed to like that idea no more than she did.

"Great. And why am I so blessed?"

"I have no idea."

And, apparently, it freaking pissed him off. She was just so flattered. "Well, gee, that explains everything."

"I thought it might."

"No. Don't even think you can throw off all responsibility for this one. I'm not about to blame a long-dead Druid girl for this sudden birth of conscience you want to toss in my lap. You can raise your own damn conscience as far as I'm concerned. It seems to me the girl had a beef with you, reacted to something you did, so it's still all your fault." She shot him an annoyed look. "What exactly did you do anyway? Why *did* she turn to Riordan when she was engaged to you?"

He grimaced. "I'm not sure you would understand."

"You're probably right. But try me anyway. What did you do to piss off your little Druid fiancée?"

"She discovered I was engaged to someone else."

Janelle stilled. "You were engaged to two women at once. And neither of them killed you?"

"Not just any two women. One human woman— Maegth—and one of faerie blood. Alanna. She was of the Unseelie court, while I was of the Seelie. A marriage between us would have added another bond between two faerie courts that exist in an uneasy truce. But my relationship with Maegth was entirely personal." He lowered his voice to a brooding tone. "My plan was to discreetly marry Maegth while maintaining an engagement with Alanna, more a political alliance than an emotional one, until . . ." He glanced at Janelle uneasily.

"Well?" she prompted when he didn't finish. "Until when? A month later? A year? Would it be a fake engagement you'd let taper off? How did you plan on handling it?"

He shifted restlessly. "Actually, I didn't plan to break the engagement with Alanna at all. It would simply be . . . a little on the long side."

Warning bells. "How long?"

"For the duration of Maegth's human life. After, as Maegth's widower, I could marry Alanna."

The car bucked as Janelle accidentally stomped on the gas. "You . . . you . . . oh, my God." She pulled the car over amidst honking horns and parked on the shoulder. "This was the 'imagined slight' you mentioned as the motivation behind her betrayal? *Imagined?* You can't be serious. *Imagined?* I can't even begin to tell you how offensive that is."

"I said you wouldn't understand. Humans generally do not. That's why we try to keep such practices a secret from them. When those of faerie blood fall in love with humans, they do sometimes engage in the brief human marriage, even knowing that they have to see to their faerie lineage as well. They don't marry two females at once, but"—he shrugged—"it is practical to secure their future interests when opportunity arises."

"You think that's practical? Try cold. Callous. Cruel."

"Or unfeeling?"

"Yes. Completely." Janelle nodded furiously, pissed on behalf of both women. "It's like you would marry Maegth with an eye on the clock, just waiting for her to kick off. And how would Alanna manage wedding plans? How would you set a date? I suppose you could start with the average life span of a human Druid female at that time in history. Then you could just factor in all of Maegth's vices and genetic inclinations. Account for acts of God, maybe a plague or two . . ."

Kane didn't respond.

Janelle's frustration grew. "Would you start picking out the groomsmen and bridesmaids when she took to her death bed? Why, you could even start digging her grave early, just to get a jump on it. Can't you see how horrible this is? If all Maegth did was curse you, I'd say consider yourself blessed. I would have removed your little faerie testicles. With a fork."

Kane winced. "So what happened to all that compassion I so admired in you?"

"It will return after a faerie lifespan, I'm sure."

"You know, that's a lot longer than—"

"What? The lifespan of a human? Which, I'm told, is only slightly more significant than the lifetime of an insect? Yeah, I heard. Over and over. I swear, this is so outrageous. I can't believe . . ." She shook her head. "Is this done a lot? God, in the same situation, what would a psycho like Titania have—" Shocked by a sudden thought, she glanced at Kane.

He sighed, thereby confirming it. "Where do you think I got the idea? Oberon was married to my mother, a human, while he was engaged to Titania. He loved my mother."

"And when your mother died—"

"Well, he grieved. Extensively." Kane cleared his throat. "Then, he briefly consoled himself with Riordan's mother before he did his duty and wed Titania. Then Riordan's mom showed up at Oberon's door. She was heavy with child. Oberon's, of course."

"While Titania was Oberon's new bride and already the reluctant stepmother to another woman's child." Janelle leaned her forehead against the steering wheel. "No wonder Titania's scary. It's a freaking faerie soap opera." She just bobbled her head on the steering wheel in a clumsy head shake. "Unreal."

"I suppose it all seems cruel to you."

Janelle raised her head and turned a stare on him. "That's because it *is*. I mean, is this what you guys do—juggle your little humans like concubines while you contemplate cold marriage with your faerie women? Lord. Whatever idiot first defined *fairy tale* as a story of noble love, purity and honor just did not have a clue." She took a breath, forced herself to just let it go. Not her problems. Not directly. "So, this is why Oberon publicly favored you and why Titania had to tolerate you."

"Yes. At least during my childhood. When I was a grown man, I saw fit to leave court. Or at least seek out my own dwelling on the periphery. Riordan stayed with me."

"That's when he was living with you."

"Yes."

"You were an adult while he was still basically a child?"

"Yes and no. Your human equivalent, I guess, would be a teenager living with a toddler."

"Sounds like an explosive combination."

"It was. But we made it work." He spoke quietly, neglecting to elaborate.

"So. When your engagement with Maegth hit the skids, I guess you were free to marry your Alanna."

"I was free, yes."

Janelle choked now. "So you're married?" *Oh, God.* "Did I have an affair with a married faerie halfling whose wife will no doubt kick my very mortal ass?"

"I've never been married. I broke both engagements."

"Just made a clean sweep of the whole mess, huh?" Janelle pondered for a disarmed moment. Why would he do that? "No, wait. Let me guess. Alanna found out about Maegth and she was the one who kicked you out on your faerie ass."

"It wasn't like that between us. She knew about Maegth, just as I expected she had her own romantic interests. The engagement between Alanna and me was a deliberate, political alliance. To appease both courts." He shrugged. "It made sense in that respect. Alanna was Titania's niece, which made her not only a member of the Unseelie court, but also a direct blood relative to Titania. Were I to marry Alanna, we could produce a male child, potentially an heir to both courts, thereby truly bridging the gap between Seelie and Unseelie, between Titania and Oberon. When the child took the throne over both courts, a true alliance would be sealed. Peace would reign."

Janelle stared at him, feeling the tangles and politics and wondering how anyone could navigate them. She couldn't deny the logic behind such a decision, but neither could she imagine marrying for political reasons. "So this is all royal stuff. Cold political alliances. And Maegth was—"

"Maegth was my weakness. I wanted her. I wanted

some happiness, some passion in my life. I thought I could find that, briefly, in her. I thought I could serve both my duty and, for a brief while"—he smiled ruefully—"my passion? Love, perhaps?"

Janelle pondered his words quietly. There was so much wrong about what he'd done to both women, and yet . . . "I don't know what to say, Kane. I honestly don't know."

"There is nothing to say. It's in the past."

Janelle frowned. "Except . . . I get why you broke things off with Maegth. Her sleeping with your brother, that's pretty much a deal breaker no matter how you look at it. But why didn't you marry your other fiancée? Why did you break that engagement if it meant so much to both courts?"

"Marrying Alanna to appease my people and hers . . . would be a selfless gesture, wouldn't it?"

"Yeah, I guess so."

"Well, that should answer your question, then, right?" He smiled tightly. "So I was selfish. I wanted someone just for me. And Alanna was not. I felt nothing for her. After Maegth, and then to go to a cold bed—I just couldn't." He stared out the window. "And thus the fragile truce between Titania and Oberon, between my stepmother and me, was broken. It remains broken. Unlike Titania, my father understood the perils of a strictly political alliance. He forgave my broken engagement. Titania does not. She simply added it to the store of offenses my very existence represents to her."

Janelle was staring at him, completely overwhelmed. "So you're saying it's complicated?"

Smiling, relaxing just a little at her tone, Kane turned to Janelle. "Yes. It's . . . complicated." He studied her briefly, golden eyes glowing with some emotion she couldn't quite define. She pulled back into traffic.

As Janelle drove on in silence, Kane didn't bother concealing his fascination any longer. He loved to watch her changing expression, the flashes of intelligence, humor, temper and even hurt. Although he regretted being the frequent cause of the last.

But it wasn't love. It couldn't be. Because that would mean something he just couldn't bring himself to accept. That she was the one. And if she was the one, then that would mean—

But she couldn't be the one and, consequently, she really didn't need to be in possession of all the facts. She had no interest, for example, in the second half of the curse. It was true that Maegth had condemned him to never feel love for any woman but one. But the hell of it was, the Druid girl had also sworn he would never have that one woman. She could not cause him to love anyone, and she could not make it impossible for him to love the woman fated to be his one great love. But she could do—and had done—worse. She'd seen to it that he would spend his immortal life alone and genuinely longing for the one woman he could never have. He'd been determined to never meet that one woman—he couldn't pine for a woman he'd never met and loved to begin with, could he?—so he'd restricted himself to only short-term involvements. But now, with Janelle acting as his guardian . . .

It couldn't be Janelle. Fate wouldn't smile upon Maegth so fondly, would it?

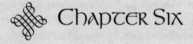

Chapter Six

Pacing from one side of the clearing to the other, Janelle glanced at her watch. *Note to self: never again schedule a report to Phil in between patient appointments.* Druids had no sense of time. She sighed. It was late afternoon, and in addition to a full schedule for the rest of the day, she was hip-deep in paperwork she needed to complete. Although, she much preferred a doctor's hectic pace to yesterday's disturbing woo-woo discussion with Kane. A practical mind could only take so much of that stuff.

Now, mindful of precious time just ticking away, she pondered skipping—

She shrieked as a hand clapped on her shoulder.

"Sorry. I didn't mean to startle you," Phil apologized. "You seemed ready to march right back to the parking lot."

"Oh. No. I'm here." Although if he'd showed up a few minutes later, she might not have been. She shifted guiltily.

"And I'm late. My apologies. I was setting something up." His voice had a meaningful edge.

"Something to do with me?" Janelle asked cautiously. "Look, I thought I was just making reports. I have to be back to work in about thirty minutes as it is."

"Don't worry. This won't take long." Phil turned and called, "Oberon?"

"I'm here, I'm here. I said I would be." And Oberon, stalking into the clearing, sounded pissed about it, too. He eyed Janelle with misgivings.

Janelle glanced from one to the other. "Why do I think this is going to suck for me?"

Oberon nodded at Phil. "Talk to the Druid. This is his deal. I'm just making it legitimate and possible."

Janelle turned a questioning gaze on Phil. "So?"

"I wanted to explain, away from the puca, some of the specifics of your duties," Phil began quietly. "As Kane's guardian, you will be in the best position to judge the success or failure of his quest. When I call him to account, it will be your job to decide whether he's changed as promised, and whether he's made sufficient amends for his offenses."

"Me? Judge him?" Janelle backed up a step. "I didn't sign on for that. I thought you Druids were going to decide."

"From afar? I don't think that's fair, do you?"

Janelle gave him a doubtful look. "And do you think it's fair to ask me to decide? Knowing I already hold a grudge against him?"

"You will be fair. We have faith in your integrity and judgment."

"And you think kissing up will make me accept the duty." She gave him a jaded look. "So I can only wonder . . . what fresh joy does this bring into my life?"

"Just that you must be on your guard." Phil sounded grave in spite of her playful tone. "We will see to it that Kane doesn't know about your role as judge, but I guarantee he realizes you will at least be called to offer testimony. He will try to sway you, most likely using any and every means at his disposal." The High Druid took off his spectacles, discreetly occupying himself with polishing them. "I think you're well aware of at least some of his methods. He has a certain reputation."

Oberon looked up in pleased surprise. "Does he, now? I guess he does. Takes after his old man in that respect."

"Oh, come on." Janelle's face burned at the implication. "You're not seriously going to warn me about—"

"Sex? Oh, yeah." Phil returned his glasses to their former jaunty angle. "I think he's going to use everything at his disposal, and I understand he has a remarkable skill set in this arena. So I guarantee he will try." The Druid paused to frown thoughtfully. "I doubt, however, that he will consummate the seduction, since that would produce sufficient conflict of interest to render you ineffective and ineligible for guardianship. That would make you useless to him, since you couldn't produce testimony on his behalf. But I do predict he will try to engage you emotionally and, up to a point, physically. You must always be aware of this possibility."

"Okay. You can just consider me warned and on my guard. So what else do you have on the agenda?" Janelle eyed him brightly, silently demanding a change in subject.

Phil accommodated. "Another warning for you: be aware that engaging in sex with anyone at all will temporarily but drastically weaken your healing gift."

Okay, that did not qualify as a sufficient change of subject.

Now even Phil blushed. "I mean, if you engage in the actual act with an actual partner. Alone . . ." He hummed. "No worries. There need to be two people involved in the act for you to exchange and therefore lose energy. Otherwise, your own energy is retained and untouched. Er, so to speak. Heh."

"Aaarrrrrgghh." Janelle turned on him in a burst of embarrassed frustration. "So does this mean you're going to be setting spies on me? In my bedroom? My workplace? Every hotel and clump of bushes in the city? My sex life is—or it should be—*my own damn business.*"

"Oh, agreed! Absolutely!" Phil hurried to assure her. "Honestly, the warning about your healing gift was strictly for your own purposes. And you're on the honor system when it comes to the guardianship agreement. I trust that you will just tell me if there is a conflict of interest and I will take matters from there."

Oh, good God. As if her life hadn't grown complicated enough. Must they also humiliate her?

"It's not our intent to humiliate you, Janelle." Oberon's voice was quiet. "That's why this part of the meeting was held privately. Basically, you're drawing on puca energy to heal, and a lot of a puca's power is sexual in nature." He shrugged. "We're a carnal people. As you've seen."

"It's a law, if you will," Phil continued. "Use up energy and you need to allow time to pass so you can rejuvenate. Twenty-four to forty-eight hours after the act and you'd be back to 100 percent. That means Friday night nookie would not interfere with Monday morning patients. See how that works?"

Janelle groaned.

"So." Phil clapped his hands in a jarringly cheerful manner. "You will secretly judge the puca at a time and place yet to be determined. Be on your guard against seduction attempts by the puca, and realize he will be cunning in this regard. And, finally, be aware that sex with another will temporarily drain your healing power to minimal levels."

While Janelle silently waited for Phil to break into a "Go, team, go" Druidic cheer, Oberon eyed Phil as if he were some exotic and mildly repulsive insect. Right. Human lifespan. But purple glasses and kindergarten clapping did nothing to discourage the buggy impression.

The king turned, amusement shining from his eyes, to focus on Janelle. "I realize my son could pluck this knowledge from your mind anytime he wished, and could, if he desired, use it against you. Understand that I believe in my son and I think he will prove himself in the end. But I want to make sure that there will be no question when he does so. Therefore, I'm granting the Druid's request that I shield your memory of this conversation and any influence it has on any of your other thoughts."

Janelle stared. "You can do that? Shield my thoughts from Kane for me?"

"In a limited manner—subject-specific only. It's a king's privilege, intended mostly to ensure confidentiality of matters whose secrecy is crucial to my people."

Damn. Wouldn't it be great if he could block off all of her thoughts to Kane?

"I can see where you would prefer that." Oberon smiled. "It's not within my power, though. What I can do is shield the subjects of our meeting today from the mind-reading powers of anyone but me. This will make it so no one else of faerie or puca heritage will be able to read any of your thoughts that are related to today's meeting with me and the High Druid. It will be as though the meeting and all of its contents never took place. This protects your role as judge, the warnings about Kane, and the potential weakness to your healing power. Any new but related thoughts you have will also be protected." Gently, he touched Janelle's shoulders and met her eyes with a golden gaze so like his son's.

And then it felt as if she were falling into that gaze. There was a light touch in her mind, soothing even, before he pulled away.

She blinked, then met his smile with an uneasy one of her own. "So it's done?"

Oberon nodded. "Good luck to you, Dr. Corrington. I'm counting on you. And on him."

"But King Oberon will not influence you or his son regarding any of this," Phil remarked pointedly. "I have his word on that. So"—he glanced at his watch—"I guess we're through here. Tee-time in fifteen, which means excellent timing." He smiled and, with a light skip-step, strode off into the trees.

Druids and golf. How about that? She wondered if there was a league. Could they chant and cast spells on the putting green, or was that considered cheating?

When she turned back, Oberon was gone as well. Thoughtfully, she returned to her car and the last two appointments of her day.

"For the record, I think this is a really bad idea," Janelle murmured futilely the next morning. Not that she had any hope of changing Kane's mind. He'd formulated this plan in the file room at the clinic, while she was off meeting with Phil and Oberon. Next time, she'd give him something a little less mindless to occupy him. Bored minds, as her mother always used to say, hatch plots.

"I realize this will be a difficult encounter. But I have to begin making amends somehow, and this is a place to start."

Janelle considered. "I think your heart's in the right place, but your head's going about it the wrong way. Some things are best handled subtly."

Kane was shaking his head. "That might work for smaller matters, but this is big. It deserves formality. Man-to-man formality."

Janelle eyed him doubtfully, but could hardly deny that men could be weird in that respect. He was a guy, so he would know, right? She wasn't a guy. All she could vouch for was that weird bluntness guys responded to so comfortably. Which, now that she thought about it, was exactly the tack Kane was taking with this. There was logic there. "All right. Let's do this, then."

Decisively, Kane climbed out of the car and slammed the door smartly before rounding it to Janelle's side. Janelle, wrinkling her nose a little at his chivalrous attempt to open her door—and trying to hide the little spark of pleasure it gave her nonetheless—was already stepping out. Unassisted, thanks.

"You're afraid to let me touch you." Kane spoke knowingly.

"Am not." *Are, too. Shut up, thoughts. He can read you.* "I am, however, a big girl, and never once have I carried a parasol. While I appreciate the gesture, I can open my own car door and stand up all by myself."

Kane, to give him his due, kept his voice and expression completely unchanged. "I never said you couldn't. I was trying to be polite. Some women, I have found, are not offended by that."

Janelle just scowled, ignoring the warmth in her cheeks. She was a *physician*, for Pete's sake. And blushing? How nauseating. *Change the subject.* "So, have you thought about your approach? How do you plan to get your foot in the door?" She turned to face the brick building, which, according to the sign out front, housed Forbes & Forbes Accounting and Financial Services.

Duncan Forbes. A hereditary but nonpracticing Druid, a descendant of Akker and Maegth, and, more importantly for their purposes, Mina Avery's estranged father. Duncan Forbes hated his own daughter on account of a situation that was completely misunderstood because of Kane's actions and words.

Presented in the right light, Kane had argued, Mina wasn't a daughter to bring her father shame, but one who should make him proud. She'd saved the life and freedom of an innocent man. Riordan wasn't responsible for the misery in Forbes's ancestry; Kane was. Kane's goal now was to convince Duncan of this, redirect his hatred to the deserving target—Kane—and give father and daughter a chance to find peace, if not a true relationship.

In this manner, he hoped to make amends to Mina, thereby crossing another name off their list. "Duncan Forbes will see me."

"Uh-huh." She eyed him doubtfully. "This ought to be interesting."

But, strangely enough, the receptionist waved them on past as though she were expecting them.

"How'd you manage that?" Janelle glanced at him as they walked down the short hallway to Duncan Forbes's office.

Kane shrugged. "I have an appointment. Isn't that how you usually reserve the time and attention of a professional?"

"Sure, if you want to pay their professional fees."

"It's just money." He pushed open the door, while Janelle eyed his back resentfully. *It's just money, he says.* Obviously a puca didn't need to pay rent or bills or insurance premiums.

Tossing an amused look over his shoulder, Kane held the door and stepped back to allow Janelle to precede him.

Probably just to needle her, too.

"Probably," he murmured as he followed her in.

Duncan Forbes was seated behind his desk and was speaking with excessive geniality into a telephone as he waved them to chairs. Janelle seated herself while Kane ignored the invitation and went to peruse a wall of framed documents and photos.

Forbes hung up the phone and, eyeing Kane with some mild and quickly concealed irritation, cleared his throat. "What can I do for you?"

"I am Kane."

"Yes. Mr. O'Brian. You made an appointment with me. Nice to meet you."

Kane didn't turn around, just ran a finger lightly along the frame of a photo. That of a young woman. Watching him, Janelle frowned.

"Who is the young woman?" Kane murmured over his shoulder.

Regarding the same photo that intrigued Kane, Forbes

folded his hands and rested them on the ink blotter centered on his desk. "That's my daughter, Daphne. Her offices are right down the hall."

"You must be proud of her."

"Very much so. One day I'd like to leave this business in her capable hands. A little more experience under her belt and that's exactly what I'll do." He smiled politely. "So, Mr. O'Brian. You need an accountant?"

"No."

Forbes frowned a moment. "Financial advice? Money marketing? Retirement funds?"

"No."

"Then—forgive me—why are you here?"

"I'm here to talk to you about your daughter."

Forbes frowned. "Like I told you, Daphne has offices down the hallway. I'm not sure what this is about, but—"

"Not Daphne. Pandemina."

Janelle cringed inwardly. And waited.

Forbes regarded him for a few silent moments. "I don't know what you're talking about."

"I did wonder how you would respond to that statement." Kane sighed heavily. "That was my least favorite choice. It lacks imagination. And spine."

"If you're just here to waste my time—"

"I'm paying for your time." Kane never raised his voice, just sounded completely reasonable.

Janelle eyed him approvingly. Those good looks were so deceptive. That was one thing she'd really liked when she first met him. Kane was both eye candy and one smart cookie. Much like when dealing with his stepmother, but for different reasons, it paid not to turn one's back on him.

"When you make an appointment with me through this office, you're paying for my professional expertise. Not information on my private life."

"So you admit Pandemina is part of your private life?"

"I admit nothing. I just want to know your part in

this. Are you the woman's attorney? What do you want from me?"

Kane turned and dipped his head in a tiny, mocking bow. "I am Kane, son of Oberon. Perhaps better known to you as Robin Goodfellow, the puca. I believe you're acquainted with my brother."

Duncan's features darkened. "So he's behind this?"

"He's behind nothing. No one is. I came here today entirely for my own reasons."

"And what might those be?"

As each spoke, Janelle shifted her gaze from Duncan to Kane and back to Duncan again. It was a cross between a soap opera and a ping-pong match. Tennis, after all, implied more distance. This thing threatened to get dirty, up close and real personal.

Kane smiled slightly. "Perhaps you haven't heard. Your quarrel is with me, not with Riordan."

"I did hear. And it sounds like my quarrel is with both of you. And neither one of you. Because of the two of you, those white-sheeted idiots are trying to drag me back into their ridiculous, completely disorganized and ineffectual midst. Once the great healers, peacemakers and wise teachers of the world, now they're nothing more than a cultish glee club."

Kane raised his eyebrows. "This isn't about vengeance for you?"

"No, it's about living my own life and getting what I want. Playing Druid bureaucrat because of a pair of puca brothers doesn't facilitate either one of those aims."

"I see. I overestimated you." Kane frowned. "The honor of two long-ago Druids . . ."

"Is dead and buried right along with their bodies. Let it rest. Let the living live."

"I can empathize with that to some extent, but it seems that the living are still plagued by the actions of the now-dead. Your daughter, for example."

"Daphne leads a full life, earning decent money and a

respectable reputation under my tutelage. She doesn't
need or want anything to do with the Druid Way."

"Again, you mistake me. I'm talking about Mina."

Duncan raised his voice. "Are you being deliberately
obtuse? I have one child. Daphne Forbes. Unless you
have legal documents disputing this, I suggest you accept what is and leave me in peace."

Janelle spoke up. "Look, buddy. Those legal documents wouldn't be all that hard to obtain these days,
and I think you know it. A simple DNA test would resolve the question to our, your, and the court's satisfaction. Do we need that, or can we talk like reasonable
adults? I doubt Mina even wants anything from you." In
fact, the woman would probably ream Kane for even approaching Forbes about this. Now that she'd met the
guy in person, Janelle had to admit she didn't blame
Mina. Maybe no father at all was better than a travesty
like this guy.

"Mina may not want anything from you," Kane interrupted in a steely voice, "but she deserved acknowl-
edgement and respect from you. She got neither. I'm
here to change that."

"If that's the case, then you can get the hell out of my
office."

Kane regarded him calmly. "I think not."

And that's when the accountant proved he didn't de-
scend from the peace-loving faction of the Druid population.

A lamp smacked against the wall behind Kane, and
Janelle ducked as another chair landed in the corner between them. For an older guy, Duncan was pretty damn
strong in his anger.

"Enough of this! Get control of yourself." Kane caught
the stapler Duncan lobbed at his head.

"Get out of my office. Now." Duncan glanced around
wildly. "And you can tell my so-called daughter that my
attorney will be seeking a restraining order and filing

complaints against her. And that boyfriend of hers can kiss his damn business good-bye. I guarantee you I can have somebody on his ass finding regulatory offenses and imposing fines and penalties until he doesn't have a leg to stand on." He snatched something off his desk—"I'll destroy them before I see them destroy me"—and hurled it.

A paperweight struck Kane on the shoulder and he braced low and angry. A *flash-shimmer* and the puca's body began to contort.

Duncan shrieked and grabbed for his phone. "Wendy! Get the police on the line. Now!" Still gripping the phone, the man gazed around wildly, obviously bent on escape. "You two have ten seconds to get the hell out of my office before—"

Kane froze midshift. Half man and half horse. It didn't look comfortable.

What the hell? Janelle, who'd sought cover behind an armchair, rose slowly to her feet and backed away from the scene before her. Duncan looked equally appalled, staring at Kane, as he stuttered nonsense. "Just . . . just a damned paperweight. Didn't—"

"Silence." The single word came from behind Janelle, who spun to face the source. A strange man met her eyes briefly, but without expression.

Janelle's breathing grew shallow, her head just a little light and her stomach queasy. Was he another Druid? A faerie? Something else?

"Breathe. Or you'll faint." Not that he cared, the man's tone stated, except for the momentary inconvenience.

Janelle inhaled roughly and exhaled on a shaky sound. "You, um . . . should I know you?"

The stranger was devastating. His features were almost too perfect to be real. Every line and plane was sculpted, from broad brow to patrician nose, to high and superbly angled cheekbones, to square jaw and stubborn jut of chin. His only softness was the sensual curve of his mouth. Dark, nearly black eyes gleamed curiously at them. Not quite emotionless, but disarming, nonetheless.

"You are the guardian. Kane's this time."

"Y-yes. And you are?"

"I am Tremayne." Black, fathomless eyes glittered at her and then focused on Duncan. The former Druid had dropped back into his chair, knees obviously giving up on their owner. "You would be wise to tread more cautiously. This puca has a temper." Tremayne smiled humorlessly. "Just ask his younger brother."

Duncan stared, eyes wide and jaw hanging slack. He nodded slowly.

Tremayne turned to Kane. Finally his features held expression: vague curiosity. And sharp contempt. "If you are ready to be reasonable, puca, I will release you."

Peering anxiously at Kane, Janelle detected awareness in the puca's eyes. And anger? *Come on, idiot. If you can hear my thoughts, then control your damn temper. I don't think we want to mess with this one. Do you?*

Kane's eyelids drifted closed, then lifted again in silent assent.

Tremayne blinked in response—a silent taunt?—and Kane was free, his human form fully restored.

His voice controlled, along with his expression, Kane turned to face Tremayne. "What the hell are you?"

Tremayne smiled, but even that seemed flat. "You don't recognize me?"

Kane slowly shook his head. "I know who I think you are. But you're different somehow. I remember you as Riordan's jailer, and that Akker originally summoned you."

"Is that all you know of me? I'm not surprised. The puca brothers have never been known for their courtesy and care of others. It will work against you."

"You have a problem with me?" Kane asked.

"I do. You and your brother. I don't like you." The simplicity in his tone implied this was the understatement from hell. "Apparently, it's my curse to forever shadow the puca brothers until one or the other is . . . contained."

Then, glancing briefly at Duncan, Tremayne faded, gone with no further drama. Frankly, no more was needed.

"Well, that went well." Seated safely in her car, Janelle cast a brittle ironic look at Kane. "Did it ever occur to you that getting thrown in jail might have a negative impact on my professional and personal reputation? Thank God the police never showed up. And we won't even go into the freaky freeze-ray action of your buddy Tremayne." She shivered.

Kane frowned. "I'm missing something there."

"Well, no kidding. He already told you that much. Apparently, you should know him better than you do. And that's not good, given his powers and his lack of affection for you. What exactly is he, anyway? A nature spirit seems awfully unlikely. That sounds too peace-loving for this guy and his freeze-ray trick."

"Like I said, I have a dim memory of Akker summoning a nature spirit, calling him Tremayne, and charging him to keep Riordan contained in that Sarsen stone." Kane shook his head slowly. "But I recall Tremayne as a simple entity devoted to a single task. Barely sentient. The guy we saw today . . . he's so different now. It's like he's evolved or something."

"And now he's holding a grudge." Janelle raised her eyebrows. "Deservedly, from what you said, and 'evolved' or not, this Tremayne seems slightly less than compassionate. Almost emotionless. So how do you make amends to an ice man anyway?"

"I have no idea. Honestly."

She sighed. "So. Do you think Duncan will pursue legal action against Mina or against us?"

"No. I think the freeze-ray trick I suffered took the steam out of his temper and his intentions. Besides, aren't such things expensive and time-consuming, not to mention bad for business? All he really wanted was for us to leave. And we did."

"I hope you're right."

"As for the rest . . . I thought we were doing the right thing by coming here. Isn't that what I'm supposed to be doing? And why is the right thing always backfiring on me?" Kane looked genuinely puzzled. "I just made things worse for everybody. Again."

Silently relenting, Janelle dropped her head to the steering wheel. "It wasn't that bad. Spooky and tense, but no real harm done. Tremayne was scary but he didn't really hurt either one of us. As for Duncan . . ." She raised her head. "Might I suggest subtlety? Maybe a little diplomacy? I get it about guys liking the straightforward, 'honorable' route best. But from what I heard, there's nothing honorable about Duncan Forbes."

"True."

"And, frankly, I think Mina's better off without him. Father or no father."

"I won't argue that, but it's still beside the point." Kane halted his own speech, his attention caught by something just past Janelle's head.

"What?" Following his eyes, she turned and stared out the side window, right into a perfect, creamy-skinned oval framed by baby-fine blonde hair. Rich blue eyes met Janelle's with interest and demand. She mimed rolling down the window.

Curious, Janelle opened the window and peered out at her. The blonde looked familiar. "Can I help you?"

"We don't know each other, but we have some mutual friends. Mina Avery, for one."

Bingo. "Are you Daphne?"

"That's me." The blonde smiled, revealing a row of nearly perfect pearly whites, with a single front tooth slightly and charmingly misaligned. She looked real now instead of plaster-cast perfect. "Daphne Forbes.

Daughter to Duncan and Violet Forbes, half sister to one Pandemina Dorothy Avery."

"Nice to meet you. I'm Janelle and this is Kane. Friends of Mina's, as you said. So what can I do for you?"

Daphne bit at her lip, looking awkward, which seemed uncharacteristic for someone so polished. "Actually, I was hoping there was something I could do for you. Or for Mina. You just left a meeting with my father, right?"

Janelle and Kane exchanged glances before Janelle responded. "I guess you could call it that. It seemed more a barroom brawl than anything so civilized as a meeting."

"Hmm." Daphne looked thoughtful. "He's been a little on edge lately."

"Yeah?" Janelle shot Kane a speaking glance before turning back to Daphne. "Why's that?"

Daphne glanced over her shoulder and then through the opposite window past Janelle and Kane. "How about we go somewhere to talk privately?"

"Are you sure you want to do that?" Janelle studied her warily. "I mean, given the situation, I'm thinking your father will be drawing a line in the sand very soon and asking you to pick sides."

"He did that a long time ago. Only, I wasn't given a choice. And Mina wasn't given so much as a chance. So, forget Duncan. Let me buy you coffee."

When his recent visitors disappeared between cars in the parking lot, Duncan released the slat of his window blinds. His fury had cooled, as had his terror, leaving him shaken and jumpy.

Thank God they'd left on their own. He'd bluffed earlier about calling the police. The last thing he wanted was the bad publicity and unwelcome questions such a visit would invite. And now he needed a drink, damn it.

Such a close call. And then for something as deadly as Tremayne to tag along? Not good. He shivered.

"They've left?"

Startled by the voice, so familiar and so detested after all these years, Duncan pivoted as though stung. In his haste, he thwacked the back of his hand against the desk.

Feminine laughter, brief and self-satisfied, met his ears. "It's wonderful that you still react to me this way."

Scowling, Duncan rounded his desk and stood behind it. It was a control position. He *was* in control. He had ambitions. Plans. No damn puca or other faerie freak—and certainly not some pretentious human jerk—would be manipulating his life this time. Never again.

"What did they want?"

"Who?" He was just buying time. They both knew it. Just as they both knew who his visitors had been.

"Don't be coy, Duncan. Why were they here? Were they looking for another liaison to the Druid circle?"

"Hardly. And if that's what they wanted, this wasn't the place to look for it."

"Shall I share your distinctly un-Druidic sentiments with your little receptionist?"

Duncan shifted, his discomfort nearly outpacing his annoyance now. "You know about that?"

"Of course. And I'm devastated. Sincerely." The scorn and laughter in her voice suggested otherwise. "And, really, Duncan. Is it age? Is that why you have to fall back on the overblown mystique of Druid wizardry in order to get a girl in bed? I know it worked in the past, but I would have thought, after all these years, you would have new seduction ploys, new leverage to offer. How boring."

"Not everyone requires foreplay as twisted as the kind you demand."

Amusement again tugged at those ageless lips. "As I recall, you enjoyed the kinky stuff every bit as much as I did. Craved it, in fact. Don't you remember?"

"Don't remind me." He closed his eyes, feeling his heart pound as the memories rushed past his defenses.

More laughter.

Damn it. Wasn't it enough that she'd brought him to his knees in the past? Must she realize how susceptible to her he still was?

"Relax. I'm not here to torment you. Even if it would be fun. I have other purposes. I think you and I might find some of those purposes are common to us both."

Duncan stilled but didn't respond. It could be a trick.

"They involve a recently punished puca. And his reluctant guardian." She smiled.

His doubts vanished. Not because of the smile. But because of the fury he saw playing in her beautiful eyes. His heart pounded. He picked up the phone. "Wendy. Please hold all my calls for the next hour. And no visitors. No exceptions. Understood?" He hung up before she responded, then rounded his desk. Slowly this time. It was a weakness for him. She was his weakness. Damn her for knowing it, too.

# CHAPTER SEVEN

On the other side of town, Janelle, Daphne and Kane were sitting in a coffee shop. Janelle was winding down with a summary of the morning's events, but a summary amended to accommodate the ears and sensibilities of normal humans leading normal lives. The shape-shifting and freeze-ray action, for example, were completely omitted. "And that's when Duncan lost it."

"And probably sent Wendy into a tailspin by asking her to call the police. Why he thinks his space cadet of a receptionist could effectively bounce anyone is beyond me." Daphne looked amused. "I'm sorry I missed the fireworks. I just saw the two of you leaving the office when I was on my way back from an int—a meeting. With a client."

"An int . . . erview maybe?" Janelle eyed her curiously. "As in, job interview?"

"I didn't say that." Daphne relaxed back in her seat, stirring her coffee with a little red straw. Her eyes were sparkling, though. "And even if you tried to call me on it with the great Duncan Forbes, no way would he believe you over me."

"I won't argue that," Janelle murmured. "So why are you interviewing?"

Daphne shrugged. "Just to see what's out there. Give me leverage with the old man, that kind of thing. Hey, the guy's on a power kick and he's locked in a lifelong battle of wills with my mom. I'm tired of dodging their crossfire and their constant manipulations, at home and on the job. I swear, when your personal life and your professional life are one mixed-up mess on a 24/7 basis . . . nasty." She forced a laugh. "Ever work for your parents?"

"No," Janelle replied shortly.

"Yes," Kane replied at the same time.

Daphne glanced from one to the other, a smile twitching at her lips. "And nobody looks happy with their situation. So I don't have the market cornered on family and career quandaries?"

"Not even close," Janelle allowed, although her own quandary was worlds different from Daphne's. What she wouldn't have given to be able to work with her parents, or at least know them longer than the twenty-one years she'd had.

Nodding quietly, Daphne turned to Kane with a mild frown. "You know, I recognized Janelle from some pictures my—well, from some pictures. But you. Kane. You look really familiar but I just can't place it. Should I know you?"

"Riordan is my half brother. I've heard there's a resemblance between us."

Daphne's eyes widened. "You mean you're a dead ringer for the guy."

"Not completely." That from Janelle, which drew Daphne's attention.

Daphne glanced from Janelle to Kane and back again. "So it's Mina and Riordan, and now it's Janelle and Kane? That's sweet."

"Gee. That's not a little patronizing." Janelle scowled in discomfort. "And no, it's not 'sweet.' It's complicated."

Daphne raised her eyebrows. "More Druid stuff?"

Surprise, surprise. Janelle blinked. "Yes and no."

"So it's like that again." Daphne sighed. "It would be great if you guys would just fill me in on the whole story, instead of everyone just feeding me bits and pieces of it. Sounds like my father's right in the middle of this stuff. If you tell me what you're trying to do, I might be able to influence him on your behalf. Or at least snoop a little. Give me something. I'm a little desperate for excitement here."

"Is that why you're interviewing for jobs?" Janelle prodded. "Because you're bored?"

"Aren't we cagey? Which is foolish, because I think we could be on the same side. It just takes somebody laying down her cards." Daphne smiled a little wickedly. "So how about it? I'll show you mine if you show me yours."

Janelle cast a sidelong glance at Kane. "She's talking information, puca, so don't get too excited."

Daphne's smile faded. "Puca? You said puca. What's going on?"

Janelle eyed the girl warily. *Ugh. Smooth move.* But what could she say? There was just something about Daphne that Janelle had liked immediately, and she'd let her guard down.

"He's a puca? Really a puca?" Daphne turned her attention to Kane.

"And if he is?" Janelle watched cautiously.

Daphne gave her a wry look. "It's not like I could tell anyone about your puca here and have them believe me."

"But you do know what a puca is?"

"Sort of. I read about them in my father's journals."

Kane straightened. "Your father's journals?"

"Sure."

Kane's voice sharpened. "He wrote about pucas in journals that he left someplace public enough that you could get your hands on them?"

"Oh, God no." Daphne looked appalled. "They were

in a safety-deposit box. And that was years ago. I'm guessing he's either switched boxes or hid the journals elsewhere. I just know I went in recently and the key I had copied no longer worked."

"You had a safety-deposit box key copied?" Now it was Janelle who was disturbed. "Isn't that illegal?"

"Complicated, too." Daphne shrugged. "I'm resourceful." She offered a cheesy smile. "My father always says so."

"Your father wrote about pucas," Kane mused. "That information might have come in handy a few weeks ago. So what did your father say in these journals?"

She shrugged. "It was mostly angry ranting. He was rebelling against the whole family cult thing and wanted his daughter completely clear of it."

"So he's never been involved with the Druids?"

"Oh, he used to be hot and heavy with all of them. He wanted to lead. When Phil beat him out as leader, though, Daddy took his toys and went home. If he couldn't lead, he didn't want anything to do with them. And he refused to even court the idea of involving me in a cult run by anybody other than himself." She tipped her head, looking speculative for a moment. "But I do think, if he could find a way back to leadership, he'd go back to them in a heartbeat. Power's like a drug to some people. He's one of them."

"So noted," Janelle responded thoughtfully. "Back to the puca part, though. What did he say about pucas?"

She frowned. "Well, he never actually mentioned more than one. It was always the one puca. The one they had to isolate, whatever that means. These were older entries, too. And very cryptic, as if he were afraid someone might read the journals, even though he did his best to hide them. You'd think that, if he were that worried about being found out, he wouldn't write in a journal at all."

Kane nodded slowly. "And he never mentioned a second puca."

"No, not that I recall. I mean, it's been a while, but the reading was pretty fascinating. I think I'd remember a second puca."

Pondering another possibility, Janelle turned to Daphne. "What I want to know is if there was another mentioned in your father's journal. Not a Druid, not a puca, but another. By the name of Tremayne."

Daphne looked startled. "Tremayne? Funny you should mention that name. I met this guy . . ." She shook her head. "Well, it's just a name, right?"

"A name has power," Kane allowed.

Janelle rolled her eyes. "More importantly, the name isn't all that common. You met a Tremayne. What's he like?"

"Other than hot?" Daphne twisted her lips in a half-hearted grin. "Ruthless. My guess is he's a private investigator, with my parents as the subject of his latest investigation. They must have done something really ugly this time. Yet another reason to skip town while I still can."

Janelle glanced at Kane. "Think it's the same guy?"

"Either that or a huge coincidence, which I don't favor."

Kane turned back to Daphne. "Does your father mention Tremayne in his diaries?"

"Not likely. This guy's about my age, and those diaries are probably twenty years old. He would have been a child at the time."

Kane nodded. "That would make it unlikely, then, wouldn't it?"

He changed the subject, but the conversation wound down pretty quickly anyway, with Daphne checking her watch and murmuring about an appointment. They went their separate ways soon afterward. Once Janelle and Kane were alone in the car and headed toward home, Janelle mentally replayed and reviewed the conversation. After a while, she turned to Kane.

"So what do you think? Was it the same Tremayne?"

"I think it's likely."

She shook her head, pondering her current situation. Yup. She was on weirdness overload. Thank God for normal life. "Well, guy, I'm afraid it's time to stop being otherworldly and let me earn my way in this particular world. I gotta change clothes and get to work."

So saying, she pulled into her usual parking spot, only to see a familiar car parked right next to hers. Riordan. He didn't live in this complex anymore. And God knew she'd missed him—or at least Teague, her old friend. Not in a romantic way, but she'd taken some pleasure in coming home from a bad day and bitching to a friendly ear. Even if he did always return the favor by inundating her with tales of magical woo-woo.

"Something wrong?"

Janelle shook her head, then nodded at the car next to hers as she shut off the engine. "Riordan's here."

"Checking up on me?"

"Maybe. He probably thinks you turned me into a goat."

"Now that's something I can't do. But wouldn't it do fun things to my karma?"

"Just boggles the mind to imagine." She got out of the car, waiting for Kane to follow suit before she locked up. Then she followed Kane toward the stairs leading to the second floor of her building.

Before Kane reached the steps, Riordan was already jogging down to meet them. No welcoming smile this time, however.

"Wasn't it enough that you fucked with my life all these centuries? Now you have to go and fuck with Mina's too? What did she ever do to you?"

"Hi, and nice to see you too?" Janelle inserted.

Ignoring her, Riordan glared at Kane. "I gave you Mina's father's name so you could use him to gain your freedom. Not so you could humiliate Mina by begging for him to recognize her as his daughter. She needs him like she needs a hole in the head."

"Oh, that." Kane grimaced.

"Yeah, that." Riordan looked incensed. "Mina just had a shouting match over the phone with him. The bastard made her cry, too. And that's your fault.

Janelle plopped her butt on the bottom step and shot Kane a disgruntled look. "I told you talking to Forbes was a bad idea."

"Yeah, over and over. You've made your point." Kane's voice was low and disgruntled. No doubt he was less than pleased with the I-told-you-so, but she was pretty sure he was mostly wracked with guilt that he'd made things so awkward for Mina.

"Somebody want to tell me what the hell is going on?" Riordan sounded seriously harassed. "If you knew it was a bad idea, why did you do it?"

"It was Kane's idea. And, once again, he was trying to do the right thing, even though it didn't quite work out that way."

"Gee, there's a surprise." Riordan gave his brother an unfriendly look. "So why is it, when you try to do the right thing, somebody always gets hurt?"

"It's the damnedest thing, I swear." Kane shook his head, looking equal parts baffled and defensive. "I just thought if I showed Duncan that I was his enemy, not you, then that would remove an obstacle between himself and Mina. I thought I could mediate peace between them. I was wrong. I'm sorry."

"Who asked you to be our mediator?" Riordan took an angry step forward.

But Janelle got to her feet, ready to clobber away in Kane's defense. "He *said* he was sorry."

Riordan, obviously recognizing the look in Janelle's eyes, just balled his fists and held his ground. He turned back to Kane. "Well, fine, damn it. You didn't mean harm. But you still caused it. Don't do us any more favors. Got it? Stay away from Mina's people."

"I guess that includes Daphne," Janelle muttered. She had a feeling Daphne could be useful in getting to Duncan, too. Whatever Daphne thought of her father, the man had a mile-wide soft spot for her.

"Yes, including Daphne." Riordan shot them a warning look, then strode back to the parking lot.

"You know, my buddy Teague used to be a lot of fun," Janelle grouched after him, her voice raised intentionally to reach Riordan's ears. "Now that he's turned human, got himself a girlfriend and a new name, he's edgier than an adolescent with jock itch."

An inordinately loud slam of a pickup door met her declaration, and an engine revved to life.

"Cranky brat," Janelle grumbled after him.

"I'm sorry, Janelle," Kane murmured quietly to her. "I suck at this amends business."

"He'll get over it. Come on." She stood and started up the stairs. "The real world awaits Dr. Corrington."

A few days after the encounter with Forbes and then Riordan, the telephone ringing startled Janelle out of an exhausted sleep. Blearily, she swiped a hand across her nightstand, found her cell phone and brought it to her ear. Nothing. The ringing continued. Her land line?

She reached further and managed to knock the receiver onto the bed, scrambling to find the damn button.

"Hello?"

"Janelle Corrington?" asked a muffled but probably male voice.

"Y-yes." If it was a telemarketer, he could say good-bye to his hearing. What time was it, anyway?

"MD? And . . . guardian?"

She frowned, trying to the clear the fog from her head. "Who is this?"

"You need to do something about your charge."

"What are you talking about?" Flipping the covers back, she swung her legs around and sat up.

Hearing a step—sensing it, really, deep in her belly—she glanced up. Kane stood in the doorway. Janelle stilled. By unspoken agreement, they'd kept a distance between them while alone in Janelle's apartment. Probably because they were both aware of the last time they'd touched. The power and the temptation. This situation, for example, with her sitting on her bed while dressed only in panties and a little cami, should be completely off-limits.

But she didn't say so.

And he didn't leave.

No, his gaze roamed the length of her bare legs before settling with a great deal of interest on points northward. Two of them. Well, she was cold, damn it. That's what any doctor could tell him would happen to a woman's breasts when cold. She tugged the covers up and glared until his gaze shifted to her face. He raised eyebrows questioningly.

Giving him a speaking look, she forced herself to attend to her caller. ". . . not doing your job," the man continued, his voice unrecognizable and just a little whiny. "The guy's a menace. Nobody's safe from him."

"Who is this?" She spoke over him, finally.

"Just a concerned and knowledgeable citizen."

"Oh, aren't we righteous? How about a name, buddy? If you're making accusations, at least be man enough to stand behind them."

"Never mind me. Have you seen the paper today?"

She scrubbed at her eyes then squinted at the clock. Glowing blurs gradually settled into figures. It was five thirty. In the A.M. She wasn't on call. Wasn't on duty. And some idiot called her at five thirty in the freaking morning to complain about a puca problem? Well, how bad could the problem be, when the only puca she knew was standing right in front of her, staring at her boobs? Actually, now that she thought about it . . . really bad. But mostly from her perspective.

"No. I have not seen the paper. I plan on not seeing the paper until I've had at least three more hours of sleep. Go away."

"Wait! You have to look. It's in the metro section. Second page, halfway down. Find it. Read it. Then do your job and report it. We don't need that insanity running loose in our city." A click and the line went dead.

She stared at the phone. "Oh, fine. He wakes me up from the best sleep I've had in weeks and *he's* the one who's angry? Kiss my ass." She dumped the receiver on the nightstand, hauled her legs under the covers and buried her head back in the pillow.

"What did he want?"

She groaned and pulled the covers over her head. "Take a hint, puca." She spoke through sheet and blanket. "Go away. I'm tired." And way too weak to be dealing with potent puca machismo.

He just waited patiently, obviously refusing to leave without information, but for once too polite to grab it out of her head. It was that bit of courtesy that had her yanking the covers back down. "Something about the newspaper. It was an anonymous caller wanting to tattle on you. Probably some bitchy Druid, since nobody else knows about the guardian thing."

Kane moved further into the room. "Somebody called to blame me for something? What did I supposedly do?"

"He didn't say. Just that it was important enough to merit space on the second page of the metro section. Now may I sleep?"

Without responding, Kane left the room. A few moments later, she heard the apartment door opening and closing. Then footsteps retraced the path to her bedroom.

She growled, "Oh, come on. Can't you read it out there

and tell me about it later? Say, in two or three hours? I'm a physician. My sleep deprivation is bad for my patients."

"It's Saturday. You're off until Monday afternoon. Remember?"

"So I'm catching up." She burrowed under the covers—only to yelp when he turned on the bedside lamp and skitter backward when he dropped onto the mattress beside her. "Hello? Boundaries? We do not share a bed in any form, for any reason. Got it?"

"I'm just reading the paper." He flipped through the stack of newsprint until he found the appropriate section, dumping the rest onto the floor. Then he returned to the page that held his interest, scanning until his eyes came to fold level. He stopped and focused.

Despite herself, Janelle watched nervously as he read. "What? It can't be that bad. You didn't do anything."

"Are you sure about that?"

"You ask me that question . . . why? What the hell did you do?"

He met her eyes over the newspaper. "I didn't say I did anything. You just seem so sure that I did not. It's . . . surprising."

"Not all that surprising. Just logical. We've been joined at the hip since the Druids sent us on our merry way. That severely limits your opportunities for mischief."

He studied her for a few moments. "You might think so. But there have been pockets of time where you were busy with patients and I was free to roam."

"Not really." She frowned. "I would think you'd have to stick pretty close to me, wouldn't you? That's how it worked with Riordan and Mina."

He was already shaking his head. "I can leave you."

"What—?"

"It's just not a good idea for either of us if I do," he explained patiently. "Besides doing your guardianship duties"—he grinned slightly—"along with playing conscience for a puca with a bad track record, you're also providing me with an alibi should Druids come calling with accusations."

"Accusations like that one?" She nodded toward the newspaper.

"Yes."

She sighed. "Okay, I get it. So just tell me, then. What does it say? You robbed a bank? Flashed a little old lady? What?"

He turned the newspaper around and pointed to a headline in the center of the page:

MYSTERY HORSE TERRORIZES CARYTOWN

Eyes widening, Janelle reached for the newspaper to continue reading. Apparently, a black stallion doing a great impersonation of a rabid dog galloped down Cary Street in the fashionable Fan District of downtown Richmond. Besides terrorizing locals with a lot of showy rearing, it busted out windshields and dented the sides of several parked cars. It even damaged storefront facades and shattered apartment windows.

As the newspaper went to print, police were still canvassing the area for information on the animal and its owner—presumably to charge the latter with violations and fine him or her for damages.

Janelle raised her gaze to meet Kane's. His expression was blank as he quietly awaited judgment.

"Well? Did you do it?" When he didn't respond, just looked at her, she held up a hand. "And don't even try to feed me some guilt trip about how, if I knew you, I'd know you weren't capable of something like this. See, the thing is, I *don't* know you. But what I do know about you is that you're absolutely capable of some really twisted offenses if you deem the victim deserving."

"Point taken. But I didn't do this. There was no reason to do any of this. Random violence and destruction are a waste of energy and resources. There are better ways."

"You would know."

"I would know." His gaze never wavered.

Sighing, she leaned back against the headboard. "So, what's going on then? Just a freaky coincidence?"

"A black horse running wild down Cary Street? Does that happen every day?"

"Well, no. But it could happen. I guess. I mean, what else could it be? How many of you guys are there?"

"Like I told you before, I thought there were only two: Riordan and me."

"So in that case, now just you. And, if I'm to take your word for it, it *wasn't* you. So there must be some other explanation. Perhaps even that coincidence I mentioned?" She murmured the last on a hopeful note.

But Kane was already shaking his head. "I have a hard time believing in coincidence."

"So what should—"

The phone rang again. First her land line and then her cell phone started chiming. And forty-five minutes later—none of them spent peacefully asleep in bed—Janelle was discreetly exiting her apartment with Kane right on her heels.

She unlocked the car and climbed into the driver's seat. When she'd slammed her door closed and heard the corresponding slam of his, she clasped her seat belt and started the engine.

"So."

"Yes?"

She put the car in gear. "You're absolutely sure you don't, well, sleep shape-shift . . . or anything like that?"

"Sleep shape-shift?" He sounded amused, confused and mildly disarmed. As though somebody had suggested something utterly outrageous. Like, for example, that faeries and pucas were real.

"Hey, it's a legitimate question. Humans sleepwalk, sleep-eat, and from what I hear, even have sex in their sleep. I would think a puca could, theoretically, do the stallion thing in his sleep."

"Have sex in their sleep? Really?" He looked intrigued.

"Oh, good God. I accuse you of playing rabid horsey down Richmond's main drag and you take a mental detour down Pervy Lane. Hello? Get with the program and answer the question. Ever shift in your sleep? Could you have done this?"

He sighed. "No, I didn't do this."

"Well. Okay. There's a simple solution to this. We'll just go take a look and"—she groaned—"see what my new Spidey senses tell me about the stallion's path through town." And that was just weird. The Druids had claimed she would be able to tell if mischief was the act of a puca, that she could sense the energy patterns left by puca magic. That's how Kane had explained it anyway: energy patterns. Almost like a footprint, each was different. But how would she know if this weirdo talent was even working?

"You'll know."

"You sound so sure of that. Did you used to have this sense?"

"No. It's a Druid gift. Empowered by—"

"Puca magic," she intoned, almost singsong. "Yeah, I get it. You know it's scary when I can predict the next weirdo comment to come out of your mouth."

He shrugged. "If it makes you feel any better, I'll know if your power's working, too."

"Yeah? How's that?"

"Well, it is my energy you're sucking up."

"Energy parasite, that's me. And if I have to use somebody, it's downright fitting that you be the someone that I use."

"That does seem to be the consensus."

"So tell me: the stallion thing." Janelle glanced at him. "Why do you guys do that, anyway? And I'm not saying this particular stallion incident was in any way related to you. I'm just asking out of curiosity. And obligation, I suppose. I need to know if this is an undeniable urge or what. And what you might do while under the equine influence."

"Equine influence?" Amusement glittered in his eyes.

She shrugged a little defensively. "I'm just asking. Is it a feral thing—like the werewolf legend—or are you capable of reason?"

"I guess you do need to know more about me if this thing's going to work." He frowned thoughtfully for a moment. "To be honest, I haven't pulled the puca ride trick in centuries. Longer even."

"Why?"

"The puca ride usually springs from an innate desire to reform someone. It could be that the desire to reform is a positive urge. Maybe to help somebody see the light when they're in the wrong. Or it could be less altruistic."

"Ooh, wait." She breathed the words in mock excitement. "Let me just take a wild guess. Could it be . . . *revenge*?"

His lips twisted wryly. "Yes. But on a much smaller scale than the kind of revenge I was practicing—which is actually part of the answer to your question. My revenge efforts have all been focused on Riordan. For a very long time."

"And there's really no point in taking a cornerstone on a puca ride?"

"Well, it is kind of illogical, don't you think?"

"That's one way of looking at it."

Kane peered through the windshield with a frown. "Is that a sign for Cary Street ahead? Looks like it's blocked off to through traffic. The police, I presume."

Eyeing her options, Janelle pulled into a metered parking place just shy of the intersection and shut off the engine. The sun would be up soon. It was best that they conduct their business in darkness, just in case there was something woo-woo that would show itself or need resolving. Whatever that meant. So it was now or never.

She steeled herself and glanced at Kane. "So, I'll just know somehow if whatever happened here was due to puca magic?"

"That's right."

She paused, bracing herself. She honestly didn't believe he was responsible for what had happened here. For all of his faults, Kane had made sense earlier when he argued his own position. And she'd believed him. Still did. So it couldn't be him, couldn't be the influence of puca power. Her doing the Spidey sense thing was just for form's sake. And to satisfy all those damn phone calls this morning. Hell, they'd come from everyone, including High Druid Phil and an agitated Mina, both wondering if Kane was on the warpath after all. Janelle reached for her door handle.

But Kane had already exited and rounded the car. Next thing Janelle knew, he'd opened her door for her. Janelle glanced up, directly into his eyes. Eyes that didn't glance away from hers, eyes that said he had nothing to hide.

All right. That was okay, then. She swung her legs out of the car and, using a distracted fumble with her keys as an excuse not to accept his extended hand, rose from her seat. Not commenting—what was the point, when they both knew why she avoided his touch?—Kane slammed her door and quietly walked beside her.

As they approached, they saw a small figure huddled under an overhang, just past the line of sawhorses and orange traffic cones blocking off the street. Seated on the filthy, glass-strewn pavement, the figure was rocking. His hands and much of his body trembled violently. Janelle immediately began a mental rant against drugs and families who didn't take care of their children.

"Janelle—"

"Hush." Kane no doubt intended to stop her from doing what she had to do, but damn it all, she was a doctor and this person was very likely some kid living on the streets. He was probably no older than Shawn, her humiliated teenage patient, whose biggest concern in life was the aftermath of a failed make-out session. Meanwhile, this boy—

He looked up and she froze. This was no teenage boy.

Chapter Eight

Easing past the makeshift street barrier, Janelle approached the huddled man carefully, even as something unfamiliar, something very much like dread, sang along her nerve endings.

"It's the Druid from the grove. The runty one who insulted you on our walk back to the car." Shrugging off the jacket she'd thrown around her shoulders, Janelle glanced up at Kane. "And I don't think it's drugs. I think he's suffering from shock. If I'm not mistaken about what I'm feeling right now, he's just experienced a puca ride from hell."

"You're sure?" Kane's features were set and his voice was hard.

Carefully, she settled her jacket around the man's shoulders and watched his fingers clutch convulsively at the material. She didn't know how she could be so sure, but she was. She slowly nodded her head. "Puca magic. I can feel it everywhere here, and the remnants practically throb from this poor guy. But how can it be? If it wasn't you—"

"It wasn't me. I don't know what happened here, but I didn't do it. It wasn't me. I swear it, Janelle. You have every reason to think the worst of me, but I didn't do this."

She studied his hard face, feeling torn. "Oh, who the hell cares who's responsible for this right now. I don't know who to blame. All I know is I have to help this man."

"Yes. You do." And Kane's voice had taken on a meaningful edge.

Comprehending, she turned a troubled gaze back to the little man, who seemed completely unaware of their presence. Nothing seemed to touch him, he was so lost in his private hell. "The glamouring, you mean?"

"Yes."

She felt everything inside her rebel at the idea. "I assume that means you're going to give me the abridged version of the lesson right here and now?"

"Why don't you have a go at healing him first?"

Duh. Who was the doctor again? Healing should have been her first instinct. She knelt next to the little Druid. She'd swear he didn't weigh more than she did. It would take a really cowardly person to pick on someone this size. Carefully, she touched his shoulder, feeling chaotic emotion wash over her.

She steeled herself. "Hi." She tried a gentle smile—the one she used to calm her youngest patients. "My name is Janelle. I'm a doctor. What's your name?"

He didn't respond.

"His name is Browning," Kane murmured quietly. "That's what he goes by."

Janelle nodded, although Browning never indicated that he'd even heard the exchange. "Hi, Browning. I'd like to help you if you'll let me."

No response. His gaze never even flickered in her direction. His mind was completely traumatized. Who would do that?

Still, he hadn't objected to her touch. Feeling the waves of chaos continue to wash over her, she mentally braced herself and raised her other hand to touch his temple.

He never moved.

At contact, she nearly fell back onto her butt. Kane steadied her from behind.

Inhaling deeply and shakily, she let Browning's emotions—mostly terror and bafflement—cascade around her until they'd dissipated somewhat. Then she felt for his vitals. He was deep in shock. The man was overwhelmed and his body strained beyond its limits, thanks to his emotional state.

Janelle groaned. "Kane?"

"Easy, Janelle. You can do this."

"No. No, I don't think I can. I've never—"

"Your headache. You healed that, remember? This is the same."

"No, it's not, damn it! That was just me inside me. But this is *his* head and *his* body. I can't feel . . . how could I possibly even know, much less address—"

"Just focus. It worked last time, remember? Think about the source. Try for the source."

Flinching mentally and physically, Janelle tried to follow the waves, which seemed to be crashing everywhere around and on top of each other. "I couldn't possibly follow any of this."

"Focus."

Focus. Of course, focus, damn it. But he didn't have to do it. She was the one who had to chase down the insanity and repair the physical damage it had wrought. If she even could.

Still, the mental harangue steadied her and she was able to see past the smaller patterns to the overwhelming one. She followed it. His vitals were a mess, so she would deal with those first. She soothed his blood pressure back into normal range; calmed his heartbeat to a steadier, less dangerous pace; adjusted his body temperature to a more comfortable level; eased the pounding in his head, his ears, his body. And bruises. He'd been handled roughly. Not beaten, but no care had been given to his frailty.

After a moment that felt like forever, Browning seemed

easier, his skin more pink than white. And, slowly, he turned his head to meet her eyes. "I know you."

Janelle swallowed, still shaken by her own experiences. "What happened to you?"

His attention drifted over her shoulder, then up, until it fixed desperately on Kane's face. "Him. Horse!" He swallowed convulsively, and Janelle struggled to keep up with his laboring heart.

"What?" Janelle spoke quietly, hoping he could convey just a word or two more for her. Something to exonerate? To convict?

Browning's gaze fixed obsessively on Kane. Terror radiated from every part of his being. "The puca. He's evil. He tried to kill me. No, worse. He tried to drive me insane." Browning swallowed audibly. "I think it worked."

"Kane." Janelle spoke low, but her panic was building. "He can't take this."

"Get him to look into your eyes and, when he fixes, tell him he must sleep."

Too frightened for the man to do anything else, Janelle met Browning's eyes, felt him latch onto her gaze almost desperately. "You're tired, aren't you?" she asked.

"Yes."

"Wouldn't you like to sleep?"

"Yes." He held her gaze.

"Tell him, Janelle."

Making it an order seemed so wrong, so—

"Necessary for him. Tell him."

"You must sleep now. Sleep."

Browning immediately slumped, and Janelle sagged in relief.

"Good." Kane bent and carefully leaned the Druid into a more comfortable position against the wall. "He'll keep while I show you the rest." He held out a hand for her, but, avoiding Kane's touch, she scrambled to her feet without his aid.

"He said you did it." She eyed him cautiously. "That

you did this thing to him. To drive him crazy. Out of revenge."

"Is that what you think?"

She swallowed, remembering. He'd sought revenge against Riordan. Cruel revenge, and long lasting. But somehow, with the Druid, the revenge had seemed particularly devastating. Total destruction. If Kane hadn't destroyed Riordan, when Riordan's offense was so much greater, why would Kane retaliate against the Druid so viciously as payback for the lesser offense of insulting him? It didn't add up.

And yet, it was puca magic. And Kane was the only puca—

"I don't know. I just know we have to help Browning. The question of who did this to him is secondary. Can we help him?"

Kane nodded patiently. "But he needs to forget. This memory will keep him locked in the same destructive loop unless we take it from him."

"By using the glamour." Setting aside the question of blame in favor of a possible solution, however repugnant, she stared into Kane's eyes. Tried to let her mind truly grasp the idea of tinkering with somebody else's thoughts. With someone else's memories. Could she really do that? It felt like such a violation.

"It's not. You're not trying to hurt him or unnecessarily invade his privacy. He's seen something he can't accept, something completely at odds with his reality. To fix his world, he needs you to take that anomaly away from him. Completely. Basically, you're creating a logical, acceptable lie for him—the same kind of lie you might try to tell him without the aid of glamour—and just ensuring that he believes it. You're eliminating the middleman, bypassing his doubts and reality and giving him the lie directly."

"Wholesale lying. I see." It felt so wrong. A total violation of the man's privacy and integrity.

"It is an intrusion, I'll grant you that, but it's a minimal one and intended for his own well-being. You're telling him a little white lie so he and you can go on with your lives as productive, sane members of society."

"Supposing I buy into this train of thought—and I'm not saying that that's what I'm doing at this point—just how would I go about . . . glamouring somebody?"

"It varies over time and with experience. Eventually, you'll grow accustomed to it and it will simply be a matter of making a soft connection with another mind and whispering a few instructions."

"Look, I don't ever want to become accustomed to doing something like this. Suppose you tell me how to take care of a onetime occurrence? This one in particular?"

"That's a start, I suppose."

When she opened her mouth to argue more, he just held up a hand and shook his head. "We'll deal with the here and now. First, you need to make the connection."

"And I do that how?"

He stepped closer. She automatically stepped an equal distance backward, at which point he grabbed her hand. She jumped, her fingers instinctively gripping onto his as her body went into complete overload. Jangling nerves, mixed emotions, trembling hands all coalesced into one chaotic mass of needy awareness. She felt him, heard him and even—slightly—*was* him. Felt the hard warmth of his hand and the slender pressure of her fingers around his.

"This is the connection," he murmured. *I can speak to you this way, too.*

She swallowed heavily and tried to ignore the accelerating beat of her heart.

"You watch the pupils. Between you and me, because of our power bond, the connection is immediate, based on touch. With anyone else, you would need to make eye contact and hold it. The other person will want to hold it. This is part of the gift. They want to hold the contact once you initiate it. When the pupils dilate, contract briefly, then dilate more . . . you're there. That's when you exchange the information."

"Exchange . . ." She shook her head dazedly, but never broke eye contact. She couldn't.

"It's a blind moment for the human. Well, the other human. The person is open to you, responsive to any question and willing to accept as truth any information you offer, no matter how contradictory it might seem otherwise."

"It works like hypnosis?"

"In its purest form. This is no mere suggestion. As long as what you're saying fits logically and comfortably into the world concept the human holds, then the human will absolutely accept your statement as fact."

With a jerk, Janelle broke away, backing up a step or two, her breath coming in gasps now. She couldn't even look at him. The connection had been so intimate. Would it be like this with a glamour victim?

"The person is not a victim. Unwitting of your actions, perhaps, but as long as the intent is pure, you are not victimizing the human. And the thing between you and me . . . the intimacy . . . is different entirely. I can't glamour you. It's just not the same thing."

She hazarded a panicked glance at him. "Then what is it? This connection between you and me?"

His lips twisted just a little. "It's many things. Fate. And forbidden."

"At the same time?" She was appalled. Then shook it off. "Never mind. Here and now. Glamour. Finish the lesson."

He dipped his head in acquiescence. "You state facts clearly and concisely. He accepts them. Then you break the connection. And ease back into reality."

"And he'll believe what I tell him? Anything I tell him?"

Kane nodded. "As long as it fits into his own reality."

"So as long as I lie well, you mean. That is so wrong. Completely dangerous."

"Dangerous, yes. Wrong? Depends on the who and the what." Kane glanced down at the sleeping man. "And something or someone left this man with an experience he can't get past. Glamour, in this case, would be a blessing. Merciful." He met Janelle's eyes. "Agreed?"

She glanced down at the Druid, remembering the agony she'd experienced secondhand through the man's thoughts and emotions. He couldn't endure long without aid of some kind.

"And you can provide that aid."

Yes. She could. And so she must. It all just came down to that. Resolute, she knelt next to the man, touched his shoulder. "Um. Wake up?"

He opened his eyes instantly and looked up at her. Intent and mindful of Kane's instructions, she caught the man's gaze with her own and waited a moment. His eyes dilated once, then twice, and he leaned toward her, as though drawn almost obsessively. She leaned backward, disarmed when he followed.

"Make the exchange," Kane murmured.

"He's creeping me out." For he seemed perfectly fine.

"Make the exchange," Kane said again, but urgently.

"But what do I say? This is so James Bond-y, with a side order of stalker victim."

The Druid's hands were actually reaching for her.

"Exchange!"

"Spit? Words? Phone numbers? Life stories? Exchange what?"

"Tell him he never saw a horse on Cary Street. That his experience was nothing more than a dream brought on by spirits."

Abandoning her panic, she grabbed the man's hands as an anchor, held his gaze and spoke quickly. "You never saw a horse. Your ride was nothing more than a dream. Brought on by, um, evil spirits. You'll wake up with your sanity intact and no memory of this conversation with me or with Kane."

The Druid leaned closer.

"Do it now. Wake up." She dropped his hands and scrambled backward until her back met brick wall and she rose to her feet.

"I said spirits. Not *evil* spirits." Kane murmured this in her ear.

"Does it really matter?" She was watching the Druid, who, thank God, had stopped approaching her like some flesh-eating zombie eyeing his next feast.

Janelle saw the man blink and look around himself in bewilderment. The horrible glazed look was gone, as was the terror he'd previously broadcast from his very soul. Puca power still clung to him, but it was no longer a malevolent force. Just an influence. That was good, right?

"Probably." Kane was watching him, too.

"You." Browning narrowed his eyes. "I know you." He glanced from Kane to Janelle. "Both of you. What am I doing here? Where are the other Druids? I thought we were in the grove." He shook it off before continuing distractedly. "I had a dream. Someone must interpret my dream. I think it means something. A prophecy. Evil spirits stalking our city's horses. I must warn James."

"James?" Janelle eyed him with dazed horror.

"Bond." He paused, unblinking. "*James* Bond."

"But you're not him."

"Of course I'm not him." He eyed her with disgust. "I'm just a Druid."

So saying, the little man scrambled to his filthy bare feet and wiped off the back of his pants. Then he hurried down the street, muttering about malicious spirits and protecting the country's farm animals and recreational stables. He was a man on a mission. A hobbit on a mission? No, not a hobbit. A Druid. And was that so much better?

Janelle leaned weakly against hard brick. "So, is he looking for Druids or a fictitious spy?"

"Both, I believe. It's just possible that he now believes James Bond is a Druid who can cast spells to deliver us from evil spirits preying on farm animals. Perhaps we'll get lucky and there is a Druid named that."

"I don't think I have that kind of luck." Janelle swallowed. "Dear God. What have I done?"

"Did I mention that it's critical to think carefully before speaking when you are in the middle of a glamour?"

"Uh, no, you somehow neglected that part."

"I thought it would go without saying."

"Nothing, but *nothing*, goes without saying where you're concerned. And don't you dare go getting mad at me about this one. I've never glamoured before. As a human, I shouldn't be able to do this."

"But you're a smart woman. A smart woman who knows she has a vulnerable mind open to her every suggestion isn't going to suggest idiocy, now is she?"

And the censure behind his words raised her ire and her very own malicious tendencies. "Gosh, I don't know. Can I glamour *you*?" Now, that would be entertaining. No barhopping performer of a hypnotist could hope to compete with Janelle's creativity, given an entranced Kane at her mercy.

"Is that what you want? To be able to glamour me?" He was close to her now, hands grasping her shoulders. Fingertips brushed the bare skin over her collarbone.

Janelle jumped. She felt the zing that preceded a virtual full-body inferno as his thoughts, frustration, worries, arousal battered at her conflicted conscience, fears, concerns, leaping arousal and *terror* of all of the above.

"You fear me? No, you fear *you*. And us together. What we can do and what you just did. But you don't fear me."

"Don't kid yourself," she choked out. "I fear the hell out of you."

But she was lying, trying to build a wall that could not

be built. Their emotions, open for both to see and exchange, collided and mingled. Unbearably intimate and so explosive.

"If you were to glamour me, what would you do?" He spoke low, his eyes flaming with something between temper and pagan desperation.

"H-horrible things. Humiliating."

Unable to look away from his eyes, she saw and felt the moment temper gave over to something different. Eroticism spiced with amusement. Even affection?

"Really." She forced her lips to move. Dry lips. She licked them, felt her head spin just a little as the look in his eyes intensified. "Humiliating." So now he was laughing at her and it was turning her on?

It's turning me on, too.

And then he was reaching for her and Janelle was trying to decide how to field another pass. Could she weather another encounter with Hot Stuff? Especially given how the one eight years ago turned out?

She remembered still. It had been amazing—and she stood not a single chance against him in all his glory. Even without the mind-meld stuff that currently sizzled her insides. Kane didn't need mind melds to torch every cell in her body. He was devastating just as he was, no puca tricks necessary.

Be on your guard against seduction attempts.

The memory of Phil's words stopped her cold. She held up a hand to halt Kane's progress—and was grateful he didn't make contact. "Consider this me halting you in your tracks. I'm back in control here."

"Temporarily, anyway."

She gave him a disgruntled look. "That's not helping matters."

"I'm just being honest." His eyes still burned with emotion.

"Well, try this for honesty. Beyond the hormones, mentally, emotionally and logically I realize you're bad for me. I just have to keep all my little soldiers on alert when you're around. No more relaxing of the defenses. No more smiles and touches and kisses. Got that? Just be your usual obnoxious self, don't read any libidinous challenges into my words, and we'll get along great. Just a reluctant guardian and her vengeful yet horny puca ward."

"Is that how you see me?" He eyed her quizzically. "Just horny and vengeful? Nothing deeper? No character at all?"

"I didn't say that." She glanced away. "Those are just the parts of you that I need to stay away from, the parts I need to keep fresh in my memory so I don't weaken again."

"So how do we keep *me* from weakening?" His voice, so intimate, suggested total impossibility.

She gave him a cool look. She would not be manipulated. "That's easy enough, especially for you. Visualize the worst-case scenario, should I lose guardianship of you. What would they do to you if I were out of the picture? Cage you for millennia like you did Riordan? Even if you got lucky and were assigned a new guardian instead—which they seemed really reluctant to do—my replacement could be a complete nightmare."

"Worse than you?" He raised his eyebrows, just a little mockingly. "I'd think you would be my worst-case scenario as guardian. Think about it. You're the onetime lover I skipped out on without a word. Remember that part?"

"How could I forget?" She gritted her teeth. "But you need to consider other possibilities. What about our buddy Duncan? He'd make a great guardian. And heaven only knows how many woo-woo types could be pulled into the pool of possibility. Huge selection, in all likelihood. Especially given your royal status. Envy, anyone? Power plays? The possibilities for puca torture are endless.

"As the deal stands now, at least you have me abiding by my oath as a physician, which means a certain leash on at least physical torture. That means you're relatively safe with me unless you push me too far."

"Good point." He shoved his hands in his pockets.

Janelle tried to ignore the way the denim stretched taut between the pockets. As taut as it could, given Kane's physical state.

When Kane cleared his throat, Janelle realized she'd been a little obvious with the focus of her attention. *Good move, guardian. Can we just call you Dr. Hypocrite?*

Kane waited patiently until a blushing (again!) Janelle met his eyes. "If this is your way of keeping me in my place, it's not working very well."

No kidding. It was completely unfair that he could walk around in her head anytime he pleased, that she couldn't hide a single damn thought from him. Then add that to their history and a stupid attraction that seemed alive and well in spite of that history. . . . "Tell me, Kane. Why didn't you glamour me before you walked out eight years ago? Why didn't you make me forget you?"

He stared at her a moment before turning slightly away to survey the nearby buildings and vehicles. Dented and damaged cars, three of them right in a row, lined the right side of the street. On the left, several store windows had been shattered. "The damage here was deliberate. He had to go out of his way to damage both sides of the street. It wasn't just along his path. Why?"

"You didn't answer my question."

Absently, Kane bent to pick Janelle's jacket off the ground where the Druid had abandoned it. He turned back to Janelle, handing it to her. "There was no need to take the memory from you. All you remembered was a fling that ended a little callously. There was no puca magic involved in our encounter, and nothing that couldn't have happened between two consenting and fully human adults."

She stared. "That's all? That's the reason?"

"What more do I need? Do you honestly wish that I'd unnecessarily fiddled around in your mind, taking and changing your memories?"

No. She didn't. Her gaze trained on the jacket she held, she carefully folded it over her arm. Of course she didn't want him manipulating her mind like that. She just wanted to believe that he'd done it out of respect or even affection for her, not just for the sake of practicality.

He eyed her quietly. "All right. It wasn't just practicality. Can we let it drop?"

And was that a lie to shut her up? As if she'd ever know. He could read her every thought, this coldhearted jerk who didn't bother with her feelings. *Hear that, puca? Just keep your distance and a strict leash on that destructive temper of yours.* His jaw twitched, but that was the only sign that he'd received her silently poisonous message.

Just as she narrowed her eyes, a challenge poised on her lips, she saw his attention shift abruptly. "What are you doing here?" he called out.

Janelle shifted her gaze to a shadowy figure standing just beyond the makeshift street barrier.

He was watching them.

Chapter Nine ✤

Duncan Forbes. Great timing.

Stepping around the nearest sawhorse, Duncan approached them, a disturbing smile crossing his face. "Call me crazy, but what I've been seeing between the two of you doesn't look like proper guardian/ward etiquette. Almost incestuous, don't you think? And perhaps against the rules?" He shook his head, making an annoying and less-than-masculine *tsk-tsk* sound.

Janelle glared over Kane's shoulder at him. "Are you following us?"

"This is a public street. Maybe you should think of that before you start breaking the rules. Or maybe you already did. Maybe a guardian is trying to rid herself of a puca? Or maybe a puca is trying to manipulate his guardian. Do you know? Do you wonder?"

Janelle felt her cheeks burn.

"No and no," Kane responded coldly, and presumably, for both of them. "So tell me. Were you the one who called to report this incident?"

"What incident? Oh, about the horse you mean? I read about that in the paper." Duncan shook his head. "A wild horse running loose in downtown Richmond. Can you imagine?"

"Couldn't even begin to." Kane sounded equally dis-ingenuous. "Any idea who might have done it?"

"Me? How would I know anything about it? Oh, be-cause I work just a couple blocks over? Hmm." Duncan feigned thought. "Or maybe, just maybe, it's because it had something to do with puca magic? Is there some-thing you need to confess to the Druid Council?"

Janelle raised her chin. "What, are you speaking on behalf of the council now? I thought you'd rejected your heritage, Oh Mystic One."

"A man can change his mind, can't he? Especially when he sees a need for his support." Duncan eyed them pointedly. "Meanwhile, I suggest you pay more atten-tion to the rules. They included something about arm's length, if I'm not mistaken?" With a last, pointed look at Janelle and Kane, he turned and leisurely strode off.

Watching him, Janelle growled under her breath. "He wants something."

Kane, still watching Duncan, murmured quietly, "Even more importantly, he seems to believe he's on the brink of getting it. He seems a lot more confident than when we confronted him in his office. Smug, even."

"That sounds bad for us. And I don't know why. A few weeks ago, I didn't even know Duncan Forbes ex-isted."

"And then you were saddled with me."

"And fun times were had by all."

A sudden frown on Kane's face distracted her and she followed his line of sight.

A shadow. And somehow a familiar one?

"It's Tremayne." Kane raised his eyebrows. "I think he's been here the whole time. Watching everything." He glanced at Janelle, who eyed the shadow uneasily as it disappeared around a corner "And now he's follow-ing Duncan."

"Daphne said he was a private investigator."

"Hardly."

"It's possible. Maybe some of your kind get bored and take on a hobby or two. Private investigating might be a fun way to occupy yourself for part of an eternity."

"He's not one of my kind."

"So I gather. But he's not one of my kind, either."

Kane nodded. "I wonder what he's after. I'll ask Riordan what he remembers about him."

And she'd damn well let him ask. Investigating woo-woo types did not fall under the job description of puca guardian. Other matters, however, did. She'd focus on those.

"So, about the Druid." She was very proud of the even tone of her voice. "What will happen to him now? I mean, because of the James Bond and evil spirits thing."

Kane's lips quirked, as though anger had dissolved into reluctant amusement. "Since that wasn't really a suggestion or command, more of a comment, it shouldn't do much more than temporarily confuse him."

"But he'll still believe what I told him about the horse ride? That it never really happened?"

"You commanded it, so yes. And his own subconscious will reinforce the command. His mind doesn't want to believe his experiences were real. It's much easier to accept a bad dream than to deal with a nightmarish reality. He will willingly believe the ride was a dream, and the James Bond foolishness will fade. He'll experience a little embarrassment along the way, maybe, but that's probably it."

Janelle nodded, relieved. "Good. So. About the horse he rode. The puca." She met his eyes in question.

"This is where we start attaching blame?"

"Well, it is the job assigned to me as your gullible guardian. Correct?"

He shrugged. "Go on."

"This was the same Druid who annoyed you so much you recklessly shifted shape in that park, mere minutes

after the Druids condemned you for other vengeful behavior. Remember?"

"Yes."

"Yes? That's all you have to say?"

"Yes, I remember the incident in the park—and
Browning—but no, I didn't do this."

"Then who did? Riordan? Not hardly. We have evidence of puca magic used against somebody who drove
you to rage not too long ago. Some people might already
be convicting you—the only known puca on the planet—
without even considering any defense you might offer."

"Are you one of them?"

"Maybe."

"Liar." He turned back to her. "You're mad at me about
a lot of things, but you don't really believe I did this.
Logic tells you it would be difficult." He paused, eyes
locking with hers. "And your gut tells you it wasn't me.
And yet you don't trust your gut. Not anymore. Thanks
to me."

"Get the hell out of my head." She could actually feel
him in there. Snooping even beyond what she might actually be projecting.

"I had to know. That's all."

"What do you care what I really believe? You ought to
be more concerned with what I report back to your
Druid buddies about this incident. I have to report something, you know. Your High Druid Phil is awaiting my
conclusions."

"What will you tell him?"

"What, you didn't already read that in my head?"

"I stayed away from that. I just wanted to know what
you personally believe."

That made no sense. "What do you care what I believe? Honestly. What do you care?"

"I just care. If you despise me, I'm doomed. If you
think I'm innocent, maybe you'll help me find out what
really happened here."

"Why would you need my help to figure that out? I already did all I can do. I sensed puca power. That should be the end of the story. You are, after all, the only known puca around here, right?"

"With *known* being the operative word. I wonder if there are others."

"You mean, now that it's convenient to believe there might be others?"

"I didn't do this. Another puca must have done this. Which means there must be another puca somewhere. If there is not, then I have no defense. Yes, it would be darn convenient to find admissible proof that someone else could have done this."

"Just for the sake of argument, let's suppose there is another puca walking around out there. What would this puca be to you? Who can sire a puca? Oberon, obviously. What about you or Riordan? Other faeries?"

He was shaking his head. "To be honest, I've only ever known of Oberon being fertile with a human female. I suppose Riordan, as a human himself, could father children with Mina now. But those children would be human. Anything prior to that . . . odds are it would have been a sterile union. Unless he mated with someone of faerie blood."

"And did he? Did you? Hey, if you have an unacknowledged, illegitimate child running around, I could see him or her being a little peeved with deadbeat Daddy the Faeriest."

"You're hilarious."

"And even better, I have a point."

Kane nodded. "Except that I never had unprotected sex with a woman if the union was potentially fertile."

"That you know of."

"You are particularly fond of that phrase."

"Just trying to include all possibilities."

"You want to believe that the little Druid is the victim of my long-lost child?" He gave her a disbelieving look. "Or maybe you think the Druid *is* my long-lost child."

Janelle pondered. True, the Druid seemed to have a major chip on his shoulder for the Goodfellow brothers, but as for resemblance . . . Browning resembled an underfed troll.

Kane gave her a wry smile. "I suppose he could resemble his mother?"

Janelle tried to picture a mother who, crossed with Kane, could produce something as objectively unattractive as the little, runtlike Druid. It wasn't pretty. "And she managed to talk you into bed *how*?"

"I'm pretty easy."

She flinched inwardly. "That's what I hear." She deliberately dismissed the subject.

"I said I'm easy. But I don't take sex lightly either."

"You took it lightly enough with me." And why the hell did she have to say that?

"Because it is a good point."

"Out. Out of my head!"

He nodded in acquiescence. "For the record, I didn't take it as lightly as you might think."

Right. "So let's drop the past and this stupidity we have going between us. We need to address the situation at hand. We have puca magic and only one known puca. A Druid enrages that one known puca. Same Druid shows up later, a victim of puca magic." She paused. "If you didn't do this, I don't think we can deny that somebody set you up. This was too elaborate and yet too damning to be a coincidence."

"I'll go along with that. So. Who would set me up? And how?"

"The how . . . I'm not sure. You're the puca. Suppose you tell me how?"

"If I knew, you'd be the first person I'd tell."

"So let's take it from the 'who' approach." She paused in thought. "You've obviously made a few enemies in your lifetime. Anyone I know? Can we collect a dossier on you? Maybe some blurbs on these people, just summarizing past events and the current status of the relationship?"

"Now who sounds James Bond-y?"

"Hey, I'm just doing what I think is logical. If you don't want my help, though, I can draw the obvious conclusions and make a straightforward report to Druid Phil."

"Is that a threat?"

"It's just a simple statement and you know it."

He nodded. "Still, that leaves me wondering exactly what you will report to Phil. Even if you are giving me the benefit of the doubt here, he's still going to have to know something."

"So we spin it. For now."

As it turned out, they didn't have to spin anything. Phil was missing. They couldn't contact him, and all of the Druid underlings to which she was subsequently routed were cagey on his behalf. Disconcerted, Janelle hung up her phone and looked at Kane.

"I guess we just pursue this thing on our own then."

Kane, now lounging on Janelle's ugly gray couch, eyed her with interest. And not just because she was wearing a fitted little T-shirt and had neglected the camouflage of a bra. The woman insisted she had no breasts—he'd heard that thought more than once in her head—but quantity notwithstanding, he found them dangerously distracting just as they were. "What, you're not going to accuse me of killing Phil?"

"You mean, just for my own amusement?"

"Or revenge." And she had plenty of cause for it, given that, as she'd pointed out, he'd neglected to take her memory of him. He'd never been able to make himself do that. Telling her why would serve no purpose, just cloud the real issues and problems. The woman didn't need to know that he'd left her memory intact for the simple reason that he couldn't stand the idea of her not remembering him or the one night they'd shared. All *he* could think about was her, so why should she be spared? A kind man would have taken the memory from her. A generous man would. Kane had not. So he was selfish. Not exactly a news flash.

Janelle shook her head. "You know, people are occasionally motivated by emotions and factors other than revenge."

"Like what? Take you, for example. What would motivate you to reject the obvious solutions?" He was genuinely curious. "That I'm the one who did the puca ride with the little Druid. Or that I might have taken out the guy who condemned me to the juvenile existence I'm currently leading. The motivation of revenge might suggest that I'm the one responsible for both."

Janelle frowned, obviously not thrilled to have the disturbing details thrown in her face all over again. "Logic alone would sway me. After all, *you* were the one who condemned yourself to this situation we're in. Not Phil. You *chose* to confess. Phil didn't force you into it. You chose to accept punishment. So hurting Phil would serve no purpose. Besides, for all we know, Phil found some little twenty-year-old who had a thing for purple specs and Druid types and he's off having a fling with her and her roommate."

He smiled reluctantly. "Now that's an imagination." And he'd known that imagination intimately—both in action and in thought. He'd missed it.

She shrugged.

"So, do we try to locate Phil?" he asked quietly.

She made a face. "Actually, I was told in no uncertain terms that Phil's disappearance was 'Druid business' and to keep you out of it. I think there's a trust problem."

"No kidding. Somebody apparently has a high opinion of my ability." Kane's tone was dry. "It seems that I can play runaway horse *and* kidnap a High Druid all at the same time."

"Your point is so noted," she mused.

"So what now?"

She tapped a fingernail to her lip. "I think we should see if anyone knows of any other pucas in existence. Any idea how we'd manage that?"

"Yes."

His face impassive, King Oberon settled onto the couch by his oldest son. "You called, son who is not my son?"

"What, is that his new title? A couple of words and, bam, Kane goes from Prince of All Faerie to 'son who is not my son'? You are cold, buddy. Ice cold."

"It was his decision." Oberon's expression and tone remained neutral.

Which only served to annoy Janelle more. "Yeah, well, a father who realizes his son is making a bad decision doesn't just go along with that bad decision. He tries to talk him out of it."

"That would be beneath me and disrespectful of him."

"Dignity, pride." She waved a dismissive hand. "Big freaking deal. All I'm saying is—"

"Janelle, it's nothing personal," Kane interrupted, but not impatiently. "He's just reminding me of his limitations where I am concerned—limitations I invited by asking that he disown me. And right now we're wasting royal time."

Oooh, tick-tock goes the royal clock. Janelle rolled her eyes, but not before she saw a spark of amusement in Kane's eyes—mirrored in Oberon's?

Kane turned to his father. "I'm going to have to be blunt. And understand that I have good reason for bringing up this subject."

"Consider me warned. Continue."

Kane met Janelle's eyes before turning back to his father. "Are Riordan and I the only two pucas in existence?"

Oberon looked surprised. "That is an odd question."

"But necessary. I'll explain in a minute."

Oberon was slowly shaking his head. "I know of no other puca besides the two of you. One of you, now. But I couldn't absolutely rule out—"

"Oh, good grief." Janelle was beside herself. "Is there no faerie equivalent of Planned Parenthood? Or a Society for Keeping Your Royal Highness's Pants Zipped? To be unsure of the existence of any other child—"

His Royal Highness looked to be on the verge of a royal tantrum. "I have fathered no children other than those I currently acknowledge. They know who they are and they are aware of each other. I cannot, however, speak for everyone of faerie blood."

Janelle frowned. "But I thought a union between a human and one of you guys was generally an infertile one."

Oberon shrugged. "Usually it is. The odds are against such a conception. It is not impossible, however." He nodded at Kane. "As evidenced by—"

"The son who is not your son. Yeah, I get it. But the faerie in question doesn't have to be of royal blood?"

Oberon attempted modesty—and failed. "The royal part's not important. Virility is."

So, the faerie king was packing heat. "Oh, gag."

Kane snorted, his amusement beyond his own containment.

"I'm sorry if this embarrasses you, young lady." No one could patronize quite like an extraordinarily fertile and self-satisfied King of All Faerie. "I'm just trying to answer your questions. Did you have others?" And he seemed eager to answer every last one of them. *Great. Thus the closet exhibitionist emerges from his hidey-hole.*

Kane cleared his throat. "I have questions."

Oberon, currently entranced by his own potency, turned

reluctantly to the other male in the room. His son. Who was not his son.

"You say you have no evidence of other fertile unions between a human and one of faerie blood. How about rumors? Possibilities? Anything we could follow up on? Any way to tell at all whether another puca might have been conceived?"

Oberon sobered and regarded his son quietly. "Suppose you tell me why you so desperately hope another puca exists."

Kane sighed. "There was an incident. In downtown Richmond."

"Oh. *That* incident."

"You knew about it?"

Oberon shrugged. "I know what's reported to me. I assumed it was nothing more than sensationalized coincidence. This is not the case?"

"I sensed puca magic at the scene," Janelle reluctantly admitted.

Oberon looked grave now as he turned to his son. "Evidence of puca mischief. When you're on probation. Not good."

"I didn't do it."

Oberon regarded him quietly but didn't comment.

"We need to list our suspects. Or at least increase them to more than just the one. Otherwise . . ." Janelle shrugged.

"And that's why you need the potential existence of another puca. I see." Oberon seemed thoughtful now. "I can ask around, but you would get better information from another source. Assuming you could cultivate it."

"And who might that source be?"

"Titania."

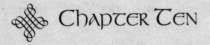 ## Chapter Ten

"So, when do we contact Titania? And how?" Flopping down on the now-vacant couch, Janelle eyed Kane patiently. Oberon, pleading royal duties, had left after sending up virtual mushroom clouds with his suggestion.

"You're kidding, right?" Kane, slouched in a chair opposite Janelle, regarded her cynically.

"Uh, no. We are kind of desperate here, you know?"

Kane was already shaking his head. "We will never be that desperate or self-destructive. Titania would cheerfully dance on my grave. In fact, nothing would make her happier, other than preceding my death with exquisite torture and assorted heckling. She would not help me. If anything, knowing what I was seeking would just give her ammunition to use against me. She'd know what to keep from me—or what to hold over my head."

"Wow. That's one twisted relationship you two have."

"What, that she hates my guts and I don't trust her not to knife me when I turn my back?"

"Yeah, that one. And I can just hear the love in your voice, too."

"You mentioned that great wellspring of evil." He shrugged, his jaw tight. "That's about as accurate a description as any I've heard. Hugging her would be like hugging a python. Deadly."

"Yeah? Whatever happened to 'too beautiful to look upon'?" Janelle gave him a wry look. "I thought men dropped like flies around her no matter what she did."

He grinned reluctantly. "That only applies to humans. She doesn't fool anyone of faerie blood. At least not so completely. The taint of power is unmistakable."

"She couldn't fool Mina or me either," Janelle mused.

"Maybe it's the gender. Or, it could be a side benefit of playing guardian to a puca. Her beauty is a glamour, so maybe she can't fool you completely, even if she can sustain the facade for you."

"Wow. So what does she really look like? Without the facade, I mean."

"You wouldn't believe me if I told you." He waved a hand, dismissing the subject. "The point is, consulting Titania would do more harm than good."

"Only if we were honest about our reasons. Maybe we could trick her into giving us the information."

"You're actually considering tricking the Queen of All Faerie. And you've even met her. You've seen what she's really like. Are you nuts? You're mortal, Janelle. You couldn't withstand what she'd throw at you."

"Is she allowed to hurt me? I mean, I'm human and therefore not one of her subjects, plus there's the wild card of me playing puca jailer."

"Oh, so now you're my jailer?" He snorted, every inch the royal prince. "And here I thought we were on the same side."

Janelle froze. "That's *it*. It's perfect."

"What?" He looked alarmed.

She sat forward on the cushions, eyes wide and heart pounding. "I have to convince her that I'm out for blood. Your blood. That I want to torture you. I need her to believe that finding this other puca would be in your absolute worst interest."

Kane stilled.

"Think about it. Heck, given our history, it wouldn't take much at all to convince her of my intent to hurt you. We laid the foundation at the trial already. Remember when they assigned guardianship to me? I think I made it clear to everyone exactly what I thought of you and the prospect of being your guardian. Some might say I wasn't just annoyed, but downright pissed. Or even a little . . . *vengeful*? Anyone? Anyone? Come on, Kane. You're a bright boy. Can't you see the connection? The possibilities? Is it that much of a stretch to believe I might want to hurt you for blowing me off eight years ago?"

"No, but—"

At his reluctant agreement, she pressed on. "Isn't it what Titania would do?"

"Seek revenge for rejection? Oh, at the very least. Heads would roll. But—"

"After all, Oberon's infidelities with your mother and Riordan's mother constituted repeated rejection of Titania. With your mothers gone and the king above her jealous rage, she's punished you and Riordan as stand-ins for your father for your entire, millennia-long lives. My wanting to make you suffer for rejecting me eight years ago would seem only logical to her."

"Yes, no question. But Janelle, there are other concerns. If she thinks you're trying to trick her . . ." He shook his head, his eyes dark with his thoughts. "I don't know if I could protect you from her. Not with my powers as limited as they are. And not with her under Oberon's protection, reluctant as it is."

"So she doesn't have to know." Janelle shrugged. "I just have to be good at it."

"And how long do you think that will last? She can read your mind as easily as I can."

Janelle winced. "Okay, that could be a problem." In fact, it was downright repulsive. Imagine the evil faerie stepbitch wandering at will among Janelle's thoughts, secrets, longings, weaknesses. She'd have access to everything and anything.

"If she busted you early on, she might be amused by the plan—right before she used our intentions against both of us. That's not great, but we might survive her wrath. On the other hand, if you pull this thing off halfway—just enough to gain some semblance of trust from her—her fury would be unimaginable. Titania detests being embarrassed or shown up in any way. We would suffer for it—you even more than me. She has great contempt for humans, even as she's drawn to them in a twisted way. It brings out the worst in her."

Janelle stared. "This is your stepmother. The queen. And she's this vindictive?"

He shrugged. "Different culture, different species, different rules."

"But that's such a rip-off. How'd we go from amoral fetish-queen faeries to the magic of fairy tales?"

"Doesn't Titania qualify as the evil stepmother?"

"Sure, but wouldn't that necessarily cast you in the role of Snow White or Cinderella? Do you sing to mousies much?" She shook her head, the ridiculous visual tugging a smile to her lips. "I still say we're onto a plan worth trying. Suppose you teach me how to shield my thoughts? If we're successful—"

"Then we're still dealing with a long shot. The possible existence of another puca."

She glared at him. "You know, for a puca of faerie blood who wields magic and lives in a world where the impossible is possible, you sure act the skeptic when you want to. What else do we have to go on here? The puca ride happened. You say you didn't do it. I'm inclined to believe you. But if you didn't do it, then somebody or something else must have done it. Who could that be? Somebody else who wields puca powers. Hence, the potential existence of another puca."

"Unless it's Riordan."

"Don't even go there." Janelle glared at him. "He wouldn't do that, even if he could."

Kane frowned. "I was just thinking that maybe—and I know I'm reaching here—you had a point with your sleep shape-shifting theory. I wonder if it's possible for him to have retained power and not know about it? Except in sleep, when normal inhibitions relax."

Janelle was already shaking her head. "Even in his sleep, Riordan wouldn't go after some helpless little man like that Druid guy."

"You're right. In his right mind he wouldn't. Who's to say he was in his right mind?"

"Come on, Kane, let's play odds here. Don't you think the existence of another puca's a little more likely—not to mention desirable—than thinking your brother is some Jekyll-and-Hyde nightmare of a former puca?"

"I still say it's a possibility we should consider."

"Fine. You look into it. But only after you teach me how to shield my thoughts from you and your scary step-mommy. Speaking of whom, I can't believe, with glamour at her disposal, she doesn't project an appearance that's a little more believable and a little less manga stripper. Yech." Janelle shivered. "Those eyes. Shouldn't she at least attempt to look human?"

Kane smiled reluctantly. "That must be part of the guardian thing. She appears less, well, manga to your average human male. The stripper part . . . I'll admit that's what she's deliberately projecting. But it works for her."

"How depressing. So. Shielding of the thoughts. Let the lessons begin."

"If you insist." He paused, obviously positioning his words. "To shield your thoughts, you have to be deliberate and you have to be always on guard. That's why it would be bad to fall asleep or ill or unconscious in front of someone of faerie blood if you don't trust them. Shielding your thoughts from a faerie is much like holding your tongue, but before you even speak. Never let the thoughts fully form. Stray wisps you can probably get away with. Just don't let them develop beyond a casual, unformed concept. Does that make sense?"

"A little, but probably because I'm hoping it's not as difficult as it sounds."

He pondered a moment. "Okay, try this, then. Think of that tip-of-your-tongue phenomenon, where the memory is just out of your grasp. A fleeting reminder of something you sense but don't quite remember. That's the state where you leave your thoughts."

"Seriously?" She stared. "Is it even possible to do that on purpose?"

"It takes training and practice, but yes, it is possible. There is another method, which is slightly easier but not as effective. Basically enclosing your thoughts inside a mental container you consciously maintain. That works for Riordan. Somewhat. With me, with the queen—your being human—it won't work at all. Titania would just laugh as she mentally collapsed your container and took what she wanted."

Janelle shuddered. "What was it like to grow up with that?"

"Difficult at times." Kane shrugged. "It taught me discipline fairly early in life, though."

"The receiving of or the practicing of?" she retorted.

"Both."

"Riordan wasn't raised by her."

"No."

She pondered. "With his container thing, he probably wouldn't have stood a chance with her."

"Probably not."

"Does he know that?"

"Does it matter?" Kane waved off the question as unimportant.

Royals and pucas. Dense as doornails sometimes. "Of course it matters. Especially if he ever thought living with her and Oberon was preferable to living elsewhere or with you. And if he knew what you went through as a kid, I think he'd understand you a little better."

"There's nothing to understand." Kane's voice rose with impatience. "For over two thousand years, we haven't been part of each other's lives, except as cause and effect. Why would that ever change? In Riordan's eyes, I will always be the reason he lived inside a Sarsen stone fragment for two thousand years. He has good reason to hate me. I earned his hatred."

"Maybe, but knowing what he was spared and what you endured as a kid might alleviate some of those hard feelings." And she had to believe there were occasions when Kane had prevented Stepmommy Dearest from destroying his young half brother. Kane had seemed only too aware of what could happen with the container strategy. And Riordan was completely unaware. Was it because Riordan wasn't exposed to Titania? Maybe even completely sheltered from her?

Oberon would likely have been too busy acting as head of state to bother with domestic issues like rocky relationships between his wife and sons. No, smart money was on Kane acting in a suspiciously protective manner. Very much, in fact, like an older brother protecting his younger sibling from what he himself endured on a regular basis. So there, in her mind, was proof Kane had loved his younger brother. It must have hurt like hell when Riordan slept with Kane's fiancée. Kane might have gone overboard—okay, way overboard—in retaliating, but he *had* been hurt.

"It's pointless to pursue this." And Kane's tone suggested that he was done with the subject. "So. You understand the concept of disciplining your thoughts, correct? And if you must have a thought, at least hide it behind others."

Janelle raised her eyebrows. "Mary had a little lamb . . ."

"Crude, but yes, that's the general idea. For a more

subtle approach, though, try imagining something mundane but nagging, like a grocery list or a to-do list, or work duties. Anything you'd prefer someone else see over what you're actually thinking. Then keep it uppermost in your mind—mentally repeating it or shouting it to drown out the dangerous thoughts. This is not easy."

"Not easy? There's an understatement."

"Exactly my point. For now, let's try just wiping the slate clean of thoughts."

"Okay. Here goes nothing. Literally." Janelle frowned and closed her eyes.

"Clear your thoughts. Picture a blank, clean slate. Nothing else is there. Everything is easy and carefree . . ."

No thoughts. How did one have no thoughts? Even now, she was thinking about having no thoughts, which only made her mind want to race to other, more complicated thoughts. . . . "Maybe I ought to give yoga a try." She inhaled deeply to calm her mind.

"Wouldn't hurt. How's the slate coming along?"

Inhaling again, she spoke on the exhale. "You tell me. Can you read anything?"

He met her eyes briefly, meaningfully, and glanced away.

"And that would be a yes." She smiled, unamused. She'd tried—apparently with no success—to banish the question that had plagued her mind for most of the day. And several others preceding it.

"Am I supposed to answer your question or shall we start again?"

"I believe you already gave your answer. That it was unnecessary to glamour me. My puny thoughts were mundane enough that you didn't need to adjust my memory of our tawdry little one-night stand."

"That's not exactly what I said, but it's really a moot point." Kane's voice was every bit as expressionless as he wanted her blank slate to be. "As for the mind shielding . . . Let's try something else, just to see if it works.

Try batting around a wisp of a thought, so we can see what's visible and what's not. For now, let a thought breeze by you of a single letter, number or word, and in about fifteen seconds, I'll go probing."

Her thoughts. She flinched. So he'd just go poking around in her head to see what he could see. Hell, she'd rather do stirrup duty at the gynecologist's than submit to a mind probing. By anyone.

"This was your idea."

"And you started reading early."

"I did not. You threw that thought right at me."

"Oh, good Lord. Start ten seconds from now."

Kane hummed a complicated little tune she half-recognized as she carefully calmed her thoughts and maintained her mental layering of concepts.

When Kane turned to look at her, staring hard, she could actually feel the mental touch and sense his question—his *unanswered* question. She let herself smile. It was working.

"I dreamed about you last night." The bald statement emerged as a husky whisper.

Her layers collapsed on themselves and her breath escaped in a rush.

"The number eight," he murmured with calm assurance.

"That was cheating."

"You bet." He shrugged. "But justified and necessary. Titania won't play fair. I had to show you how impossible this plan is. You mean well, and I can't tell you how grateful I am that you're willing to take such a risk on my behalf, but it's just too dangerous. I can't risk you."

"You can't—"

"No, damn it. I can't risk you." He turned from her, obviously more affected than he'd let on. Then, tipping his head back, he murmured a phrase in a foreign, musical tongue. After a twirling of tiny lights, a young woman appeared.

Janelle, who thought she was used to this by now, took three steps backward. "Who are you?"

"What do you mean who am I?" The petite woman looked down her pointy nose. "Who are *you*?"

Janelle slid a cautious glance at Kane. "Is this a friend of yours?"

"Yes and no." Kane looked equal parts resigned and exasperated. "Janelle, meet my sister Breena."

Janelle studied Breena with interest. "Another puca? But I thought—"

"Hardly." Breena snorted and rolled her very large—not cartoonish, just gorgeous—green eyes. "I'm pure faerie, baby. Unlike my mongrel half brother here."

"Mongrel? Gee, there's love for you." But Kane's voice was mild.

"Actually, not even half brother, according to the latest." She turned her curiosity on Kane. "So Dad's finally disowned you, huh? And now we have to claim a human as the royal heir? Yuck. They're already half corpse as it is." She grinned evilly at Janelle. "We call it kissing carrion."

Kane's lips twitched, both at the term and Janelle's silent outrage. "Bree, cut it out. Janelle's a friend."

Breena narrowed her eyes at him. "Cut what out?"

"I mean quit with the attitude. You're wasting time and there's no need."

Her expression cleared and she regarded Janelle more closely. "That's interesting. Should I know you?"

"I doubt it. I'm one of those half corpses you mentioned. Carrion? And if you try to kiss me, I'll clobber you, faerie or not."

Breena laughed. "Okay. So whatcha need, brother dear? If it's spying on Mom again, I'm going to hurl, though. Like I want to watch her getting it on with her little boy toys. Blech."

Janelle, eyes wide, regarded brother and sister. "Interesting family you have here, Kane." When he shrugged and opened his mouth to respond, she cut him off. "I get it. Different culture, different mores. It's just a faerie kingdom of orgies. Do me a favor, huh? Attempt *not* to enlighten me more than necessary. For completely understandable reasons, I'm suddenly feeling sheltered and impressionable."

Still grinning, Breena glanced at her brother. "I like her. Maybe we should keep her."

"Titania would eat her alive."

Breena pouted a moment. "Not if we all protected her, she couldn't. I have tons of ammo on Mom. Why, just the other day—"

"No, Bree."

"Hello?" Janelle finally worked her mouth around some coherent words. "You know, the half-dead corpse can still speak for herself. I don't want anyone 'keeping' me. I admit I don't know what it means for a faerie to keep a human, but I think I'm smart enough to expect the worst by now. So let's just skip it, shall we?" She glanced from sister to brother and back again. They wore identical, benignly amused expressions.

To think, most of the world was unaware of their existence.

"Most of the world doesn't *want* to believe in our existence, at least not the way we really are." Breena sounded cynical now. "We don't go and exchange baby teeth for quarters, for example. Humans have watered down our reputation to an embarrassing degree, especially over the last century."

Century. That word again. Why did they have to keep bringing that word up?

"So now they have this distorted vision of angelic creatures." Breena snorted and glanced at her brother. "Silly humans."

"Yeah." Janelle laughed weakly. "Silly humans. So, did we have a point to this little chat?" Faeries were scary.

Big green eyes twinkled with amusement.

"She's reading my thoughts," Janelle complained.

"Yes, but you're the one projecting them." Kane fought a smile. "We discussed this, remember?"

Breena stepped closer to Janelle and spoke in a wide-eyed stage whisper. "I think the 'point' you're looking for is this: Kane wants me to intercede for him with Titania so you won't feel compelled to confront her. He's protecting you from her wrath."

"He'd send you instead of me?" Janelle raised her eyebrows. "So you're saying Titania wouldn't eat her own young? You surprise me."

Eyes sparkling with laughter, Breena turned a cheerful pout on her brother. "Please let me keep her. I'll be so good."

"That's highly unlikely." Kane spared his sister a wry look, then turned back to Janelle. "She's right about Titania, though. Let's let Bree see what she can find out."

"What am I looking for?" Breena fairly sparkled with curiosity.

"What, you didn't find that in my puny little brain when you went poking around?"

Kane grinned. "I think she's attempting—belatedly—to be polite. She likes you. Bree, I want to know if Riordan and I were the only two pucas conceived. I need to know if there is even the possibility of the existence of another puca in this world."

"Hmmm." Breena narrowed her eyes thoughtfully. "Wouldn't that be fun. Okay. I'll snoop. It'll cost you, though." She pivoted lightly, her twinkling image gone before she completed the circle.

Janelle swore she could hear a faded peal of laughter. Faerie types apparently loved their own melodrama.

"Scamp." Kane was shaking his head.

"So I gather. But not malicious, right?" Janelle asked carefully. Hopefully.

"No malice, but mischief in spades. She's young still."

"And I think she likes you"—Janelle raised her eyebrows—"in spite of the act."

"She does, but don't kid yourself." Kane's lips twisted in a wry, yet somehow admiring smile. "She pretends hostility to protect me and to protect her position in the family. If any of the others were around, she would have verbally gone for the jugular."

"Others?"

"My half sisters. Breena's the most normal of the six. And the most likely to sneer at the crown and anyone who wears it."

"So you trust Breena?"

"Sure. She knows I'm good for it."

"Because of that price she mentioned."

He smiled.

"Do I want to know—"

"Probably not."

"Yeah." Different cultures, different values . . . So what *would* constitute payment from a puca to his faerie half sister? The possibilities just boggled the very readable mind of a near corpse like her.

Clouds of gray swirled close and suffocating, then gradually dissipated to reveal familiar features. So pale, and laboring for breath. There was pain—unspeakable pain. God, how much could she take? And he could feel it with her, wracking her body with a fiery agony she couldn't tolerate for long. This was his fault. He'd done this. Somehow. Why did this happen? He screamed for her to stop—

And she did. She stopped. Eyes wide and flat and . . . dead.

Kane bolted upright in the darkness, his breathing nearly violent as he shoved the blanket off his perspiring body. Helpless to stop himself, he stumbled to his feet and staggered down the hallway. Trembling, he quietly opened the bedroom door and peered inside.

Janelle. Her breathing soft and even in sleep. She yet breathed. He closed his eyes. But time was running out.

CHAPTER ELEVEN ❧

Janelle was at work when the next call came, just a few days later.

"He did it again. And this time he's gone too far," the muffled voice on the line said. "You're not doing your job."

"Who is this?" Still reeling from a dizzying schedule of morning appointments, Janelle had just taken a break to scarf down a sandwich. She had a staff meeting in ten—no, make that nine—minutes.

"I'm not your concern. The puca, however, is."

Janelle dropped the sandwich. "What happened?"

"I suggest you go visit a friend's house. You remember your friend Riordan? Used to be Teague? He has a bit of a situation on his hands and might be in need of a good doctor right now. Just in case. Even better would have been a decent guardian watching over his brother, but apparently he didn't rate that kind of—"

She dropped the desk phone in its cradle, grabbed her purse and cell phone, and raced out of the office. As she passed the reception desk, she raised her voice over the dull murmur in the waiting room. "Kane. Is he back yet?"

Startled to attention, the receptionist glanced at her

watch. "No. He's been gone well over an hour, but he did have quite a list."

Crap. "I'm leaving. Family emergency. Could you inform the others for me?" Close friends like Riordan and Mina qualified as family, Janelle rationalized to her guilty inner voice. "I'll try to be back for my two o'clock."

Looking concerned, the receptionist nodded.

Janelle pushed the door open with one hand, while she dialed her cell phone with the other.

"Riordan? What's going on?"

"Funny you should call right now." He didn't sound amused.

"Somebody called me. Anonymously. He said there had been trouble and implied you might be hurt."

"Well, the call wasn't from me. I'd have called you five minutes from now, though, and I'd have given you my name and a strong invitation to come see me. Now."

"Okay, I'm on my way. So why don't you just tell me. What happened? Where are you? Is anyone hurt?" She grabbed her doctor's bag, climbed into her car, slammed the door and rammed the key in the ignition.

"I'm at Mina's house." His words were clipped. "My company of contractors is here, working on the roof, finishing up renovations and repairing a new leak we found."

Janelle mentally mapped her route to Mina's house. "And something happened?"

"Sometime in the last hour—lunch break for my men—somebody kicked ladders down, tromped all over fresh lumber, kicked in windows, tore the hell out of some shingles. Even compromised some of the support beams. Hell, some of my tools are missing or busted up, too."

"Was anyone hurt?" Fingers clumsy with strain, Janelle signaled and merged into traffic.

"No." Riordan sighed. "Like I said, the house was empty. Mina was at work, I was on another site, and my guys had gone out for fast food."

"Thank God for that."

"Or cowardice. You'll notice I said all this stuff was *kicked*, right?"

Janelle groaned inwardly. "Yes. I noticed."

"Hoofprints, Janelle. Hoofprints from a horse."

"That's not good."

"No kidding. Where the hell is Kane?"

Janelle gritted her teeth. "He's running errands."

She could almost hear Riordan grinding his own teeth as he bit back whatever he wanted to say. "Look. I never agreed with the Druids forcing guardian duty on you. Nobody should be handed that kind of burden without their permission. Not Mina and not you. If I could, I would have taken the responsibility from you when the decision on Kane was handed down. For better or worse, he's my brother."

"I know you tried." And that solid base of decency in Riordan was why she felt blessed to call him friend. He was a good man and he'd meant it when he offered to take Kane on. "And I know it's because of you that I was given the healing gift."

"Yeah. Well. If anyone could put that to good use, it would be you. But that's beside the point. I'm not holding you responsible for Kane's actions. I'm not. But if you see or hear anything against him, please don't protect him out of some misguided loyalty. The guy has issues, okay? Two thousand years' worth of vengeance is bound to take a permanent toll on a guy's moral fiber."

She couldn't argue with that. "Don't worry about my loyalty. I consider you and Mina at the top of that short list and I won't tolerate Kane hurting anyone. If it turns out that he's still on some bender of a vengeance trip, then he needs to be stopped. I'm supposed to be some kind of puca magic detector, so I should have answers for us once I get there."

"Okay. See you soon then."

As soon as Riordan clicked off the phone, Janelle called the clinic. "Is Kane back yet?"

"He just walked in. Here."

A shuffling noise, and then Kane's voice came on the line. "Janelle? What's wrong? Where are you?"

"Where have you been for the past hour?" She kept her voice level, her hand steady on the steering wheel.

Silence. "So it's like that, is it?"

"Just answer the question."

"I've been running errands. On foot, since they were all in the immediate area. If you want to check on that, I can give you a list, along with people I spoke to. I can't glamour anymore, so inventing alibis would be beyond me. That doesn't mean, however, that everyone will remember me, or that they'll know what time I was there." He paused. "You'd have to take some of it on faith."

How much could she take on faith? Where should she draw the line? How many more coincidences would have to stack up before she'd have to wake up and smell the puca?

And why the hell was she so unreasonably sure right now that Kane was telling the truth? Damn it.

"Janelle, just tell me what's going on. There's been trouble, hasn't there. Who and what?"

Janelle sighed. Then, in a split-second decision she hoped she wouldn't regret, she swung the car into a left-turn lane. When traffic cleared, she executed a quick U-turn. "I'm coming back for you. Five minutes."

"I'll be here."

Ten minutes later, Kane was sitting in the passenger seat. "So what'd I do this time?"

"That's not funny."

"You're telling me."

She shot him a look, saw the frown knitting his brow as he stared straight ahead, and let her temper ease back. "Somebody vandalized the construction work at Mina's house."

Kane glanced over in alarm. "Is she okay? What about Riordan?"

"They're fine. The place was vacant at the time."

"Thank God. How much damage is there?"

"Enough." Janelle grimaced. "The problem is . . . there are hoof marks everywhere. Horse's hooves, according to Riordan."

"Of course. Why wouldn't there be?" Kane scowled out the window. "And you naturally assume I did it."

"Well, given the evidence, it was either you or a wild stallion running free in Richmond. You tell me."

He shrugged. "Wouldn't be the first report of a wild horse around town."

"Yeah. And we both know how that's turning out for you."

"For the record? I didn't do it. Any of it. Also for the record, I think you know I didn't do it. The evidence is getting to you, though. Just stacking up against me. And it all very clearly points to me as the culprit. Maybe even too clearly? Almost like I'm trying to convict myself?"

Janelle frowned. "Well, there is that. A guy would have to want to get caught to be that obvious about it. So maybe you're on some whacked-out mission of self-sabotage. Which is really sick, by the way, so cut it out if that's what you're doing."

"Now you're the comedian."

"Yeah, and see how we're both laughing hysterically? This is bad, Kane. Really bad. And the fact that the victims are Riordan and Mina this time, after everything they've gone through already . . ."

He sighed. "Yeah, that really sucks. They deserve a break from this and here I am bringing more to their door. That's the last thing I want."

And poof went the self-destruction theory. He might be willing to self-destruct if he considered himself past saving, but he wouldn't take Riordan and Mina down with him. That was just making matters worse, both for them and for the guilty conscience that would motivate self-sabotage. Illogical. Again.

"Okay." She sighed. "We'll see what we see."

Twenty minutes later, she pulled into a driveway, slowing to a halt right behind Mina's ancient sedan. Riordan's pickup was parked in the street. Turning off the ignition, Janelle looked around. The mess was already evident. Even the roof looked like it had been damaged beyond prerepair condition. Shingle work was scuffed and dented as though something had tromped all over—but a horse on the roof? Well, *of course* on the roof. Where else would a puca gallop, after all? The whole scenario looked worse and worse for Kane.

As Kane and Janelle approached, they heard yelling and a crash, and a general shifting of debris at the side of the house. More yelling. She took off at a run, Kane right on her heels. "Riordan! Mina! Are you guys in there? Everybody okay?"

"Janelle!" Riordan's furious voice rang past the already-open front door. "Inside! Some of the supports fell. Mina's been hurt. She's bleeding!"

"Oh, God." Janelle put on speed, leaping up the stairs and charging through the front door. There she found Riordan carefully settling Mina on a rug in the center of the living room. He held a towel to the leg he was elevating.

Hearing footsteps, Riordan looked over his shoulder and froze. He saw Kane. "You. Get the hell out of here. Now."

"Fine. I'll go." Kane raised both hands in a universal palms-out, mean-no-harm pose. "I didn't do this, but I know it's not the time—Look, I'll be sitting in Janelle's car. If you need me, call." Turning with obvious reluctance, Kane took a few steps.

"Freeze!" This from Mina, who sounded strained. "Kane. Get your ass over here and plant it."

Riordan looked ready to protest again.

"If he did this to our house, damn it, I don't want him disappearing on me." Mina sounded ready to rip heads off and feed them to their owners. "I love this house. Somebody's done their damnedest to try and wreck it. I'm putting a stop to it."

Riordan looked torn. Kane decided the matter for him, discreetly seating himself in a chair a few feet away.

"Riordan, if it makes you feel any better, I think there's more to what happened here than just an extension of an old grudge." Janelle spoke quietly, seeking temporary peace. "Don't jump to conclusions. Or at least, wait until I help Mina before you start doing it. She needs you and Kane's not going to do anything right in front of his guardian. Agreed?"

Riordan nodded, but his attention was on his brother. "I'm watching you."

Kane nodded.

Janelle glanced at the damage just beyond the room, where it appeared the house was falling in on itself. "You're sure the roof over us will hold?"

"Yeah. It was the overhang off the side of the house that came down. That's the part we were working on and it's where most of the damage is. The main roof's stable."

Hearing the certainty in his voice, Janelle dismissed the worry and moved closer to Mina. "So. Once again you tricked me into a house call," Janelle murmured lightly. "What happened this time?"

"You mean, besides an idiot puca scampering across the roof and playing hopscotch all over Riordan's equipment? And then the damn overhang collapsing when I wasn't expecting it, busting out a window and sending a fun shard of glass into my leg . . ." Mina scowled and raised her head to see the damage to her limb. Her face drained of color and she dropped her head back on the floor with a painful-sounding thump.

"Mina!" Riordan sounded panicked.

"God. Don't be such a mommy." Mina choked the words out. "I'm okay. Just . . . woozy." She kept her eyes closed.

"Love the sight of blood, do you?" Janelle teased her gently.

"Yep, you found me out, Doc," Mina replied. "So, is the leg a goner?"

"Yep. I'm cutting it off at the armpit. We're gonna need a length of leather for you to chew. How's the dental insurance?"

Mina chuckled a little shakily, bracing herself as Janelle lifted the blood-soaked towel from Mina's injured leg. Janelle's heart pounded as she saw the depth of the gash. Felt nausea actually well up.

"Janelle?" This from a surprised-sounding Riordan. "Are you okay? You went all white." His voice sharpened. "Is it that bad?"

"No. It's . . . it's textbook. A simple wound with clean edges. The glass didn't nick anything too crucial or there would be a lot more blood than we're seeing now. I just, um, skipped lunch today. Dumb move." *Good Lord, Janelle. What's your problem? A doctor getting nauseous over a leg wound? Get control of yourself. Use your training.*

She cleared her throat and glanced at her patient. "Nice one, Mina. Unlike the head wound you showed me not too long ago, this one looks deep enough for stitches."

"Aw, crap." Mina sounded miserable.

"But as it happens"—Janelle swallowed past a tightness in her throat—"we have a special going." She looked around. All the men but Riordan and Kane were well out of sight and earshot.

"A special, huh? How does that work? Two stitches for the price of one?"

"Even better." Janelle glanced at Riordan. "With your permission, I'd like to do something a little unorthodox."

Mina opened the eyes she'd squeezed shut. "You mean the freaky Druid thing? You know how to do it now?"

Janelle nodded. "Yep. No drugs, no needles, and even better, it doesn't leave a scar."

"Well, you know my vanity and all." Mina attempted verbal flightiness.

Janelle smiled. "You mean needles freak you out as much as the sight of blood does?"

"Oh God, you have no idea."

Janelle glanced at Riordan, and he nodded silently.

"Then let's skip those." Gently, she settled her hands against the bare skin on either side of the wound and let the sudden disorientation absorb her completely. Waves of pain, curiosity, anger and fear battered her consciousness. Carefully, Janelle sought the pain, submerged herself in it and rode it to the source. There she examined the damage. No infection that she could detect. A little muscle damage, but nothing critical.

Cautiously, she let the magic take over, surrendered totally to its overwhelming power. The waves crashed against her with increasing strength before reaching a crescendo and, finally, diminishing. When even the remnants of a dull throbbing eased to a neutral state, she opened her eyes. She was relieved and even surprised to find herself in her own body. Her own very shaky body.

There was still blood on Mina's skin, she saw, and a faint line where the gash used to be, but the wound looked a month old now, rather than fresh. It looked as good as, if not better than, a plastic surgeon's work, she decided with detachment. She wouldn't take credit for the skill, would just be grateful for it. Especially given the fact that she'd nearly lost her composure earlier. All over a simple cut. It wasn't often that she treated someone she knew. It was so different when it was a friend.

Mina, meanwhile, eyed her with leery wonder. "So it's done, huh? It doesn't even hurt. I mean, I could feel something, something besides the pain when you touched my leg, but . . ." Mina stared. "This is amazing. Think of what you could do with that kind of gift."

Janelle smiled a little. "Yeah, that's what I thought at first. And it is amazing. But . . . well, it's complicated." Janelle paused to glance at a still-concerned Riordan, who'd moved nearer. "As for the leg, I realize it looks a little gory still, but I really think she'll be good as new in a couple days."

"Thanks to Janelle," Mina said.

"No, actually, it's thanks to the Druids who gave me this gift, and thanks to Loverboy here who gave them the idea in the first place."

"It was a moment of true genius." Mina smiled at him.

"I don't care what it was," Riordan murmured. "I'm just grateful."

"No argument there." Mina spared a glance down at her blood-smeared but miraculously healthy limb. "I can't believe you did this. It looks almost as good as new, if a little disgusting with the blood and all. But the gash before. It was so . . ." She swallowed convulsively. "Yech."

"As your doctor, I recommend no more stress for you today. I'd really love to check you out at my office after you've rested. Give you a tetanus shot if you're not up-to-date."

Mina rolled her eyes. "No need for any shots. I had to have a physical recently to qualify for readmission to the school's insurance plan. They were so thorough I felt violated."

"It seems to have worked out in your favor now, though. And I didn't detect any infection, but we can keep an eye on it. As for the blood loss and the woozy feeling, I'm not too worried. It doesn't look like you lost all that much blood, but I hate to take any risks since I'm not admitting you or anything." She frowned. "Let me just get the afternoon off and I'll keep an eye on it."

Mina shook her head. "That's not necessary."

"Yes, it is."

"No. It's not." Mina frowned. "You don't even keep a twenty-four-hour watch on your real patients. Riordan will watch me and if he thinks it's necessary, he can always call you. Right?"

"But . . ." Janelle was being irrational. Even she knew that.

"You *are* being irrational." This from Kane, who had remained silent for the entire procedure.

"Get out of my head, faerie boy."

Kane turned to Riordan. "Has she always been this prickly?"

For a moment, the brothers seemed in complete accord in their affection for Janelle. "No, actually, she's the only woman I know who could take a blood geyser in stride. I've seen it happen. She was cool as a cucumber. Totally rational."

Janelle chose to keep her gaze on Mina's leg in order to avoid curious eyes. "It's just that I'm not used to handling medical emergencies that involve my friends." She gave them a warning look. "Now don't go all mushy on me. It's just a different situation, okay? Dealing with strangers, it's textbook. The head knows that it's best to back off, that skill can accomplish a lot more under pressure than sympathy can. Dealing with a friend . . . it's just different."

"The heart won't back off," Kane murmured. "And other, deeper instincts kick in, too."

Janelle nodded, still a little shaky. "I've never done it . . . the healing thing . . . quite like this. It was weird." The rush had been so complete. The rush of pain, the rush to counter and correct. She hadn't expected that. To cure her own headache and the Druid's mental distress, she'd had to concentrate to employ her gift. With Mina, she'd felt almost possessed by the magic.

"Magic is often fed by emotion. The more you believe,

the more you feel, the more momentum behind the magic."

Riordan eyed Kane with challenge. "Hence the power of a two-thousand-year-old grudge."

Janelle groaned. "Let's not start pounding our chests now, okay, guys? I want Riordan to move Mina into her bedroom—assuming the roof there is stable. Kane, I'm going to need antiseptic, some gauze . . ." She reeled off a list of items, most of which she didn't really need if this healing was as complete as it seemed now. But she was learning as she went along. Until she knew more about this gift, she would be backing up the magic with whatever traditional medicine seemed appropriate. Cleaning the site, supervising the patient—these seemed appropriate precautions. And, sure, they gave Janelle a little peace of mind as well.

While Riordan lifted Mina, Kane headed off to the bathroom to collect the supplies Janelle requested. Five minutes later, he delivered the bundle to Mina's bedroom. Janelle immediately bent to her task, quickly becoming absorbed in it.

As Kane backed out of the room, he felt a familiar and discreet grip on his forearm. Bowing to the inevitable, Kane quietly followed his brother through the living room and out of the house, closing the door behind him. He turned to hear Riordan out.

But Riordan led with his fists. "You son of a bitch."

Kane didn't dodge the blow, and it caught him in the stomach. So did the one that followed. He was just glad Janelle wasn't there to get involved.

"Come on, you coward. Fight back at least. Or are you going to hide behind this probation you're on?" Riordan landed another blow.

Kane grunted, his temper flaring. "I didn't do this." But he kept his fists down.

"Oh, no? What, some other puca's running around

screwing with my livelihood and putting Mina in danger?" Riordan shoved him, clearly trying to get him to fight back.

"I wouldn't do that."

"Sure you wouldn't. Just like you didn't blame me for something I didn't do and just like you didn't go back and try to kill me later." Riordan circled him.

"I didn't try to kill you."

"Bullshit." Riordan landed another punch to Kane's gut. "I was there when you went on that little rampage in Avebury. I didn't really get it at the time—why you were so angry—but you busted the hell out of some of the stones. You were trying to get at me in the stone where I was imprisoned, weren't you?"

His breathing harsh as he avoided his brother's continued assault, Kane still didn't raise his fists. He would not. "Not to kill you, Riordan. I'm not a killer. But I was angry. I'd just found out that Maegth had died in childbirth. And the babe she carried . . . it could have been mine. Or yours."

Riordan stumbled. "A child?"

"The babe was stillborn," Kane explained. "A boy."

"A boy. So that's what . . ." Riordan's voice was hoarse, his eyes distant and glazed. "That explains some of what I overheard. It was all fragmented, the conversations so confusing, but I wondered . . . So, it was true. And maybe the child was mine. And they were both dead. The mother and the babe."

"Yes."

Riordan's eyes took on a nasty glint. "A child that could have been mine. I might have guessed some of that. I didn't know it was Maegth. Didn't know it was your fiancée. But I did know there was a woman, and I might have suspected some of the rest . . . Nobody, not even my own brother, had the decency to come right out and tell me. I had to guess and wonder without ever knowing for sure. And with no way of escaping that stone and finding out for myself, while you pounded and busted away at it. Once again, you saw *yourself* as the injured party. And once again, you took it out on me." His fury palpable, Riordan stalked Kane in earnest.

"Maegth was dead," Kane said. "The babe never even breathed. Once I got over my anger . . . it seemed futile to wonder about paternity." He gestured pointlessly. "But I'm sorry. I should have told you. If not before, then certainly now."

"Yeah, you damn well should have told me." Riordan launched a wild roundhouse, which Kane ducked and sidestepped. "A child that could have been mine. And my own brother kept the truth from me. Damn you for that." His breath coming in gasps, Riordan circled. "So that's when you destroyed that old cabin, too. I heard about that. Just part of the same tantrum, wasn't it? You put on your little horse and ape show and terrified all the villagers, going ape-shit over those stones and then trotting all over the cabin roof. Then you set the damn thing on fire. Managed to burn up half the grove."

"It was the cabin where I found you two together. You might forgive me for wanting it gone. Besides, I owned it and it was empty. It was mine to burn." Kane paused, feeling a moment of remorse. "Destroying part of the grove was a mistake. I compensated the Druids."

"So, is that what you were trying to do here, too? Destroy the home I share with Mina? I saw the hoofprints on the roof. Were you going to burn it down, too? If we hadn't come home . . ." Riordan rammed his fist into Kane's stomach.

Kane reeled away and dodged the next lunge. "No!"

"I don't believe you." Riordan attacked again, knocked Kane's feet out from under him with the swipe of a foot. Kane dropped and rolled but didn't engage.

"What the fuck? Fight back, you idiot, so I can beat the shit out of you."

"No."

"Why not?" Riordan shoved at him again. "Waiting for your guardian to save your ass? Coward. Sneaking around, still making me pay for the past. Why'd you even bother confessing if you weren't through punishing me?"

Kane ground his teeth. This wouldn't be a fair fight. They'd fought plenty when they were younger and more evenly matched, but now his brother was human. Kane had to pull back, even if it killed him. Even if he was being unfairly accused now, and even if his brother had a future, freedom, Mina, a friendship with Janelle . . .

Base instinct demanded Kane fight back, but he mastered it. At the same time, he didn't have to take a complete beating.

"Is it Mina? Is it that you want her now, too? Do you have some clever scheme cooked up to discredit me and steal her?" And Riordan landed another punch, mostly because his question floored Kane.

"No, damn it!" And finally, Kane shoved Riordan away from him.

"Then what? Why are you doing this? Why would you act unselfishly for once and then cut back and destroy it all? You can't stand it that I'm free and you're not? It was *your choice*, you idiot."

"I know. And I deserve my punishment and more."

Riordan didn't seem to hear. "Whatever you do, Mina's mine. You can't have her. We love each other. You won't—"

"No, damn it! I don't want Mina. I don't give a shit about anyone except—"

Riordan hesitated in mid-punch. "Except? Don't stop there."

Kane stared at his brother, and he was amazed at how similar Riordan looked to himself while angry. The similarities were always striking, but when angry . . . And Kane had always been angry.

Of course, now Kane wasn't angry, he was just desperate. Desperate to keep that years-old image from replaying in his head over and over again. With more detail each time. He could feel the clock ticking, the days marking themselves off. God. To keep that from ever becoming a reality . . . How? At this rate, he'd never get the hell out of her life in time to stop it.

Frowning, obviously bemused, Riordan lowered his fist. "What? *What*?"

"It's Janelle."

"You have a thing for Janelle?"

"Yes. No. That's not it. That's not the problem."

"It sure as hell is. You stay away from her, too, you jackass. Like you didn't hurt her enough before?" Riordan raised his fist again.

Growling, Kane grabbed it. "Just stop, damn it. I'm trying to tell you. What happened to your house and to Mina . . . I didn't do it. It doesn't make sense for me to do it. Screwing with my karma would be the last thing I need right now. Think about it. And I need to get this amends business done so I can get the hell away from Janelle before I hurt her."

"Hurt her and you'll deal with me."

"Did you not hear me? I'm trying my best *not* to hurt her. That's the whole point, damn it. I *saw* something."

Riordan froze. "What do you mean, 'saw'?"

"*Fore*saw. Eight years ago. November first. And several times since then."

Riordan swallowed, all the wind taken out of his sails. "Oh, shit. What did you see?"

"Janelle's death. At my hands."

The color drained from Riordan's face.

"Yeah. That's why I have to get this done. So I can get out of her life before the damn thing comes true. I can't . . . I couldn't live with . . ." He lowered his voice. "If it makes you feel any better, especially since you seem to think I'm after Mina . . . well, I'm in love with Janelle."

And that was a surrender in itself. He'd acknowledged his own doom: to love one woman always but never have her. So much promise dangled just out of reach. Tantalizing him, and always, always out of reach. He wished he'd never seen anything dangling there. So much easier if he'd never seen. It could dangle into eternity without touching him. But it was clear as day to him now: Here was a woman who was beautiful, perfect—everything he wanted. And everything he could never have.

He lowered his voice. "I loved Janelle on sight. I didn't want to. I told myself . . ." He shook his head. "It just happened. In spite of everything. Now, eight years later . . . if anything, I love her more. She's stubborn, brilliant, self-sacrificing and noble to a fault, heartbreakingly generous even if she covers it up with sarcasm and calm practicality. It's humbling. Hell, she inspires me. She makes me want to be a better man. And I'm trying to be that man, even though I know I can never have her. So, yes, I love her. I always will."

Obviously stunned, Riordan sat back on his heels. "And you're destined to kill her?"

"Yeah. Nothing like a traditional happily-ever-after, huh?" The reality was torture. He had two choices: Janelle's death at his hands or perpetual banishment from her. He was utterly screwed. Either way, he lost Janelle. Maegth had completely outdone herself with her curse.

His brother studied him for a moment. Then, sighing, Riordan shrugged. "That's too completely fucked up to be anything but the truth." Shaking his head, he ran a hand through his hair. "I believe you."

"Well, there's a switch." Kane sighed.

"What, you don't like it when everyone believes you guilty of something you didn't do?"

Kane twisted his lips at the irony. "It kind of sucks, actually."

"No kidding."

"Riordan . . ." Kane hesitated, then gripped his brother's shoulder and met his eyes soberly. "I'm damn sorry about the child. I am. I'd like to think that . . . if the babe had lived . . . I would have told you. We could have worked it out. For the child's sake." Kane eyed his brother, remembering how, at one time, it was the two of them sticking together, with their mothers dead and their father constantly locked in combat with his angry second wife. They both knew how *not* to raise a child. He hoped that lesson would have overcome the anger.

"Yeah." Riordan frowned, the childhood memories clear in his own eyes. "Me, too." Then his lips twisted. "Maybe we could have asked Titania for parenting suggestions."

Dropping his arm, Kane groaned good-naturedly, as his brother had obviously intended. "So is this . . . Are we good now?"

"Yeah."

And Riordan slugged him one last time in the side, though not too hard.

Kane scowled at his brother. "Enough. I had a lot of that coming, but I have my limits."

"Yeah, but it feels so *good*." Riordan rubbed his swelling knuckles.

Kane shoved him. "I'll bet."

Riordan laughed as he stumbled backward, but then his amusement faded. "So . . . what did Janelle say when you told her? About the prophecy, I mean."

"I haven't told her. And I won't."

Riordan studied him. "Do you think that's wise?"

Kane stared hard at the house in an effort to stave off other visions that still taunted his mind's eye. "I don't know about wise. I hope it's kind. With any luck, she'll never need to know. I'll be gone before it has a chance to be fulfilled."

"That's the plan? That's it?"

"It's all I have. Unless you can think of an alternative." Kane raised an eyebrow.

Riordan just shook his head slowly. "I know a curse can be broken. Can a prophecy be avoided?"

"You sure spent a long time inside that rock, didn't you? How much have you forgotten? A prophecy only reveals a likelihood, not an inevitability. It's hard to avoid, but it can be done."

"So why don't you warn her? Tell her what you've seen. She's smart. She'll be able to take precautions that way, right?"

Kane was already shaking his head. "Telling her could lend strength to the prophecy. The humans have a good term for this, although they don't comprehend the full nature of it. If I told Janelle about the prophecy, I'd be setting up a *self-fulfilling* prophecy, which would *not* be all in her head. Basically, she'd be racing toward that oncoming train instead of standing in place and waiting for the collision to come to her. So this way, by not telling her, I'm buying some time. But the longer I spend around Janelle, the more likely . . ."

Riordan nodded. "In that case, it does sound like finishing your business and getting out of town is your best option. Crazy, that you ended up with her as your guardian. What are the odds? If you need any help, call me. And I mean that. Janelle means a lot to me. I don't want to see anything happen to her."

"So I gathered." There was an edge to his voice that even Kane himself could hear.

Riordan grinned evilly. "You know, Janelle and I were damn close before I met Mina."

Kane ground his teeth. He'd known that. He knew Janelle and Riordan were friends before, when Riordan was Teague, and he couldn't blame Riordan if they'd—But he damn well wanted to blame him!

"Oh, just chill. We were friends, nothing more. In

fact . . ." Riordan laughed at a sudden thought. "In fact, when we first met and I made the mistake of asking her out, she refused to even consider anything beyond friendship. You wanna know why?"

"Because you felt like a brother to her?"

"Nope. It's because I resembled a certain ex-boyfriend of hers. *You.* According to Janelle, looking like Kane Oberon was the biggest turnoff there was."

The sun was setting when Riordan walked Janelle and Kane out to the car. Janelle had called her office several hours before to say she would be gone for the rest of the afternoon. She'd explained that the "emergency"—well, damn it, it was an emergency, and family at that, even if no common blood bonded them—had taken longer to resolve than she'd planned. After she'd finished with Mina, she'd wandered around, surreptitiously examining the damage to the house.

Honestly, Janelle knew she was being overly cautious, that Mina was probably okay. But the doctor in Janelle couldn't help wondering if she'd overlooked something, wondering if the magic would be enough. And the friend in Janelle . . . well, the friend just couldn't turn off her worry that fast. So Janelle had stayed mostly to reassure herself, until an exasperated Mina had told her to go home and go to bed.

Which, frankly, sounded like a darn good idea.

As Kane rounded the car and climbed into the passenger's side, Janelle turned to say good-bye to Riordan.

He returned her gaze. "So, what's the verdict, Doc?"

"Your Mina will be fine." Janelle smiled wearily. "I'm almost positive of it."

Riordan nodded. "I know. And I'm glad. But I was talking about all of this. The vandalism. Was it puca magic? Was it Kane?"

Janelle studied him. "I . . ." She frowned.

"What?"

"Damn it, it's just odd. No, *off*." It had been bothering her all afternoon, too. She rubbed aching temples.

"What's off?"

Janelle gestured vaguely. "The magic. I'd swear it's the same as before, but now it feels like I can see it—no, not see it, but sense it—more clearly." She frowned and shook her head. "And now that I have a clearer impression, it feels wrong. Off. Just . . . off. On the surface I'd say it's puca. Pure puca. But it's so . . . shallow. I don't know. There's something wrong there." After a moment she added, "Not that I know what I'm talking about."

Riordan regarded her thoughtfully. "No. That's damn interesting."

"So is your response." She eyed him with suspicions she hadn't yet voiced. "So, why aren't you condemning Kane anymore? You were ready to kill him earlier. I noticed a few marks on his face, too. Although, given what I've learned of puca metabolism, I'm sure any bruises he has will be gone before morning. I'm assuming that while I was cleaning Mina up, you two had a lively conversation? You know, for lack of a better term to describe a juvenile fistfight." She knew the two were hotheads.

"That's about what happened. As for being less condemning . . ." Riordan shrugged. "Well, we eventually talked. And I believe him. I'm inclined to think he didn't do this."

"Really?" Janelle suddenly felt hopeful.

"Yeah. But that means something else is going on. *Someone* did this. Who? And why?"

Janelle nodded. "That's about as far as we've gotten with our theories, too. Still, it's reassuring to hear you say this. I thought maybe I was just being a blind optimist."

"Or a woman still in love?"

Janelle blanched. "No! God, no. Do I look stupid?" She shook her head, completely rejecting any and all possibility. "History aside, we're not even the same species. As a physician, I'm well aware of my gene pool, and we're swimming in totally different oceans. I don't want to mix the brews."

Riordan grinned. "Everything worked out for me."

"No, you abandoned your ocean in favor of Mina's."

"Whatever it takes." He considered her. "Although I'll admit ours were different circumstances."

"Very different." Riordan was innocent, while Kane had admitted his guilt. He might even be guilty now, in spite of Janelle's own hopes and beliefs, even if Riordan had just reinforced her optimism. And she was too damn tired to consider the situation in any positive light. Optimism was for energetic types, and she just wasn't one of those right now.

Waving in farewell to Riordan, she climbed into her car and started it up. With the care more likely to be found in a very frail, very old woman, she backed out of the driveway and directed the vehicle toward home.

After a few moments of odd silence, Kane spoke. "So, you refused to go out with my brother?"

"Hmm?" Janelle glanced at him curiously. A powerful attraction washed over her. She was exhausted, and every nerve ending in her body jangled with the aftershocks of healing Mina. If she so much as touched Kane right now . . .

"Riordan said he asked you out a few years ago and you turned him down."

Janelle frowned, trying to recall. "Oh, that. Yeah, but I think asking me out was just a reflex action on your brother's part. You know, single female no uglier than your average dog, conveniently located in the same apartment building." She shrugged. "I seemed eligible, if only marginally. He seemed less than heartbroken when I turned him down."

"Maybe because you told him he reminded you of an ex," Kane remarked.

"So, he told you that, too?" Janelle didn't know whether to be amused, annoyed or embarrassed.

"Riordan thought it was hilarious." Kane's voice had a surprisingly hard edge.

Janelle gave a laugh. "And you didn't like that at all."

Kane didn't respond. He didn't have to; she could sense his dismay.

Not that she cared. Honestly, she was so damn punchy at this point, she didn't care about anything. She pulled into the parking lot of her apartment building. Thank God. She was ready to drop.

She pulled into a parking space—any space, any damn one of them—and turned off the engine. Hell, she could sleep here.

"No, you can't." But Kane's voice was soft. He opened his door and climbed out.

Obviously, he was picking up on her exhaustion. She watched as he walked around the car and opened her door. He bent low and grabbed the keys from the ignition.

"Given that even the air is heavy with it," he said, "how could I help but notice how tired you are?" He slid his hands behind her back and under her knees.

A woman with any self-respect would have objected at this point.

"Just pretend you're asleep." He bumped the door closed with his hip and pressed the remote lock for her car on the keychain she was holding. The headlights blinked. "You could even tell yourself that maybe I glamoured you into obliviousness. I didn't. I can't. But you're too sleepy to know that, so just go with it."

She chuckled in spite of herself, even let her head drop onto his shoulder.

He cradled her close as he headed toward the stairs. As he walked, he murmured, "I'm glad you didn't go out with Riordan. I would have had to kill him, and fratricide's hell on karma."

"I'll bet." She was smiling against his shoulder. "You wouldn't, though. You don't have it in you to kill him."

She spoke low, but with sleepy, matter-of-fact conviction.

Then she shocked him by admitting, "I don't know whether I'm going to pass out now or go into spontaneous orgasm." She met his eyes, her own feeling heavy with fatigue and overstimulation. "You might want to put me down before nature makes the decision for me."

Carefully, he set her on her feet in front of her door and steadied her with a hand on her sleeve-covered elbow. He took the keys from her, inserted one into the lock and opened the door. When she looked up into his eyes, it was to see a full-blown inferno in their golden depths. Even a completely normal human, one with no experience with magic or magical beings, could have felt the waves of power rolling off his big body. Heat. Frustration. Attraction. But would he act on that attraction?

"No. And not just because of the guardianship business. If I'm going to screw up my life in one encounter with you, I'd rather not do it when you're too tired to participate. If I'm going down, I'd like to take one good memory with me."

Janelle licked her lips, unwillingly pondering the creation of such a memory. Would it be worth it for complete damnation? Why did her heart say yes?

"Go to bed, Janelle."

She continued to stare at him, and he groaned and gently took her shoulders and steered her into her bedroom. There they stopped.

Janelle found herself hoping he'd make a move. Now that they were in the bedroom, would he—?

"No. He *won't*."

Janelle just nodded quietly, her eyes devouring him. He was the most beautiful man she'd ever known.

"Will you be okay?" He looked hesitant. All but his eyes. They said he knew what she wanted. What he wanted, too. "I'm not a saint, Janelle."

She nodded. And just stood there.

With a frustrated noise, Kane walked to the dresser, opened one drawer and then another, pulling out clothing. Sweats, she saw. Underwear?

"No, *not* underwear. I couldn't..." He gritted his teeth. "Arms up."

Trembling, her will weaker even than her knees, Janelle just raised her arms and watched him approach. He tugged the hem of her blouse out of her pants. No scrubs today. She'd expected only routine office visits. So a simple blouse.

Which he was now unbuttoning. She caught her breath as cool air met bare flesh, her belly flinching with every brush of material. Awaiting his touch on her skin.

"Which I will do my damnedest to avoid." Kane's teeth were gritted. His eyes looked like melted amber. She could feel the heat of his body so close to hers, the rigidity of every muscle. It was pure fire underneath that T-shirt, those jeans belted with a Celtic knot.

She swallowed at the reminder. There were consequences to every action. Kane's very fate proved that. She remained docile.

He gently tugged her shirt open and lowered her arms.

Why'd he do that anyway? Arms up?

He smiled tightly. "It kept them out of trouble."

Oh.

He tugged the sleeves of her blouse down her arms, let the fabric pool on the floor. Then, carefully avoiding the touch of skin, he unbuttoned her pants. Gripping the zipper tab, he tugged it down, loosening the fabric on her hips. The slacks sagged as the zipper lowered, then finally, they slid down her legs unaided.

Kane took a long step backward. Unnecessarily long. His chest seemed to heave once, and then again. His belly muscles went taut with restraint above a suspicious and impressive fullness in his jeans—his desires and hers—restrained by a heavy Celtic knot.

Dressed only in a bra and panties, Janelle closed her eyes.

After a moment, she felt him step close again, felt soft material slide over her head. Instinctively, she bent her arms and fished for armholes, which he guided toward her hands. Cloth floated down to cover breasts and belly. She stepped into equally soft pants, felt a glancing brush of cotton as he raised them high over thighs and hips. Elastic snapped securely to hug her waist. All this he'd done without touching skin.

Not even once.

God. Not even once. Why not once? Just once. She needed—

A harsh sound from Kane. "Janelle. Please."

She opened her eyes and stared at him. "Just a kiss."

The fire in his eyes seemed to flare higher as he stepped close—an involuntary move on his part, she could tell. His jaw hardened and the muscles of his arms and chest bunched as if to stop himself, but it was a struggle.

"Lie down, Janelle. Here." With jerky movements, he reached toward the bed behind her and tugged the blankets down to reveal the sheets beneath. "Come on." His hands careful, he touched her now-clothed shoulder, and she could feel the warmth of his hand through the thin material. She let him coax her into sitting and then reclining on the bed. Even let him draw the covers over her. She loved the feel of him caring for her. Protected: that's how it felt. She hadn't felt protected . . .

In so long. A long, long time. She shouldn't want it even now. She was an adult. She was independent. Just tired. Needed bed.

"I like protecting you. I will always protect you." His voice was low, gently rough and yet clingy-soft. Like the feel of suede against supersensitized skin.

Or was that his belt? Soft, textured leather was rubbing against the skin of her belly. A harsh groan—his; her sigh. At last. Oh, she'd wanted—

He had, too. He wanted her. So much. Her shirt rode high as his hands slid to touch her stomach. Fingers softly fit between the lines of ribs and glided higher to carefully peel back her bra and cup her breasts.

Janelle lost her breath on a whoosh and arched higher back. A mouth came down softly to take the peak of a bared breast deep into moist warmth, drawing deliciously until she shuddered from it. She tipped to offer him the other, which he accepted as if starved.

She felt abrading cloth, and hands—her pants, now coming off—sliding over her hipbones, which she raised. She wanted. Oh, how she wanted.

Warm suede and cold pewter slid against her hip, her thigh, even as a whiskered cheek brushed at her ribs, her belly. Breath rasped hot against her hip bone. Roughened hands parted her legs, slid high on her thighs. Soon they combed through hot, moistened curls. She could feel, almost hear the rasp of his stubbled cheek against her skin, his hot breath on her hotter, hungrier flesh. . . .

Keening, she lifted her hips high, ready and wanting what he would give her: that hungry mouth, that tongue, those hands. Sensations blended in a fevered rush, and she felt a tightening begin deep in her belly. Soon she screamed—

"Janelle?"

—and sat up in a rush. Darkness. She blinked, her breath coming rough and fast, as she felt tears slicing cold paths down her cheeks. Hot sensitivity tingled on intimate parts of her body.

Which was fully clothed.

It had just been a dream?

"Janelle, are you okay in there?" *Kane.* He was in the living room, not the bedroom?

She licked her lips, then cleared her throat and tested her voice. "I'm fine. Just a . . . a dream. Sorry I disturbed you."

Shaken, she lay back down, hugging blanket and pillows close, wishing they could ease the ache. It was a long time before she fell asleep.

Out in the living room, Kane stared at the ceiling, wondering exactly when his sanity would shatter around him into a million jagged pieces. He'd lived that dream with her! Unwillingly and then willingly. Touching . . . but not really. And wanting to, so badly. He must have a masochistic streak a mile wide. To actually walk through the dreams of the woman he loved—that was both the fondest fantasy and worst torture known to a man condemned never to have her.

And there was nothing to be done about it.

Chapter Twelve ✥

Janelle couldn't live like this. She'd always been a take-charge kind of woman, and that's exactly what she would do now. According to the office manager, Kane would be gone for at least another fifteen minutes, which should give her plenty of time. Plenty of alone time she desperately needed. The first real alone time she'd had for days.

This healing gift was completely overwhelming her. Nobody had told her she'd be climbing the learning curve with the velocity of a space shuttle. Mentally, she just couldn't keep up. Whatever happened to conscious control? Shoot, earlier today she'd cured a baby just on contact. She'd done no more than touch the inconsolably crying—and, as it turned out, unimaginably gassy— baby Lexie, who'd immediately found a rather loud relief. Lucky for Janelle, the baby's expression—poor kid had seemed as shocked as her mom by the sudden and outrageously extended eruption—had caused such amusement as to distract anyone from questioning the incident.

Then there was Janelle's ten o'clock appointment, a woman with a migraine. And, yep, it happened again. One touch to the forehead to check for fever and it was bye-bye, migraine. Sure, it was great that these people were finding relief through her gift. The baby felt better. The migraine patient felt better. But where was the control? Where was the deliberation, the caution? She couldn't know exactly what she was accomplishing if she wasn't consciously aware of the steps taken toward healing. With the magic, she had no clue what steps were taken and not taken. The healing was instantaneous. It felt so reckless. She was too new at this, too ignorant of possible consequences, and could only guess at the degree of thoroughness. Were the patients healed completely? She hoped so . . . but she couldn't know for sure.

And she felt so petty for questioning good fortune. She was healing! With a touch! Remember the Holy Grail of medicine? She'd *wanted* this. And so far, it was working. So why did it feel like the medical equivalent of vigilante justice? Maybe the end was spectacular, but what were the consequences of skipping or mutating the process? Bailing on logic in favor of magic? Even as the woman in her who wanted only to ease suffering reveled—no, rejoiced!—in the gift, the scientist in her was freaked out by the whole idea.

Maybe she should talk it over with Kane. Maybe he could help her make sense of it.

She groaned. Or maybe, once she was face to face with him, she'd lose the ability to think or speak about anything except the other night. Yeah, the other night—the time when she threw herself at him.

Things had been strained the past few days, ever since the accident at Mina's. First had been the worry over Mina's injury and the cause of the vandalism. And then . . . well, Janelle had been shameless that night, which was humiliating to recall. She was no prude, but she'd never been the type to throw herself at a guy, especially when so much was already on the line.

Of course, Kane had fielded her advances with perfect

gallantry. He'd gently cared for her and pushed her away, while at the same time assuring her she was desirable. He wanted her—he'd made no secret of that—yet he hadn't taken her when she was vulnerable. That said something, didn't it? He *cared* for her.

Either that or High Druid Phil was right about Kane's cunning seduction techniques. Coming to her in a dream like that—assuming he could deliberately initiate such a thing, heaven help her—would be the perfect way to thoroughly seduce her without technically breaking any rules. If they never physically touched, she could remain his guardian and yet become utterly biased in his favor. Unless she learned what he was doing.

A perfectly devastating strategy, if that's what it was. It had felt so real. But no, it was just a dream. She knew that. Yet she was also certain that it had been more than just a normal dream. She'd felt him—could *still* feel him—in her memory.

It was just too distracting. She needed to focus. To be rational. *Be on your guard,* the Druid had said. And the best way to be on her guard was to proactively seek the truth. That's how a smart woman would handle this kind of thing, instead of waiting around for the truth to fall on her head. For more people to get hurt. So . . . snooping. It was time to get to it. No more waiting for others to do her investigations.

Inhaling deeply, Janelle exhaled and looked around. *Hello? Any questing minds out there? Sex. I am sooooo horny. I shall get myself off right here and now. Anybody want to watch?*

Having given her best attempt at long-range thought projection, she waited a heart-pounding moment. Nothing happened. No sign of prying minds. So, she was good to go. Or as good as she'd ever be.

Quickly, she pulled her cell phone out of her pocket and hit speed dial. She glanced around nervously until a man answered.

"Riordan? Hey, it's Janelle."

"Mmmph."

"Huh? Are you all right?"

"Just eatin'."

Janelle grinned. Her friend had always had a voracious appetite, and it had doubled since his two halves recombined. "Again? You're going to get fat and Mina will leave you."

"I can't help it. I'm just so damned hungry all the time. Good thing I still have a puca metabolism, huh?"

"Yeah, good thing. I know a few women who'd probably wring your neck out of jealousy. To be able to eat like a pig and gain not a single pound . . ." Not that she could blame the guy. Two thousand years' worth of hunger. If she hadn't eaten in that long, she'd probably gobble up her entire apartment complex, then munch on the landscaping for dessert. "How's Mina?"

"She's great! You can hardly see a mark."

"No discoloration, unexplained fever . . . ?" Janelle's voice rose in question.

"Nope, none of that. You're amazing."

"No, the gift is. I'm glad she's okay. Continue to keep an eye on it, though, okay?"

"Will do." He cleared his throat, obviously focusing on their conversation now. "So, was that the only reason you called—to check up on Mina and catch me pigging out again?"

"I did want to check on Mina, but I'm also in need of information."

"Yeah? What kind?"

"How do I contact Titania?"

Walking swiftly to her car later that day, Janelle glanced carefully around. She'd given Kane the slip again by pleading mysterious feminine requirements that would only embarrass them both if she explained. Interesting, that such things applied so universally. She was also very proud of herself for holding her real reasons just out of his mental grasp. She'd been practicing what he'd taught her, and she thought she was getting pretty damn good at it, too.

"Not all *that* good at it."

Janelle jumped, then pivoted, her gaze darting everywhere for the soft female voice.

A sigh followed. "Up here."

Surprised, Janelle looked up to see Breena, Kane's half sister, sitting on a low tree branch. She gazed at the girl a moment before smirking just a little; she couldn't quite forget Breena's earlier disdain for humans. "I guess you know how stereotypical that is, right—a faerie sitting on a branch of a tree? Although, normally we picture you guys a bit smaller. More like Barbie doll–size."

Breena easily slipped from the branch to land lightly on the ground. "We know. It's entertaining. Know what else is entertaining? The idea of you fooling Titania into anything at all. Sure, you can fool my brother. He actually *wants* to give you privacy, idiot that he is. I don't know when he got all softhearted. It was probably right around the time he let Riordan out of his rock."

Janelle's amusement faded. "You sound so blasé about the feud between your brothers. Isn't a millennia-long fight a big enough deal to be of concern to all you faerie types?"

Breena smiled—amused once again by the near corpse, no doubt. The smile blossomed into laughter. "I swear, I'm going to convince Kane to let me keep you. Unless, of course, he keeps you first."

Janelle started, then mentally shied away from the idea. "Tell me about your mother."

"What? Are my brother's secret yearnings not a big enough deal to be recognized by you *human* types?" the faerie mocked. But after a moment she acquiesced. "All right. We can drop the subject of Kane and discuss my mother. She's . . . not here. Not coming. Once I found out what you were doing, I had her called elsewhere just to be on the safe side. And, no, I won't tell you where. Suffice it to say, she'll be occupied for a while. Long enough for me to help you understand what you're risking here."

"What?" Janelle was shocked. "I went to all that trouble to call her—"

"Yeah, I know. It was brave of you. My assistant thinks you're really cool, by the way. For a human."

"But I talked to Titania. I know I did."

"You *thought* you did." Breena smiled. "It was just my assistant, though. Let it go. My mother's temper is a bigger deal for you at the moment than the details of faerie culture."

Janelle shook her head, bemused. "Probably not as interesting."

"Oh, I wouldn't go that far. Mother's temper is legendary. Just ask Oberon. That sorry SOB will pay for the rest of his life for keeping Mom in the wings. And that's a long time, in case you didn't know."

"So I've heard." Janelle lowered her voice cautiously. "So, what exactly would your mother do to me?"

Breena shrugged, and the gesture seemed oddly prosaic. "First, she'd snag all those little thoughts you have hanging around the edge of your consciousness. Wouldn't even break into a sweat doing it. She'd know what you were doing and she'd use it against both you and Kane. That's why Kane wanted *me* to work on this angle for you. Why can't you let me?"

"Because I need this thing over. *Now*. Kane needs his freedom back, and I need my normal life."

"Ah. Tempted, are you?" Breena actually leered, the little twit. Obviously, she'd gone deep-sea fishing in Janelle's thoughts and memories and landed some doozies. No doubt she'd located fears and trust issues a mile wide, along with several other mixed emotions that should have damn well remained private.

Janelle scowled.

Breena, no doubt witnessing the painful blush on Janelle's cheeks, exhibited rare mercy and let the subject drop. "So, how's the healing thing working out for you? I'll bet you're getting good at it."

Janelle shifted uneasily. "Yes. Very good at it. Almost too good. I don't even have to think about it or try anymore, and poof. All better." She shook her head. It had been amazing, really. Colicky babies were suddenly very happy, ulcers spontaneously healed, migraines eased . . . Hell, she'd even fixed her car that morning. She really hadn't known what was wrong with it, just knew she should touch some weird thingy under the hood, clear some icky junk off with a thought and then reseal it, and *boom*: the car drove like a dream.

"I healed my car this morning. My *car*. How can that be?" she asked Breena.

The faerie grinned. "The Druids' gift is a bigger concept than just knitting skin and bone. It's more . . . realignment. Enhanced realignment and order. It's just that gifts are best applied to your already-existing skills. For you, that would be healing. You apply order to bodily disorder." She gave Janelle a wicked look. "Of course, in your free time you'd now be a damn good mechanic."

Janelle glanced uneasily at her.

"As far as your progression to healing without conscious direction . . . that's a good thing. You just have to be careful about it is all. You have the glamour ability, so that can work for you—if necessary. You'll get the hang of it."

Somehow Janelle didn't think so. The skill seemed to be constantly shifting, always refining itself until it was beyond her control and comprehension. It seemed a difficult thing to master—and to hide from others. And the consequences to her patients . . . She hoped for the best, but she just didn't know. Janelle shook her head. "Tell me about Titania. Have you asked her about the possibility of a third puca?"

Breena puffed out her breath in frustration. "Honestly. I can't just ask her that question. I have to circle it. I have to dance around it and flirt with it or else she'll figure out what I'm up to. I'm getting there. We've been discussing hot faerie guys, past and present. It's her favorite subject, so she doesn't mind. I've got a list started." She shrugged her shoulders. "It's kind of lengthy."

"And this list will get you where?"

Breena gave her a patient look. "Titania has slept with nearly every faerie in the kingdom. Literally. The only ones she consciously excludes are the ones related to her—and then only because it icks out Her family members. That's how far gone she is: Her family barely claims her. Anyway, she loves to discuss her guys' sexual preferences. And sex with a human . . . well, it takes a certain kind of faerie to want a human."

Titillated in spite of herself, Janelle hung on every word. "What kind? Good? Bad? Weird?"

"The kind who can step in and step back quickly. With his heart, I mean."

"You're talking about the lifespan difference."

"Yes, that." Breena shrugged, then eyed Janelle with amused speculation. "It's also kind of on the fringe, sexually."

"Why do I think I'm going to need a shower after this conversation?"

Kane's sister laughed. "Oh, I don't know. Because you've slept with a faerie type before and really have the hots for one now?"

Janelle sighed. "I'm going to hate myself for asking this, I know I will. Why and how . . . 'on the fringe'? I mean, when humans talk about on the fringe, it's just a term for really kinky—often verging on sick stuff."

"That's it exactly."

"So you all think Kane's pervy. Like his dad. And his brother."

"Sounds genetic, doesn't it? Genetically perverted? And,

ooh, I'm *related* to them. Look out, humans, Breena's on the loose." She laughed.

"I think . . . I'm speechless."

Breena grabbed Janelle's hands, then tugged her around until they were face-to-face. The faerie was no longer laughing; she was dead serious. "I've been playing with you a bit. I've enjoyed it, too. And I have this silly hope that someday you and Kane—Never mind. But I'm dead serious about Titania. You will get *hurt*. And so will Kane. If not directly, then through you. You can't do that to him now. He's counting on you. You have to stay away from my mother."

"But—"

"Look, if you must do something active to help, try focusing on the Druid faction. There's something there. I can feel it. Kane feels it, too. Focus on them, see what they have at stake and what they're trying to gain. You do that while I handle Titania."

"What about Kane?"

"I have a feeling my brother already has a plan in motion."

"What do you remember of Tremayne?" Kane asked his brother. After Janelle had left on her mysterious "feminine" errand, he'd slipped out as well. Lacking any other option since Janelle had taken the car, he'd used magic to transport himself to his brother's house.

"Hmm?"

Kane sighed. "Riordan, this is getting comical. You don't have to eat nonstop."

Riordan finished chewing the last of the dinner roll he'd brought with him when he'd answered the door. "I'm hungry." The response was exasperated. "And a guy should be able to get a meal down without somebody interrupting and interrogating him. First Janelle, then Breena, both disturbing me from my lunch, and now you dragging me out here in the middle of—"

Kane verbally pounced. "Janelle called you? What did she want?"

"Well, she asked about Mina, naturally. But then she also wanted to know how to call Titania."

"She *what*? And you told her?"

"No. Give me a little credit, would you? I had her call Bree's assistant. That girl's a wonder of resourcefulness. She'll keep Janelle clear of Titania, no problem."

Kane frowned, but didn't argue.

Riordan leaned against the doorjamb. "So what is it that required you interrupting my meal?"

"I came to ask you about Tremayne. What do you remember of him?"

"You probably know as much as I do, if not more. Everything I know about my sentencing is based on hearsay, and Akker saw to it I remembered very little."

Kane nodded quietly. "Anything you know, anything you remember could help."

Riordan shrugged. "He's some kind of nature spirit Akker summoned to cage me in the stone. I'm pretty sure Tremayne was bound to the stone in some way, too. Maybe Akker's doing. I'm not sure. You know, Tremayne witnessed your little tantrum at the stone circle, just like I did. You were pretty murderous. And Tremayne seemed . . . I don't know . . . in some kind of agony over it. And before you ask, no, he didn't say anything to make me think that. It was just something I sensed."

Kane nodded thoughtfully, remembering the incident anew. He'd been nearly insane, thinking Maegth might have been carrying his child. Or Riordan's. And then to lose the child and Maegth . . . She was gone. Just gone. "Tremayne was with you for the whole two thousand years?"

"Yep."

"So, then, if he spent all that time with you, maybe against his will . . . where's his loyalty?" Kane eyed his brother shrewdly.

A voice from within—Mina's, sounding impatient—suggested Riordan get his butt back to the dinner table or face the consequences. Distracted by the threat and obviously taking it seriously, Riordan shifted backward a step. "That, my brother, is a very good question. Why don't you work on answering it, and let me go back in and finish my dinner. Mina's getting pissed. She doesn't like being left alone at the dinner table. It's bonding time for us."

"Oh. Dinner conversation?" Kane pondered that. It was actually hard tying a domestic image to the scamp his brother used to be. "How sweet. Like an old married couple discussing their day."

"Nah," his brother replied. "Food sex."

"That knee should be plenty numb by now." Janelle smiled reassuringly at her patient. After today's focus on puca and faerie business, what she needed most this evening was routine—something simple but useful that reminded her of her worth as a human. Stitching up a knee, ironically enough, was a welcome task. "Let me help you onto the table and we'll get started. A little antiseptic, a few stitches, a bandage, and we'll have you out of here in no time."

The girl didn't move from her chair, just eyed Janelle with distrust. "What if it leaves a scar?"

"Well, I'm not promising that it won't, but we'll try to keep it neat and as small as possible. And there are worse places to have scars than on your knee. Everybody has a scar on their knee from some childhood adventure or another."

"I'm not a child."

Janelle eyed the eighteen-year-old with suppressed humor. A skateboarding injury sounded pretty childlike to her. Even if the child in question sported a very adult-looking butterfly tattoo on the side of her calf, mere inches south of the injured knee. "Of course not.

So please just take your seat and present your knee so we can finish up and stop wasting your valuable time. Sound good?"

"Of course." The girl sat carefully, chin held high, and propped her leg on the table in front of her.

"Comfy? Ready for me to begin?" Janelle held her hands wide. She'd already donned latex gloves, had thread and needle, and was ready to go. Latex was a necessity, she'd discovered. Not just to prevent the transfer of germs, but also to reduce the incidence of skin-to-skin contact with her patients. She'd had a few incidents regardless.

Helping an elderly woman into the clinic yesterday—an innocent and well-meaning gesture—had turned into an unintended healing session right there in the waiting room. A simple touch to the woman's bare arm, and Janelle had involuntarily dissolved a couple of gallstones. Hell, even the woman's nasal passages, congested thanks to seasonal allergies, had cleared. But she'd been lucky; the incident was weird but not overtly magical. Even better, nobody had formally diagnosed the gallstones to begin with, so there was no record of their existence requiring follow-up.

So for now she was in the clear. But repetition of such weirdness—like the gassy baby and the migraine patient—could invite suspicion. Shoot, if every potential patient healed spontaneously upon coming into physical contact with Dr. Corrington, people would begin to wonder. People like Dr. Hoffman, for example, who was still watching her like a hawk. When would he let up already? She'd seen him check over her case files, question her patients, question her nurse . . . He was just looking for something to trip her up.

Patience, Janelle. He'll ease up in time, she told herself.

The girl before Janelle now gave her a doubtful look. "I guess I'm as ready as I'll ever be."

Janelle steadied her mind and her hands, then bent to carefully set the first stitch. She was distracted by a muffled sound from above her shoulder, and when she glanced up she saw her patient was white-faced. "Are you okay?"

Slumping weakly, the teenage girl shook her head. She swayed dizzily into Janelle, her cheek brushing Janelle's forehead.

Janelle immediately felt a rush of nausea, embarrassment and fear, with thready pain underlying a mildly numbed portion of leg. She identified the discordance and, uneasy with it and unable to help herself, reluctantly, inevitably reordered it. The girl leaned backward, moaning and staring at the ceiling.

Dread pooled in Janelle's belly. She glanced down at the wound . . . which was gone. Naturally. Only a thin pink line remained, and even that would disappear way too soon.

Okay, this wasn't good. Well, it was good that the girl was healed, but really not good in that there was no rational explanation this time. Colicky babies could mysteriously find release. Gallstones, not visible and undiagnosed, could mysteriously dissolve and probably nobody would question it. An open gash healed before she could even set the stitches? Tricky.

And oh, God. The tattoo was gone! Not that any doctor was thrilled to ponder the idea of a patient subjecting herself to the risk of infection and disease at the hands of a less than qualified tattoo artist . . . but the damn tattoo was gone! The kid was going to freak. Janelle had "healed" a tattoo into nonexistence. The skin was smooth as a baby's bottom now, no sign that any needle had ever touched the girl's calf. How on earth would she explain this?

Janelle's thoughts raced. "Um. Don't look. Just keep your eyes averted and it will feel better. Deal?" She hurriedly slid gauze over the iodine-stained skin and taped

it in place. As a panicked, really desperate bandage for
her own situation, she let the tail of a long piece of tape
cover where the tattoo used to be. "These are dissolving
stitches. They do a great job. And they're almost invisible."

"You're finished already?" The girl sounded bewil-
dered and hopeful.

"Yep. You might have spaced out for some of the experience, being all woozy like that. It happens sometimes.
Just be grateful. Meanwhile, keep the wound covered as
long as you can." That would buy her some time at least.
"When you finally change the dressing, don't be alarmed
or overly reassured if you don't see anything wrong at
first. The stitches are small and I set them pretty carefully." Lie, lie, lie. What else could she do? "I also applied some topical antibiotics, so that should help reduce
any scar tissue formation. You'll be as good as new before you know it." And wasn't that the truth? "Now do
yourself and your doctor a favor and the next time you
skateboard, please remember the knee and elbow pads,
along with a sturdy helmet, okay?"

The girl nodded ruefully.

Her nerves jangling and adrenaline frothing in her
veins, Janelle rose from her stool, peeling her gloves off
in a practiced motion. Thoughts racing, she scribbled up
some mild prescriptions—precautionary—and set them
on the table next to the girl. "Take these with you when
you leave. The nurse waiting outside the door will show
you where to find your mom. She's filling out forms, I
believe." Desperately needing air, Janelle left the room.

What did this mean? If she could unconsciously "heal"
a tattoo, she could probably close piercings. Not exactly
a tragedy, but certainly unexplainable. And she couldn't
help but wonder what other "cures" she could accidentally precipitate. Suppose a touch to the wrong person
reversed a gastric bypass? Or ejected a hip replacement
or pacemaker? And would the same touch also heal the

health problems that made those artificial aids necessary? What about tattoos used for radiation patients? Would she heal the cancer along with the tattoo or just make it harder for the cancer to be treated without the tattoo to guide the technician? Would the consequences be positive or negative? Not just in terms of public exposure, but what about her patients' health? Or the health of a stranger on the street, someone she unknowingly touched in passing?

She just didn't know yet. With this alarming lack of control combined with blind ignorance . . . her patients at this point were little more than guinea pigs. She couldn't condone that. It was irresponsible, possibly even unethical.

How depressing. Even alarming. Is this how it would work now? Had the gift become a curse? How would she practice? If every time she tried to use traditional methods the nontraditional took over, she wouldn't go long without exposure. Then what? The gift was a wonderful thing, but wouldn't she end up in some laboratory or freak show?

She hurried down the hall, barely nodding at the receptionist as she muttered "break" on her way out the front door. At seven o'clock, it was already past sunset, and streetlights illuminated small pockets in the darkness outside. She took a small walk around the building.

"Oooh, are you on break? Excellent timing," came a low voice over her shoulder. She jumped and glared at Kane, who was following her. He continued talking and walking without pause. "I was just thinking that I needed to consult the good Dr. Corrington about a friend of mine. She has this martyrlike, self-destructive bent. She really needs help."

Janelle groaned. "If this is about Titania—"

"Of course it's about Titania!" He dropped the sarcastically chatty tone. "Damn it, Janelle. I told you—"

"I know, I know. And Breena stopped me, so no harm done. She was quite clear just how easy it is to trip me up. And how powerful your stepmother is. I get it." Janelle paused. "I just . . . I'm afraid. This gift . . ." She shook her head helplessly. "I can't control it. What if I end up hurting someone through my lack of control or my ignorance? I don't know the healing gift's limitations or how it will evolve. With standard medicine, at least we've run tests and encountered potential outcomes. We can stop midway through a procedure if things appear to be going wrong. I have no control with the magic. And virtually no experience.

"And what if I'm faced with a situation where healing means exposure for me while not healing means death for the patient? I couldn't choose *not* to heal someone traumatically injured—not and live with myself. But then, if healing resulted in my gift being exposed, I wouldn't be able to help anyone at all. They'd lock me up for study or fraud and so much for the gift. And then what would happen to you if something happened to me? I just don't know what to do. I don't know what's right anymore."

Kane was silent a moment before he sighed in surrender. "You want to save the whole damn world. It's both your virtue and your downfall. I just wish you'd occasionally take a break from everyone else and see to Janelle. You're a good person, one of those rare doctors who would give their very soul to help another. That's why you are both the best and worst choice to be responsible for this healing gift."

Janelle winced at the reminder.

Kane glanced at her. "What, did you just deal with a difficult patient?" Not that there was any surprise in his voice. Naturally, he would have sensed her current upset, along with the reason for it.

She laughed at the irony. "I wish. This patient was all too easy." And, speaking of easy, she wondered what everyone thought when they saw her with Kane, the two of them constantly leaving together.

Kissing cousins. Naturally. Ugh.

Kane spoke: "I'll bet they think we're dealing drugs on the side. You have the access, I provide the muscle, that kind of thing. We're off to the sleazier part of town to push and distribute," he suggested with a wink.

"That is completely repulsive." Janelle made a face.

"It was either repulse you or kiss you."

"And of course that's the last thing you want to do." He hadn't kissed her the other night—not even in that dream. And she shouldn't want it. It was wrong to want it. How could she be so foolish to want it so very badly? But she was. And she did.

Kane reacted in an instant. He turned, big hands gripping her waist to lift her high against the brick wall of the clinic. Face-to-face. Carefully, his golden eyes holding her gaze helpless, he leaned his big body into hers. His hard chest pressed into her breasts, his hips rocking into and under hers until his body weight supported her. Then, inevitably, he pressed closer until his face blocked out everything around them. Anything beyond them. And then his mouth was on hers and she was bonelessly melting into the wall, into him.

Janelle's heart stuttered. God, but the man could kiss. And the rest—It was liquid heat, electronically charged. Charging all around her. She felt his excitement, the urgency, the arousal. Even, surprisingly, tenderness. Her arms slid around his neck and she poured herself into that kiss, that emotion. And returned it. He cared. She cared. *They*—

His fingers raked through her hair, sifting through strands, scraping deliciously across her scalp. It sent tingles down her nape, down her spine. Down his spine. Slanting her mouth across his again and again, she arched into him, feeling those tingles return full circle, threefold. Her heart raced, unable to keep up with his, or with his arousal. She couldn't breathe. He pushed closer, increasing the carnal zing of their contact. Intimate, sweet—and not enough.

Needing more, she ground against him as he kissed her, felt his responding desperation, his throbbing hardness that drove her own ache so much deeper, that nearly buckled his knees. Wisps of dream memory floated through Janelle's mind: the feel of him, the feel of her. And the fullness of that memory proved that it was shared. *Oh, to make it real.*

Groaning harshly, Kane bucked helplessly against her, and the sharp edge of his belt buckle dug into her belly. She winced. And with that, the spell was half-broken. With a growl, Kane pulled back to let her sag against the wall. Then he rolled out of reach. She could almost feel the heaves of his chest, could almost taste his breath.

"Janelle." The word was a warning.

Her breathing harsh and almost painful, Janelle leaned her head back against the wall. She couldn't look at him now. But what was the difference? He knew what she was thinking. "This can't go on. We can't keep doing this without—"

He groaned again. "Don't say it."

"Well, damn it, it's true. We'll both go insane if we don't do something about this."

"I thought you never wanted to make love with me again."

She took a moment to compose herself, then said, "Who said make *love*? I'm talking out-of-control bodily urges. We need to fix them. And I'm not some giggly coed who needs roses and pretty words to have an orgasm." Well, she wouldn't be. She refused to be.

He shook his head, half laughing. "Gee, that sweeps me right off my feet."

"Oh, shut up. If anyone around here is jaded about the opposite sex, it's you. I'm allowed to keep pace. For my own sanity at the very least."

"So, what do you suggest?" His voice was low.

"I think you know."

"Maybe I want you to say it."

She cast him a resentful look, one born of pure frustration. "Maybe you suck for making me say it."

"Maybe with talk that juvenile, you sound like an adolescent. One who'll require roses, sonnets and wedding rings before you'll even let a guy inside your bra." But there was a real smile in his voice now.

His amusement seemed to take the edge off both of their moods, and Janelle chuckled tiredly. Resignedly. "Think so?"

"You tell me."

She sighed. "Okay. I'll tell you. I'm a doctor, so it behooves me to be blunt and shameless. Ready for it?"

"I'm all ears."

"Oh, that's so not true. You're definitely not all *ears*." She could still feel the other parts of him grinding against her. She would never recover.

He groaned, sharing her arousal. "Stop that."

"Just a leeeetle bit of revenge there, boy," she joked. "You know about that. You do remember revenge, yes? Two thousand years of it . . . ?"

He stared at her. "I'm waiting for the blunt doctor talk. I'm hoping it will distract me from what's ailing me."

She grinned. "Hardly. It's about what's ailing you. What's ailing us. But maybe I'm talking to the wrong guy."

"Excuse me?" He gave her a furious look.

She laughed aloud at his obvious jealousy. "The wrong guy to answer my doctorlike questions!"

"Oh. Well, why don't you let me be the judge of that?"

She shrugged. "All right, you asked for it. I'm . . . I'm looking for a definition of sex."

"A definition of sex? Didn't you go to medical school? I think they probably covered the birds and the bees at some point. Or were you absent that day?"

"Funny guy. I'm looking, specifically, for the Druid definition." Her eyes widened. "Although, I seriously can't picture asking index-finger-dancing High Druid Phil."

Kane guffawed. "If you do decide to ask him, can I watch? It would really make my day."

"Pucas are so twisted." She shook her head. "But I'm serious. Since we have this attraction and it doesn't feel like it's going anywhere . . . I'd like to know where the line is. Then we could, um . . ."

He grinned. "What, enjoy some dry-hump action? Be still, my faerie heart."

She laughed, enjoying a moment of their shared humor. "It could be like teenage sex, maybe. Third base and no farther." She hoped he knew that metaphor.

He seemed to. "Oh, come on. Let me at least dance around home plate."

"See? That's what I mean. Can we do other stuff?"

He stared at her, his beautiful eyes hot with amusement and desperate arousal. It was a heady, knee-melting combination. However would she last?

"You? What about me?" he complained. "I have the torture of being able to walk around in your fantasies. And still I have to restrain myself." His eyes darkened to a deeper amber. "Like now, for example."

Her fantasies—? Like the other night. She'd been right about it being more than just a dream—he'd shared it.

"Yes." One word. Pure steam. And she could see both the memory and knowledge in his eyes. "I thought I would go insane."

Feeling emotionally naked, Janelle broke eye contact.

"Janelle Corrington, MD. Blushing." But his words were soft with affection. They grew even softer. "Like I said, it was torture getting through that without going to you. The sweetest torture known to man. I think you fried every last brain cell I had left."

She savored the wondering sincerity in his voice. It

was so . . . respectful. Admiring. Adoring even? No, that
would—

"Adoring works. I do . . . adore you, I mean. Just so
you know." He inhaled and pushed away from the wall,
then offered her his arm. "So. The girl with the gash in
her knee."

Janelle gave him a dazed look as she waited for her
brain cells to realign themselves into a moderately capable whole. She cleared her throat. Watched his smile
widen. That smile was pure happiness. It did something
to her that made her feel whole and energized and
healed.

Healing. The girl inside. The patient. The one who
doesn't need stitches anymore, Janelle reminded herself.
Then she groaned inwardly in renewed memory.

"Yeah. Well, I accidentally healed her. Which is a completely illogical way of viewing this whole thing, I know,
but I can't just openly heal, and that makes me mad. I
even made her tattoo go away this time, which I'm going
to have a hell of a time explaining." She cast Kane a sidelong glance. "And, as if that weren't enough, whenever I
do heal somebody, I have to steer way clear of you or
else we end up in a stupid clinch." She shook her head.
"I feel like a prostitute. Healing power for sex."

"Interesting way of viewing the matter," Kane remarked.

"More like horrifying. How did things come to this?
Six months ago I would have sold my soul to be able to
heal people instantaneously. Now . . . now I have to try
not to heal them. It's ludicrous."

Kane thought a moment. "This was supposed to be a
gift. A blessing. A compensation. And now you see it as
only a burden." *Like me,* she heard him think.

"Not like you. Well, okay, yeah, like you. In a way."

He grinned ruefully. "It's great that you're so decisive
about all this."

"See? This is what's become of me. A doctor can't

afford to be indecisive. Especially in an emergency. If I'm worried about—"

He half laughed. "In a medical emergency, I guarantee you would not be indecisive. We're talking about magic right now. A scientist confronting her newly gained magic. How could she not be thrown off balance?"

Janelle shook her head. "I'm not just thrown off balance; I'm an ethical mess. Yes, I want to heal people. But this gift is so far out of my league. Totally beyond my control. What if somebody really gets hurt by it just because I don't understand its potential? And then there's the risk of public exposure, which means I have to hesitate to use my gift and then use it only in secret. There will be lies upon lies upon lies. I'll slip up. How could I not?"

"Are you saying you regret the gift?"

"Yeah. In some ways." She chanced a glance at him. "How selfish is that?"

"You're asking *me* about selfish?" He smiled ironically. "Look at my track record."

Kane suddenly glanced over his shoulder. He hurried her forward a few steps, but his attention was obviously on the shadows.

"What's wrong?" Janelle asked.

"Somebody's there," he murmured quietly, then raised his voice. "Hello? Why don't you come out into the open and talk to us. I'm not promising we can give you anything, but I have time and if I can morally help, I will."

Janelle glanced at Kane. His tone was wry, but he really meant what he'd said. He would help—a stranger, a friend, a relative, an enemy. A girl could tell that just by looking into those golden eyes, which led straight to a strong and loyal heart.

Janelle mentally pinched herself. Where the hell had that idea come from? This was Kane. The guy who'd ensured that his brother never saw the light of day for two millennia. The guy who would have married a human while secretly staying engaged to a faerie fiancée. He'd actually picked out his second wife before he'd even made the first one official.

"It was complicated," he remarked.

"Get out of my head."

A man's voice rang out behind them. "Perhaps mind reading is something they shouldn't have allowed a condemned puca."

Janelle whirled, only to have Kane shove her behind his back.

"Hello, Kane." It was Tremayne, speaking in his curiously uninflected voice.

"Planning on freezing me again?" Kane eyed the man warily, his body still shielding Janelle's.

"Hurts, doesn't it?" Tremayne smiled almost companionably.

Hurts? Janelle looked at Kane. It had hurt Kane when he froze like that? What the hell was this Tremayne guy, anyway?

"And I can see where that's breaking your heart." Kane held out a hand, palm up. "Why don't you just tell me what you are and why you're spying on us. And on Duncan."

Tremayne leaned casually against a post. "Maybe I just needed a hobby."

Kane stared at him. "Daphne Forbes said you're a private detective investigating her parents."

The man just smiled. "Is that what she thinks? I suppose that's partly accurate. I am investigating her parents. But they're not the only ones I'm investigating, Kane. A puca wielding magic to harm others should be held accountable, don't you think? And we both know you're more than capable of a vast amount of destruction with those powers of yours."

Kane considered Tremayne. "You're talking about the damage I caused in Wiltshire, England. At the Avebury Circle. The stones and the cabin."

"And an ancient grove." Tremayne murmured, "Yes. All of that. In fact, you might say investigating the causes of puca damage is my job now."

"You're working for the Druids?" Janelle guessed.

"In a manner of speaking." Tremayne's face was still expressionless. Alarmingly so.

"And you're all set to permanently condemn Kane for everything that's going on," Janelle concluded.

"I'll give him the benefit of the doubt . . . for now."

Kane raised a cynical eyebrow. "You have that power? That right?"

Tremayne gave him a mild look. "What do you think?"

"I think you're on a power kick."

"Well, somebody certainly is." Tremayne's features hardened. "It's my job to put a stop to it. Anyone who gets in my way will be dealt with."

"So, that's your purpose?"

"That's as much as you need to know about it, yes. I'm watching you. And yours." Tremayne pivoted without another word and strode off.

Janelle stared after him. He'd disappeared into the darkness long before his footsteps faded.

"Did you ever ask Riordan about him?" she asked Kane.

"Yes. And he knows little more than I do. Except . . ." He grimaced.

Janelle cleared her throat. "Yes? Is this the part where you tell me all about the destruction Tremayne mentioned? I'm assuming you had a good reason for not telling me about it."

"Depends on your definition of a good reason. It was painful. I regret it. I . . . Well, it happened several months after the ceremony condemning Riordan. I found out that Maegth was pregnant."

Janelle's eyes widened. "With another puca?"

Kane glanced away. "I honestly don't know. I don't know if it was my child, Riordan's child or, frankly, somebody else's child that she carried. But she died in childbirth, as did the babe. A boy, I was told." His features were stark with remembered anguish. "When I found out, about the pregnancy, the birth, the deaths . . . I lost it. It was too much. I'll admit it's a good thing that Riordan was already caged in stone where I couldn't get to him. I did, however, shatter his stone and several others."

"That's when it was made into a cornerstone."

Kane nodded. "Then I destroyed the cabin—it was on my property—where I'd found Riordan and Maegth together. I burned it to the ground, in fact, and ended up setting part of the grove on fire. Nobody was hurt and I compensated the Druids to their satisfaction later. But I understand the sight of me and the devastation I wrought . . . well, it traumatized a few villagers. I shifted into horse, ape, whatever shape seemed handiest. I don't remember all of them. It's a bit of a blur even now." Kane swallowed and inhaled heavily. "Riordan said he was aware of what I did to his stone. And it's a good bet Tremayne was aware of it, too. Riordan said whatever I was doing seemed to be harming Tremayne in some way."

Janelle nodded slowly. "I suppose it's occurred to you that that long-ago rampage bears some resemblance to the more recent destruction everyone wants to blame on you? The terrorized Druid. The enraged horse. Mina's house."

"Yeah, it was a little hard to miss. And, even better, both Riordan and Tremayne made that same connection. I think Riordan understands now. But Tremayne . . . well, he's seen me violent, I caused him pain and he's still obviously holding a grudge. That's not good. You know," Kane mused, "add all of the above to that freeze-ray trick of his . . . I'd really hate to go up against Tremayne in a fight. I don't know that I could win."

"More powerful than a puca. That's so reassuring." Janelle stared off into the dark, then turned her wondering gaze back to Kane. "But of course there's the big-money question: is he on the side of good or evil?"

"Good question. I wonder if Oberon knows."

"Or Titania," Janelle suggested. "Hey, angry or not, there's no denying that Tremayne is hot. Maybe he's one of her boy toys."

Kane gave her a look. "Shouldn't you be getting back to the clinic?"

She smiled, amused by his jealousy—and a little pleased by it. "You seem a little out of sorts. Was it . . . something I said?"

Grimacing, Kane just slipped her arm through his and steered them back toward the clinic.

As they walked, Janelle studied the shadows. She still sensed eyes watching them. Was it Tremayne? Or was it someone or something else?

Chapter Thirteen ❦

"Janelle?" Dr. Hoffman poked his head into her office the next morning. "I need to have a word with you."

Janelle set her file folder down and glanced up. "Sure. Come on in. My next patient's not for another fifteen minutes. Will that work?"

"I hope so."

Hoffman closed the door behind him and turned a sober look on Janelle. Her heart thudded.

"Is there a problem, Dr. Hoffman?"

"The eighteen-year-old who was seen for a gash in her knee last night . . . I understand you treated her?"

Janelle forced herself to breathe. "Yes."

He frowned. "Stitches, right? And you wrote her up a prescription for antibiotics and painkillers?"

"Y-yes." Very mild ones, though, and only as a pre-caution. Although healed, the girl might still ache a bit, and Janelle could only assume there might still be risk of infection. Magical healing powers really should come with their own instruction manual. Or at least a FAQ section.

Hoffman nodded.

Oh, shit. This was it. She'd been found out. "Yeah, about that . . ."

"The insurance company was balking."

"Insurance?" Janelle mentally stumbled. How did that figure into anything?

"Next time you write a prescription, ask if the patient would prefer generics. The co-pay's a lot less and the insurance company keeps its nose out of it."

Janelle blinked. She must have forgotten, in her flustered state, to ask that very basic question. But, that was it—co-pays and generics? That was the problem, not magical healing and gaping wounds closing on their own? "I can't believe I forgot to do that. I'll make a point of remembering from now on. Thanks for bringing it to my attention." She could breathe again.

"And then there's the matter of Mrs. Fischer."

More insurance problems? True, Hoffman was a stickler about all of this. He knew how to work the system—both inside and around it. Usually for the patient's well-being, or so Janelle hoped.

"Mrs. Fischer? I'm afraid I didn't treat a Mrs. Fischer that I can recall—"

"Yes, I know." Hoffman closed the file he'd perused. "She's always been my patient. And while I hadn't run her through tests yet, all her symptoms pointed to gallstones. But then something amazing happened. She talked to you and somehow her symptoms mysteriously and spontaneously disappeared. No treatment necessary."

"Oh. Well, that's a good thing, right?"

"Oh, but the wonders don't end there. I talked to our nurse Cindy, who mentioned yet another amazing piece of good luck. She was babbling on and on about baby Lexie Goldman—with a suspected bowel obstruction. The child was on her way to the hospital for emergency care when mother and child encountered you and, *poof*, all better. The staff is still amazed. And the mother was deliriously relieved that our suspicions and fears were unsubstantiated."

"That's even better news. Nasty things, bowel obstructions." Oh, God, so this was the baby from the other morning? Their contact was so brief she'd thought it was just gas.

"Yes. So we have another patient magically spared medical intervention. You do get lucky, don't you, Dr. Corrington?"

"Yeah." Janelle laughed a little weakly. "I must have the touch."

"Or perhaps it's just the lucky presence of your . . . mascot." He eyed her speculatively.

"Mascot?" Janelle frowned.

"Your . . . cousin."

"What about him?"

"Kane, you said? Kane O'Brian?"

"Yeah. Is there a problem? He's just doing some errands and office chores for me. On an intern basis. I think he wants to know if a medical office is a good place for him, professionally. For us, it's free labor, and the office manager seems pleased with his assistance."

"Did anyone perform a background check on the man before we allowed him access to sensitive case files?"

Oh, boy. "I'm sure somebody must have. In any case, I don't let him deal directly with the confidential stuff. It's mostly copying. Stuffing envelopes. Running errands. By the way, would you like him to pick up some lunch for you today? He offered to go for me earlier and I took him up on it."

Hoffman stared at her a moment. "No, thank you."

"Mmm. Okay." *Help.*

The phone buzzed. Janelle silently blessed it. "Hello?" With seeming reluctance, as Janelle held the receiver to her ear, Dr. Hoffman left her office.

"Problem, Dr. Corrington?" It was Kane.

"Possibly."

"I heard your thoughts. Maybe you'd like to ride along and order your lunch yourself?"

"That sounds like a good idea." Trembling, she hung up the phone and concentrated on regaining her composure. Deep breaths. At this rate, she'd definitely be needing to take up yoga. Stress relief, clean slate practice and the whole breathing thing. Inhale. Exhale. That part used to be fairly routine for her.

They chose to walk to the deli instead of driving.

"Your Dr. Hoffman seems to be keeping a close eye on you," Kane commented.

"Tell me about it. I felt like I was walking on eggshells."

"You were. I have the feeling he's not letting up anytime soon. He seems to have fixated on you."

She frowned. "I know. We'll just have to be extra careful. You channel 'human and harmless intern' at all times. I . . . I will wear latex gloves and long sleeves. So. Once again, instead of using my gift, I'm trying to stifle it." She couldn't help grumbling, "What is the point if I can't even use it to help people?"

"It can be used," Kane replied. "You *know* it can be used. It's just trickier than you want it to be. I know your feelings on the subject, but I think you have to admit that there is a time and a place for all magic—both the healing and, by necessity, the glamouring. Take your Dr. Hoffman situation, for example. I think it's time you seriously consider—"

"Oh, no. Don't even think it." Janelle picked up her pace, as if she could run from the idea.

Kane grabbed her sleeve, drawing her immediate and supremely focused attention. The placement of his hand was intentional, she was sure, touching her sleeve and avoiding skin contact with her. She was grateful, and yet something wild inside was tempted to test the waters again. Had their explosive attraction dissipated at all? Had it grown? Was such a thing possible?

"Don't go there." At his growl, she glanced up in

shock, and was just in time to catch a spark of responding wildness.

"Kane." She was so drawn to him, could not bring
herself to put distance between them, emotionally or
physically. So the answers were no, yes and yes. This
chemistry between them was explosive.

Kane spoke as though the words were wrenched from
him. "Your definition. I checked on it."

"Definition . . . ?" She broke off, her heart outpacing
her breath.

"Yeah. Sex. According to my discreet Druid source . . ."
He moved in closer until heat from his body invaded her
space. "The definition for sex in this case is very specific.
It would entail"—his eyes glittered dangerously—"so to
speak, me being inside you." His pause was deliberate
this time, just as his gaze was too intimate, too invasive.
She knew he was visualizing, his every nerve ending no
doubt imagining the intoxicating sensations of his body
surging into hers.

She caught her breath, found it impossible to let it out
or take more in.

"But also for us both to surrender to it. *Two* climaxes."

No air. The possibilities! Lips, tongue, heated flesh,
wild-eyed thoughts and words all merging and losing
themselves in the grinding urgency—

"Breathe, Janelle."

Oh, but what about hearts and—She quelled the rest
of it.

"We'd have to leave hearts completely out of it. For
both our sakes."

Stung by the bald statement, she broke free and stumbled back a few paces. Chest heaving, she couldn't even
look at him. The things he'd said and the things he'd
read in her mind, not just the sex, but the other . . . The
other was worse. For him to know she secretly wanted
more and to deny it aloud and so bluntly. Painful, mortifying. And even now she couldn't stop the thoughts.

"Get out of my head, get out of my head, get out of my head!"

She let out a furious breath, chancing a glance at him as she sought her own fury to deny the hurt. "You're not welcome in my thoughts. Just as I'm not welcome in anyone else's head." And there she found her rationale. "It's not right. It's a very personal violation to invade and manipulate someone's mind without their express consent." She began pacing, working out her anger and finding her strength and her logic. "And don't give me those 'greater good' and 'controlling the Bedlam population' arguments. I can't do it. Changing people's minds and memories—ethically, I just can't do it."

"You used a glamour just fine on Browning, that Druid damaged by his puca ride." Kane, his voice and demeanor calm but for a roughened edge, still watched her every step.

Janelle shook her head. "That was different. I wasn't just lying to him. I was helping his mind heal. He wouldn't have healed without the glamour. But what you want me to do is wrong. I can't go messing around in Dr. Hoffman's head just to avoid inconveniencing myself."

"So, what will you do then?"

She frowned, her thoughts racing. "Just as I've done before. I just need to be more careful."

Kane looked skeptical. "But you've already had some close calls. What if something catastrophic happens and you're forced to reveal your gift in front of him?"

"Then . . . then I'll come up with something." She hoped. "Something logical he'll accept. And then I'll offer to take weekend duty off his hands. I'll call it an apology for the misunderstanding. That smoothes a doctor's feathers every time."

"So he likes his weekends free, then."

"Who doesn't? And, well . . . he has an active social life." She spoke carefully.

Kane narrowed his eyes. "Does he now? Why do I get the feeling he's tried, more than once, to make you a part of that social life?"

Janelle scowled at him. "He's a guy. That's what your gender does, remember? Are you going to condemn him for trying to do exactly what you did?" She didn't particularly like Dr. Hoffman, but she also didn't want Kane so jealous that he'd overreact.

Kane's eyes darkened. "It's not the same."

"Oh, no? How is it different? At the very least, he's human. No magicky baggage like a millennia-old grudge against a family member to hold him back. He's just a doctor struggling to do his job and maybe have a few moments of fun along the way." She shrugged. "He can ask me out all he wants. I just say no. Simple as that."

"So you turned him down?"

"Well, he's my colleague. And he's a full partner and I'm just salaried, so he outranks me. Of course I turned him down. It was a no-brainer."

"I bet that bruised his ego. Maybe that's why he has it in for you so bad."

The censure she heard in his voice irritated her. "What, I should have gone out with him just to soothe his tender ego?"

Kane sighed. "No, I'm just saying he has reason to pick a fight with you. All he's looking for now is ammunition. This could get dicey, and quickly. You need to head it off. A few simple suggestions and he could be put off the scent entirely."

"But I won't use this glamour mind-meld trick to serve my own purposes. It's . . . it's just wrong." Janelle pivoted and walked away.

Kane stayed put, though she felt his gaze on her. "I agree. It would be wrong if done callously or dishonorably. But I think you could glamour him with care. You know his priorities and his skills, and you value both them and him. You also value your own abilities. It would be a shame if your healing gift went unused or your medical skills went to waste because some stupid suspicion caused you to have your license revoked."

"Ooooh. That's not fair." She turned and paced back toward him.

"With every gift, with every power, there is responsibility. Is it ethical to risk giving up your opportunity to help others when you know what you can do? When you know you possess extraordinary ability? Think of the greater good."

Janelle slowed, reluctantly, a few steps away from Kane. "But I don't want that sort of power. Sure, I can often tell what's in my patients' best interests and act on it. But that's different. Usually I lay out for them my diagnosis, their options and my recommendation. But the decision's not mine. It's theirs, unless the patient is incapable and has no advocate."

"Yes. I respect your ethics. They suit you very well, and are one of the reasons you're in the position you're in. But you've moved on to the next stage of power and responsibility. This is not so much about your job description as a human doctor"—he paused significantly—" as it is about your rights and responsibilities as a Druid healer."

"Druid healer? Get real, buddy. I'm no Druid. I'm just—"

"A Druid." He smiled and shrugged. "Or at least you're an honorary one, with honorary powers. And it *is* an honor, make no mistake. They take their gifts seriously, and they don't share them indiscriminately. Apparently, Dr. Corrington, you passed muster. They believed in you or the gift would never have taken. And look how it's flourished!"

She stared. "But they did it because—"

"Because my brother suggested it? Because *I* suggested it?" Kane shook his head. "Think about that. We're not their favorite people. They wouldn't take our word. I'm sure their decision was based on who you are and their feelings about what you'd do with the power." He shrugged. "Consider it a compliment. And understand that they're trusting you not just with the healing, but also with the glamour. It's the potential for evil that bothers you, if you're honest with yourself. That someone *could* use glamour for evil. That's true. And that's why not everybody is trusted with it. The Druids trust you to use it for good. Why can't you trust yourself?"

Janelle shook her head in instinctive rejection. "It just feels so arrogant. Tyrannical."

"And so it is if done carelessly or disrespectfully. You are neither careless nor disrespectful and the Druids know this. Accept the gift of glamour for the tool that it is. Have the courage to use it, and accept the moral risk you take every time you do use it."

Her movements jerky, Janelle turned, paced a step, then, undecided, paced right back. She didn't know what to say, what to think or how to feel.

"Just start with the here and now. Let the rest grow on you a little."

Here and now. She could deal with the here and now. But the here and now seemed to involve deception. "You think I should do what they gave me the power to do. What you say they actually trust me to do. To . . . use this glamour."

"For the greater good. Yes. Just as you used your healing gift for good. None of this is evil, Janelle. In fact, I'd bet your average human would consider your healing gift a miracle. The glamour gift simply makes it possible for you to use magic in a human world that doesn't easily believe or accept the unexplainable."

Janelle nodded slowly, still feeling shaky on the inside. And—she stared at her trembling hands—on the outside. She had shaky hands. She, a doctor? That was a sure indication that her world had tipped upside down.

"Take it easy. You're just reacting. You're a doctor, true,

and now a healer—a Druid healer drawing on faerie-based puca magic, whether you accept that yet or not."

"Faerie magic?" Druid and faerie and puca and doctor. "But—"

Kane, the bastard, looked on the verge of laughter! "But you're also human," he continued. "You're allowed to react."

"React? I'll give you react. How dare you laugh at me? This is a serious matter. I'm contemplating messing around inside a grown man's head. The head of a man responsible for the health of the public. That's serious."

He sighed. "Lighten up, will you? The Druids trusted you with the power. I trust you with the power. And Dr. Hoffman trusts you with the health of his clinic's patients."

Janelle snorted. "Sure, he loves me. And when he sees me heal a gash with my fingertips—"

"Yes?"

She cringed. "Well, even if people saw I'm truly gifted and not delusional, they'd ship me off to a bunch of weirdo scientists. Before you know it, they'd be running tests to see if I can resurrect the dinosaurs or turn our enemies' capitals into Zombie Central." She shivered. "So much for the miracle gift."

"I'm not sure about zombies and dinosaur resurrection, but the scientist scenario is certainly possible." He paused significantly. "Unless you actively prevent it."

She made a face. "By becoming a 'glam queen.'"

"Not quite how I might have phrased it, but yes. That's what I believe."

"I'll think about it. That's all I can promise."

Heart pounding, Kane fought his way out of a trance to find himself staring out the window of the clinic business office. Seeking another image to replace the horrors in his mind, he stared at a clump of neatly groomed bushes, their shadows cast long by the late afternoon sun. Still his heart thudded in sickly recovery. These visions were getting more intense, seizing his waking moments now and not just his sleeping ones.

And it was always Janelle. That beautiful face, so pale and lifeless. The same as before and yet not quite. Even in the darkness surrounding her in his vision, he'd been able to see a faint purplish bruise blossom on her chin. Had he done that to her? Was he the one who'd hit her? How the hell did she die? And why?

He was afraid of what it could all mean. Given the frequency, intensity and increasing detail of his visions, he had the horrible feeling that something would happen very soon. He had to get the hell away from her.

"I have the information you wanted." Mina's voice was a low murmur over the phone. "I just don't know if giving it to you is doing you a favor or sealing your doom."

Janelle glanced around carefully before replying. She'd had a bad night's sleep to ponder all of what Kane had told her about sex definitions and being an "honorary" Druid healer. In search of a (dangerous) distraction early this morning, she'd called Mina with a request. Now, a mere two hours later, Mina had delivered. The woman worked fast.

And her timing was perfect. Kane had just left to run errands for the clinic. "I appreciate the concern. I do. But I honestly know what I'm doing here."

"And that's why you put me on a snooping mission instead of just asking Kane outright how to call Step-mommy Dearest? Because you know what you're doing?" Doubt rang clearly in Mina's voice. "It sounds to me like you're afraid he would object to you seeing her—and probably with very good reason."

"Fine, so I'm keeping this secret from him. It's for his own good, though. He has this unreasonable paranoid streak where I'm concerned. He's so terrified, always, that something might happen to me." She shifted, peeking out the door of her office before gently closing it. "You know, given that the guy dumped me without a thought way back when, I never dreamed that he would become so damned protective."

"Mmmmm," Mina replied, sounding unconvinced.

"Trust me," Janelle said. "But I really do need that information." She glanced at her watch. With any luck she could set something up before Kane returned. He'd be none the wiser until it was too late. And since Breena had so far failed to provide the information she wanted, this was Janelle's only choice.

Mina sighed. "Okay. I'll give it to you. But only if you promise to call me immediately afterward. I'll worry otherwise."

"And you want a full report."

"Yeah, that too. So, do you have a pen?"

"I'm ready."

"First you call this number." Mina rattled off nine digits.

"On the phone? Nine digits?" Calling such a number was what she'd done last time, and she'd gotten Breena's assistant.

Mina sighed. "This is a faerie queen. Do you really think she's bound by the usual standards?"

Janelle sighed, not wanting to give away the fact that she'd tried this already. She made light of the situation, and hoped things would be different this time. "Well, we're talking phone lines, not tap my toes together three times and take me to the faerie queen. I figured some of the rules would apply."

"Nope. Dial those numbers. Let it ring once. Then hang up. Then dial the last three numbers over again. Wait for the pick-up. Then hang up again. The phone will ring immediately. That's your contact."

Janelle frowned. This method was slightly different than last time. "You're sure about this?"

"Heard it from the horse's mouth."

"Ha. The horse or the faerie?"

Mina snorted. "How about the horse's ass?"

"Oh, you mean the faerie queen."

"Yes! And have I mentioned she's become downright chummy lately? She's been popping in and out at odd times on the faerie prince and me. Yech. And her timing is exquisite. We were rolling around on the kitchen floor Tuesday night and—"

Janelle groaned. "Nice image. Thanks for giving me one more thing to wipe off the slate."

"Huh?"

"Never mind. Listen, thanks for the contact info. This might actually get me somewhere."

After saying good-bye, Janelle hung up. She stared at her scribblings for a few moments, absently retracing some of the digits. She really had no choice. Breena hadn't contacted her. Things were progressing. Were Kane in her shoes, he'd call. She knew he would.

Inhaling deeply, she picked up the phone. She'd been practicing her mind shield a lot—even on Kane when he wasn't suspecting. She could do this. Blank slate . . .

She dialed. Hung up. Dialed again. Then hung up again. The phone rang.

"Hello?"

"You called?"

"Yes." She paused, feeling like an idiot. If this wasn't the right number, if this was another faerie giving her the runaround or it was some human and a misconnection . . . Oh, what the heck. "I wish to visit with Titania."

"And who are you to believe yourself worthy of a visit with the faerie queen?"

Ha! This was the right number. "Tell your queen that the guardian of her stepson wishes to exchange information. It could be helpful to both of us."

There was a pause. She wasn't exactly put on hold so much as the line just went silent. Just as she was becoming certain the phone was dead or the faerie peon had hung up on her, the voice returned. "Her Highness will meet you. You are familiar with Druids' Grove, I believe?"

"Yes."

"Thirty minutes."

"All right." Janelle hung up, then exhaled long and deep. *So far, so good.* She'd managed the faerie servant. Could she manage the faerie queen?

Chapter Fourteen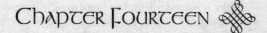

"Well. If it isn't the little guardian. And how are your patients, Doctor? All healing as quickly as you would wish?" Titania smiled, her breathy voice mild as a summer breeze and yet provocative as a high-priced hooker's.

"My patients are my business."

"Of course. But the gift? It brings you good fortune? And healing to your patients?"

"Again, that's confidential. I'm here strictly on faerie business. And puca business." Janelle didn't want to give this woman any more information than she had to.

Titania shrugged. "The faerie business I understand. Puca business, however, is completely irrelevant to me."

Janelle pictured a very clean slate, keeping her mind entirely blank. "*Is* it? Completely?"

"What do you mean?" Titania turned huge eyes on her, their glow almost overwhelming.

Clean slate. A completely clean slate. But for revenge. Janelle projected revenge.

"Oh. My." Titania's eyes sparkled as she laughed. "What are you planning, little guardian? I think I smell a betrayal."

Clean slate. Her heart pounding, but: clean slate. "Maybe you do. Maybe you're interested."

"Betrayal of the puca. Yes, I might be interested. If you're sincere."

"Do you think I'd be foolish enough to be anything but? You're the faerie queen. I'm mortal. We're alone. If I'm insincere, I'm basically screwed, don't you think?" And that was so completely true. Only a foolish mortal would try to fool a faerie queen, so it was a darn good thing she was only out for revenge. Very excited about revenge, in fact. Could feel her heart racing, her breathing roughening, but it was all out of sheer excitement. Sweet revenge!

"Very screwed." Titania's huge eyes glittered. "Only a fool would try to fool the faerie queen. So, what do you have for me?"

"I have a plan to get even with Kane."

Titania laughed. "Better and better. You seek to get even with Oberon's heir."

Janelle maintained focus. "Oberon's heir? I, um, thought that was Riordan now. Kane was disinherited."

"Well, yes, but since Riordan is mortal, he's not eligible for the throne. The elders ruled on that yesterday and Oberon acquiesced. He hasn't formally reinstated Kane, but I'm sure it's just a matter of time. So, yes, Kane will again be Oberon's heir. And you wish to betray him. His own guardian. This is delicious."

Inhale. Exhale. Inhale. Exhale.

"This makes you nervous?" Titania was even more amused.

"Well, royalty and all. I guess that part of it's nothing really new, though, is it? Kane was always a prince—being Oberon's child and all. Even if it was a love child."

Titania raised an eyebrow, looking annoyed. "Tell me again about the betrayal. What is this plan of yours? Will I like it?"

"I think you might. It serves both our purposes. I believe you're aware of what he did to me eight years ago? And of the inconvenience he represents to me now?" Shoving all else aside, Janelle batted those two offenses back and forth in her mind. Over and over. To the exclusion of any other subject.

"Yes. But you always struck me as such a . . . moral creature."

"Moral doesn't mean self-martyring. I want my life back." Tired, she was so tired of being pawn to a puca's whims. Like he hadn't already used her and broken her heart. He should pay. Why shouldn't he pay? He made everyone else pay. Even now that some justice had been handed down to him, Janelle was being forced to pay right alongside him. Why was she being punished? She'd done nothing wrong, and yet her life would be a wreck before she got rid of him. "I don't deserve to be tied to a puca's penance," she added.

Titania nodded. "I can see your dismay. So, what is this plan of yours?"

Janelle paced slowly, thinking on her feet, her thoughts supremely, intentionally focused. "I bribed one of the Druids for a secret."

The faerie queen stilled. "Bribed a Druid? But, they never tell secrets. I can't even touch their secrets, with mind power or anything else."

Janelle shrugged. "Druids are human. We know each other's weaknesses. And I'm not constrained by the rules of the faerie realm in my personal dealings with them. It just so happens that I had ammunition against one of them, and he shared a secret with me."

"A secret."

"Yes. He said he could cast a spell for me, stripping Kane of his remaining powers, his immortality, all of it. But—"

"A Druid spell?" Titania interrupted.

"Yes. A Druid spell. Enabled by the karmic debt Kane owes me."

"Oh. Yes, that could do it," the queen murmured. Then she glanced suspiciously at Janelle. "But why are you telling me? What do you want?"

"To do this, I need access to another puca. I can't do it on my own, and I can't use strict faerie power. It has to be like power, along with the debt Kane owes me, facilitating the Druid's spell."

"So, you need a puca. One of equal power to Kane," the queen murmured.

"Yes."

"I suppose somebody already told you that Kane and Riordan are the only known pucas in existence."

Janelle focused solely on her quest for a cooperative puca. "Yes, that's what I was told. But surely it's possible there's at least one more. Unless you think you can talk Riordan into betraying his brother. But oddly enough, despite everything the two did to each other, I don't think that's very likely."

Titania began to pace. "Suppose there were another puca. What sort of access to this mysterious third would you need? A simple relaying of instruction? Or something more?"

Janelle's heart began to pound. *Excitement*, she told herself. It was access at last to vengeance. She just wanted revenge. She needed this third puca for revenge against Kane. "In-person access. My Druid friend wishes to remain anonymous, so I'd be the liaison between them. If another puca really exists."

Titania slowly nodded, her eyes distant, almost feverish. "A Druid spell plus karmic imbalance plus puca power. That could work." She started pacing, mind obviously busy as she spoke her thoughts aloud. "I could orchestrate a conception as before. Put a spell on the male every bit as powerful as the one I put on Duncan to create Mina, and kick-start my own little puca war."

The implications shocked Janelle, disrupting her focus and loosing a flood of thoughts and emotions. *Created* Mina? Dear God, Titania was behind all of it: Mina's parentage, the puca brothers' feud—

Titania whirled as Janelle became aware of her tactical error.

"Error is right."

Janelle swallowed, watched that great wellspring of evil reveal every bit of itself. So much for facades.

"You thought to fool me—the Queen of All Faerie? I've outlived civilization as you know it. And you thought to fool me?" Titania backed Janelle up against a tree. "Did you think there would be no consequences?"

"I might have hoped?"

When Titania just smiled, Janelle shivered. She had always thought manga-style illustrations looked mildly demonic. Like the gremlin creatures from that weirdo kids' movie. Cute but creepy.

"And now you insult me? Demonic? Gremlin? Creepy?"

Janelle backpedaled. "Noooooo, more like recognizing your . . . your *depth*. A certain aura of power."

"Evil," Titania corrected.

Yeah, that, too. Aw, shit. "No!"

Titania's eyes darkened. Sparks appeared and began to whirl everywhere. As Janelle braced herself for whatever the hell constituted retaliation, suddenly a masculine bellow interrupted the scene.

"Cease!" Oberon stepped into view, and his eyes, virtually crackling with fury and power, were trained on his wife. Titania stumbled backward, her sparks dissolving. In the face of her husband's fury, she looked almost cautious.

Suddenly, another set of hands grabbed Janelle and shoved her behind a broad back. Kane! Oh, he was going to be pissed off. He'd been right, too. Maybe repeating it in her readable thoughts over and over again would soothe the savage beast.

Not even a little. And Kane furious.

Meanwhile, Oberon had backed down his wife and

was glaring at her. She'd managed to regain her former composure, however. She eyed the faerie king with some amusement.

"So what if I meddled in the love affairs of a couple of pesky humans? Big deal. Hey, it was due to my planning that Mina was conceived and able to grow up to free Riordan. The way I see it, you should be thanking me. I served justice." Her eyes glittered with malice.

"Justice? More like you were moving pawns around, setting my sons against each other."

"Oh, give me a break. They were bred to butt heads from the moment they were conceived. Different mothers, one loved and one not, one son so obviously favored . . ." She was needling him, and it was clearly working. Oberon looked darkly uncomfortable for a moment.

"I had not—"

"You didn't intend to show favoritism?" Titania delicately, pityingly inserted. "Maybe not. But it was there all the same."

"That's done now. My sons are equal in my eyes. And you are pure poison."

"Oh, don't be so melodramatic. I didn't put anything in motion that wasn't already foreseen. Your own sons foresaw most of it anyway. I just wanted to ensure that it was fulfilled." The queen shrugged. "And so it was. Fate didn't question, and my karma is pristine as always."

Oberon glared. "If you'd laid a hand on Janelle—one iota of faerie magic—it would not be."

"You are *so* right." Titania sighed in mock remorse. "My temper. Thank you so much for stopping me. I really must keep a leash on that silly thing." She smiled at Janelle. "My apologies if I frightened you, little guardian. I do hope I would have pulled back before harming you, but I'm glad my husband and stepson—er, formerly recognized stepson—were here to make sure of it."

She waved. "Ta-ta!" And then, with a whirl of sparkles

she was gone. Oberon followed, disappearing in a lightning flash of rage.

"Ooooooh, boy. There's going to be one hell of a marital spat at home tonight." Janelle felt shaken up by the encounter herself.

"And so you should feel shaky," Kane said, staring at her. "Titania might have to defer to karma in a literal sense, but she has many ways around it. She always has. Don't kid yourself. You might have been dead by now. Or worse, wished for death."

"He's right." This from overhead. Breena. The girl hopped down from a concealed branch. "I warned you to stay away from her, too. But did you listen? Oh, no. Why listen to me? What do I know? She's only my mother." Breena made a face. "You realize, of course, that if Kane and Dad hadn't shown up when they did, *I* would have been forced to step in—and I really would prefer to hang out below her radar." She glanced up at the branch. "Or above, I guess you could say."

"Would you have stepped in?" Janelle asked curiously.

"And now an insult, too. Some thanks." Breena rolled her eyes, dismissing Janelle, and turned to Kane. "You're one of my two favorite pucas in the world, but you really have dangerous taste in women."

Kane gave his sister a wry look. "Speaking of pucas and our number in this world, any luck with that search for a third?"

Breena pouted. "Not even a little. Mom has that sycophant assistant of hers tailing me everywhere. It was just chance that I could sneak away today. But Mom's not talking, not about faerie men or human men or anything. At least, not to me. She's acting really paranoid, like she's trying to hide something. Weird, even for her. So I've been searching online, tracing rumors and matching our records to human records, but all I'm finding are dead ends. And the sheer volume of info . . ." Breena shrugged. "I don't know what to tell you."

"Online?" Janelle asked, startled. "Faeries surfing the Internet?"

"Information is information. Although I might be a little handier with the mouse than you." Breena gave her a mischievous look before turning to Kane. "So, want me to keep looking, brother dear?"

He sighed. "Yeah. I'd appreciate it. But don't get yourself in trouble on my account, okay?"

She winked at him before fading into sparkles.

Kane turned back to Janelle. "See? Even Breena fears Titania. With good reason."

Janelle nodded, not doubting it. "I'm afraid to ask, but . . . how could Titania manipulate Duncan and Mina's mom? What would she do, exactly?"

"To make them conceive? A simple love spell would do the trick. No doubt she made Mina's mom utterly irresistible in Duncan's eyes—for a brief period. As for Mina's mom . . . Titania probably ratcheted up the wish Lizzy always cherished to give birth to the child prophesied to free my brother. I'm sure it wasn't difficult. Fate was headed in that direction anyway."

"So it's not an offense in your culture?" Janelle shook her head, perplexed. "Wow. I just don't understand that. It's *wrong*, Kane. Even if things were headed that way, your stepmom had no business manipulating things. And for what reason? To put you and Riordan together in some puca version of a cockfight. She'd been waiting for it to happen and wasn't to be denied. Classy."

Janelle's anger seemed to dampen Kane's, or at least his expression of it. No doubt he was still furious with her, but apparently he could see that she knew very well how stupidly she'd behaved. Thank God he'd shown up when he did. Protective pucas were occasionally very handy. Handsome, kind, protective pucas.

"Oh, just stop it. Kissing ass in your head is still kissing ass," he muttered. But he couldn't hold back a rueful grin.

"Hey, I'm not the only one keeping secrets. Your *heir-ship*. When did that change?"

Kane looked uncomfortable. "It hasn't yet. Not formally. Oberon just told me about the elders' joint opinion. They refuse to accept a mortal as their ruler. So . . ."

"You're not surprised." She eyed him and couldn't help pondering this development. He'd wanted that throne. Never said as much, but giving it up certainly hadn't been an easy gesture for him. And now he had it back. So, either he'd given it an honest shot in the hope that Riordan would be accepted . . . or he'd really been counting on the elders' rejection of Riordan as future king. They'd discussed it before, and maybe Kane really had done it all to gain brownie points for good intentions.

"I'm *disappointed*. Riordan deserves the throne—well, at least to be our father's heir." Kane raised his eyebrows pointedly. "Not that I'll be distracted by royal talk. Do you even realize what a close call this was for you? Titania has powers you can't even imagine."

"Okay, okay. Seeing Titania alone was a dumb move. I admit it. You and your sister warned me. I'll also admit that I have never been so relieved in my life as I was when you and your faerie dad showed up to save my damsel ass. I don't know what Titania was going to do with those sparks, but they sure didn't seem friendly. Still. I'm trying to do what I can. I'm trying to move things forward. Can you at least admit that I came pretty close—"

"To getting yourself killed? Yeah, I heard. Just be grateful. Mina's worry over your safety overrode her discretion, and she told Riordan what you were up to. He called me and Oberon. As for the rest . . ." Kane gave her a dark look, reluctant respect lingering in his eyes. "Okay. I don't like the risk you took, but you were close. You did fool her. Briefly. I could tell by how angry she was. So . . . did she ever say if there was another puca?"

He didn't look hopeful. He knew it would have come up in the conversation with Breena.

"Well, no." Janelle grimaced. "Titania didn't come right out and say there wasn't one, either, but she mostly talked about manipulating the future conception of another puca."

Kane nodded, plainly disappointed. "And that led to the revelation of Mina's conception."

"Basically." Janelle frowned. "But you know, that still doesn't mean there isn't another puca somewhere. I thought it was interesting that her first question was how much contact I would need in order to put my plan in motion. I said I needed to be in direct contact, to act as liaison. That's when she started talking about manipulating the conception of another. Almost as though she'd tried one idea in her mind, found it objectionable and moved on."

Kane was nodding slowly. "So it's just possible that there is a third puca. I suppose I have to hope."

"Dr. Corrington, I need to see you. Immediately." And, unlike his manner the other day, Larry Hoffman, MD, wasn't casual in his request. It was pure command.

Janelle nodded, though he couldn't see her over the phone. "I'm on my way." Silently pondering possibilities, Janelle strode quickly to his office.

Once she'd closed the door behind her, Hoffman rose from behind his desk and took his glasses off. "Dr. Corrington."

"Yes?"

"Janelle." He paused, as though gathering his thoughts. "I had a visit today. From a girl who claims she might never have had stitches. In fact, there's no sign that the knee was ever even injured. And yet she was charged for both the visit and the stitches. Well, her insurance company was charged." He paused and eyed Janelle strangely. "Believe it or not, that's not even the real reason the girl was kicking up a fuss. You see, she claims that not only did she not have stitches but that you secretly removed her beloved—and permanent—tattoo."

"What?" Janelle's heart pounded.

Hoffman laughed shortly. "I told her mother that there's no way you could have removed a permanent tattoo without laser surgery and a significant amount of scarring on the site. Besides which, we don't handle that here. But the daughter insisted I confront you with this."

Janelle gave him a helpless look. "I'm at a loss."

He nodded thoughtfully. "The real issue here, though, are those stitches. It's a real mystery. Even worse, there's a paper trail supporting both the girl's visit and her dispute of the procedure—money paying for the disputed charges actually changed hands, and a claim for such was formally made to the insurance company. What are we going to do about this?"

Janelle just stared, panic beginning to choke her.

After a few strained moments, Hoffman lowered his voice to an intimate tone. "To protect the clinic's reputation and because there was no physical harm done, I covered for you. The girl said you told her they were dissolving stitches, and I backed that up. I said that occasionally, when the skill level is high, they are virtually unnoticeable."

"Did she . . . ?" Janelle swallowed.

"Did she believe me? Yes, both mother and daughter bought that explanation. And, frankly, the mother seemed secretly pleased about the missing tattoo, although I have my doubts that any permanent tattoo ever existed. The point is, I doubt she will make any further noise on the subject. I also verified the suturing procedure with the insurance company. There will be no more questions. They are now very pleased with you and with the clinic, as your record to this point has been unimpeachable."

"Thank you. I—"

"But now *I* need to be satisfied."

Janelle squeezed her eyes closed, cursing inwardly.

Hoffman considered her thoughtfully. "What I need to know is this: Were you trying to swindle the patient, the insurance company or the clinic?"

Janelle's eyes flew open. "Swindle? Nobody. I swear! I *did* help that girl. She came in with a huge gash. I treated her and she's mending. And apparently she's healing very well, too, if she doubts she ever had stitches at all."

"There were no puncture marks, Janelle. When I examined the girl's knee, there was no evidence of any suturing. I didn't tell them that, but you and I both know the marks are unmistakable, especially when they're this fresh. Even if the stitches themselves dissolve. But I just can't understand why the patient and her mother would issue complaints if they were part of your scheme all along and helped fake the girl's injury. Consequently, I believe their confusion is genuine. I think this whole scheme comes back to you. What's your angle? What did you do and what are you trying to gain?"

"No angle. I think . . ." Desperate now, realizing the point Kane had tried to make on the last occasion Hoffman confronted her, she looked into her employer's eyes. Waited. But his gaze didn't connect with hers. He met her eyes but kept his distance even as he continued to speak.

"You have a better explanation? A backup to use in case the first one didn't take?" He eyed her curiously. Doubtfully.

"No, I . . . Look, I wasn't trying to cheat anyone. I care about my job, my patients, this clinic. I would never endanger anyone or act unethically"

"Then what happened with that girl?"

She drew a blank, even as her mind raced.

"As physicians, we are constrained by a strict moral

code . . . " he droned on importantly. As usual, he was clearly more in love with the sound of his own voice than intent on dealing with the issues.

A rational explanation. That's what she needed. Something. Anything. But she didn't have one. She had nothing but the truth.

Don't do it, Janelle.

Kane! she realized, and was filled with gratitude. Maybe he would help. *Where are you?*

Right outside the room.

I'm going to tell him the truth. I have no choice.

It won't work, Kane replied. *Think about it. How are you going to tell him you healed that girl with Druid magic? That you repaired a gash serious enough to need stitches with a simple thought? Will he buy this? He's a scientist, right? He's a doctor, and at heart he's a scientist. He won't buy magic. And remember the tests they'll do on* you.

Janelle tried to picture Hoffman's face while she told him of pucas and Druids, tried to imagine talking him into not sending her to a loony bin or some government test facility. Tried desperately to believe he'd be amazed, impressed, filled with wonder—and psyched to let her practice healing quietly in their little clinic. It just didn't happen. She just kept envisioning pink slips and white jackets with overly long sleeves best worn knotted behind her back. As much as she hated to admit it, Kane was right. The truth would be a bad move with Dr. Hoffman. And any other explanation—

She really had no choice.

Heart in her throat, Janelle tried to catch Hoffman's gaze again. Tried. Waited for the pupil enlargement and constriction that she knew was part of the technique, but she waited in vain. His attention and focus never wavered.

It wasn't working. He wasn't the least bit susceptible to her. He didn't even fall into her gaze as he was supposed to.

Kane, why didn't it work? I did everything that worked last time.

It didn't work because you didn't put your heart into it. It feels wrong to you to glamour him. So you won't let yourself.

That's all? That's why? It's all psychological?

Kane gave a mental sigh. *It's deeper than that. It's at the heart of your character. You believe it's wrong, and won't let yourself open up to him. I was afraid of this. That's why I tried to convince you earlier.*

"Janelle." Hoffman interrupted her thoughts, gave her what he probably believed to be an understanding and very suave look. "I'm willing to be reasonable. I'm willing to let you explain at your own pace. If you need time to think about it a bit . . . why don't you take the afternoon off, get your recollections straight. You can meet me back here at six and . . . and we'll go someplace close for dinner. That way we can discuss this civilly without being overheard or interrupted by co-workers."

You're not buying that line, are you? Kane sounded furious.

I don't have any choice, Kane. I don't buy the line, but maybe I can convince him anyway. He's not completely without reason.

No, but if you go—

Can it, Kane. I have to do this. It's the right thing to do, and I'm doing it.

"I'm sure we can work this out. So . . ." Hoffman smiled, completely confident now. "I'll see you back here at six."

At this rate, Janelle decided later that evening, she wouldn't have to worry about those nonexistent stitches and time in any government institution; she'd be too busy building her legal defense for assault and/or murder. Sad but true, Dr. Hoffman was driving her to it. Kane had been right. Her employer hadn't expressed any demands outright, but he was downright implying that she owed him for his discretion. He seemed to think she should gratefully conclude their working dinner by falling naked into his flabby arms.

". . . And I'm sure we could come to a mutually beneficial solution to this situation."

Yes, she knew what that solution would be—at least in terms of what he wanted. Spineless, manipulative bastard. This excursion had been a mistake from the get-go.

She bared her teeth in a forced smile. "Listen, Larry. I appreciate your cooperative attitude." Gee, what a euphemism. She nauseated herself with the PC. "I'm hoping you can turn that toward evaluating my work at the clinic. I'm a good doctor. You know that. My patient list is growing by the day. I've had no other complaints—"

Hoffman gave a slimy little laugh. "Okay, I'll be honest, Janelle. I didn't ask you to dinner to discuss work. I don't consider your job to be in jeopardy. Frankly, now that I intervened"—*hey, don't bust your arm patting yourself on the back,* she didn't say—"we're in a better position professionally than we were before. The patient's happy. I'm happy. Everyone is satisfied. As long as no further questions are raised, all is well. As for tonight . . . as I think you've guessed, I'm strongly attracted to you."

"Dr. Hoffman . . ." Janelle felt the sudden and nearly irresistible urge to flee.

"Call me crazy, but I think you feel the chemistry, too." Leaning forward, he grabbed her hands and held them even as she discreetly resisted. "I know you've been fighting it out of respect for our working relationship, but there's no need. We're adults. We can—"

Her patience ended. "No. We can't." With a less-than-discreet yank, Janelle freed her hands, grabbed her purse and slid her chair back. Furious at his attempts to strong-arm her, she rifled through her bag for cash and tossed a couple bills on the table to pay for the dinner she hadn't eaten. "Consider this me calling you crazy.

What we have is purely a working relationship. Nothing else. And I resent you even bringing up the subject."

Her cell phone buzzed in her pocket, drawing immediate attention. At first she thought it might be Kane, but then she realized he probably would have just shown up and spoken into her mind if it was. And he'd seemed pretty angry when she'd decided to go to dinner with Hoffman and left him at the apartment. No, it wouldn't be him.

Neither she nor Dr. Hoffman was on call tonight, but a doctor didn't just turn off and tune out. And it was the clinic on the phone, she saw from the display. It was after hours, true, but occasionally some of the staff stayed late to catch up on paperwork. Janelle flipped it open and put the phone to her ear.

"This is Dr. Corrington."

It was Cindy. "Janelle! Oh, my God. You've got to get over here. Someone—some*thing*—is tearing up the waiting room and . . . Oh, my God."

"Are you alone?" Janelle asked, her heart pounding in her chest. "Get out of there!"

"I can't. I'm trapped in the back. I tried to call the cops, but I couldn't get through. You're on my speed dial and you're the first person to pick up."

Janelle grabbed her things. She hoped this didn't have anything to do with the puca. "I'm on my way. Five minutes." Thank God they'd chosen a restaurant close to work. Too damn bad they'd chosen to walk. She growled at Dr. Hoffman, "Come on, Romeo. Emergency at the clinic. Sounds like all hell's broken loose." She just hoped it wasn't puca inspired. She wished, tonight of all nights—*really* wished, given her evening—that she hadn't been so short with Kane earlier.

A little over five minutes later, Janelle was hurrying across the parking lot of the clinic. Dr. Hoffman, hampered by the spare tire of fat encircling his self-satisfied, middle-aged middle, huffed along at a distance behind her.

Just as she rounded the corner and reached the main door, a figure rushed past, arm swinging wide. An elbow connected with her chin, and Janelle stumbled backward, holding her jaw and blinking.

"Sorry. Accident." The voice was slurred. And . . . familiar?

"Tremayne!"

He gave her a dazed look, seemed to stagger, then vanished, just before Dr. Hoffman came distantly into view. What in the world? Oh, this was going to be so bad. She could just tell.

CHAPTER FIFTEEN

Stunned and shaking off the ache in her jaw, Janelle carefully pushed through the front door of the clinic. The glass had been shattered, obviously to allow entry. Inside, she glanced around the silent waiting room. The place was completely trashed: chairs overturned, broken glass everywhere, instruments and supplies scattered on the hallway floor, blood—

Blood? Holding her breath, Janelle followed the obscene trail to find Cindy sitting in a shadowy corner between exam rooms. She appeared dazed, with one arm tucked close under the bulk of her sweater. The garment was darkly stained.

"Cindy?"

The nurse shifted her attention and glanced up. "Janelle. Thank God. Is it gone?"

"Is what gone?" Janelle didn't really want to know. Gently she raised Cindy to her feet and half-carried her into the exam room where she boosted the nurse onto a table. Groaning, Cindy gingerly lay down. Blood soaked the side of her scrubs from neck to midthigh. Janelle braced herself but kept her voice calm. "Let me see what we're dealing with here."

"I've been applying pressure."

Janelle almost smiled at the nurse's practiced calm. Cindy was damn near bleeding to death but still coherent, still diagnosing, still updating the doctor. What a trooper.

"It was a monkey, Janelle. An honest-to-God chimpanzee busted through the door and started tearing up the clinic." Cindy shuddered. "And he had this horrible hammer-hatchet thingie. It looked like a carpenter's tool."

"A monkey? Loose? With a hatchet?" *No. Oh, no.* Until a month ago she would have assumed this to be a hallucination due to trauma or blood loss. Now . . . now, she couldn't help but recall Kane's prank the first time he shape-shifted in front of her—into a chimpanzee. And wielding a carpenter's tool? She vaguely recalled Riordan mentioning missing tools when Mina's house was vandalized. That would connect the two events. Which would be bad. Very bad.

Janelle cleared her throat and tried to sound natural. "How could that be? Is the zoo really that close?"

"I don't know. I called you just before he came at me, and I was going to try the police again, but then my phone was gone and the blood—"

Cindy winced and cried out. Janelle was lifting the balled-up sweater Cindy had pressed to her wound. Janelle stared in horror. The damage was far beyond what she'd expected.

"The monkey. It's like it was possessed. I would swear it even laughed and talked while it went, throwing and smashing things." Cindy was almost babbling now, probably to block out the pain and shock. "And I wasn't hurt yet, so it wasn't a hallucination. It was like a monster, really, slashing right and left with that wicked hatchet thing." The nurse paused, gritting her teeth. "And eventually, that side of the hallway was right and I—my shoulder, my arm—was left. And after he cut me down, he just kept going."

Cindy's upper arm and shoulder were sliced all the way to the bone. Her assailant had laid her open from collarbone to upper arm and, given the way the bones appeared out of line and the way Cindy held her upper body, the clavicle and scapula were probably fractured. The humerus . . . Cindy's whole upper arm was shattered. Only multiple surgeries and screws and a hell of a lot of luck would restore full use of her arm. And then only after a long, painful rehabilitation.

Janelle trembled as she took stock. It was a miracle Cindy had remained conscious. A miracle also that the arm was still attached. Only flesh and skin and compromised bone held it together. And dear God, what if the blow had been six inches higher? What if it had struck her neck or head? Cindy could be dead right now. Janelle couldn't think, could only feel. The doctor was gone. All gone. And right now Cindy's arm—the nurse's future, her lifestyle, her ability to hug her own children—was in her hands.

Janelle's breath caught in her throat. She'd never wanted this. She'd never set herself up for this. That's why she'd become a general practitioner in the first place, damn it, in spite of her technical skills, in spite of the mentor and instructors who'd tried to steer her toward her strengths. But a surgeon's job—their recommendation—would have been her worst nightmare. She couldn't handle facing, possibly every day, the prospect of someone dying on her table. As her mother had died on some other surgeon's table.

But Cindy, a single mom with five-year-old twin girls and a mischievous three-year-old boy who already showed a love for tree climbing—They needed their mother, needed a fully functional, happy, healthy mother. They deserved that, and if Janelle could give that to them . . .

The odds were against Cindy dying if Janelle acted quickly. And she would pray like hell for the arm. This was something that would really tax her power, but it was also exactly what her power was made for. Shaking and only a little reassured, Janelle reached for the nurse's limb with every part of her being, thinking of no one and nothing but the injury.

But what if she failed? What if Cindy lost the arm? Her friend, a nurse, with her skilled hands and kids to coddle . . .

Touching the nurse, she felt Cindy's pain slam into her, nearly buckling her knees. Near unconsciousness tugged at Janelle's awareness, and she wavered. She fought past the agony, past the fog, through the panic, and she focused.

"Oh, my God. Cindy. What happened here?" Dr. Hoffman peered over Janelle's shoulder. *Wonderful.* "What the hell?" His voice was hoarse. "Janelle?"

Swaying, Janelle opened her eyes in time to see Cindy's eyes flutter open on a groan. Bracing herself, Janelle looked down at the nurse's wound. It had healed, leaving only a long, pink line surrounded by smears of fresh blood.

"Is this . . ." Dr. Hoffman's voice had risen high and thin. He cleared his throat and began again, but was trembling now with shocked fury. "Is this some kind of sick joke? I could have your license for this!"

"No. Not a joke." Janelle glanced sharply at him. But her eyes were drawn inexorably to Cindy, who watched Janelle with exhausted gratitude. And more than a little awe.

"Janelle? How did you—"

"Shhhh. Just stay calm." Quaking inwardly, Janelle could only wonder herself. That much blood. That kind of injury. Surely Cindy needed follow-up care. They couldn't just send her home alone as though nothing major had happened. But this was Druidic magic. This was a miracle. This was . . . inexplicable.

Dr. Hoffman glanced from Janelle to Cindy and back

again. "Dr. Corrington. A meeting in my office. Five minutes."

Janelle inhaled deeply, hoping to restore her composure. "Make it twenty and I'm there." She spared him a glance. "This is not a joke. I'll . . . look, I'll try to explain. Just give me a few minutes to see to my patient, please."

Dr. Hoffman raised an eyebrow, then turned sharply on his heel. He was headed toward the reception desk. "I'm writing a note for reception to have all of your appointments canceled until further notice."

"But—"

"My office. Twenty minutes." He turned and strode down the hallway.

Oh, shit. True, he shouldn't be able to cancel her appointments like that, not without consulting the other partners, but the man had her in a bit of a tight situation. He'd seen too much. Right before his eyes, unquestionable evidence that a woman had recently suffered traumatic injury, which Janelle had obviously treated without using a single, standard, acceptable medical procedure. She'd spontaneously healed a woman using sheer magic (read: quackery) that no respectable, science-based medical clinic could condone. Yep, spun the wrong way, this story really could mean investigation and possible revocation of her license.

"You've been keeping secrets." Cindy's thready voice drew Janelle's attention.

"I . . . yeah. Sort of." A reluctant smile was tugged from her, because she was glad the gift had done something wonderful. Cindy closed her eyes a moment, still catching her breath. As she did, Janelle reached with one hand, saw that it was smeared liberally with blood, and retracted it. She tugged her coat up slightly to find a tuft of clean material and dabbed at the tear tracks on Cindy's face. "I bet that hurt like hell."

"You *know* it did." Cindy opened her eyes. "I felt you feel it." Her gaze was both probing and wondering. "I

don't know how you did what you did. But I know it was
you. Inside me somehow."

Janelle blinked. "You felt that?"

"In my arm. And in my head, just a little."

"Oh. That's not good."

"Speak for yourself." Cindy raised her once-injured
arm, carefully moving the fingers. They cooperated,
which seemed to fascinate her. "Even the tendons and
muscles. The bone itself. Everything. You didn't just
make the bleeding stop and the gash go away. This . . . I
couldn't move any of this a few minutes ago. Now look
at me."

And Janelle did, almost as dazzled as Cindy. "That's . . .
God, I'm so glad." She shook her head. "I swear, I saw
you here, saw your arm like that and forgot I was a doctor. I didn't have a clue what to do. Just . . . instinct." And
it had been a purely magical instinct to use her Druidic
healing. Which, now that the crisis had mostly passed,
was again scaring the hell out of her. She'd abandoned all
of her training, her composure, her skills as a physician,
in favor of a magical gift that was an impossibility.

"You're a miracle. You could heal the dying and the
incurable. Become rich and famous. We can call the me-
dia: the newspapers, television, medical journals—"

"No!" Janelle panicked, then lowered her voice to a
more moderate tone. "We can't do that. Nobody would
believe me. Or you. They'd call me a quack. They'd say I
was deceiving patients, endangering their health by using unapproved medical practices, then scamming them
by taking money from them for my so-called services.
I'd lose my license to practice medicine. And then where
would I be? In jail for fraud. Even if I proved this wasn't
fraud, I'd just be put on display as the next big circus
freak."

Cindy stared at her. "But you can't just bury this ability. It's amazing. When did you start doing this? Have
you always been able to do it? How can I help?" Avoiding

Janelle's restraining hands, Cindy raised herself on her healthy elbow, hugging her newly healed arm close. "Hell, you could open up your own clinic, call it alternative medicine and simply be mysterious. We could wow everyone while you healed impossible cases. I'd be your nurse, of course, because I know better than anyone how . . ." Her words slurred and she swayed. "Oh. I'm a little light-headed." She closed her eyes and rolled onto her back again.

"Blood loss." Janelle eyed her with concern. "You need fluids and rest."

"But we need to talk about this. This is amazing. Momentous. The things you could accomplish—"

"I know. Believe me, I know. But you've suffered trauma. You need to recover."

"But—"

"Rest now, talk later. I promise." Seeing the mutinous glint in Cindy's eyes, Janelle narrowed her own. "You're a nurse, Cindy. Suppose you had yourself for a patient right now. What would you be recommending?"

"That's not fair."

"It's exceptionally fair. Now lie still while I decide what to do with you."

"What do you mean?"

"Well, I can't keep you here. I'll have enough explaining to do without Dr. Romeo examining you for evidence."

Cindy raised her eyebrows. "So, he made a pass at you, too? The man just can't keep his hands to himself."

Janelle scowled but refused to let the subject be changed. "Look, I know your arm is going to be fine, but I can't in good conscience just send you home. I don't know for sure that you're in any condition to be alone. Shock, emotional and physical trauma, flashbacks, blood loss." She just shook her head. "And I can't send you to a hospital, which I'd prefer to do, because a hospital wouldn't take you without explanations."

"Just call my mom. She can come stay with me and the kids. No questions asked."

Cindy's mom was a nurse, too. That might be the best option. "All right. But I'll want to keep tabs on you."

"No problem."

"And you can't tell people about this."

"Wouldn't say a word."

You can't rely on that, Janelle.

Janelle jumped. She had thought she'd first felt Kane's presence when she entered the clinic, but she wasn't sure and had almost hoped against it; she didn't want any more evidence that he might have been involved. He'd remained silent. When she'd frozen to stare helplessly at Cindy's wound, she'd felt his presence strengthen. It had been a warmth. A reminder of power. Her power. It had been deliberate, she was sure. Otherwise, he'd stayed in the background, she supposed in order to let her make her own decisions whether to wield her—*their*—magic.

Where are you, Kane?

I'm just outside the door.

The door ... Her thoughts sharpened in renewed memory. *Kane, I saw Tremayne just outside the clinic when I arrived. He seemed dazed and then he just disappeared. Do you suppose he did this? Is he the one framing you? Out of revenge or some vigilante justice or something?*

Silence. *It's possible. I'll have to follow up. But we have more urgent concerns right now. Cindy. You know she won't be able to help herself. She'll have to tell someone what happened. Someone she trusts not to tell. But then that someone will tell someone they trust not to tell ... and soon you'll have rumors. We'll have rumors. We can't have rumors.*

You want me to glamour.

Yes. I know how you feel about that, and I know you have great respect for this woman, but you have no choice.

But—

She also has the horrific memory of a chimpanzee willfully vandalizing this clinic. Even talking and laughing. That's too odd not to raise questions. Besides which, she's going to have night-mares, and her mind is going to reject this all at some point.

Like the Druid?

Maybe not as badly. This wasn't a puca ride. But there would be some damage. When reality and expectation are so completely divergent . . .

He was right. Again, damn it.

You understand that it's not that I like to be right. Well, not exclusively.

You're trying to humor me. Or worse, kiss up. It won't work. We still need to have a chat about that chimp. I've seen you do *chimp.*

Apparently somebody else has too. Or else they pulled that memory from your mind.

Tell me you had nothing to do with this.

His voice in her mind sounded disappointed. *Would I slice off Cindy's arm, Janelle? Do you honestly believe—*

Oh, God, of course not. She didn't know how she'd ever considered it, now that she'd actually heard the question put into words. It wasn't in his nature. Part of her knew his nature as well as she knew her own. *You wouldn't de-liberately hurt anyone. But—*

She frowned, as something else finally registered. There had been magic performed here. And it was defi-nitely puca magic. But—she shook her head—it was off, somehow. Like at Mina and Riordan's.

How could it be puca? There was only Kane. And he wouldn't do it.

Or would he? Was she being seduced by her knowl-edge of him, by the attraction she felt to him? Wasn't that what Phil had warned? Maybe Kane had acted, knowing he could rely on her to heal his victim? Maybe he'd been trying to expose Janelle, punishing her for disagreeing earlier and forcing her to use a glamour when she didn't want to. Maybe he was punishing her for going out with—

No! She wouldn't believe that. An accident, then? He'd

shown up, did the damage, expecting only property to be at risk? But even that felt wrong. There was no logic to it. And it was just—

Damn it, he was innocent. She believed that with all her heart.

Thank you for that much. But Kane managed to sound deeply offended. *Quite the vote of confidence, if it took you a while to get there. So generous of you to admit that I wouldn't terrorize and nearly maim an innocent woman.*

Okay, okay, I get it already. You didn't do it. See? This is why you shouldn't walk in people's heads. If you'd kept your nose out of my thoughts, you could have avoided all the arguing that led to my conclusion. Now that we have that conclusion, we need to find out who's really behind what happened here.

Yes. We do. But first we have something else we need to handle.

Janelle groaned inwardly. The idea of walking through a friend's head without permission was truly repugnant.

You must.

Yeah, I get it. Do you mind keeping it down while I try to concentrate?

"Janelle? You're so quiet. Like I said, I think this healing touch of yours is the coolest thing in the world. A miracle."

"Yeah. A miracle." And she couldn't begrudge the miracle, given Cindy's limb, but the complications were, well, complicated.

She looked into the nurse's eyes. Held her gaze. The pupils enlarged, constricted, enlarged more. Cindy was open to suggestion now.

God, Kane, what do I say. I didn't even rehearse—

Tell her a human burglar broke into the clinic.

"Cindy, it wasn't a monkey in the clinic with you. An adult human male broke in and started busting up chairs in the waiting room. He was saying—" *What was he saying, Kane? Quick.*

You just had to go into detail. He was saying . . . something about insurance, maybe?

"He was blaming the insurance companies for the health care crisis." That made no sense. "No, *doctors*. He's blaming doctors for squeezing insurance companies." She narrowed her eyes. "It's just possible that he really hates Dr. Hoffman."

Janelle, no! Think of that karma.

Like Hoffman's karma is pristine?

I'm only worried about yours.

Janelle scowled. So much for that. *This is why I shouldn't be walking in somebody else's head, puca.* "Scratch that. He doesn't know any of the doctors here. He just saw the clinic, flew into a rage. He hates all doctors, not just Dr. Hoffman. Seemed nuts. On drugs maybe. Possibly was even looking for drugs.

"See, now that's a more likely scenario. Some idiot broke in, looking for drugs, couldn't get at them, got angry . . ." She glanced around, looked outside. "Saw people approaching and took off. Those people were Dr. Hoffman and me. Okay?"

Now, the healing part. You must conceal that, too.

Which ought to be fun. "He cut your arm, but it was a shallow wound." She pondered a moment. "And it will look normal to you. You'll keep it covered for a week, especially at work. And you'll take care of yourself, treat yourself as you would a patient who suffered blood loss and trauma. But you won't describe it as such to anyone." She frowned. "And the human who broke in here and did this had a bloody nose. A really bloody nose."

Oh, good grief.

Well, I have to account for the sheer volume, don't I? "Okay, he actually sliced himself open. Accidentally. No, that won't work, because the blood could be tested by the cops. You won't concern yourself with the amount of blood. It's inconsequential only on this occasion." In fact, Janelle would mop it up herself. She would launder the scrubs Cindy was wearing and give her something clean to wear to her mom's house.

You're getting better at this. Soon you'll be a natural.

Kane's remark infuriated her. To be good at feeding pretense to another human being by manipulating her mind? Bleh. "Lying to her sucks. Doctors shouldn't lie to their nurses, and doctors shouldn't try to strong-arm their colleagues into having sex with them. Ethics. It's all ethics. If you break down at one spot, you'll break down at another."

Janelle—

"Chauvinistic bullies like Larry Hoffman should have their penises chopped off and fed to them. God knows how many times he's harassed Cindy. If it weren't for—"

Stop!

"Oh, I'm done. Cindy, wake up."

The nurse blinked and sat straight. "You chopped off Dr. Hoffman's penis and fed it to him? I won't say he doesn't deserve it, especially if his nuts were on drugs." Cindy frowned, looking confused.

Kane!

She heard the puca sigh. *Just leave it alone. She's too loyal to you to say anything about the doctor stuff to anyone else, and it will fade anyway because it confuses her.*

Right. Okay. "Can you tell me what happened here?"

Cindy looked around. "A man broke in. I can't remember what he looked like. Just . . . he kept ranting about health insurance and squeezing doctors." She lowered her voice. "I think he was on drugs. That's probably what he was looking for."

"A druggie looking for a fix." Janelle nodded, wanting this to stick. It was a sufficient explanation. "Did he get any?"

"N-no. No, he didn't. That's why he was so mad. He started tearing up the place. And then he did this." She raised her arm. "It's just a scratch. I'll be fine but I think

I need lots of rest and fluids. My mom will help. Did you call her?"

"I will. After we get a change of clothes for you, though. Let me help you."

It was another half hour before Janelle found her way to Dr. Hoffman's office. She'd had to get Cindy cleaned up and settled in her mom's car, then quickly clean up the blood on the floor without disturbing anything else. Then she'd taken a quick look around—for fur or telltale chimp evidence—before making that dreaded walk down the hallway.

She'd have to glamour Larry, too, she realized. While her complaint about glamouring someone being disrespectful no longer concerned her as much, she didn't like the idea of walking around in a mind as filthy as his. Frowning, Janelle opened the door to his office and found him seated at his desk.

He looked up. "Where's Cindy?"

"I sent her home with her mother. She's a nurse, too, so Cindy will be in good hands."

"Good. So, just tell me. What the hell happened out there? What did I see?"

Janelle caught his gaze with her own, watched the pupils.

Which didn't budge.

She stared harder, felt her stomach heave and nearly stumbled backward. *It feels like a sickly heave in the belly. . . .* A sudden memory of Kane's words ran through her mind.

"Janelle? Are you ill?"

No, but she was going to be. It hadn't worked. It wouldn't work—no, *shouldn't* work, according to karmic rules. That belly heave Kane once described . . .

Kane? Are you there?

I heard.

Larry was staring at her. Hard. He said, "Look, I don't know what was going on out there, and so far you haven't explained a damn thing to my satisfaction. Whatever it was, whatever you did . . . it wasn't medicine. It wasn't natural. What's going on?"

So glamour was out. She'd have to try the logical, happy-ending-justifies-any-spooky-means argument. "Does it matter so much? Honestly? Cindy's fine now. Isn't that the whole point?"

"This is a medical clinic, not a freak show. We do things by the book here. What you did . . ." He seemed shaken. "Look, I'll just go straight for the bottom line. Are you going to tell me what happened out there?"

Janelle paused, but then said, "No. I can't."

Dr. Hoffman took a deep breath. "I've seen too many tragedies where critically ill patients have been cheated of life or limb by quackery. They're terrified or desperate and they think poking needles into their foreheads or smelling pretty candles will cure them of cancer. Next they'll be coming to you with your weirdo crap." He took a shaky breath. "You'll treat them and afterward they'll believe they're cured. Hell, maybe you'll believe it, too. And then what if you're wrong? What if they die when traditional medicine could have saved them or offered them a few precious months? What then, *Doctor* Corrington? Well, I won't have that here. Not at my clinic."

Janelle was shocked. "What are you saying? You're firing me?" He couldn't be. He wouldn't. But he clearly intended something.

"No, I'm still of the opinion that you shouldn't have been hired in the first place. You lack the experience the rest of us have and I question your background. You've dabbled in this sort of thing before. I was worried that you would try it again. What you did here tonight convinces me I was right to question you. You're a seemingly responsible, hardworking person and the other partners have seen that. I would have a hard time convincing them to fire you. They didn't see what I saw or feel what I feel. But that doesn't mean I can't have you investigated—as you should be investigated. What went on out there would have to be pursued. Unless . . ." He raised a hand, no doubt to gesture, but at its obvious trembling he laid it back on the desk.

"Unless what?"

He carefully folded his hands and met her eyes. "Unless you just walked away. You do that, just turn around and walk away from this place, and I won't say a word about what I saw."

"I can't do that." She shook her head and backed toward the door. "No, I can't leave. I just began my professional career and . . . no one else would hire me if I left now. I couldn't practice."

"Your chances of any career in traditional medicine would be even worse if I started an investigation. Tell me, Dr. Corrington. What would we find if we investigated? I hope you don't have anything in your past that you don't want dredged up."

She would be a one-woman freak show. Her life would turn into a circus. Everything would happen exactly as she'd feared, and who knew what the ultimate consequences would be? And Kane. She had a feeling the Druids would penalize Kane for this—for not talking her into using her glamour correctly.

But, if she left, if she walked out of here right now, her very silence would draw suspicion. Larry's silence would damn her, too. So she was finished. One way or the other, she was finished.

Janelle . . .

I have no choice . . . other than begging? Seeking compassion? "Obviously, you know you've put me in an untenable position. Lose-lose, and no choice whatsoever."

Dr. Hoffman looked unmoved. "I didn't do this. You did."

"Was I supposed to let her lose the arm?"

Her employer looked away. "I will say it again. This is a traditional and respected medical clinic, with traditional, trained physicians practicing proven, science-based methods of modern medicine." He paused, then grudgingly continued. "Unscientific methods of healing might have their place"—his tone said he clearly doubted as much—"but I guarantee you it's not here."

Why couldn't I glamour him, Janelle pondered. *Why?*

It's karma in action. Sure, Hoffman's a jerk with a hefty debits column, but he's also a human who genuinely thinks he's doing the right thing in this case. So we can't touch him with magic. Remember the whole checks and balances system protecting the weaker species from the more powerful magic wielders? Consider yourself checked. Kane sounded sad.

But he's blackmailing me now. Surely that screws with his karma.

"Even if our moral and ethical standards relaxed sufficiently to let you continue with your experimental practices," Hoffman droned on, "I guarantee you the insurance companies would all have a fit. I mentioned this before. Malpractice premiums would go through the roof. Health insurance companies would have to reclassify us and possibly remove us from their list of providers. That would hurt us and our patients."

Sure, the blackmailing would affect his karma, except his intentions here are mostly pure. He's doing what he believes is a good deed, using the only means available to him. Everything may have started out as a personal beef with you, but in this instance, his perspective has shifted from personal goals to a higher one. The greater good, as he sees it. You're a wild card, one the clinic can't afford in his opinion. He's protecting his patients as well as his reputation and the reputation of the clinic. It's responsible to fire a doctor who heals with a touch.

Responsible, but not logical. Not right.

In his own way, he is right. We apparently can't fight that.

But I'm right, too!

Yes, but erasing his memory, eliminating his purpose, is not. That's why you can't glamour him. You could override the check, but it would be unwise. As I know.

But you're the one who wanted me to glamour him before. You apparently thought it would work.

I think it would have then. But circumstances have changed. Unlike before, your Dr. Hoffman isn't out to trap you this time so much as to do the right thing by his patients. For once his heart is in the right place. Ironic, I know.

Great. So she was foiled by yet another newborn conscience. More irony. Although, she supposed her own hesitation to glamour Hoffman in the past played a role in this, too. If she'd glamoured him when Kane pushed for it, she might have avoided this. Was she right to hesitate before? Was she wrong? God help her, she still didn't know.

Reluctantly, she turned back to Larry, who had fallen uncharacteristically silent. He was watching her closely, as though fascinated and repelled at the same time.

Janelle gestured aimlessly. "I guess I'll leave, then. Can I count on you for a reference at least? I haven't been here a year yet. Leaving is bad enough. Leaving without a reference is career suicide."

Larry was already shaking his head. "I'm sorry. I am. But I cannot associate my name with yours in any way. You've proven yourself a fringe element, and I have my career and the reputation of this clinic and its other physicians to consider. I can't give you a reference."

"So that's it then. That's just it." She was through.

"I'm afraid so. I wish it could be different." But his tone suggested otherwise. This was exactly what he wanted. How convenient for him that it also seemed the right thing to do.

She wondered if he'd still be so determined that she leave if she'd slept with him as he'd pressured her to do. Given the repulsed part of his expression, she'd wager he was relieved he'd never had a go at her. The other part, however, seemed downright intrigued. Perhaps the man was yet corruptible.

Just drop that line of thought. Now. I'm trying to be good and let you handle this yourself, but if he puts one hand on you, I won't be responsible for my actions.

Maybe if I hadn't turned him down so brutally.

You were no more brutal than he deserved. Don't blame yourself for this. He's always had an agenda. Yes, you are part of it, but you threaten him, his beliefs and his livelihood. He wants you gone. He might have liked to use you first, but you'd still be gone eventually.

I suppose you're right. She focused on Dr. Hoffman, who was still speaking.

". . . And we can mail the check to you as soon as it's cut. So. We're through here, then?" He stood up with a casual smile, as though he'd just rearranged their meeting schedule instead of successfully edging her out of her career.

Devastated, Janelle didn't respond, just turned and left his office.

Letting the door swing shut behind her, she rushed down the hall. As she turned the corner, she felt a familiar hand slide around her back, tugging her close to the shelter of a hard, warm body. Feeling needy and really hating that about herself, she leaned into Kane's strength and let him lead her down the empty, littered halls and out the door. Then he settled her in the passenger seat of her car and rounded the vehicle to sit in the driver's seat.

Not questioning anything, she just closed her eyes and shut out the world.

Glancing briefly at his silent passenger, Kane directed the car back to Janelle's apartment, even as his mind, heart and less refined body parts warred with each other. He knew what he had to do. He knew what he wanted to do. The two paths were one and the same until the very end, where they diverged sharply.

He loved Janelle with every fiber of his being. Maegth had foreseen that, canny Druid that she was. Leaving Janelle would be the hardest thing he'd ever done, harder even than the first time. Unfortunately, that was exactly what he had to do—but not before he released her from a promise she shouldn't have been forced to make in the first place.

He knew one sure way of doing that, one way that would sever the agreement and release her from his guardianship duty for good: sex.

Okay, so technically he could just walk away from her without breaking the guardianship bond. But she would always feel that bond, always feel obligated. That unrelenting, to-hell-with-self honor code of hers.

This was a lie, too. Sure, she would feel the obligation unless he took it from her, but he wasn't thinking of her good, only of his. No surprise there. The fact that his physical wants and her honor-driven needs coincided just gave him tacit permission to shamelessly take what he wanted so badly. What he'd been fighting for days now.

Of course, what he really wanted wasn't just sex. Not really. Okay, so he wanted the sex. He wasn't a saint. And he knew exactly how good it would be with Janelle. But damn it, he also wanted more, so much more than that.

He wanted to make sweet love to her, so sweet and so consuming that she would forget that he'd ever hurt her, that anyone had ever hurt her. To make her forget that he would—because he had to—hurt her yet again. He wanted to make her forget anything but pleasure and what they could be to each other. And then he wanted to stay with her forever. Never lose her.

But he couldn't have forever with her. He saw it as clearly as he saw anything. And despite that, tonight he could and would say a very thorough good-bye—thus proving, for anyone who might have doubted it before, that Kane Oberon was still the selfish sonovabitch he'd always been.

Chapter Sixteen ❧

Janelle drifted in and out of wakefulness, her thoughts and fears and dreams braiding into an ugly length of nightmare poised to whip her for the rest of her life. She'd sought escape from reality only to find worse in her dreams, then sought to wake from her dreams only to ponder a terrifying future. Again and again she repeated this cycle, until . . .

Until a new and welcome body slipped into her bed. Until a soothing touch brushed her with sweet thoughts and warm lips. Long, soulful kisses told of love and appreciation, of admiration and reassurance. She would survive this, just as she'd survived everything before. She wasn't alone now. Even if she felt alone in the future, she never would be. Not really. She would always have him. Kane would watch over her always, see to her happiness and safety, no matter the cost to himself.

Their kisses grew fierce and Janelle opened to them, welcoming the brutality. She wanted him, only him, had only ever wanted Kane.

She opened her eyes to darkness, lit only by the warm gold of Kane's eyes near hers. "Hi." He lowered his mouth to hers again, lips teasing, plucking, clinging. Wanting her and needing her. Loving her, so much and so long. "I thought we'd test out that definition. You know, dance around home base a few times."

"Kane," she breathed. She felt his familiar arousal beating at her, heating her from within until her own need threatened to devour her.

He slanted his mouth across hers and did the honors. He delved deep, even as his awareness rocked her very foundation. He'd always loved her. Always. Wanted never to leave.

"Then don't." She groaned, amused, but then flinched as her nerve endings twanged, one after the other, beneath his touch. He'd removed her coat, was plucking at the buttons down her shirt, the straps of her bra. Fingers, long and rough, slid into the cups to lift her breasts.

He dipped his head, taking a tip into his mouth. *Sweet, so sweet.* Their thoughts echoed each other, and Janelle cried out.

"Yeah, just like that." He whispered against damp skin, his breath tickling, raising goose bumps, before he turned his attention to her other breast. And Janelle found sweet relief, sweet joy of all things, especially after—

"Shhhh. None of that. More of this." Kane drew on her nipple, tugging it deep in his mouth, and Janelle felt a keening ache all the way to her core. As she arched under his mouth, he tugged the blouse off her shoulders, but left the sleeves to trap her arms to her sides. Then, with a smile she could feel both in her mind and against sensitive skin, Kane abandoned the material. He let tricky fingers wander deliberately over tender flesh and sensitive ribs.

"Hey!" A reluctant laugh came as Janelle, half-bound in her sleeves, shifted helplessly to avoid the ticklish caress. He was driving her crazy!

Next his mouth drifted low and nibbled on those same hypersensitive spots. When she squirmed more, he only grinned. "Sometimes it pays to walk around in-side a person's head," he suggested.

"Oh, *bad*." She broke off on a gasp as he drew deli-cately on flesh just below her rib cage.

His fingers slid lower, trailing exquisite pangs across sensitive flesh. Her belly, her hips. Her pants loosened. "Kane? Careful. We shouldn't—"

"Mmmm. But I must." He murmured this against her lowest rib, the vibrations drawing keening sounds from her throat as they arrowed low and intimately. When had God connected the rib cage to the pelvic nerves, any-way? And who'd forgotten to tell Janelle? Damn medical school.

Male laughter followed as Kane trailed his lips lower yet. He paused to teethe lightly at the skin covering her hip. Gasping, she flinched and arched away, even as she felt a slip of material slide low on her hips, thighs, briefly hang up on toes, then whisper away. Her panties. She felt his hands sliding high along naked thighs, separat-ing—

Naked? But they couldn't . . . What if he didn't stop in time?

Fingers delved deep, scattering her thoughts. Warm, wet, slick. Janelle could feel the exquisite probing and yet feel her own flesh under his fingertips. Her pleasure, his, combining and heating and increasing. The pres-sure built inside both of them. She heard her own pant-ing breath echoed by Kane's, as his wicked fingers pressed deep in a rhythm he plucked from her fantasies. Carefully, deliberately, he adjusted the angle.

"Ohhhhh." She lost her breath in a whoosh. "Not. Fair."

"Mmmmmmmmmmm." He was vibrating the tension higher.

"Gah! You can't!" Oh, she wanted. Him. Deep. Now. Hard. Fast. She felt so empty. So hungry. So alone.

Not alone.

Sheets rustled as his chest and belly slid higher, the warmth and friction exquisite with anticipation until . . . Filled. She was filled. Oh, good. It was *so* good.

"Yes." He groaned, lifting her legs to wrap around his hips as he arched and drove yet deeper, stretching and filling. She felt his length, felt her own muscles taking him even deeper, milking him.

Kane groaned. He wanted her arms—

"Then release them, damn it!" Janelle cried out, and she felt him lift her hips on a thrust, loosing the material so she could slide her arms free of the sleeves.

She circled her arms around his neck and pulled him close, wanting to wrap all of herself around all of him. Dragging him down for a kiss, she slanted her mouth across his as he licked into hers and explored. They shared surfaces, textures, tastes. Mirrored and mingling. And she could feel him feeling her. Enveloped and enveloping. It was driving her crazy. Lifted her hips as he thrust, seeking more.

More?

Now! And she screamed as the pressure burst and she came. And then again. And, her nerves already on overload, she felt him coming! Long, hard, so good. Pleasure bursting against pleasure and rebounding for more. It was more sensation than a body could endure without sending the mind screaming for sweet release, even from pleasure.

He groaned in agreement, letting his face fall to the nook between her neck and shoulder, which seemed made just for him. Warm, moist, and smelling just of Janelle. That smell, he remembered it. Would always, always remember it.

"Mmmmm. Me, too." Janelle murmured sleepily. Thoughts clouded and floating. So lovely. Never wanted to move again. Not her arms and not her legs. All of her entwined with all of him. This was the kind of braid she could plait through her heart and her life, blissfully entangling them for always. Murmuring thoughts drifted freely as she surrendered at last to peaceful sleep.

Listening to Janelle's breathing deepen, Kane pressed his lips to her skin. Warm and soft. He could stay here forever and be so happy. If he could have anything at all—one thing in the whole wide world, just for him—it would be Janelle. Brave, true, stronger than she believed, witty, resilient. And even better, she loved him right back. He could feel it, hear it, smell and even taste it. He'd never had anyone of his own, not like this.

And . . . not even now. He sighed into her neck. He didn't want to leave this spot. It should be his. Right here. But it wasn't.

Carefully, his movements slow and gradual, he unhooked her ankles from behind his hips, smiling a little painfully as he did so. He'd heard it, just before she drifted off: she wanted to braid her very soul with his. That would be his greatest wish, too, if it were allowed.

Hands gentle and craving, he lowered her legs beside him, lingering to touch. Her hands had relaxed their grip as she slept, so he more easily slipped them down to her sides. More difficult, he had to slide himself free of her body. He didn't want to leave. She looked and felt so peaceful. It hadn't been half this painful the last time he'd walked away from her, and that had felt like a stake was driving through his gut. What he felt now was unspeakable. He wondered if she would realize that later, when he was gone. Would she understand what he had done or would she hate him? Oh, but it was selfish to wish for understanding.

In careful, reluctant movements, he rolled himself away from her and off the bed. Turning back, he gently tugged the blanket from beneath her feet, where they'd kicked it, and tucked it up to her chin. When she rolled her head in her sleep, hands moving slightly as if seeking, he stilled. Would she waken now? Part of him wanted her to. Most of him knew that was a bad idea. Waiting would just make it harder. Letting her hate him would make it easier for her. So that's what he would do. He would repeat—

He closed his eyes as his gut twisted.

Yes, *repeat* what he'd done to her eight years before. She would hate him and forget him and move on with her life while the Druids assigned him to another guardian. Or, more honestly, when they decided his fate immediately. The cards were stacked against him. He would of course fight a conviction, but it didn't look good. Especially given his actions tonight.

Instead of making amends to Janelle, he was compounding his offenses against her. It wouldn't matter that he was freeing her from obligation and leaving her in order to escape a prophecy of her death. That prophecy was only the fulfillment of a curse that was, at the heart of it, his fault, too.

Turning, he found his pants where he'd dropped them on the floor at the foot of the bed and tugged them on, buttoning the waistband. The belt, with its Celtic knot for a buckle, hung open.

He traced his fingers over that knot, the heavy pewter cool to the touch. Funny, how something that had once come so easily between a man and a woman, stopping them before they moved past the point of no return, was absolutely no barrier at all once the mind and heart knew what they wanted and realized they could take it. Now, it was just a buckle. And with practiced ease he secured the belt and reached for his shirt, sliding his arms into the sleeves.

Quickly buttoning up, he strode to the doorway. Just as he reached it, the phone jangled on the nightstand. It startled Janelle awake.

Her gaze locked immediately on Kane, first with confusion and then with cold accusation. Never shifting her focus, she switched on the lamp and reached for the phone.

"Hello?" Her voice was husky. Then her expression changed and she sat up. "Riordan? What's wrong?"

The alarm in her voice halted Kane's thoughts and plans. "What is it?" he asked.

Janelle held up a hand for silence. "What? The grove? Why? What kind of ans—" Her eyes widened. "No, but wait—" She halted her own words, pulling the disconnected phone from her ear. "Damn it!"

"What's wrong? Is Riordan in trouble? Or Mina?"

"I don't know, and maybe." She sighed. "He wants us to meet him at the grove. Immediately. He says we might find some answers there. He seemed in a rush, though, and hung up without giving me too many details."

Kane nodded. "You stay here and I'll follow up—"

"Not even in your dreams, puca. I'm going. I want answers from Riordan and then I want answers from you. You will tell me why you keep sneaking out of my bed—especially when you're the one who initiated what happened here tonight." *Two climaxes.* The words vibrated in the air between them. Tonight had certainly fulfilled every nuance of the definition, from total surrender to mutual satisfaction. Ah, but hearts . . . She broke off her thoughts, looking away. "I can't believe you were going to do it again, but you were. Just like before. You were going to just walk out. And don't tell me that's not what you were doing."

He didn't even try. "You don't have to go to the grove. This isn't your problem anymore. If I need help, my brother will be there."

Janelle shook her head as she kicked free of the blanket. "I have to go. Riordan thinks it's possible that whoever's framing you will show up."

"Does he suspect someone in particular?" Kane asked. "Tremayne maybe?"

"I don't know. He didn't tell me any names. What he did say is that he wants me to see if I recognize any magic present. Remember how I said I could tell it was a little different? Off, sort of? I think he wants me at the grove to see if the footprint of magic is the same there as it was at Mina's and the clinic." Still naked, she climbed out of bed, seemingly oblivious to Kane's watchful eyes, even as they both knew better: they were both aware.

Kane glanced away. "But this isn't your problem anymore," he pointed out again. "I can meet Riordan myself, leave you out of this entirely. You know . . . I could even tell them. The Druids. What happened here. That the guardianship bond was compromised. It would free you of all of this."

"Try, and I'll deny it. I will look any Druid or faerie in the eye and lie through my teeth." And by the look in her eyes, she meant it.

"What happened to your honor system?"

"It slept with my footloose ward and got really, really pissed. That's what." Flashing him an angry look, she lunged into jeans and a T-shirt and chased her tennis shoes around the room. "So, we're off to see Riordan. You get to go as a penitent puca and I'll be your guardian for the evening. Get it?"

"I can't risk you." He ground out the words. That's what it all came down to. And now he could see the bruise darkening her chin. Just as in his vision.

"You keep saying that." Locating the second shoe and stepping into them both, she turned back to Kane.

"It's true."

"But, see, it's not your choice. It's my life to risk." She grabbed her phone and ID and shoved them into her pockets.

"Janelle—"

"Give it up. I'm coming. Arguing is just wasting time, and we're supposed to be in a hurry."

She was right about that. Was it possible that they could conclude this quickly and he could be far from her, forever, before everything came to pass? He would confess. He would plead guilty. He would beg for another guardian. Anything. But this would be done quickly. "How far is the grove from here?"

"Thirty minutes by expressway. Closer as the crow flies." She was grabbing her keys.

Closing his eyes, Kane focused his energies. "So let's take the crow's route."

Even as her stomach and heart—hell, all of her—ached from the betrayal she'd seen for the second time, Janelle stood transfixed. This would never, could never, become routine. Kane seemed to glow, his colors and textures shimmering and blurring, his shape changing as Janelle looked on in helpless awe. A moment later, a tall, muscular stallion was nosing her shoulder.

Let's go.

Janelle paused. "So, I have a stallion in my apartment and I'm just going to lead him out the front door?"

I decided it was safer to shift in private than down in the parking lot. I can't glamour, Janelle, and frankly, your mastery of it is questionable. It's dark. Leave the lights off and maybe we can get out of here with no one seeing us. If someone does see us, I'm just a horse. Weird, but not otherworldly weird.

Certainly eviction weird. "Okay. Priorities. Screw the rest. Let's go." Flipping off light switches as she went, Janelle quietly exited the apartment. She glanced both ways before quietly motioning Kane to follow.

Luck finally with them, they managed to exit the building without encountering anyone. Down in the parking lot, Kane wasted no time and nosed Janelle into climbing onto his back. Then they were racing cross-country.

"So," Janelle began with cool determination. "This would make you my cornered suspect and me your bitchy interrogator. Why were you leaving me?"

"Do we have to do this now?"

"Considering your first instinct is to leave without explaining, I'm thinking now might be my only chance.

So, yeah. Now. Why were you leaving? Explain yourself.
I thought the sex was good. You seemed to enjoy it. Did
you think I was going to make you get down on bended
puca knee and propose to a human? Ha. That knee is
calloused from past proposals, anyway, and we already
know where those got you. In bed with me and no ring
on anybody's finger. So, good sex, no strings. What more
do you want?" Did she really want to know? Could she
have been so wrong about him? She'd thought—

What *had* she thought?

Another near-sex adventure instigated by Kane might
have convinced her that Phil was right: Kane was seducing her just short of the full deal in an attempt to win her
loyalty while still maintaining the integrity of the guardianship bond. Consummated lovemaking on the other
hand meant . . . what, exactly? And then his trying to
leave her? What the hell was that about? There was no
logical explanation for any of it.

The guardianship. What was Kane trying to accomplish by making her ineligible as his guardian? Why sex
and then escape? Why not sex, then hide the fact from
the Druids and expect her libido to speak on his behalf?
Why not dream-sex or almost-sex that still won her over
but allowed her to speak effectively and positively on
his behalf? All worked in his favor and none entailed his
leaving her. In fact, leaving her would hurt his cause, not
help it. She was missing something.

"Just tell me why, Kane."

"I had to leave. This guardianship gig is wrecking your
life. Admit it. Your clinic's been vandalized and your
friends have been assaulted, all because of me and this
stupid bond created by Druids. If it weren't for that, this
guy who's framing me wouldn't have any reason to go
near you. And that's not even counting the job you lost.

"And, God. What if it had been *you* at the clinic?" he
continued. "What if it had been *you* he hurt so critically
instead of Cindy? Could you heal yourself of an injury

that grave? What would happen if the injury itself had left you unconscious and unable to heal yourself? Can't you see? You getting hurt or worse is unacceptable to me."

Janelle's frustration welled, and she barely heard him. His excuses were weak. He was still missing the point. He'd tried to *leave* her! Just as he'd done before. He was going to just leave while she slept. Devastate her all over again. No, even worse than before. Because she loved him now.

"So, you're going to play the martyr and take whatever sentence the Druids give you. Or are you hoping for a new guardian despite what they told me, about this being your last chance? Such sacrifice. Isn't that sweet. Or could this possibly be a subtle attempt at making amends to everyone around you? Play the martyr for a selfless cause, invite pity? Well, I hate to break this to you, but I don't think it'll fly. Take me, for example. I'm mostly just pissed. Not a drop of pity in sight."

"Yeah?" He gave her a provoking look. "Well, if you're so pissed at me, why are you still trying to help? The best revenge would be to let me be framed as I framed my brother all those years ago."

"I've told you before. You're the one who lives like that, not me. I don't base all of my life decisions on revenge. I like to solve things, make people better, not create problems and suffering."

She could almost hear him grinding those big horsey teeth as he responded. "Has it occurred to you that you coming to the grove with me is *causing* problems and suffering?"

"You mean for you? Excellent." She spoke with false brightness. "Two birds with one stone. I get to find my answers and make you squirm while I do it. Sounds good to me. Turn here." She pointed left.

He did so, then glanced back at her. "I thought you said you weren't vengeful."

"I'm not. At least, not on a grand scale. Mostly just the

whiny stuff. You squirming, for example, would please me."

He was silent a few moments. "Janelle, please. I'll squirm. I'll beg. I'll do anything you want if you'll just walk away from this. Get as far from me as you can and stay that way."

Janelle caught her breath and couldn't speak for a few moments. Then, carefully, she tried a few words. "You want to get away from me that badly?" Talk about commitment shy. And she hadn't even asked for one.

"Yes. I want that more than I can say. I *need* to get away from you."

Janelle flinched again. Then she heard him in her heart. *More than he could say.* So, he couldn't say. And he couldn't risk her. So he wanted her away from him and he couldn't say why.

Dear God, but she'd almost convicted him in her own head. In spite of conflicting evidence. In spite of what her heart told her. While all along he—"I swear I will strangle you myself, puca. Okay, just tell me what the hell it is you're keeping from me. You're shoving me away in order to protect me. Don't give me some bullshit about my inflated ego or your habitual selfishness or my tendency to leap to Pollyanna conclusions. I know I'm right. You're the one who's always saying you can't risk me. So right now you can't risk me. And you need me away from you. You know what that sounds like to me? That for some reason you believe you bring danger to me."

He was silent, still loping along, but she could have sworn he stumbled a little.

Bingo. She sighed. "I'm an adult, Kane. Don't treat me like a child. I don't want to be hurt and I don't want to die. Consider me an ally on the whole not-risking-Janelle mission and just fill me in. The more I know, the more I can be on my guard and make smart decisions."

She could almost feel his brain churning through

her words, his desires, his fears, her anger. Then she heard him—more mentally than audibly—sigh in surrender.

"Thank you, God. Now speak, puca. We're almost there and I bet you have a lot of words to spit out before we arrive."

"Eesh. Guardians get bossy when you sleep with them." But there was a smile in his voice. Both sadness and relief, she sensed. And a wealth of the affection he'd been hiding from her since she woke up.

"I don't know. Maybe Riordan was right. Maybe it would be better to warn you. You're a logical woman, would think with your head instead of running off half-cocked." He was pondering aloud.

"Riordan knew? And you didn't tell *me?*"

He groaned. "Honestly, that was not a slight. It wasn't. I was trying to protect you and you might notice that he didn't tell you either. There is good reason for this if you'll let me tell it."

So it wasn't the time for petty grievances, she allowed silently. "Okay, okay. So tell me."

"Before I get into all this, please just remember your promise to adhere to logic, not emotion, not heroism. We're playing the odds. Agreed?"

"Within reason. Bottom line, I'm sticking close to you unless you can convince me to do otherwise."

"Stubborn." He paused, changing direction slightly, before racing forward. "I already told you about Maegth's curse. In a roundabout fashion."

"I remember. She said you would feel nothing romantically for any woman, with the odd exception of me."

"Yes. But the second half of that curse . . . was that I could never have you. You would be the only one for me, but you were forbidden to me."

Janelle scowled. "Well, she's got it right so far. But how does that change anything?"

"That's not all. Eight years ago when I left, the date

was November first. Do you know what that day means to a puca?"

She frowned. "Not really. All Saints' Day? The day after Halloween?" She tried a smile. "Was it that we skipped trick-or-treating?" The joke sounded as lame as it felt, but she could hardly bear the tension. She felt brittle enough to shatter like glass. Whatever he was going to tell her, it was worse than the curse. It had to be.

"The first day of the eleventh month is called November Day. The Puca's Day."

"That's vaguely familiar. Mina might have mentioned it. It's when Riordan had his trial."

"That was an unusual version, but yes, that's the gist of it. On November Day, the puca must be civil and speak the truth, and he has the power to prophesy. Well, that's what I did, eight years ago."

"Speak the truth?" Her lips twisted. "Couldn't tell it by me."

"I know." His words were low.

"Hey, that was a joke, dummy. As far as I know, you haven't lied to me—not since I was declared your guardian. You're no saint and you keep secrets, but I thought we were past lies."

He was quiet, as though taking in her words, the faith implicit in them. Faith in spite of the doubts this morning's behavior inspired. She believed in him. She couldn't seem to help herself.

He cleared his throat. "So, the prophecy. Eight years ago, the morning I woke up in your bed, I foresaw . . . Janelle, I saw your death." His voice shook.

Janelle stared. She didn't know whether to be relieved he was leaving for her own good rather than because he hated her or—well, terrified. He'd seen her death. "Well, I guess I knew it had to be something this drastic. So, my death, huh? I'll bet that was a mood killer. No wonder you ran like hell."

"My intent, before and now, was to be gone from your

life, one way or the other, to prevent that prophecy from being fulfilled."

"You can still prevent it?" Her heart pounded.

"It's not easy. I'm basically second-guessing fate and hoping my decisions this time around are different from ones I might have made otherwise . . . but yes, it can be avoided."

"And you're saying the best way to avoid it is for you to leave before I die. Maybe to keep me from dying? Does that mean you're there when it happens? How do I die?"

"I don't know."

But she sensed it was will rather than fact that forced the words from him. "Oh, come on, Kane. You saw me die but you don't know *how* I die? You must know something. If I'm going to die and you think you know how it happens, don't you feel just a tiny bit obligated to give me some details?"

"Why? So I can turn a prophecy that can still be avoided into a self-fulfilling prophecy? Hell, no, I've given you enough information to convince you to be on your guard. I hope. But any details beyond that would serve only to strengthen the prophecy. I'll be leaving just as soon as we see this through. There's no reason to continue risking you now. Not with the Druids thinking you unfit as a guardian."

"No reason to . . ." And he sounded not the tiniest bit regretful about it, either. That was it. She could trust her heart, what she'd begun to suspect all along. "You planned it, didn't you? You and me and sex tonight. Just so you could break the guardianship pact." Relief flooded her. That was it. He was leaving in a desperate attempt to keep her safe. He cared. Period.

He turned his majestic head and glanced back at her, the raging gold of his eyes magnified in equine form. She'd even say he looked gorgeously tormented if it didn't sound so melodramatic. He turned his head back and spoke into the wind. "Now don't you go turning me into some martyr for the cause. I made love to you because I damn well wanted to. I've wanted to every day for eight years. Do you want to know why I never took the memory of me from you? Because I couldn't stand it if you forgot me. You're all I've thought of for eight long years. I never wanted to leave your bed. If there were any other way . . ." He broke off.

"Kane?"

"There's no point to this. The last thing I want is to rip at both of us before I leave." He bit off the words. "Just know that my leaving is your best chance at avoiding the prophecy."

"Why do I get the feeling that there's something else you're not telling me? Something big. And it's because you're trying to protect me from something. Again."

"Maybe it's because we're of different species and this isn't the first secret I've kept from you?" Still, he sounded evasive. "Hell, maybe I have simple commitment issues. I do, actually. Two thousand years of doing what I want, when I want. And now, to share the remote control?"

"Kane," she interrupted quietly. "Tell me. *How do I die?*"

"No!" he burst out. "Why the hell would you even want to know?"

"Maybe to brace myself? Prepare myself? Opt to avoid a certain intersection at 10:12 A.M. on March fourteenth of next year?"

"Relax." He sounded exasperated. "You don't get hit by a truck."

"Well, gee, that narrows it down. How about a VW bug, then? A parade float? A herd of wild antelope? What?"

He didn't respond, but the turmoil in his silence spoke volumes.

She sighed in frustration. "Fine. This is where we can access the park. See the fence?" *Damn it.* But she supposed, even if they hadn't run out of road and time, he wouldn't have told her anything more. She would at least have spent a few more minutes slamming her head against that brick wall just to make sure, though.

Kane slowed to a walk, then carefully, and seemingly weightless—almost *flying*?—leapt the fence. They were inside the park. Janelle felt a whoosh of power, a moment of free-falling, and then she was lying calmly in Kane's arms. Against his very manly broad chest. Damn, but she would miss that chest. He couldn't leave.

Kane was eyeing her with surprise. "You didn't even flinch. I shifted under and around you and you didn't even flinch."

"Yeah, so maybe I'm getting used to you and your weirdo ways."

"And maybe you're drawn to them. That's kind of kinky."

She scowled at him, although a smile reluctantly tugged at her heart. They'd come so far. Was it all for nothing? "Put me down."

"Yeah, okay." He did so. "And, for the record? The only reason I'm not tying you up and shipping you off to China right now is because you have that healing gift. It's not something I'd rely on long-term, but for now . . . maybe you'll come in handy. You can heal yourself, right?"

She cleared her throat, suddenly remembering the Druid's words. Sex would weaken her power to minimal levels. Thank God for Oberon's shield trick or Kane would be having a coronary. Right before he shipped her off to China "for her own good."

"Yep," she said. "Remember when I had that headache and made it go away? You were there. You saw me do it. I'm better than aspirin."

He nodded, looking marginally relieved. "Okay." Then he glanced around. "I thought you said Riordan would meet us here."

"I did, but maybe I misunderstood. Maybe he went right to the grove."

"Figures. He always was a cocky SOB."

Janelle frowned. She hoped that's all it was.

"Why? Do you think it's more?"

"I'm concerned." She pursed her lips, frowning and feeling like the most evil bitch in existence.

"No, that would be my stepmother. Remember? She was made for the role of supreme evil bitch."

"Right. Manga stripper faerie stepmother. How could I forget?"

"Exactly. So, tell me what worries you."

She scowled at him, barely able to meet his eyes. "You already know what I'm thinking."

"Yeah. I just want to know how you'll phrase it," he responded.

She stopped and turned to face him. Looked over his shoulder.

He tipped her chin up so she had to meet his eyes. "It's okay. Just go with the facts. We both know what they suggest."

"I feel magic, and it's just like what I felt before. It's all puca power. It's . . . off. But it's so familiar at the same time. What it all comes down to is, it's got to be either you or Riordan wielding the magic that's causing all the trouble. But damn it, I don't want to believe either case. Is it Riordan? Would *he* betray you? Consciously or sub-consciously? Is he doing the sleep-morphing thing?"

"Or . . . is it me," he finished quietly.

Janelle groaned. "See how impossible this is? This is why the Druids said no figure-eighting. I can't do this."

"What exactly are you doing?"

Janelle looked away, scrubbing at her eyes, before turning stubbornly to face Kane. "I've become totally irrational." Screw guardianship. Screw evidence. Screw objectivity. She was following her heart. "You didn't do it. So it has to be Riordan. Unless there really is that third puca like we thought."

Kane sighed. "How can you be so sure it's not me? I still am the most likely suspect. We're talking puca powers, and only one known puca can still wield them. Add motive, opportunity, history of similar crimes. It doesn't take much to connect those dots. Hell, maybe I'm the one doing it in my sleep."

"It's not you." She was sure.

"But how can you be so positive? Your 'Spidey' senses? Some other gift I don't know about?"

"Love." Damn it, she hadn't meant to say that. Not now. Not to look like the sappiest, most gullible jerk that ever picked up a syringe and healed with her fingertips instead. But not everything could be explained. "I know you. I love you. Even if you royally piss me off with your insistence on keeping me in the dark for 'my own good.' I know you're not the one behind the puca ride downtown, Cindy's accident at the clinic, or any of the other stuff. It wasn't you. You were framed."

The look on his face indescribably tender, Kane lifted a hand to touch her face. He traced her cheekbone as his gaze caressed hers. "I shouldn't admit it. Not now. But you have to know, since you seem able to pry almost anything else out of me. I love you, too. I knew it eight years ago and I know it now."

"Because of Maegth?" She held her breath.

He shook his head, hearing her fear before she spoke it. "Maegth didn't curse me to love you. She cursed me to not experience lesser feelings or romantic inclinations toward other women. She could not *make* me fall in love with you and she could not *forbid* me falling in love with you, because we were fated to fall in love. As she knew. You were fated to be my one great love. She did, however, tell me I could never have you and that I could never bear to settle for another woman in your place. And she was right. I do love you. Only you."

Kane paused, then spoke with low fervor. "That's why, as soon as we're through here, you have to let me let you go. Before it's too late. I don't want to see you die. Please. I can handle anything else the Druids want to dish out as punishment, and maybe they'll give me another guardian—if I'm impossibly lucky. But I don't think I could survive watching you die, knowing I could have prevented it."

Janelle gazed up at him, unable to look away, much as it hurt. So, he would still leave her after this. Even after they'd exchanged words of love aloud. He'd already said he would leave, so she shouldn't have been surprised. "But, with the healing gift . . ."

"Don't even go there. Even a Druidic healing gift isn't infallible. I won't risk you. If I stayed, I would be proving that I'm the same selfish ass who condemned his brother two thousand years ago. Thanks to you, thanks to love, I'm . . . well, I'm *improved*, at least, if not completely reformed." He gave her a crooked grin that faded at the edges. "I have to go."

She narrowed her eyes at him. "You can go anywhere you want to, puca, but that doesn't stop me from following." The fact that they both knew he could elude any pursuer just rendered her stubbornness more an ache felt deep in the heart than any real threat. "I love you. I always will. There must be a way for us to be together."

And somehow, she felt that any chance they might have would be found here.

She took a deep breath and faced facts. "So. Let's find Riordan. And hope he has some answers we can live with."

Resolute, she backed away a step, then, turning a little awkwardly, strode off down a familiar path. She stepped over tree roots, shoving branches aside to clear her path, until Kane slipped an arm around her waist and halted her. Turning her, he met her mouth with his.

"What?"

"Shhhhh," he whispered against her lips, stealing her breath. "Let's approach this a little cautiously, all right? And, not to challenge your independence, but maybe you could let me go first?" He moved and smiled against her cheek, his changing tone obviously intended to distract her. "As the superior immortal around here, I can take anything thrown at me. You . . . not so much." He cast her a pitying glance.

"Gosh, you're right. I'd forgotten about all that." She gave him a wide-eyed look, but didn't let his silly ploy succeed. "That whole immortal thing and being superior and all—so, tell me, do immortals start to stink after they've been around for a while? You know, like aged cheese? Come to think of it, you probably have centuries-old toe jam and fingernail grime."

"Gross. Aren't you supposed to respect your elders? I do have at least two thousand years on you. You should stand in awe of me."

She sniffed in mock disdain. "Yeah, but I've seen you with your pants down."

He burst out in laughter. "Yes! Even more reason to admire me. You should be starstruck, in fact. My very own groupie." His eyes soft with affection, he reached out to rub his thumb over a damp streak on her cheek.

A wet cheek? She didn't know how it got wet to begin with. Scowling, she rubbed it against his hand because she just couldn't help herself. And she grunted, "Just move it, oh egotistical one."

He set off again down the path.

As she followed, Janelle couldn't stop her mind from wandering unwelcome routes. Where was Riordan? Why had he called them there? Was it a trap? A confession? Something else?

"I personally vote for something else," Kane remarked.

"God, me too," Janelle concurred.

"So keep the faith."

They rounded a bend and Kane suddenly stopped, reaching behind him to still Janelle as well.

Footsteps. Very faint but growing louder. Closer?

Behind them!

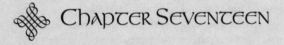

CHAPTER SEVENTEEN

Kane grabbed Janelle's hand and pulled her off the path and behind a bush. The footsteps continued to approach. Quick, long, heavy strides. A man's gait. Janelle held her breath as the footsteps grew louder and closer. He was going to walk right past them. Was it Riordan?

The footsteps rounded a curve and a strange sweeping sound accompanied them.

A robe.

Janelle stared. Was it Phil?

The head turned.

No, it was Tremayne!

Feeling Kane stiffen in surprise as well, Janelle ducked lower behind the bushes. Tremayne swept past them without pause, seeming completely unaware of their presence. Kane and Janelle remained motionless until he was almost out of sight.

Kane finally tugged at Janelle's hand, motioning for her to follow. He led her quickly and quietly, keeping the footsteps in earshot, though the figure was just beyond their sight. When the sounds grew fainter, changed and stopped, Kane stilled, as did Janelle.

Voices: a woman and a man. Janelle strained to hear, but at first could not. Then . . . a tinkling laugh.

Titania? Janelle glanced at Kane, who looked as startled as she felt. Tremayne was meeting Titania? But, that didn't seem right. And as she listened, the tone, the lilt of the woman's voice, seemed slightly different than the faerie queen's.

Janelle tugged at Kane, gestured, and they moved closer, trying for a better view of the female. She wore a hood and cape made of some diaphanous material, clinging and sparkling and seeming awhirl even as it settled against her body. Next to her knelt a familiarly robed figure, larger than the woman. He kept his head low, his face shadowed by his hood as he bowed before what looked to be a makeshift altar.

Robes and altars? Oh, boy. This couldn't be good. A little satanic ritual, anyone? Human sacrifices? Bloody orgies? Hey, at least they had a doctor on site, one with a few tricks up her sleeve at that. But could she reattach a head? And how the hell would they get past a faerie and her otherworldly henchman with sicko freeze-ray powers?

Kane cast her an exasperated glance, obviously reading her thoughts.

So, she had an imagination. Acting as guardian for a halfling faerie puca tended to enlarge a girl's perspective on the world. Especially when said girl had wallowed in science and fact for her entire life.

The words being spoken were still indecipherable and possibly further muddled by the thoughts racing through Janelle's head. Kane, obviously frustrated, tugged her hand and repositioned them yet closer. Then he cast her a hushing look. No doubt he wished she would quiet her mind so he could listen, and also so that she wouldn't risk projecting her thoughts to the faerie in the clearing.

"Humans are so silly that way." The woman's voice was low, raising goose bumps along Janelle's spine. "Did you honestly think we would let you keep those powers? What if you used them against me or mine?"

His robes draped around him, the kneeling Tremayne gazed up at the woman, though his features were still blurred in shadow. "I wouldn't use them against you." His murmur was barely audible. "It's power that I seek, not revenge. Revenge is a waste of time. But this power . . . it could bring me everything I want."

"I can empathize with that. I don't trust it, but sure, I can empathize with that kind of thinking. And yours is such an inventive little mind, what with all the tricks you played. That stallion charging through Carytown was especially amusing. You were an inspired choice as host for these puca powers."

Puca powers? Tremayne was host to puca powers? Maybe that's why the freezing thing had worked: a puca could cancel out another puca's powers, especially if they'd been crippled by Druidic restraints. She wondered if that was the case.

"If you'll recall," the kneeling figure murmured, "I was the one who stole the cornerstone in the first place. You were nowhere near the clearing when Riordan rejected his powers, returning them to the cornerstone. I was there. I was the one who took the initiative of watching the whole thing from a distance. And I was the one who took the risk of stealing it when everyone's attention was distracted. So the cornerstone and the powers it contains belong to me already. I just needed you to help me claim them. That was the agreement, after all."

"I suppose."

"And you said you were pleased."

"I was." The woman's voice hardened. "Except for the casualties. I specified property damage, not slashed nurses."

"Um, that part wasn't exactly intentional. Maybe if I were at full power, I could limit the damage somewhat. These half-powers . . . their limited nature . . . they make my head hurt. I'm not always in control of my actions. If I possessed full puca powers, though, I think I would have full mastery of myself and them. That's the problem. You gave me most of the shape-shifting ability, but not the control. The beast without the brain."

The faerie hummed in thought.

"Just think how much more effective I could be in defense of our cause," the robed figure coaxed, his voice growing stronger. "Give me all of the powers now, not just some of them on loan. Release them to me permanently. Once I regain my supporters, we could be your soldiers. Followers. Anything you need."

"Hardly." The faerie was laughing low. "You don't want to be my little follower any more than I want a bunch of fawning idiots trailing me around. I can't imagine you following anyone."

"But I could be useful to you."

"How?"

"Kane. In spite of the rules, he's grown very close to his guardian. And I'm talking *very* close. Almost breaking-the-rules close, if they haven't done that already."

There were a few moments of stunned silence before the voice, now brittle, responded. "And I care about this why?"

"She's his weakness. You want to hurt him? Go after her. Send me after her. Give me the powers and let me hit him where it hurts most."

"Let me get this straight," the female faerie murmured in a low, emotionless voice. "If I permanently endow you with not just the limited puca abilities you have, but the full extent of them, you'll use them against this Janelle Corrington. This human guardian."

"That would be the deal."

"You'd be willing to do anything I asked you to do. Even against an innocent woman."

"Anything. You name it. But you have to give me the powers." There was now a feverish note in his voice. "Let me have them for real, not just on loan. I've already cast my spell to make it happen. It just needs a faerie push, which you can provide. . . ."

"I *could*." Raising a hand high, she caused sparks to swarm at her fingertips, swirling faster and faster, building as if preparing for a grand fireworks finale. Then she lowered and aimed at Tremayne. . . .

Kane shoved past Janelle and dove straight into the robed man, breaking the couple's connection. Even as he did so, however, another figure was in motion, leaping from the other side of the clearing right into the path of that sparking stream. This caused a dazzling light show.

"Riordan!" It was Mina's cry, and it came from where the new figure had appeared.

The dark shape that was apparently Riordan sizzled, sparks lasering outward and upward from his body as though repelled by an opposing force. The onetime puca turned, and Janelle saw Riordan's eyes glow and burn, his face shimmering in and out of view, and then he collapsed on the ground.

Avoiding the tangle of male bodies on the ground before her, the female faerie rushed forward, right into Janelle's path—or rather, right into a swift kick in her faerie shin. The woman did a neat somersault to land on her back, displacing her hood. As her face was revealed and she met Janelle's eyes, her own glittered with panic and adrenaline.

The faerie's eyes widened, as if in stunned recognition. Even vulnerability. "You're her, aren't you? You're the human he fell for. They told me, and I still can't believe it." She shook her head and her voice hardened, cold anger replacing shock. "He fell for a human. Again. Just how much insult must a faerie—a well-connected, not to mention fucking beautiful faerie at that—have to take?" And with a sparking snap of her fingers and a flash of her overly bright eyes, she vanished. The resultant shower of sparks dimmed and evaporated in the smoke.

Smoke? Janelle's mind was still reeling with suppositions and a brand-new lesson: kicking a faerie's legs out from under her was about as permanently effective in containing her as swatting a helium balloon at the ground. Janelle focused. There was smoke, and not just due to a couple of faerie sparklers. Part of the grove was in flames.

Kane, recalling Tremayne's threat against Janelle, grappled with the robed figure on the ground. Part of him expected to be frozen at any moment, but instead his opponent showed fear and rage—and surprising physical strength. Kane took a chance and settled the issue with a well-placed uppercut to the jaw, snapping the man's head back and knocking his hood free.

It wasn't Tremayne! But Kane did recognize the man. "Duncan Forbes! Making pacts with faeries and wielding puca powers in your spare time? Interesting hobby for an accountant and ex-Druid."

The man gave him a look of pure malice. "You think you've won, don't you? You think you can pin everything on me now and save yourself? Well, let's get real. That's just not going to happen. Look around you. All of this was caused by puca power. And who could have done it?" Duncan sneered. "Let's see. I'm not a puca. Your brother's now human. And my cohort is nowhere to be found. Meanwhile, I see a fire in the grove, while I, a hereditary Druid whom you hate, lie here injured thanks to your unprovoked assault."

"Enough!" This from a controlled but furious-sounding Tremayne, who had appeared out of the shadows. Kane gaped at him in surprise. Duncan did the same. "Druid. You're coming with me," Tremayne declared. Then the shadowy figure glanced almost reluctantly at Kane. "See to your brother. I'll deal with the fire and the Druid."

Something about Tremayne's voice—reliable, strong, full of authority, and even principled—inspired vague memories. Trusting the man for some unknown but instinctual reason, Kane just nodded and shoved Duncan to his feet. Tremayne grabbed Duncan's arm and hauled him off into the woods. Almost immediately, Kane saw the fire begin to dim, its fury draining. He felt a wave of relief.

Then Kane turned to his brother, and he saw the reason for Tremayne's generosity. Riordan. His brother was lying on the ground, body limp and blackened.

"Riordan?"

It was Kane's voice. Hearing the strangled note in it, Janelle hurried across the clearing.

"Janelle! Thank God." This from a tearful Mina.

Janelle looked down at Riordan, and her stomach dropped into her feet. Riordan wasn't just unconscious, but burned. Everywhere. No one could survive—

"Please," Mina begged. "You can heal him, right? You have to. He has to be okay."

There was near devastation on the face Kane turned to Janelle. She dropped down next to him. If she'd wondered at all before, the answer was right there, written in soot, sweat and his tearing eyes: Kane loved his brother.

"Can you help him?" His voice was raspy. "He's . . . he's not dead yet. So close, but—"

"I don't know if I can help. But I'm damn well going to try." Janelle settled carefully on her knees, as close to Riordan as she could get. Kane and Mina moved back to give her room. Praying for a miracle, Janelle gathered herself, concentrating on the still body.

Dear God, but he looked like death. She had healing hands, true, but this was one of the ugliest cases she'd ever seen. Her worst nightmare had become terrifying reality: she held her onetime best friend's life in her less-than-skillful hands, while the woman who loved him sat nearby, looking on with complete faith and hope. The irony was tragic. The timing. Twenty-four hours ago, Janelle could have healed him without a doubt. It had worked for Cindy. But now, having just made love with

Kane, being drained by that coupling in the way the Druids had warned . . .

He could definitely die. He could die under her hands. Die on the table. Cold and stiff and just gone, like her mother in the hospital. She hadn't been able to save her mother and—

"Janelle?" Kane murmured urgently. "We're losing him. *Please.*"

Fighting past the terror, she focused wholly on Riordan. He wasn't dead. Not yet. And if she could stop it, she would. Lifting trembling hands, she deliberately, carefully, pressed her palms to the ex-puca's smudged and stubble-roughened cheeks.

A zinging shock pinged through her system before it was eclipsed by a choking tightness that banded around her chest and squeezed. She couldn't breathe. Pain scorched its way down her arms and along her back. Still she pursued, would damn well fight her way past all obstacles. Then the rest of her seemed to go up in flames. These overwhelmed her, and she felt her mind buckling under.

She stiffened, threw all her strength into keeping her focus, keeping her composure. She would not lose Riordan. She couldn't. But the darkness and the numbness and the—

She heard a distant roar, a protest deep in the gut. "No, Janelle! Back off! It's too much!" This was Kane's voice. Fire and pain rushed through her body, and smoke belched furiously from her lungs. His lungs. It was Riordan's cough. Limbs weakened and grew numb. Hers. His. A maelstrom of raw energy burned her from the inside out. Then darkness closed in around her and she knew nothing.

When Janelle slumped over Riordan's body, her stillness identical to his brother's, Kane looked on in growing horror. "No!"

But she'd already toppled onto her side, her head lolling back. The pale, lifeless face and bruised chin were the very picture of his prophecy. Death. She was dead. He'd asked her to heal Riordan. When her power faltered, he'd shoved everything he had at her—powers, energy, strength of will, everything—hoping to boost her up. But the draw of Riordan's pain plus the wild influx of Kane's energy had overcome her. She couldn't control any of it, and the raw energy—*Kane's* raw energy— was eating her alive. Kane had killed her. Just as he'd foreseen. This was her death at his hands.

No. Kane reached for her. Anything but that.

"Stop." A low voice from behind halted his actions. "Think carefully, puca. If you do this, it cannot be undone." This was from Tremayne.

"Who said I wanted the damn thing undone? I know what I'm doing." He gritted it out. "This is my choice."

"I swear to God, if you killed her to save me, I will kill you myself. Wasn't it enough that you chained me to that damn rock forever? And now, to risk her for my life! I've lived a long damn time and she's only had—" The voice broke off on coughing.

More voices rumbled in Janelle's ears, jackhammering at an already pounding head, and she groaned.

"Janelle!" A woman's hand touched her neck and then her forehead. "Will you two idiots stop fighting and get over here? I think she's coming around."

Her chest unbearably tight, Janelle took in a shallow breath. She opened burning eyes to see three faces peering down at her in the dawn-touched darkness. Two were nearly identical, with just tiny differences. Eye color. The two were brothers.

"Hi." It was an overly deep, raspy excuse for a voice. The golden eyes looked too bright. "You're back. I thought . . . damn it, I didn't want . . . I thought it was the prophecy. I thought I'd failed and it had won."

Unable to bear the pain she saw in Kane's face, Janelle reached up to cup his cheek. "Kane." The one word sent her into a wracking cough. "God. I sound like a three-pack-a-day chimney. And my head . . . God, it's a mess. I can't remember how or why . . . What happened?" She looked around in confusion. She recognized the place. They were in the park, up the path from the clearing where the Druids met.

"Well." Clearing his voice, Kane obviously tried for a normal tone. "Riordan here fielded a phone call from Daphne, telling him that her father was headed toward the grove. That he was meeting somebody. That's when he called you and asked us to meet him there. When Duncan arrived before you and I showed up, Riordan took it upon himself to follow him to the clearing. Meanwhile, Mina was following Riordan, and then we followed Tremayne . . ." Kane paused to watch her face. "Are you keeping up?"

Janelle nodded, remembering more now: the robed man, the faerie, the words exchanged before the fight.

Kane nodded. "When the faerie started that transfer of powers, I went after Duncan—that's who was in the robe, kneeling, not Tremayne. At the same time, Riordan, who seems to have a hard time remembering he's human now, damn it, jumped in front of the faerie." He turned to his brother and gave him an annoyed look. "That was an extremely stupid move, by the way. What were you thinking?"

"The same thing you were: break the connection. Given the fact that I used to have those powers and rejected them, I thought they couldn't hurt me. I figured I would repel them when they hit me, like light bouncing off a mirror, and they'd end up back in the stone where they belong." Riordan grimaced. "What I didn't count on was the powers throwing a tantrum and raking me from the inside out before rebounding. Remind me never to try reclaiming them. I think they're holding a grudge."

"Yeah, so we saw." Kane turned back to Janelle, who was goggling at both of them. He seemed not to notice. "You know the rest, really. You tried to heal Riordan and it was tricky . . ." He broke off, looking sheepish.

"Go on. Tell her the rest." This from a grim-looking Riordan. "We nearly lost her. Just so you could save me. Did I ever ask anybody to sacrifice themselves for me? No. Do you think I could have lived with myself if Janelle had died and I had lived? I can't believe you let her—"

"Will you just shut up?" Mina scowled at him, her face blotchy and tearstained. "Do you honestly think Kane could have stopped Janelle from trying to save you? Just like you couldn't have stopped me from following your heroically stupid butt out here. Just like I couldn't have stopped you from playing the hero by jumping in the way of faerie and puca magic. Those sacrifices are what we do when we love people." She stared at him a moment before continuing.

"Kane did try to pull her back when it was going too far, but Janelle wouldn't come back. She was pursuing it to the end. And she was doing it for you, her friend, not because Kane told her to do it. What, you think only men can be heroic? Just accept the gift, say thank you, and then shut up. Men, with your Neanderthal, prideful bellyaching. I swear."

She gave Janelle a speaking look, which Janelle would have returned if she'd felt capable. Then Mina rose to her feet, snagged Riordan's hand, and hauled him several yards away to give Kane and Janelle some privacy. Riordan mouthed a silently sheepish thank-you over Mina's shoulder. Then he bent to listen to Mina's whispered conversation.

Janelle stared after them. "If Riordan was so near death, shouldn't he be the one flat on his back, not me?" She was lying in the grass, the smell of smoke still heavy in her nostrils. The air around them was hazy with it. No sign of flames anywhere, though.

"Riordan came around almost immediately after . . . well, afterward. He's fine now, just a little shaky. But you were unconscious for over an hour. When Riordan woke up and you were still out cold, we weren't sure you would ever wake up. We brought you up here because the smoke was so heavy in the clearing. We thought fresh air might help. But you still didn't come around. I was afraid . . ." Kane shook his head. "I thought the prophecy had finally come true. That I was too late to leave you."

He stared for a moment, the nightmares still shining in his eyes. "Damn it," he burst out. *"I didn't leave in time."*

Instinctively reaching up to play her fingers soothingly through his hair, she studied him a moment. "But I'm alive, right?"

"You nearly died. It was so close. I still don't know what happened, why your healing gift gave out like that."

Janelle cleared her throat, the guilt washing over her. "Yeah. About that. There's this thing with my healing powers. Sex . . . well, sex drains them." She braced herself, hoping her near-death experience still inspired enough sentiment to keep him from strangling her.

Kane looked surprised. "You knew this and I didn't? How the hell did you pull that off?"

"Well, that's just a little something Phil and Oberon arranged for me. They provided me a little privacy from you on a couple of delicate subjects. That was one."

"There are others?"

"So, Riordan nearly died, huh?" She coughed, trying to sound pitiful.

"Yes. And so did you." And his eyes glazed over as he obviously lost himself all over again in thoughts of that nightmare he'd been having. He shook his head. "You did die. Both of you. For a moment." He shook his head. "To be honest, I had no idea you could do what you did.

Janelle, when I pushed all that extra power through you, you didn't just add it to yours like before. You multiplied it. The total power increased almost exponentially."

"What are you talking about?" She gave him a wide-eyed look, overjoyed that he'd dropped the subject of—

"I only dropped that subject temporarily," he warned. "We will return to it. As for the rest . . . Usually, when you heal, you're using the gift the Druids gave you. I sit there passively, while you draw power from me. This time, I felt your power fade—which, by the way, scared the hell out of me. Don't you dare take a risk like that again. If I'd known you were working at minimal power . . ." He paled.

Janelle sighed. "Mea culpa. Seriously. But you have to admit you've kept a few secrets from me 'for my own good,' so I thought, hey, I'd spare you for a change. So, back to that other thing. What do you mean about pushing your power through me?" That sounded alarmingly like . . .

He scowled. "As your abilities faltered, I tried to help by giving my energy to you. I wanted to save you, to stop that spark from going out."

Janelle focused, and vague memories returned. "I do remember. It was an overload of energy that seemed to pulse and grow even as I tried to wield it. There was so much. I couldn't control it." She shook her head, then looked up at Kane. "Yes, I felt it when the healing power started giving out on me. It was scary, but at the same time exhilarating. You see, I've been so afraid lately. It's almost irrational, but I feared that the part of me that's a doctor—a good doctor—got all tangled up in the gift, and that if the magic ever left me, so would the parts of me that make me a good physician. The skills, the instinct, the nerve. Every time I've healed someone lately, the magic has stifled those and taken me over. I had no conscious control.

"But this time . . . well, I swear it was different. Maybe it was because I was so weak," she mused, "but I had to consciously mold that rough surge of energy into something useful and almost manually implement it to help Riordan. It was weird and great at the same time. Sort of the magical equivalent of an understaffed, power-surging triage unit." Glancing up into his eyes, she flushed a little, realizing she was talking a mixture of tech-speak and mumbo-jumbo, and feeling like an idiot.

"You're *not* an idiot. And you are a doctor, through and through. It's more than training and implements, more than steady hands. It takes a mind-set and a will . . . hell, a selflessness and a total focus on other people. You've always had that. It's just that the magic was snatching the instinct you already possessed and going about its business before you could consciously direct it."

Janelle cleared her throat. "Ah. Well, this time . . . we um, well . . ."

"Yeah. I pushed magic through you, thereby forcing the combination of our powers. And they merged into something greater than their sum. It was huge, even with your own powers originally so drained. I see now why the Druids forbade it, why such a combination has to be so strictly limited. In our case, it was a dangerous thing because as your power gave out, you were less able to control mine. The concentration of raw energy inside of you built to a lethal level. It was killing you, even as you shared in the trauma of Riordan's injuries." Kane's eyes looked overly bright again, and he shook his head and noisily cleared his throat. "You were so close—I could feel it! But then you went down when Riordan did. And I did what I had to do. Dear God, but I nearly lost you. And him." He bowed his head. "And it would have been my fault. Mine. Just like the prophecy." He met her eyes. "*I would have killed you.*"

Janelle's eyes widened and her mouth formed an O.

"You killing me. Wow. That's a good one. I feel pretty alive right now, oddly enough. So much for the prophecy."

He shook his head, his eyes glowing with self-directed anger. "I shouldn't have let you come to the grove with me."

She snorted. "What's this 'let' business, like I'm not a free agent?"

He raised an eyebrow. "I'm a puca. I have means."

"Okay, so maybe you could have used force, but what if I had stayed behind like you wanted? Sure, you have puca power, but you can't heal. By rights, those burns should have scarred Riordan horribly—and that's if he even recovered. The most serious of the burns were on the inside. Without the healing gift from the Druids, he probably would have died. Would you prefer that?"

"Of course not, but the risk to you . . ." He shook his head.

"Wait a minute." Ignoring the pounding in her head and his gestures to shush and lie back down, she rolled to her side and propped herself up on an elbow. Distantly she heard Mina and Riordan approach, but she'd be damned if she let anything derail this conversation. Some of his words were just beginning to register, and she had a bad feeling about them. "What you said earlier, about Riordan and me being dead for a moment. What do you mean you 'did what you had to do' to save us? What did you do? What *could* you do?"

He didn't respond.

"Kane? Tell me." She sat up.

"He gave up his life for ours," Riordan said. "Didn't you, Kane?"

Kane still didn't speak.

Janelle couldn't catch her breath. And not because of her sore lungs and throat either. "You . . . What do you . . . ?"

Riordan came closer, a wide-eyed Mina following

slowly. "His immortality. He gave that up. I don't know how the hell he managed, but I can feel it." Riordan shook his head and turned to his brother. "You gave part of yourself to me. And, I'm assuming, to Janelle."

"But the Druids said immortality was something that couldn't be given to someone." Janelle eyed Kane in disbelief. "It's just not possible."

"No. The Druids can't give anyone immortality. They don't have it to mete out," Kane explained simply. "I do have it, and even I can't bestow it upon someone. But I can share it. I can share my unlimited life force."

"Not share," Riordan inserted pointedly, turning from Kane to Janelle. "Give. He *gave* part of his life force away. And once you do that, it necessarily becomes limited. It's like interrupting a circle. It's no longer endless. He's no longer immortal."

Janelle darted a horrified look at Kane. "Is he right? Did you do that—snip your circle to save us?"

Kane looked disgruntled. "I did what I had to do. And I gave what I had to give. It was my choice. And it's not like I died to save you both. So stop looking at me like that." He glared at Janelle, Riordan and Mina.

"No, but you agreed to die one day so we could both live. That . . ." Riordan shook his head, obviously speechless.

Mina stepped forward. "You know what that is? *Amends*, damn it. To Riordan, to Janelle, to me. More than amends. You gave Riordan back to me, and that puts me eternally in your debt." She dropped to her knees and threw her arms around Kane, nearly knocking them both over. "Welcome back to the family, puca."

A reluctant and rueful Kane steadied them both, then gently set Mina back on her feet. "Thank you. For the gesture, I mean. As for the rest . . . I pleased myself. You owe me nothing." He turned to his brother. "I never wanted you dead. Never. Not even all those years ago."

"I know." Riordan held out a hand, which Kane gripped warmly. "And that's why we're square now, you and me. And family. I'm glad to have my brother back. Thank you."

Nodding briskly, his emotions obviously strong but leashed, Kane turned back to a staring Janelle.

Although touched, she was downright appalled by his sacrifice. She couldn't wrap her mind around it. "But you're going to *die* now."

"Now?" Kane raised his eyebrows, humor finally sparkling in his eyes again. "Like, right now? Why? Are you going to kill me? I believe you threatened that once, but at this point it would just be copying."

"Funny guy." She scowled. "I don't mean *now* now. But someday. And you wouldn't have before." She looked down. "It was always so reassuring, you know. That you could just bounce with anything that came at you. You were indestructible." She'd been awed that he could love her, make her laugh, make her cry. She'd been annoyed that he could make her hopelessly want him for eight long years. But foremost, she'd secretly loved that he could never scar her with his death, as her parents had.

Kane, obviously aware of the path of her thoughts, squeezed her hand. "I'm alive and well. Healthy. Basically, I'm just your average, thirty-something mortal male—although I have a few lingering tricks up my sleeve. Remember him? From the beach? You met someone like that a long time ago." He offered a wry grin. She tried and failed to return it.

"What about the throne?" Janelle eyed him in horror. He'd wanted that throne—his heritage—even though he'd tried to give it to Riordan. Now, there was no one to take it. "Kane, the faerie world won't accept your rule if you're mortal."

He smiled at her, a surprisingly sweet and peaceful expression. "I'm okay with that. I would not be okay if you and Riordan had died. Just know that I don't regret this sacrifice. I don't regret anything I've given up. Nothing. I want you to remember that."

Janelle, though touched by his words, eyed him quizzically. She sensed she was missing something still. "I guess that's good . . . for your sake, I mean. But why do you sound so odd right now? So—I don't know—final? Like you're saying good-bye. Why? I mean there's no need for you to leave now, right?" She glanced around their little group, which had grown. It now held a silent Tremayne and an enigmatic-looking Duncan. Everyone seemed to know something she didn't. "You've made amends," she said. "To Riordan, to Mina, to me. And we know someone else is responsible for all the trouble around town. You're innocent. Hell, we even beat that prophecy of yours. I'm not dead. Victory, right?"

Kane and Riordan exchanged looks, before Kane turned back to her. "I'll still be facing consequences imposed by the Druid Council." He met her eyes. "I don't regret it, but when I pushed my powers to help you and Riordan heal—when I deliberately combined them—I was breaking some serious laws. Phil mentioned this, remember? There are rules governing this kind of thing, the use of rogue power. I did what I had to do, even knowing it was against our laws, so I'll face the consequences without regret. But those consequences . . . well, they're not light."

"So what you're saying is . . ."

"If I leave the council meeting as a free man, it will likely be under someone else's guardianship."

"If?"

"Yes. If."

"Kane, tell her the rest of it. She has a right to hear it from you, not some idiot Druid with an axe to grind." Riordan glared over his shoulder at Duncan.

"Oh, God. There's more?" Janelle glanced from brother

to brother. "Yeah, tell me. Get it over with while I'm still numb."

"You didn't sense it? When we were in the clearing, healing Riordan?"

"Sense what?"

"Puca magic. And lots of it."

Janelle frowned. "Well, sure. There was a ton of it, and all brand-new. But it wasn't you. And it wasn't Riordan. The rock . . . Damn it, we have witnesses. Everyone here knows what happened."

She glanced around in mute appeal. Nobody said a word. She turned frantic eyes back to Kane.

He was nodding. "If the council chooses to accept the testimony, then yes, I do have witnesses. Assuming they'll all speak the truth." He glanced at Tremayne and Duncan.

But there was also Mina and Riordan. Janelle was certain the two would testify in Kane's defense. Of course, it was possible that the Druids might not see them as entirely unbiased now. It was one thing to have completed his task of making amends, but it was something entirely different if he'd been acting irresponsibly in other ways.

Janelle had a sudden sinking feeling. "Oh, God. They're not going to believe you without that other faerie woman in custody. They're still going to say you did this. And . . ." She looked down toward the scorched obscenity that used to be a green and wooded grove. "The fire. Burning down the grove. Revenge on Druids. They'll see that as motive." Not only that, they'd see it as Kane simply repeating his past crimes. Vandalizing his brother's trysting place, terrorizing locals with shape-shifting and violence, and now burning down part of a Druid grove—just as he'd done almost two thousand years ago.

Kane nodded once, agreeing with her words as well as her thoughts.

"Viewed in the context of all the other incidents . . . they could still convict you for all of it." Janelle stared at Kane in horror. He'd been framed—and thoroughly.

There was almost no warning, just a whisper of cloth, a snap of a twig, and Janelle and Kane were approached by a mob of robed figures. She didn't think this was going to end well.

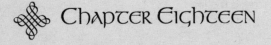 Chapter Eighteen

From the crowd, High Druid Phil stepped forward. "Kane Oberon. Your presence is required by the Druid Council. We'll meet back in the grove." He turned to Janelle and gave her a curious look, but didn't ask obvious questions. "As his guardian, you may accompany us. The other two will stay behind."

"But—" Riordan stepped forward.

Phil held up a hand. "Your trial is over, Riordan. Be content with what you have and leave your brother's fate to"—he shrugged—"fate. If he's innocent, his karma should see him through."

Riordan still looked like he wanted to protest, but Kane shook his head. "If I need you, we can summon you. Okay?"

Mina took Riordan's hand, tugging at him from behind.

"Where have you been?" Janelle stared at the High Druid.

"I'm a businessman. I had overseas matters to address."

"Oh. Well that was anticlimactic."

Phil cast her a distracted glance. "You were expecting high drama? Kidnapping, perhaps death?"

"Well, it *would* be typical of Kane's luck lately."

"True." On that negative note, Phil signaled and the white-robed group surged until Janelle and Kane were surrounded. It wasn't a hostile escort, but a quietly insistent one that led them back to the grove. The dawn-touched clearing was still hazy with smoke but free of flame. In unspoken agreement, the Druids formed a tight circle around Kane, Janelle and Phil.

Suddenly there came a curious rustling and a parting of the white robes. Oberon stepped into view. "I assume I haven't arrived too late?"

"You're joining us?" Phil asked, clearly somewhat nervous.

Oberon glanced at him. "Yes. I regret not attending the last judgment against one of my sons. I won't miss this one."

Phil shrugged, then nodded. "With your understanding, however . . . well, I'd like you to step back from these proceedings. I don't intend to involve you. I will ensure that the hearing is fair, but I think it's understood that you cannot be objective."

Oberon made a soft noise of acquiescence. Then he said, "But I will step in should I feel the need."

Phil cleared his throat, and the Druids drifted into a loose semicircle behind him facing Kane, Janelle and Oberon. The High Druid raised his voice. "Let the trial of the puca, Kane Oberon, commence. We're here today to judge the puca's progress toward atonement and reformation, and to hear his defense on other matters of importance to the Druid community."

Rebelling against the doom implied in Phil's formal tone, Janelle noisily cleared her throat. "Before you start hurling accusations, as Kane's guardian I'd like to remind everyone that Kane came of his own free will now and before. He *created* the opportunity to make amends for what he's done in the past. No one forced him to do so. Even now, he could be going on his merry puca way, and Riordan could still be locked inside that stupid rock. But that's not the case. Thanks to Kane's conscience."

My conscience, hmm? That would be you. It was a whisper in her mind.

No. I might have served as a reminder, but you have your own conscience. You are not evil.

There came a whisper of thought, a caress in her mind. It was wordless, but she knew what it was. Love. Janelle relaxed into it.

"Your point is well taken, Dr. Corrington," the High Druid murmured. Then he continued significantly, "And your loyalties are so noted."

"Fine. My objectivity is completely blown. I admit it. I'm biased. I'm loyal to Kane. But I don't throw my support around casually. I think you're aware of my original opinion of him."

"Oh, very much so. I believe you once described him as, and I quote, 'Captain Revenge the puca freak'?" Phil seemed to be enjoying the memory.

Janelle avoided Oberon's and Kane's gazes, although she heard the echo of their laughter in her head. "Okay, I might have said something like that."

"And, um, 'Robin Goodcreep' was another."

"Yes. Fine." Janelle scowled. "That's my point. I think we get the idea."

"Yes, actually, I think we do." Phil was smiling outright now. "You've changed your mind about him?"

"Yes." She folded her arms across her chest.

"You would, I take it, now judge the puca innocent? Reformed?"

She raised her chin and opened her mouth to respond, then glanced over at Kane. She thought about how they'd made love. She thought about all they'd done together, and wondered briefly if any of it had been orchestrated by Kane in order to manipulate her. Then she thought about how much he cared about her, and how crushed he'd been when he'd thought he'd killed her. There was no question he loved her.

"My answer is yes. I would judge him innocent. Does it stand? My judgment, I mean?"

High Druid Phil considered. Janelle wondered if he knew she'd compromised herself, if he knew she and Kane had made love.

Kane sighed deeply from behind her. "Tell him. It's no good if you don't."

"Oh, hush, already!" Janelle waved a hand, panic lurking beneath her tone.

"Oh, no. *Tell* the High Druid." This came from Phil himself. "Honestly. Keeping it from him will not be in anyone's best interests."

Janelle remained stubbornly silent.

Kane responded for her. "She can't serve as my judge. She can't even serve as my guardian. That's done. You might say we created a conflict of interest."

"Ooooooooh." Janelle turned on Kane. "Tattletale."

"The honor code falters," Phil mused.

She scowled at the Druid. "Yeah? Well, I still say I shouldn't have to report my sex life to a grove full of Druids. As far as the rest goes, I already admitted to my bias. You were aware of that. I came clean about it."

"True." Phil sighed. "All right. Well, I'd accept a biased guardian, but a judge must remain separate. With Oberon's permission, *I* will serve in that office." He glanced up, received the faerie king's reluctant nod, then turned back to Janelle. "So. Since you are biased, plead your charge's case."

Janelle frowned. "Oh. Okay. One sec, though. We have to make everything clear. Let's go back to the punishment phase of all this, where you gave Kane a guardian in the first place. You weakened his powers and charged him to make amends to everyone he's harmed."

"That's correct." Phil nodded.

"So, let's take a look at his victims. Let's get the list

together. Riordan—he's number one, no question, since Kane's exaggeration landed him inside a rock for two thousand years. Then there's me, his long-suffering guardian whom he hurt years ago. And then there's Mina, who was yanked into the whole condemn-Riordan curse." She frowned thoughtfully. "Does that conclude our list?"

Phil surveyed a few Druids close to him, then nodded. "Those would be the primaries, yes. If he succeeded with those, we would be appeased."

"Excellent." Janelle smiled, obviously channeling a TV courtroom lawyer. "So, on to Kane's progress. That part's easy, actually. You guys showed up a little late to witness it, but Kane here seems to have made amends to all three of us with one single act." And in as concise a manner as possible, she described Riordan's injuries, her own danger in responding to those injuries and Kane's selfless intervention to save them. She skipped what had led up to the injuries, because she wasn't quite sure how to address them without bringing up the crimes of which Kane might easily be accused.

Throughout her speech, Kane remained stoic. As Janelle wound down, she began to feel cautiously optimistic, and she gave him a smile. A genuine smile. She wanted him to believe. She wanted him to be free.

"Kane Oberon," she said, "today you are my hero. You gave up your immortality to save your brother and me. In essence, you agreed to one day die just so two others could have a second chance at life." She paused to let her words sink in.

"Now, to address the sincerity of his remorse. The purity of his intent. And the general state of his morality." She turned to Phil. "To save Riordan and me, Kane did knowingly break some rules. However, these rules were not broken for personal gain, but in a selfless effort to help us. Why am I sure it was selfless, you ask? Well, in so doing, not only did he give up his immortality, but he also willingly risked his mortal future and his freedom, given the laws of your people and the guardianship agreement. And there was something else, something even closer to his heart. In giving up his immortality, Kane also gave up any chance at the throne." She nodded in apology to Oberon, who looked displeased but resigned.

Turning back to Phil she said, "Kane risked everything and sacrificed well beyond what anyone could expect from him. For my part, yes, I consider him reformed. Riordan and Mina told Kane the same. They considered his actions to constitute more than adequate and genuine amends. You can summon them if—"

Phil was frowning. "I'm inclined to believe you about this, to be honest. Given Riordan's protective attitude when we arrived, it all seems very credible. Sadly, the purity of Kane's intent does not change the fact that the puca did, in combining his powers with yours in this way, violate a serious taboo. That won't be overlooked." He turned his gaze on the defendant.

Kane eyed Janelle ruefully before turning back to the High Druid. "I understood the gravity of the offense when I committed the crime. I will say that I did not act out of disrespect to anyone here, but out of my personal feelings for my brother and for Dr. Corrington, and I will add that I do not regret having done so." He paused. "However, I know the council must—"

"Wait!" Janelle interrupted in a panic. "Before anyone makes any kind of formal admission or judgment on this, I'd like to know exactly what we're looking at here. What's wrong with what he did, and what will happen to him if he's found guilty?"

Phil shrugged. "As I explained, this is not a minor infraction. Even given the best of intents. Powers like yours, in combination, can produce dire results. We cannot afford to be lenient in our response to this kind of offense. As far as consequences to violators . . . In past cases, we have imposed exile—occasionally even death."

Janelle flinched. "*Death?* But that would be an extreme case, and one that wasn't inspired by the best of intentions, I'm sure. Okay, okay. So the point is that you really, *really* don't want the incident repeated. Right?"

"Right. That's the point. Or a point. But it's not like we can trust him not to do it again when it's in a good cause. You saw how unrepentant he was. For that matter, we aren't terribly fond of your lack of control, either." Phil raised his eyebrow pointedly. "You endanger all of us with your indiscretions and your inability to use glamour effectively."

"Indiscretions . . ." Janelle made a face. "You mean because I couldn't glamour Dr. Hoffman?"

"Yes. And while we won't take your gift from you, since you have not technically misused it, I must insist that you let us at least—"

"Wait." Janelle inhaled deeply. "Give me a minute, I'm thinking. You might want to stand back," she joked half-heartedly.

Actually, she really felt like she might explode. Could she do this? It was huge. And with her life the wreck that it currently was, having lost her job and not having anything else, this was a bigger sacrifice than ever.

She thought of Cindy and Riordan. Where would they be now if it weren't for her gift? Scarred, injured, and possibly dead. And what about the baby with the bowel obstruction? Would Lexie have died without Janelle's healing magic? This ability the Druids had given her was such a miracle, with so much potential for good.

Sure, public exposure was a constant risk for a woman wielding a healing gift, but she would be willing to risk that for the greater good. It was just the other that truly bothered her. Lack of control. Lack of knowledge. Lack of experience. Perhaps . . . perhaps this gift belonged in bigger hands than hers could ever be—more divine hands or at least hands with greater training in the Druid arts. What she had were doctor's hands. A scientist's hands.

That didn't mean the inborn healer in her wouldn't flinch just a little—okay, maybe a whole lot—at what she was preparing to do. To willingly forfeit a miracle? Was she insane? But it needed to be done.

"Suppose there were a way around the need for punishment. Say we could skip that whole banishment and"—Janelle made a face—"the other option we won't mention. Suppose I made it impossible for the incident to be repeated."

Phil eyed her curiously. "And how would you do that?"

"Well, you said you wouldn't take my gift from me. Suppose I gave it up? In exchange for—"

"Janelle, don't." Kane ground out the command.

She turned back to him. "Kane, honestly, it might even be for the best. Think about it. Yes, the positive potential of this gift is astronomical. I would love to explore and experiment, see what I could accomplish, how many I could help. But I don't have complete control of it—not the healing or the glamouring. It would kill me if, through this lack of control or ignorance, I hurt a patient I was trying to help." She eyed him wistfully, almost afraid to say the next thing aloud. "And . . . honestly, I really am a good doctor. Traditional healing comes with a little more effort and time, of course, but I'm good at it. It's what I was made to do. And while I love the idea of a miracle, well"—she tried a smile—"lab rats don't get out of their mazes long enough to perform miracles. And a lab rat is exactly what I'd be, given a few more indiscretions like the one at the clinic. Hell, I already lost that job."

She turned back to Phil. "Please. Let me do this. You forgive Kane's single—and selflessly intended, never-to-be-repeated—act of illegally combining our powers, and

I'll give my healing gift back. This would prevent future indiscretions as well as ensure that the power could never again be combined with Kane's. Can I do that? Please?"

"You would do this for the puca?" Phil eyed her curiously.

"I would."

"All right. Consider it done." He closed his eyes a moment and Janelle felt a brief sense of loss and then a lightening. Phil opened his eyes.

Janelle was surprised to find herself smiling, actually feeling freer than she had in weeks. She turned jubilantly to Kane. He eyed her with an intensity she had yet to see outside of bed.

He choked, obviously having heard her thought.

But it was true. And now she saw something else in his eyes, a glow that had grown even as she offered her gift in exchange for his freedom. Love. She never wanted to look away from that glow. It was blinding and inviting and addicting. It was what she'd wanted from him all along, what he'd been afraid to show her.

Phil cleared his throat, drawing their attention. "The broken taboo will be forgiven, as you ask. But there are still other matters to be addressed—matters that may make your sacrifice, Ms. Corrington, for naught." He glanced at Kane. "There have been several incidents around town. Incidents that are unmistakably tied to puca magic, all used maliciously." Phil paused. "How do you plead, Kane?"

"Innocent."

"And what are the reasons we should believe you? This is all fitting with your past, and you are the only remaining puca known to us."

Kane glanced at Janelle in brief apology. "I have no proof. I have only my word, and the word of Janelle, who—"

"A moment, if you please." A low voice came from

behind a partially singed bush. Tremayne! "Here are two others with information to share on this matter. Myself and this man." Tremayne strode forward, towing another man along in his wake. A light shove, and the second man, sooty and barely recognizable in his dishevelment, stepped forward.

"Duncan Forbes?" This from Phil. "But what happened to him? Duncan, were you assaulted?"

Duncan straightened, cradling an arm in a singed sleeve. "Yes, I was. That puca is a menace. He must be stopped. And it's because of your poor judgment and inadequate leadership that he was allowed to roam free." He let his gaze pan the semicircle of Druids, much as any public speaker or politician might. "Kane Oberon proved his lack of character—and the misjudgment of our own Druidic leadership—through these rogue actions. Violating laws, hurting humans, threatening our way of life and the ways of life of other cultures." He nodded to Oberon, who regarded him coldly. "That puca needs to be contained. And our Druid family needs a new leader. An effective leader. A powerful leader."

Janelle growled. "You sleazy, power-hungry son of a—"

"Silence." Phil suddenly sounded pretty darn authoritative.

Janelle bit her tongue to keep from speaking. Couldn't they all see the madness in Duncan's eyes? Dear God, he was lying to an entire grove of Druids, a couple of witnesses who could easily call him a liar, and even to the faerie king himself. Was he really so far gone in his madness that he thought he still had a chance at pulling this off? And, dear God, what if he was right? What if he somehow managed to convince them of Kane's guilt!

Phil spoke firmly to Duncan. "Your assertions against my leadership are so noted. As for your accusations . . ." He turned to Kane. "Perhaps you'd like to speak at greater length?"

"I'm innocent. I never attacked him, except in self-defense. I wasn't responsible for the stallion loose in downtown Richmond. I never caused mischief or harm at Mina Avery's home, or at the clinic where Janelle Corrington works."

"And what about the attempt on me?" Tremayne asked. "Outside Dr. Corrington's clinic, just before a woman inside was nearly slaughtered."

Kane paused in surprise. "I had not heard of that." He shrugged. "I never attempted harm against you, either. As I recall, if anyone put the hurt on anyone, it was you acting on me."

"I'll back that up," Janelle said. "I was there. Freakiest thing you ever saw. Tremayne froze Kane in his tracks. Honestly, I don't see how anyone could harm this guy. Puca included." She turned to Kane. "No offense against your manly self."

His lips twitched. "None taken."

"But then, we've already seen where her loyalties lie." This from Duncan. "I've seen them together. Like animals in heat, probationary agreement be damned."

Janelle colored and glared. Duncan leered. Kane lunged.

Oberon grabbed his son's arm and held him in place with a whispered word in his ear. Still glaring at Duncan, Kane didn't attempt to break free.

Oberon raised his voice. "You. Tremayne. Explain yourself. What interest do you have in these proceedings? Why are you here?"

"I've been tailing Duncan Forbes for weeks now in search of something that was stolen."

"What would that be?" asked Phil, sounding curious.

Glancing pointedly at Kane, Tremayne smiled humorlessly. "My chance at a life." He dropped the smile. "I followed Duncan Forbes to the clearing here a little over an hour and a half ago. Where he met with a female faerie."

"Titania?" Oberon murmured in dark question.

"I couldn't say for sure. The faerie's face was obscured."

Janelle stepped forward. "It wasn't Titania." She turned carefully to Kane. "I think . . . I think it was Alanna."

Kane started in surprise. "Alanna?"

She nodded. "Yes, your Unseelie ex-fiancée. She didn't give me her name, and I don't have a clue what Alanna looks like, but I saw the face of the woman in the clearing and it wasn't Titania. And what she said . . ." Janelle shrugged. "She sounded like a woman rejected by Kane. That's not proof, but I did get a good look at her face. If you could set out a faerie lineup in front of me, I could identify her."

"No need for a lineup." Oberon snapped his fingers, the sparks building and taking shape. They coalesced into an oval of light, and a woman stumbled free. She blinked rapidly.

"What—?"

Janelle stared. The woman's face, as beautiful as she remembered, was unmistakable. "That's her. That's who I saw at the clearing. She wore a hood and cape when she interacted with Duncan, but I, um, tripped her."

"You tripped a faerie?" Phil asked, his eyes wide behind the purple frames of his glasses. "Dear God. This whole place might have—"

"Been destroyed, if I wished. *Boom*, like doomsday fireworks," Alanna finished for him. She glanced around the circle before her gaze settled on Kane. "Long time no see."

"Not so long. Just hours ago, right?"

Alanna didn't respond, just maintained an aloof expression.

Janelle stared at her. Alanna. Kane's ex, of the faerie variety. It threw her a little for a loop. Sure, Janelle had understood matters on an intellectual level when she'd seen and heard Alanna in the clearing, enough to put two and two together and name her as the culprit, but Janelle had been a little distracted, to say the least. Now . . . Alanna was beautiful. Drop-dead gorgeous. And Kane had dumped her? Was he an idiot? How could she believe he would fall for her, a human, when this gorgeous—

Kane pinched her. *I'm not an idiot, I'm just not in love with her. I can't think of anyone but you. Remember?*

Janelle made a face, trying to hide the effect of his words, but they basically melted her insides like ice cream on a hot sidewalk.

"Alanna. You have something to tell the court?" Phil asked.

"Not in this lifetime." She glared at the High Druid, his followers, and every other person in the vicinity, mortal or otherwise.

"Alanna." It was King Oberon, his voice low and demanding.

"I'm not of your court, Oberon." Alanna raised her nose regally. "You can't command me."

The faerie king raised an eyebrow. "Perhaps Titania could make you talk."

Alanna shifted nervously, then, raising her chin, eyed first Phil, then Oberon, then Kane. "Perhaps. Perhaps not. Who do you think masterminded this whole thing?"

Oberon stilled, and it felt as though the sky grew heavy. "Explain yourself."

Alanna finally looked nervous. "Titania persuaded Duncan to give her the cornerstone. I guess he couldn't tap its powers on his own. Then . . . Titania gave it to me. She expected . . . well, you know what she expected. You know your wife. She didn't have to say anything." She pursed her lips.

Oberon grumbled. Closed his eyes. Snapped his fingers.

In a burst of light Titania stumbled forward, looking

flustered and insulted. "Hello? A little warning and a hell of a lot more courtesy, if you don't mind? The last time I checked, I was the Queen of All Faerie and not some lackey who—"

"Silence." This from her husband, whose pointing finger drew Titania's attention to Alanna. "Your niece here—"

"Kane's ex-fiancée?" Titania inserted pointedly.

"Yes. That one." Oberon sounded even more strained, if possible. "She claims you conspired with her and with the Druid Duncan to frame my son."

"Oh, but which son are you recognizing this week? First it was Kane, then it was Riordan . . ."

"Is that why you thought you could frame them? You thought I'd withdrawn my protection? Never. I recognize both of my sons. From here on out. Anyone who hurts either of them will deal with me. And I'm feeling a hell of a lot of wrath right now. So answer the accusation. Did you conspire with Alanna and Duncan to frame Kane?"

At Oberon's threatening tone, Titania seemed to actually shiver. "You can't pin that on me. I might have introduced a few people to each other and discussed possibilities, but that's all I did!" She brushed off a sleeve. "My karma is untainted, thank you very much."

A royal vein began to pulse visibly in Oberon's temple, and Kane stepped quickly forward. He cleared his throat to address both his father and High Druid Phil. "Alanna had me at a disadvantage. I broke our engagement, so karma was on her side. Against me. Titania could use that. So, my guess is, Titania gave the stone to Alanna, leaving herself and even Alanna free and clear from karmic infraction. They could act against me in this manner without fear of retribution."

Phil nodded thoughtfully before turning to the scowling former Druid. "And Duncan? Why do all this? What did you have to gain?"

Duncan remained mute, although his gaze darted feverishly from face to face. Nuttier than a fruitcake, Janelle decided. A dangerous one.

Tremayne stepped forward. "The deal, from what I gather, was that Duncan would wield the puca powers to frame Kane. This would please both Alanna and Titania. Once the faerie women were satisfied, he could then use his new assets to regain his position of power in Druids' Grove." He nodded at Phil. "He wanted to unseat you."

"Well, I guess that explains that." Frowning, Phil turned back to the rest of his group. "I move to dismiss all charges against Kane Oberon and release him from his probation, thereby reinstating all his former powers."

"That's it? That's all? A few measly weeks of mild probation and bam, he's back in action? How does that constitute justice? What about what he did to me?" Alanna sounded angry and hurt. "Kane humiliated me," she ground out. "We were engaged. Bad enough that he got involved with a human during our engagement. A fling, no big deal. I knew in his eyes ours was nothing more than a political alliance. But I thought I could win him over anyway." The faerie smiled, obviously mocking herself and her logic. "I figured, as a faerie, I had time on my side when she did not. But then, when the little Druid tramp betrayed him with his brother, *I'm* the one he dumps? *I'm* the one who gets humiliated? And now, to know some other human is bound to take my place? How much should I have to take?"

"He's mortal now." Oberon spoke with quiet finality. "True, he will have his freedom and all his former powers, but you will outlive him by centuries, even millennia. Meanwhile, your actions tonight nearly killed both Riordan and Janelle. Kane saved them from death and you from punishment for murder. All at great cost to himself. I think you, too, could call it even. If not more than even."

At the jarring word *murder*, Alanna had closed her

mouth. Now, reluctantly, she dropped her gaze and nodded.

"Alanna," Kane called out softly. "For what it's worth, I am sorry. You deserved better from me and, frankly, better than some cold political alliance. I still hope you find it."

Alanna turned to Kane, her demeanor reluctant. "You may not believe this, but I never would have sent Duncan to physically hurt Janelle, no matter what he suggested. I never intended for any real harm to be done."

"No, what you wanted was for me and only me to suffer." Kane frowned. "In spite of your intentions, innocents were hurt by your scheme."

Alanna nodded, dread clear in her eyes.

Seeing it—recognizing it—Janelle spoke up. "Let's not go there. Please. No more guardianship pacts. No more revenge. Otherwise we'll never escape this cycle. I healed everyone she hurt. She's sorry. You're sorry. Everything's even-Steven, and no permanent harm done. Can't we just put this behind us now?"

Phil sighed. "Not quite." He turned back to Duncan.

"Oh, yeah." Janelle grimaced. "Forgot about him. Geez. This is worse than jury duty."

"What?" Duncan looked hostile. "I thought we were all playing nice now."

Tremayne spoke up. "If anyone around here needs containment, it would be Duncan Forbes. Perhaps removing the puca powers from his grasp will alleviate his instability, but he still bears watching."

Obviously curious now, Oberon turned his attention back to Tremayne. "You seem to be in possession of a surprising amount of information. How did you come to learn of this situation? Who are you?"

"It was my job, my last duty as a soldier for Akker—as his slave, really." Tremayne smiled. "I was in charge of containing those puca powers. For good." He bowed. "That is my plan now. I sense that all of those escaped puca powers are back inside the stone as we speak. Of course, they're not yet bound to it. I could use Druid and faerie assistance with the final binding." When he glanced around for support, both Oberon and Phil nodded.

With a bow, Tremayne next turned deliberately to Titania. "If you please?" he said. He held out his hand, dark eyes for once blazing with strong emotion.

Sulking and glaring, Titania obviously knew what he required. She snapped her fingers and the cornerstone appeared in her hand. Eyes glittering with malice, she lobbed it toward Tremayne, who lunged for it, but the stone never reached him. Another shape had hurtled forward, knocking it out of the air. The stone landed behind some bushes in a blinding flash of light . . .

And a squeal?

Kane tackled Duncan before the former Druid could chase after the stone he'd tried to intercept. Then a female voice rose on an angry howl. It was a familiar voice, and a familiar face emerged as a young woman hobbled out from behind the bush, brandishing the cornerstone like a weapon. It was Daphne. And she was glaring at her father.

"What—so petty theft, greed, conspiracy and assault aren't enough for you? Obviously not. I've read your damn journals, which brought me all the way over here, today of all days. But did you also have to ruin my shoes? Damn it, these were my going-away present to myself, and not exactly ch—" She broke off as a blinding light seemed to emanate from her center and radiate outward. Her eyes glazed, rolling back in her head as her knees buckled.

"Daphne!" That single, strangled word came from her father. The terrible light encompassed his daughter, blinding onlookers, who stumbled back. Gradually the glow diminished behind a wealth of dark smoke that drifted to join the haze still lingering in the scorched trees. The clouds concealing Daphne floated high, leaving behind . . . nothing?

Then Janelle's eyes focused on the ground, where a cream-colored cat balanced its front paws inside an expensive, high-heeled pump.

Tremayne casually bent to retrieve the cornerstone. Then he picked up the cat, ignoring its low rumble, halfway between a growl and purr. He peered down into the beast's blue eyes, which blinked with confusion and banked rage. "So. It appears my work is not yet done."

"Why? What do you mean? Is that Daphne? Will she have to stay that way?" Janelle was horrified, even as Duncan, pinned to the ground by Kane, moaned in protest.

Tremayne shook his head. He closed his eyes and cradled the cat in one arm, and his expression again grew impassive. The air before him seemed to shimmer from shoulder to foot, until the form of a woman took shape and stumbled backward, one shoe on and one shoe off. Obviously shaken, she patted herself from head to hip, no doubt grateful to find clothes and not fur covering her body. Then she turned baleful eyes on Tremayne.

"You just watch where you put those hands. Got it?" Then, pivoting grandly, she stalked off into the trees, only a bit hobbled by her lack of one shoe.

Her audience, mostly at a loss, just watched for a silent moment.

"Can I leave now?" Titania asked in a bored voice, the sound of which seemed to startle everyone back to movement and low muttering.

"Nothing would make me happier," Oberon growled. Dismissing his wife, he turned to make friendlier farewells.

Then High Druid Phil's voice rang out into the dawn-lit clearing: "Thus concludes the trial of Kane Oberon."

"I wonder what will happen to Daphne," Janelle murmured much later, even as Kane trailed kisses along her jaw and down her neck. It was light outside, but they'd only found their way to bed twenty minutes ago. And yet, it wasn't with the intent of sleeping.

"I wonder when you'll stop worrying about everyone else and start concentrating on me. You do, after all, have a puca in your bed. Some women would give their right arm for such an honor. Even some faerie women." He winked at her knowingly.

"Oh, I'm honored all right. Nothing like a naked shape-shifter between the sheets. A girl never knows what will pop up next. Although we never tried anything like that . . . yet." Janelle's evil laughter grew breathless as Kane's lips drifted lower.

Unfortunately, that last image nagged at Janelle and she sat up. "But . . . Daphne turned into a cat, Kane. A cat! Will that happen again? Is her life screwed up now? What was with that flash of light and the cornerstone?"

"I wish I could tell you for sure, but a puca can't choose what he can predict. If you'd like an educated guess . . . I think that girl will rise to whatever situation is presented to her. She's certainly descended from tenacious stock." Kane wrapped his arms around Janelle and tugged her close. "Also, unless I mistook the look in Tremayne's eyes, she'll have a little help with it."

"I hope so. She doesn't deserve to be sucked into all this." Janelle went quiet, her thoughts on weightier matters.

"Weightier than the puca in your bed? No. Couldn't be." Kane teasingly nuzzled her bared breast.

Janelle smiled a little, but she was still preoccupied.

Kane pulled back. "Okay, what? Something's bothering you, and for once you seem more than capable of keeping it from me. I don't like that at all, by the way. Clean slates are annoying."

Janelle looked at him, really looked at him. He was hers. She wanted that so badly—for now and always. But was it really meant to be? "Maegth's curse."

"Yeah? What about it?"

Janelle leaned her forehead against his cheek and shrugged. "She said you were doomed to love only one woman and yet never to have her."

"That was the curse, yes."

She slumped. "So how can we be together now? Can you really just overcome a curse?"

"Yes, and no." Kane, who sounded supremely unconcerned, smoothed a hand up and down her back. "Maegth's curse was more than effective against the man I used to be."

Catching the track of his thoughts, Janelle looked up at him. "But you're not the man you used to be!"

"No. I've changed."

"Yeah. A lot, actually." Janelle nodded, laughing. "The man you used to be would not have given up your immortality to save Riordan and me. So . . . I would be dead. And the curse fulfilled."

"That's the way I see it." He smiled. "And that truth feels right to me. It feels like the worst of everything is behind us."

"Even if it's just beginning for others."

Kane gave a low, wicked laugh. "Dr. Larry Hoffman, for example?"

"Mmmmm." Janelle grinned. After concluding things at the grove, they'd come home just after dawn to find a crowing message from Cindy on Janelle's answering machine. Apparently one of the other nurses at the clinic had filed strong and well-documented sexual harassment complaints against Dr. Hoffman. His arrogance toward the nursing staff had finally worked against him. He'd been comparatively subtle with Janelle, but apparently had deemed a nurse unlikely to complain. He'd underestimated this particular nurse.

The beauty of the situation, however, was that the balance of power had shifted and Dr. Hoffman's own judgment was called into question. Any accusations he made against Janelle now would therefore be discarded. Since she hadn't actually quit yet, and she doubted any of the other partners had any reason to dislike her . . .

"I think you have your job back."

Janelle smiled. "I think you're right. Except, I think I'll be taking this particular morning off."

"Yeah?"

"Yeah." She dropped her voice to a low growl. "I have this craving for a puca ride. A long, hard puca ride. I hear they can change your life."

"I might be interested," Kane agreed with a twinkle in his eye. "But only if you're willing to ride bareback."

"Oh, you're baaaad." Janelle laughed.

"You have no idea."

Janelle's protest, begun in laughing earnest, dissolved into giggles as Kane rolled onto his back, bringing her astride him. She gazed down into adoring golden eyes and thanked her lucky stars. These eyes were the same ones that had seduced her eight years ago, but now she knew why he'd left and what he'd wanted. And this time, no one was going anywhere.

And yes, time with a puca could change a person's life. But she wasn't the only one forever changed by their encounter. Love had freed them both.

☐ YES!

Sign me up for the Love Spell Book Club and send my
FREE BOOKS! If I choose to stay in the club, I will pay only
$8.50* each month, a savings of $6.48!

NAME: _____

ADDRESS: _____

TELEPHONE: _____

EMAIL: _____

☐ I want to pay by credit card.

☐ VISA   ☐ MasterCard   ☐ DISCOVER

ACCOUNT #: _____

EXPIRATION DATE: _____

SIGNATURE: _____

Mail this page along with $2.00 shipping and handling to:
**Love Spell Book Club
PO Box 6640
Wayne, PA 19087**
Or fax (must include credit card information) to:
610-995-9274
You can also sign up online at **www.dorchesterpub.com**.
*Plus $2.00 for shipping. Offer open to residents of the U.S. and Canada only. Canadian
residents please call 1-800-481-9191 for pricing information.
If under 18, a parent or guardian must sign. Terms, prices and conditions subject to
change. Subscription subject to acceptance. Dorchester Publishing reserves the right to
reject any order or cancel any subscription.

GET FREE BOOKS!

You can have the best romance delivered to your door for less than what you'd pay in a bookstore or online. Sign up for one of our book clubs today, and we'll send you *FREE* BOOKS* just for trying it out... **with no obligation to buy, ever!**

Bring a little magic into your life with the romances of Love Spell—fun contemporaries, paranormals, time-travels, futuristics, and more. Your shipments will include authors such as **MARJORIE LIU, JADE LEE, NINA BANGS, GEMMA HALLIDAY,** and many more.

As a book club member you also receive the following special benefits:
- **30% off all orders!**
- **Exclusive access to special discounts!**
- **Convenient home delivery and 10 days to return any books you don't want to keep.**

Visit www.dorchesterpub.com or call 1-800-481-9191

There is no minimum number of books to buy, and you may cancel membership at any time.
*Please include $2.00 for shipping and handling.